DYING FOR MONET

DYING FOR MONET

AN ART HISTORY MYSTERY

CLAUDIA RIESS

Praise for the Art History Mystery Series

For *STOLEN LIGHT*

"A fascinating combination of suspense, art history and love story, taking the reader from Havana, Cuba to Manhattan, to Florence, Italy, and back."—Elizabeth Cooke, author of the Hotel Marcel Series

"In this art-world thriller, Riess draws the characters with a broad brush, but they have all the capabilities, chemistry and give-and-take of a strong mystery-solving duo...complex and intriguing."—*Kirkus Reviews*

For *FALSE LIGHT*

"I am captivated when an author brings expertise to a story line...Riess helps her readers learn about masterpieces, forgeries and auctions, without ever dumping information. (She got me looking into real-life forger Eric Hebborn...always delighted to be introduced to a too-strange-to-be-fiction character.) In a world filled with too much frozen broccoli and canned soup, this is a rum raisin ice cream kind of book."—Sherrie Cronin/ Goodreads

"...admirable research, sympathy for professional women wanting a family, the plight of LGBT couples, and an overall good heart for those who still believe in love in a cynical world."—Joan Baum (Easthampton newspaper: *The Independent*)

For *KNIGHT LIGHT*

"Riess has a knack of staging her scenes in such perfect tempo that you don't want to put the book down to see what lies ahead."—T.J. Clemente (Hamptons.com The Bookshelf)

"With the novel *Knight Light,* author Claudia Riess has bestowed upon my imagination a cadre of new friends…Peripheral characters made this book extra enjoyable. I would love to meet a real life Denise!"—Maureen/Goodreads

For *TO KINGDOM COME*

"This book is extremely well written, with scenes being related vividly and interactions occurring effortlessly.This author is gifted in story-telling.It was difficult to put this book down."—NAIWE-National Association of Independent Writers & Editors

"'To Kingdom Come' is a must-read for fans of the mystery genre who also have an interest in fine arts and history. It delivers a captivating story that keeps readers engaged from beginning to end with an intelligent plotline that will have you turning pages late into the night."—The Sassy B. Reviewer/NetGalley

Prologue

It was time. The mavericks, all thirty of them represented at the first Impressionist Exhibition in Paris, 1874, had passed away. Not that a clean sweep was essential to the plan, but there was a sense of closure about it, as useless yet gratifying as an account ledger balanced to the penny.

The framed canvases were propped up against the far wall of the living room like hostages awaiting their release. The overstuffed couch, with its mesmerizing pattern of exotic birds, had been moved into the dining room to clear the wall space for them. The drapes were drawn and the room was bathed in artificial light, yet the paintings seemed to be standing out in the open, beneath the sky. It was the sheer vibrancy of color that created the illusion, Elizabeth Barden thought as she surveyed the display, guilt creeping into her enjoyment of it. Though there'd been no law against it, it had been criminal to have kept these luminous visions in the dark all these years. If only she hadn't been bound by a promise!

She remembered her parents sitting her down at the kitchen table in this very home, thirty-three years ago it was, the two of them planting themselves opposite her, looking more grimly serious than she'd ever seen them. She was fourteen years old at the time and not yet settled on what to make of herself, looks and intelligence ratings still torturously pending. She imagined she was about to hear that she'd been adopted or had three months to live. What they told her was less dire, but required a more sustained focus to take in. The paintings would be her legacy, they said, but in order for this to be the case, she must follow their instructions down to the letter. She had to clasp their hands in hers—as good as swearing on the bible—and promise to do so. The mood lightened only once during the interview, and that was when she'd pronounced the artist's name as if it rhymed with "bonnet." "Monet," her mother had corrected, grinning. "Mow the grass. Neigh says the horse."

The memory did not draw a smile. How could it, when these prisoners stood before her in dutiful formation? How brilliantly they'd persevered without a trace of reproach marring their freshness! And wasn't it curious, how her gaze seemed to be drawn—and return when it wandered elsewhere—to the still life of a Wedgewood vase teeming with flowers—gladioli, lilies, wildflowers; a riot of color she would hardly call "still." Not her favorite genre, still life, but she'd felt the same sort of instant affinity to this painting as she'd had with her lover, Jacob, not at all her type, but upon an exchanged look, bound to him, body and soul. And, of course, in a manner of speaking he, too, like the painting, had been hidden for far too long from the embrace of natural light. She must free him, too, from the dark. She had been intending for a year—what was she thinking, *more* than a year—to tell her most dear but tiresome husband of her affair and the necessity for a divorce. The imminence of the afternoon's scheduled event strengthened her resolve. She would end the secrecy tonight.

Hard to believe that barely one hour from now, unless God or chance intervened, the transaction would be underway. The wealthy young art collector, Lewis Keller, along with the gallery owner who had used his networking skills to nose him out and was serving as broker in the deal, would soon be rapping at the door of the sprawling old ranch-house where Elizabeth had lived all her life, half of it with her husband, Wallace. The gallery owner's entourage of packers and transporters would be on hand as well. The collector, a bit wet behind the ears, she'd discovered when he'd first come to look over the paintings, had seemed to rely more on the gallery owner's aesthetic judgment than on his own. Like a pet owner forced by circumstances to give up her precious charge, she hoped that the man to whom she was relinquishing the paintings would treat them with the care they deserved.

Before withdrawing to her room to freshen up, Elizabeth stepped into the kitchen to see how her husband was coming along with the needless crudité platter he was arranging for their guests.

"Ah, Wally," she said rather sadly, thinking of what was ahead for the poor man tonight, "an unaccompanied champagne toast would have been quite sufficient."

"I know, Liz, I know," Wallace said, putting down the knife with which he had been slicing carrots into sticks. "But you must admit, a little gesture of thoughtfulness goes a long way." He tapped his apron-bibbed chest for emphasis.

"You're right, dear," Elizabeth agreed, gritting her teeth at his habit of speaking in aphorisms. The knife was lying on the counter unattended, and she imagined, for an instant, as fleeting and pleasant as a sunny landscape striking an Impressionist's eye, of stabbing him with it.

Chapter One

New York City

June 21, Present Day

Laszlo's Auction House had entered the art scene in a blaze of glory, even before its builders had broken ground in what had been known as The Mud Pit, a large tract of undeveloped land on First Avenue and the upper thirties. To trumpet his project, Ben Laszlo, a billionaire branching out from his casino business, had wangled a cover story in Forbes, an appearance on Fox News, and, to balance out his target audience, an interview on PBS Arts. He was outspoken and savvy, the kind of brash people sneer at and envy at the same time.

The building and the site itself bore testament to Ben's nuanced swagger. The limestone and bronze exterior, the tall windows, were a nod to its seasoned competitor, Christie's, except that Laszlo's bronze trim was a little more eye-catching; its windows, a hair's breadth loftier. The statuary in its courtyard was more of a jab than a nod. In the plaza at Rockefeller Center, where Christie's ruled, stood a hefty Henry Moore statue of Mother and Child. In the courtyard at Laszlo's, Ben had installed an even more zaftig Mother and Child by the sculptor Fernando Botero.

Although Laszlo's had officially opened its doors two years ago, the evening possessed all the star power of an opening night gala, at least to Erika Shawn Wheatley, who'd never been to a major auction house's traditional evening sale, where its most coveted art works are put on the block, the more down-to-earth opening bids deferred to the following afternoon's auction. A special pass was required to attend the premier event, and Greg Smith, board member of Art Loss Register and the Wheatleys' friend and crime-solving ally, had gotten Erika and her husband, Harrison, a couple of hard-won passes. Unfortunately, the Wheatleys' three-year-old son's nanny, Kate, was visiting her parents in Texas, and their ever-dependable elderly housekeeper, Grace, was, on this rarest of occasions, feeling under the weather and was confined to her room. Rather than call a baby-sitter for the first time in Lucas's life, each of his over-protective parents had elected to stay home with him. Erika thought Harrison, as an art history professor, was the natural candidate to witness firsthand an auction of fine art. Harrison insisted she go, and for good reason. Greg had procured passes for them mainly because he'd heard that Erika was writing a piece for *Art News* magazine on the evolution of the art market, and he thought the goings-on at this high-stakes event would provide perfect fodder for her. The fact that a Claude Monet still life had been chosen as the auction's "catalogue lot" (the painting appearing on the cover of its catalogue) had sealed the deal as far as Harrison was concerned. "Besides," he said, "I promised Lucas I'd read him *The Very Hungry Caterpillar* at bedtime." Erika would be attending the auction, and that was that.

And here she was, unaccompanied, in her pale blue satin one-shoulder cocktail dress, gracefully pressing her black clutch bag to her hip and taking it all in. Looking every bit the independent woman of the world and risk-taker that she had become, except that at her core—and this did not contradict her self-reliance, only enriched it— wishing Harrison were by her side, sharing the charged atmosphere and providing an unconditional comfort zone.

The enormous reception area must have been designed to accommodate either a United Nations gala or a sculptural installation on a par with Mount Rushmore. A less self-assured group of under one hundred visitors might have appeared dwarfed by such an imposing venue, but the present company seemed to be right at home, sipping champagne and custom-made drinks and standing about in little cliques, or cruising the parquet floor, seeking other members of the select gathering to chat up or dress down, all in bitingly good humor. Erika was about to peel off the edge of one of the clusters and gravitate toward the bar table, flush with the north wall and roughly thirty feet of carved wood wainscoting away, when a familiar voice greeted her from behind.

"*Here* she is!" Greg exclaimed, in a tone judiciously modulated for the occasion. "And looking lovely as ever!" he added as Erika turned to fully face him.

A woman was clinging to his arm. His wife, Marcia, Erika figured, judging by the tenacity of her grip. (In the past, he'd confided to the Wheatleys his having to tolerate her possessiveness. "As a trade off," he'd said, never mentioning for what.) "Greg—hi," Erika declared, exchanging a nominal cheek-to-cheek greeting with him. "Thanks again for the pass!" She took in the room with a sweeping look. "I'm excited to be here." Directing her attention to Greg's companion, she was about to address her.

"I'm Marcia," the woman preempted, sounding more confident than she looked. She thrust her free hand—her left—forward. Something resembling a handshake followed.

"I was about to introduce you," Greg put in, looking about as abashed as an Olympic skier settling for Gold. Greg may have lost an inch or two of hairline and gone up a belt size since he and Erika had first met some years ago, but his stereotypical Nordic god presence had remained intact. "Erika Shawn Wheatley, editor at *Art News*. My wife, Marcia, paralegal at Ludwig and Pierson, and love of my life." That accomplished, "Where's Harrison?" he asked. "Haven't seen the old boy anywhere about."

"Perhaps he's a vagabond like you," Marcia suggested.

"I shuttle between the Register's New York and London offices, luv. Hardly qualifies as tramping about."

Erika explained Harrison's absence as they made their way to the bar, Marcia clutching Greg's arm even more purposefully. Marcia's possessiveness aside, it was the act of balancing in her Lady Gaga-style platform heels that required Marcia's tenacious hold on Greg, Erika realized en route.

"Ah, just the fellow I want you to meet," Greg announced once they'd arrived. "Ivan—Ivan Brooks!" he directed at a small group of individuals waiting for their drinks or seeking the attention of the bartender.

The tallest member of the group turned toward Greg. "What'll you have? Make it easy—champagne all around? Looks like there's three of you?"

Greg took a vote. "Sure, thanks. Three champagnes."

Once armed with their drinks, the foursome stepped away from the bar station to a spot where they were able to chat in relative privacy. Erika discovered that it had been Ivan Brooks, a dapper gentleman in his late thirties, tops, who'd provided her with a pass to the evening's event. "Ivan was my colleague at the Art Loss Register, New York office, but Laszlo wooed him away," Greg explained. He patted Ivan's back. "In other words, a defector."

"I was drifting," Ivan said. "I needed a change."

"You mean *change*," Greg replied, jingling the coins or keys in his pocket, the sudden movement causing his wife to wobble at his elbow. He took a sip from the fluted glass held in his other hand. "Seriously, Ivan's one of the select account executives around here and the savviest of the lot. Of that, I can assure you, ladies. I'm proud of you, mate, and to be honest, a tad jealous."

Ivan fiddled with the silk handkerchief tucked in the breast pocket of his three-piece suit.

Judging from the tight smile tensing Ivan's jawline, a detour was in order. "How long have you been at Laszlo's?" Erika asked.

"Two years." Ivan ran a palm over his slicked-back hair, calling attention to the gray streak running through it.

"And do you live here in the city?"

"For now, we're in Atlantic Highlands, New Jersey, an hour's ferry trip to the dock right here at Thirty-fifth and the river. Not a bad commute, but Laszlo's been pressing me to move closer to the action."

"*Those* three seem to be having a lively discussion," Marcia segued, nodding toward a group roughly ten yards away composed of two tuxedoed gentlemen and a relatively young woman in a more form-fitting version of their attire. "The woman's half their size, but seems to be holding her own—*more* than her own."

"Good observation," Ivan said. "She's a tigress. Name's Eva Kent, runs a restaurant chain in the Midwest: Kent House. Lays low, though, when her prey's on the block. Waits for her competitors to be what I call winded before putting in her first bid. The gray-haired fellow, William Dobbs, is a self-made billionaire who's stocking a museum he's opening in six months—in his name, of course. A regular tomcat; sprays his mark on buildings worldwide. Trying to outdo Trump. The other one, Max Rayburn, is even wealthier, but more of a connoisseur. It'll be interesting to see how the three will play off each other around the Monet."

Greg smiled. "There'll be no chandelier bids on *that* one tonight."

Marcia's glance flitted up to the crystal-studded halo chandelier suspended overhead—one of eight such fixtures illuminating the hall—then back to her husband. "Explain."

"It's an unscrupulous tactic used when interest is flagging. The auctioneer nods to an indistinct area, as if to a bidder, in order to introduce a fake bid that he hopes will get the ball rolling. You see, if a reserve price is not met, the item on the block will not be sold." To Marcia's questioning look: "It's the minimum the consignor and the auction house agree is the lowest price they'll accept on an item, or 'lot,' as it's called. If the reserve's not reached, the work will be withdrawn."

Marcia took a swig of her champagne.

"So," Ivan said, addressing Erika, "Greg's told me you're writing on advances in the art market. There are many facets to the subject, from the definition of beauty to the market structure itself. Are you concentrating on one aspect, or will it be more of a smorgasbord?"

"The article's going to be about five pages. More of an appetizer."

"Perhaps you'll be inspired to explore further, on spec, so to speak. I'd be happy to collaborate."

"Why don't you start by giving her a feel of the place?" Greg suggested. "Take her to the second floor, explain what goes on up there."

Ivan checked his watch. "We've got about ten minutes—Erika?"

The pair dropped off their glasses at the bar station, and Ivan hustled Erika off to the white marble staircase near the building's entrance.

Erika wasn't about to waste a minute of the time granted her. "Speaking of 'market structure,'" she quoted, before they'd mounted the first step. "Do you find that buying art as a commodity has overtaken the art market, or is that an exaggeration?"

"I'm not a statistician, but I can tell you that buying art for speculation rather than for appreciation has increased by leaps and bounds. How could it not, when there's nothing restraining a painting's meteoric rise in value, including the vagaries of commonplace economics?" They'd reached the red-carpeted landing. "That's not to say that appreciating art and using it to accumulate wealth are mutually exclusive."

"I should hope not!"

To the right was a glassed-in shop, its shades drawn. Its name, in stylish lower-case letters above its revolving door, simply: *gallery*. "Paintings and statuary from our up-and-coming artists," Ivan explained. "Populated by the execs at PAPNEA—you familiar with the animal?"

Of course, she was. It was at that charity's gala at the Pierre Hotel that she'd met Harrison. That fateful meeting had been the harbinger of their stormy affair and mutual healing—hers, from her father's abandonment that had destroyed her belief in enduring love, and his, from a sordid divorce that had caused him to lose trust in his strength of judgment. "Yes, I'm familiar with it. Partnership to Aid and Promote New and Emerging Artists," she spouted.

"I'm impressed."

"Don't be. My husband's on the board."

"*Doubly* impressed." He glanced at his watch. "A number of our emerging artists have made it to our afternoon auctions. A select few, to the premier tier. But come, I want you to meet someone." He headed left.

The first door they came to was paneled with frosted glass etched, again in classy lower case, with the words *assets & finance*. "Are you sharing quarters with an investment company?" she asked—too sassy, in retrospect.

Ivan flashed a grin. "What were we saying about the speculative market? This is the office where you can invest in a group of paintings and never lay eyes on them."

I should be incredulous, but somehow I'm not. "Like a fund?" she asked. "As in stocks and bonds?"

"Exactly like. The general manager of finances has been quite active in the field. He started out with a single diversified art fund that included a small sampling of works ranging from Old Masters to established contemporaries, but in the last three months, he's added several specialized funds. The Impressionists, for one. African and Oceanic Art for another."

"I work for an art magazine. I should have known about this."

"You've been focused on art for art's sake. That's a good thing."

Instinctively, she found the idea of an art fund unsavory. She tried to chalk up the feeling to naiveté, but that did not dispel it. She could not help but view such a commodity as a means of bringing art into the sector of distilled commercialism, where a painting is not valued for its inherent beauty or ability to touch the soul, but purely for how it stacks up against, say, shares of Amazon. "When was the concept introduced?" she asked, hoping she was at least only slightly behind the times.

"Philip Hoffman, on retiring as financial director of Christie's, unveiled the first equity art fund back in 2001." To her rueful head shake, he added, "Don't fret. Min Cho will have you boned up in no time." To her puzzled look, he hastened her on to the next door, this one etched with the words: *general management.* He rapped on the door and charged in, Erika trailing behind. "Hello there, Min. This is Erika Shawn Wheatley. She's an art magazine editor, writing a piece on the art market. A good friend of a good friend. We've got a minute before the chime, but I wanted you two to meet." He stepped aside and pressed Erika forward with a hand at the small of her back as he rattled on. "This is Min Cho. Min knows everything about the auction house, from contracts to authentication. She's also a living Rolodex and can direct you to the person who can answer the questions she can't answer herself, which are rare as hen's teeth." He smiled with no noticeable break in speech. "Min is not allowed to go home until the action is over.

Some clients—we won't name names—need to have her around as a security blanket."

Min Cho was sitting motionless behind her sleek, ebony wood desk, looking like a porcelain doll. That is, until she popped out of her chair and reached across her desk to pump Erika's hand. "Ivan exaggerates, but let me give you my card." She fetched one from the holder on her desktop, scribbled her private cell phone number on its face, and handed it over. "Call me any time." As an afterthought: "Would you give me your number?" She smiled, pen poised over a notepaper. "You never know."

"Of course!" Erika recited her cell phone number and stuffed Min's business card into her clutch as a three-toned chime sounded from below. After a parting word, she and Ivan hurried off to join the auction attendees being ushered into an auditorium adjoining the main room. Before gaining access, each individual was being checked off the guest list by what appeared to be a footman abducted from the set of *Downton Abbey* and handed an engraved program of the evening's event. The guests listed as bidders were also given paddles, their paddle numbers duly recorded.

The large auditorium had the feel of a rich dowager's living room set up for a chamber concert, Erika thought as she passed through the wide opening created by the French doors. Two plush-looking couches with velvet throw pillows stood against each of the side walls as if they'd been pushed there to accommodate the Victorian-style straight-back chairs placed in rows of a dozen or so, maybe ten deep. The chair-seats, upholstered in brown velvet, took on a warm glow produced by the wall sconce lights, the candle-lit effect encompassing the raised stage area as well. An empty display easel stood in the center of the stage on which a long horizontal light was mounted. "The LED light picks up more colors than the ordinary bulb, soon to be extinct," Ivan informed Erika once he'd directed the threesome to their reserved seats in the second row and planted himself next to her. "It picks up more colors than ordinary light, and can be dimmed or brightened to show the art work in different settings." Erika also knew that diode light safeguarded art works more efficiently than filament light by generating far less heat, but Ivan seemed so genuinely happy to contribute to her appreciation of the event, she kept her mouth shut.

Directly left of the easel stood a podium, as yet unattended. On it sat a wood gavel and its sound block. Farther left and slightly recessed stood another podium. Behind it, a formally attired gentleman was speaking inaudibly on a cell phone. "He's setting up communications with the phone bidders," Ivan said, addressing Erika. He touched her elbow. "I'm excited for you."

Erika glanced down at her program. "*I'm* excited for me!" Signac, Vlaminck, Pissarro, Seurat, Bonnard, Monet, names converging in a festival of sunlit colors.

"I must admit I'm a little uneasy for the owner of the Monet," Ivan confided. "It's the consignor's—"

"Translation, his *client's*," Greg put in. "Ivan's his handler."

"Yes, well, it's his first major foray into the art market. He's not particularly overjoyed about it."

Greg leaned toward Erika. "They share secrets," he said under his breath, as if the remark itself was a secret.

Ivan blanched. "*What?*"

"A joke, mate," Greg assured him, his quizzical look a silent rebuke.

A gentleman in a dark suit, white shirt, and bow tie entered stage right. The presumptive auctioneer.

"Foreplay's over," Greg commented just above a whisper, before the audience's hum came full stop.

The newcomer strode to the main podium. He was carrying a folder. He laid it open next to the gavel set. "Welcome, ladies and gentlemen. I'm Vincent Trilby, and I'll be emceeing what I expect will be quite a thrilling event this evening." He grinned broadly. (*At his playful use of the word "emceeing"?* Erika wondered.) Turning serious: "Before we begin, a familiar word of caution. Please turn off or silence your cell phones and any other devices that might disturb the proceedings. Flash photography is prohibited. Taking *any* photos, flash or otherwise, of bidders, or in fact anyone other than myself or Mr. Lawrence"—he gestured toward the man with cell phone standing behind the second podium—"is also prohibited, strictly prohibited, and *enforced*. Thank you." He cleared his throat. "The first offering this evening is lot number twenty-four, *The Chatou Bridge*, a Maurice de Vlaminck oil executed in 1907." As he finished the sentence, two young women, managing to look stately in black long-sleeve jumpsuits, black sneakers, and white gloves, emerged from the passage from which Mr. Trilby had come. Between them, they bore the ornately framed Vlaminck painting as if it were a king's litter.

"The painting is eighteen by fifteen inches," Trilby went on, eyeing the women like a hawk as they delivered their royal charge to the display easel's base. "Smaller than our Fauvist's later rendition of the railway bridge but equally vibrant, one might venture to say even more so." He adjusted the horizontal light above the painting as the carriers solemnly marched off. "You see how the unblended colors are so boldly reflected in the Seine? The pinks, blues, yellows, greens, oranges?"

Erika nodded, mesmerized.

Trilby glanced at his notes. "The provenance of this painting is, in a word, fortuitous," he went on, looking up. "It was purchased fresh off the easel by Bernheim Jeune, art collector and noted gallery owner. In 1933, he sold the painting to Gertrude Stein, writer and major patron of the avant-garde in the Paris art scene. As you may know, Bernheim's gallery and private collection were looted by the Germans during their occupation of Paris in 1940. A number of Vlamincks were included in the seizure. Thus, one disastrous detour was averted by this painting. And here's another.

"In 1940, Gertrude gave the painting to her brother, Leo, another avid art collector. Upon his death in 1947, it was inherited by a close relative, in whose possession it has been to this day. In 1946, Gertrude died, leaving her estate to her life partner, Alice B. Toklas. The partnership had no legal standing, and while Alice was away from the apartment that she and Gertrude had shared on rue Christine, an acquisitive relative of Gertrude's removed the paintings and locked them away in a bank vault. Luckily, the painting before you escaped the abduction.

"And so, ladies and gentlemen, I'd say the stars have aligned for someone here tonight!" He took a giant step to the side, as if the Vlaminck was about to hop off the easel. "Bidding is open at one million two hundred thousand. Do I see three hundred?" He snapped a nod of acknowledgment to someone in the audience, then pointed to another: "Four." And another: "Five."

Erika swiveled in her seat to have a look. In an aisle seat in the rear, Eva Kent—"the tigress"—was holding her paddle casually atilt, as if her bid had been a passing thought.

"On the phone—six!"

Erika spun back, in time to catch Trilby's cohort with the cell phone to his ear in the act of lowering his raised hand.

"Seven!" Trilby sang out. This, to another paddle-bearer. Erika, facing front, wondered if it had been to Eva—or was the woman hanging back, playing cagey?

"One million eight hundred thousand, in the rear, bidder number twenty-two." Trilby glanced at phone-man, who nodded as he raised two fingers. "We have two million. Do we have two million one hundred?"

Next to Erika, a sharp intake of breath from Ivan. She jerked her head toward him as Trilby continued to announce the bids, heading toward three million, full steam ahead. Ivan was looking down at some notice on his cell phone screen, his features registering shock. The device must have been set on vibration mode.

"You okay?" Erika whispered, regretting it instantly. What business was it of hers what went on in his life?

He turned toward her, looking almost grateful for the transgression. "Got to go," he whispered back. He grabbed her wrist too firmly, his ring digging into her flesh. "Keep in touch!" Without a glance toward Greg and his wife, he rose from his seat and, scraping past several people to get to the aisle— "sorry, sorry, excuse me"—he exited the row and walked swiftly toward the exit, bending low, as if to escape notice.

Greg and Marcia had been focused on the bidding until Ivan rose to his feet. They gave Erika a questioning look, Marcia leaning across her husband to read Erika's lips.

"He said he had to go," Erika mouthed.

"Shhh!" the person on the other side of the now-empty seat cautioned, although Erika hadn't uttered a sound.

"Later," Greg mouthed to Erika as his wife re-centered herself in her seat.

The bidding had climbed to three million and was rising in increments of fifty thousand. It held at three million three hundred fifty thousand dollars, and Trilby struck the sound block with his gavel, punctuating the sale with the traditional cry: "Sold!"

The audience gave a round of applause to the anonymous buyer (or buyer's agent) on Mr. Lawrence's cell phone. No individual or corporate acknowledgment followed. To Erika, this was both a mystery and an anti-climax. The unexplained nature of Ivan's departure added to the effect, but the vaguely unsettled feeling was quickly dispelled by an excitement rippling through the audience as the white-gloved carriers reappeared onstage solemnly bearing another wonder of the world.

"Paul Signac's *The Clouds, Antibes*, 1917," Trilby announced as the vibrantly colored oil was gently placed on the easel's ledge. "Reminiscent of his *Pink Cloud*, painted the year prior. Post the short brush-stroke technique of his Impressionist period, and even beyond his studied Pointillism, or the application of pure dots of color to replicate the play of light. He seems to have acquired a greater sense of freedom here, a sense of color for its own sake. Tipping toward Fauvism, might one say?" He granted himself a little smile of self-acknowledgment before glancing down at his notes. "As for the size of the painting," he went on, "it measures twenty-two by—"

One of the carriers suddenly appeared from the wings, heading toward Trilby, who seemed to have spotted her out of the corner of his eye. She moved jerkily, clearly restraining herself from breaking into a run. When she arrived at Trilby's side, she turned to face the audience and bowed slightly, as if she were about to recite a poem. "I apologize for the intrusion," she faltered, putting on a brave face.

Trilby's expression was one of controlled ire.

The young woman muttered something to him, and his expression turned to utter shock before resolving to polite dismay. Raising a forefinger, "Give us a moment, thank you," he advised the audience in delicately modulated tones, before turning his back on it to form a huddle with phone-man, who was energetically engaged with someone on the line. An impatient oil baron, Erika pictured.

Trilby returned to his podium, leaving his cohort to deal with the phone-in client and the carrier to slink offstage. "Houston, we have a problem," he jested, forcing his lips to curl upward despite their quivering. He cleared his throat. "I've just been informed that lot twenty-seven, the Monet still life, *Wedgewood Vase with Flowers,* has been withdrawn."

A rumble of protest from the audience.

"This is a disappointment, of course, but as you—*most* of you—know, not an uncommon occurrence. The consignor has a change of heart, the lot's ownership is in dispute, the question of authenticity arises. Any number of things." He patted his chest, as if to assure himself that *he,* at least, had not been withdrawn. "What is so unusual about this particular occurrence is that it has taken place while the auction is in progress. What normally happens is that the withdrawal occurs well before the auction itself and is transacted behind the scenes, the public remaining out of the loop. I sincerely apologize for this turn of events, but I assure you, you will be seeing a good number of compelling lots on the block this evening."

"The *chopping* block?"

Heads turned to the rear, where the purported speaker, Max Rayburn (the "connoisseur," as per Ivan Brooks), had risen from his seat and had begun ramming his way to the aisle while individuals in his path wriggled to save knees and feet from injury.

"I will be sorry to see you leave, Mr. Rayburn," Trilby called to him without a trace of admonishment. "I do wish you'd reconsider."

Rayburn had made it to the aisle. "Forgive me for the outburst. I came for the Monet, only the Monet." He held up his numbered paddle. "I'll hand it to the attendant on my way out." He offered a bland smile of remorse. "Good evening, Vincent. You haven't seen the last of me." With a little flourish, he turned on his heel and headed for the exit.

The incident hardly distracted Erika, whose thoughts were riveted on her recollection of Ivan's behavior shortly before the announcement of the Monet withdrawal. It was hard to believe that the email or text he had reacted so strongly to had concerned anything other than that imminent event. After all, Ivan was the owner's account executive and must have had a significant stake in the action, financial and reputation-wise, in some ratio or another. Of course, she could understand his dismay, but why hadn't he returned after his urgent communication had ended? What had prompted him to flee the scene altogether?

"Don't overthink it," Greg whispered in her ear, reading her mind through her facial expression. "Ivan's a jumpy sort, tends to overreact. Concentrate on the action at hand. The Signac's up for grabs. Should top one mil."

His prediction, right on point: the Signac was sold for one million fifty thousand; the buyer: William Dobbs, the billionaire Ivan had dubbed a "tomcat." Two lots later, Dobbs was top bidder on two consecutive Pierre Bonnard oils: *The Sleeping Girl* and *Window Overlooking the Garden*. He also claimed for his own the last painting on the block that evening, a work never before displayed in public: *Circus Scene*, painted in 1890 by Georges Seurat, and a precursor to *The Circus*, his final—uncompleted—work, executed shortly before his death in 1891.

"Looks like Dobbs' new museum will be fully stocked, the rate he's going," Greg remarked, helping Marcia to her feet after Trilby had announced the auction's close. Turning to Erika: "Want to join us for drinks at our hotel?"

"Thanks, but I think I'll head home." She glanced at her watch. "Eight-thirty. Bill's probably been waiting fifteen minutes." To Marcia's questioning look, "Our driver," she said, voice dropping. Would she *ever* feel at ease with her life of advantage, acquired through no fault of her own? "Let me at least take you to your hotel." *At least?*

"Jolly good!" Greg replied, disregarding the offer's apologetic undertone. "We're staying at the Park Lane. You mind?"

"Not at all."

The handful of on-site buyers remained behind while Erika and the Smiths streamed out of the auction room with the balance of attendees. The threesome had chosen not to stick around for the predictable review-and-gossip session following the event, and by the time they arrived at the exit, a sizable crowd was already buzzing around the bar.

As Greg held open the massive glass door for his companions, the heavens opened up in an un-forecasted downpour. Huddling under the entrance's eave with her companions, Erika spotted Bill's gray Lexus parked curbside, directly across the Laszlo courtyard. "There he is!" she cried, pointing toward it.

Marcia unstrapped her unwieldy shoes, shoved them at Greg for safe-keeping, and made a beeline for the car, Erika yelling at her to wait. "He's coming with an umbrella!" The trunk of the car popped open. "There!"

Already, Bill was grabbing his oversized black umbrella. He slammed shut the trunk, and by the time Marcia had hydroplaned to the car door, he'd snapped it open. Marcia said something to him and pointed at Erika. Bill nodded and shot Erika a thumbs-up sign, hustled Marcia into the back seat, then slap-footed across the slick, wet granite surface to collect Erika and Greg.

When they were all settled, Greg was sitting shotgun, and Erika and Marcia were sharing the back seat. Marcia was the wettest among them, though as compensation, Greg had made sure to keep her shoes bone dry. His thoughtfulness did not go unnoticed. As he passed the shoes to her, Marcia leaned forward and gave him a peck on the cheek. "Thanks, hon."

Marcia's bending forward had cleared Erika's view out the window facing Laszlo's courtyard. She took a cursory look as Bill shifted out of neutral. "Hold it!" she cried as Marcia leaned back, once again blocking her view.

"Me?" Marcia reacted.

"No, Bill!"

Bill had already shifted back to neutral. "What is it, Miss Erika?"

"From behind the base of the statue—the legs!"

Greg and Marcia saw what she was talking about before Bill was able to. "Oh!" the driver expelled, after Greg had adjusted his position, freeing the sight line. "Must be drunk or homeless; can't just leave him like this!"

Erika had already taken out the cell phone from her evening bag and was punching in 911. After alerting the dispatcher to the emergency and its location, she was asked to describe the subject's condition.

"I don't know. We can only see—yes, I'm going to check on him now." She tried the door on her side. "Unlock the door, please, Bill."

Bill manually unlocked the driver's door. *"I'll go."*

"No, you stay here with my friends!" To the dispatcher: "I'm on my way—Bill!"

The lock popped, and she jumped out into the street and around to the other side, her heart racing, a queasy tension at the pit of her stomach. What was it, some subliminal cue—the angle of a foot, the width of a pants cuff? But how could that be? She couldn't possibly make out details in the waning light of sunset, rain refracting the glow of the courtyard lamp. "Okay, I'm here," she said, lips almost touching the cell phone screen, as she pulled up at the base of the statue.

"The umbrella!" Bill called as Greg flung open the passenger door.

Heedless, "Don't you move, darling!" Greg ordered his wife before slamming the door shut and making a run for it. Erika had already stepped around to the other side of the statue, and all he could see of her was her lower torso, visible between the legs of the larger-than-life child standing beside its colossal mother.

"We'll wait for you," he heard Erika tell the officer, before she was aware Greg had arrived. He stepped around the partially obscured figure lying on the hard granite slick with rainwater and froze.

"I knew it," Erika said tonelessly, shoving her phone back into her evening bag; saw the look of horror Greg directed at her, as if she were some devilish prophet; half believed it herself. She gazed back at him, and her numbness suddenly dissolved into tears.

Still, neither of them openly acknowledging whose body lay before them, the blood at the man's head curling away with the rainwater; Botero's mighty woman and child, their backs to him, underlying the omission. The figures were dark brown, almost black-patinated bronze, and the dead man, in his black suit, seemed part of their tableau or its discard. One of his arms was jammed against the base of the statue, the other flung to the side, the hand gracefully cupped like a ballet dancer's—the hand with the ring that had pressed into Erika's flesh. Looking down at Ivan's hand, she felt its phantom grip on her wrist, the ring's forceful dig. Impossible for that hand to have been doomed into stillness. "I felt for a pulse," she said, anticipating Greg's question. "He's gone." She looked away and saw a few people standing behind the glass door at Laszlo's entrance, waiting to be picked up or for the rain to stop. What must they make of this rain-sodden group, and what did it matter? "The way he reacted to that text or email," she directed to Greg, down on his knees, checking for a pulse, not taking her word for it; she, grateful to him for sharing the burden of proof. "I could see he was alarmed by the message. I thought he would be coming back after he was done talking or texting, but he never did. I thought it was odd. After all, his client's lot was coming up for sale."

Greg rose to his feet, a subtle headshake verifying her medical diagnosis. "And then the lot was removed."

She nodded. "It was then that I thought the two events—the message on his cell phone and the painting's unexpected withdrawal—were related. And just now, when I looked out the car window and saw…"

"You had a sense of foreboding—of what you would find. I wish we could cover him, I mean from the rain and all."

"We can't disturb the scene."

"I know. From what I can see, he was shot in the head…" Tentative, as if declaring the words would set them in stone.

"Yes."

They were silent, standing in the rain that was finally abating, and in that moment the sun completed its descent and darkness fell, a delayed reaction in what seemed an act of respect—or mimicry—of life's end.

Breaking the mood, the distant sound of sirens, increasing to a fugal blare and ending on the arrival of three police cars and an ambulance, enlivening the night in a frenzy of rotating lights.

Ivan was attended to at once. His condition was assessed; his body, hoisted onto a gurney, covered with a white sheet, and delivered to the ambulance. Before driving off, one of the attendants hastily draped Erika in a Mylar blanket, useless, except for the purpose of covering her drenched form, every contour of which had become visible beneath the pale satin fabric.

Erika and Greg were separated, each ushered into the back seat of a police car to be individually grilled by one of the officers on scene. Out her window, Erika could see another member of the squad circling the Botero, the light from his flashlight intermittently focused on the woman and child, making them appear like criminals caught in the act. After she and Greg had provided what they knew of the tragic backstory, two other officers entered the auction house to widen the investigation. From her vantage point, Erika spied the remaining officer heading over to the Lexus, presumably to gather whatever information he could glean from its occupants.

It was a little past 9:30 when Bill and his passengers were cleared to leave the scene. Erika would have liked to have called Harrison but held back for fear of worrying him before she was standing before him, safe and sound.

Approximately twenty minutes later, Bill pulled into the porte-cochère of the Park Lane. After the Smiths deboarded, he produced a beach towel from the trunk of his car and wiped down the dampened leather seats.

At 10:10, Erika, still swathed in the Mylar blanket, was delivered to the corner of 78th Street and Madison Avenue. It had stopped raining. After passing through the wrought iron gate, she tapped the familiar passcode on the door panel and entered the four-story home. As always, the Botero nude—large, plump, stalwart—greeted her in the lobby. She'd grown more or less accustomed to the figure's grandeur over the years and nowadays barely gave her notice. Tonight, the lone figure stopped her cold, taking on the identity of Botero's sculpted mother residing in Laszlo's courtyard. Here, stripped of her child. Erika was seized by a longing that could only be assuaged by the sight of Lucas.

She dropped her shoes and bag in the lobby and took to the stairs, running swiftly and evenly on the balls of her feet, not a movement wasted, until she reached the third floor and stood poised before the closed door of the Blue Room: Lucas's room.

It was the room she'd slept in that first night she'd been a guest in the Wheatley mansion. It had been named after the color of the girl's dress in the Mary Cassatt painting that had for many years graced the wall area above the headboard of the room's twin bed. Erika and Harrison had converted the room to Lucas's, replacing the bed with a crib and, in the process, replacing the painting of the girl with a gender-neutral, colorful landscape. Both of them had felt ambivalent about the decision, but, out of some irritatingly deep-rooted communal bias, had given in to it. The painting of the lovely young woman now resided in the master bedroom as a gentle reminder to expand their views.

Erika slowly turned the knob and opened the door just enough to listen for sounds, but not enough to make out any distinctive shapes in the dark, the glow of the nightlight on the far wall hardly penetrating more than its immediate area. She could hear Lucas's breathing, one tiny audible exhalation interrupting the steady rhythm of it, the response to something dreamt, maybe. She opened the door a little further so she could slip into the room without disturbing him, then gently closed the door behind her.

There they were. Her family. All three tucked together on the twin bed that had not long ago been, unlike the Cassatt painting, restored to its time-honored occupancy when Lucas had graduated from the crib. She stood there, in her crinkly Mylar cape and sopping satin dress and gazed at the trio, seeing them in greater detail as she quickly accommodated to the scantly lit space. They lay on top of the bedding; the pillow, untouched, remained propped up against the headboard. Harrison, in sweatpants and T-shirt, was lying on his back, his right leg draped over the side of the bed, pants leg partially ridden up, revealing the lower portion of his sculpted calf. Lucas lay across Harrison's chest while Harrison's arm encased his small pajama-ed body like a bar on a kiddie ride, holding him in place. Jake, the old Chocolate Lab, was pressed against the contour formed by their bodies like a puzzle piece, deciding this was where it was meant to be, utter contentment making it so.

How had they managed to arrange themselves in such an excruciatingly sweet tableau, Erika wondered. She badly wanted to slip into their midst, where she belonged. Needed to be. Especially now. Impossible, of course, in her soggy state.

Jake's head popped from its nest at the crook of Harrison's left leg, tail signaling his greeting. "Shush, boy," Erika whispered, as if it mattered, once the old pup was in motion, shuffling and heaving, knocking into Harrison's draped leg as he bounded off the bed. Charging at her as if it had been years since he'd seen her. As she fell to her knees to return the greeting and calm him, the Mylar cape fell from her shoulders and Jake burrowed into her arms, what did he care if she got her rainy-ness all over him; she was home. "Quiet, boy." She rose to her feet, grabbing the blanket. "Let's go." She started to the door, again on the balls of her feet—as if it wasn't already too late.

"Erika!" The hoarse whisper coming from Harrison.

She turned. His head was raised. Otherwise, he hadn't moved. Lucas, miraculously, still slept. "I'm sorry," she whispered. "I didn't mean to—"

"You're drenched. What are you carrying there?" Concern brewing.

"Let me dry off. Be right back. It's a Mylar blanket." What was she thinking, that Harrison was going to just lie there and wait?

"Hold it a minute," Harrison directed, carefully sliding out from under Lucas and bracing the boy at the same time. When the maneuver had been completed, he was sitting at the edge of the bed, and Lucas was lying flat on his back, his silhouette practically unchanged. "We had a busy time," Harrison explained, smiling gamely up at Erika despite the fretful brow. He rose to his feet and adjusted the pants leg. "Shall we slip him under the covers or cover him with his spare blanket?"

She was already on her way to the closet. "The spare." She let the Mylar wrap drop to the floor and pulled the folded wool blanket from the high shelf. Holding it away from her wet clothing, she brought it to him. "Here; you better."

Before taking the cover from her, he held her face in his hands and fixed her with a troubled gaze.

"I'll explain," she said simply, relinquishing Lucas's blanket as if it were a peace offering.

* * *

"Oh, God, I should have been with you!" were his first words after she'd uttered hers: an unadorned report that there had been a murder at Laszlo's.

He realized, even as the words came out of his mouth, that there had been a primal selfishness to the thought behind them, that his immediate concern was for his wife having suffered a scare, not that someone had been killed. His priority, especially stunning, now that Erika was perfectly secure beneath the covers, warm and silky smooth after her shower, her eyes betraying her desire despite her horrific news.

As she lay in Harrison's arms, Erika provided him with a full account of the events surrounding the murder of Ivan Brooks. If she was feeling a modicum of guilt for *her* selfish instincts, it did not diminish the intensity of the love-making that followed.

Chapter Two

The next morning Grace was back to her old self, or was determined to be, in her little black uniform dress and scalloped white apron, petitioning her beloved employers, in her uniquely gentle but firm manner, for their individual breakfast orders. They begged her not to bother, to allow them to serve *her* for once, but it was no use protesting once Grace's mind was made up. The only option was to team up with a no-fuss order. They settled on English muffins and coffee. Grace shook her head slowly to indicate she knew what was going on, then opened the bread box.

Lucas, still in pajamas, was sitting between his parents, strapped into his booster seat and thoroughly enjoying his advance into adulthood; the highchair banished forever. Though his rite of passage had taken place months ago, he still seemed to be celebrating it. He leaned forward, fisted his grownup's teaspoon and scooped up a couple of floating Cheerios from his bowl sitting on the wonder of wonders, actual *table*, and deftly delivered his catch intact. He grinned, delighted with himself. Jake, sitting right behind him, raised his head, ready to catch a morsel should it come his way. Not that he was fond of Cheerios, but if it furthered participation in a family activity, he was all in. So far, no luck.

Earlier, before they'd gotten out of bed, Erika and Harrison had gone over what had occurred the day before. Though neither had a deeply personal tie with Ivan Brooks—Harrison had never even met the man— they felt obligated to involve themselves in the murder investigation and confident that they were equipped to do so. The decision was more or less a given, shaped, in part, by others' expectations of them, in part, by what they had grown to expect of themselves over the past number of years. Their conversation, therefore, had focused not on *if* they should approach the situation but on *how*. Erika had wanted to step right into it with a visit to Laszlo's auction house that very day. "I've got an excuse. I'm writing a piece Min Cho offered to talk to me about. You're thinking 'too early,' I know, but I'll know what to say. I can handle it." Harrison had been determined they start off with a call to Greg. "You said the victim had been a colleague of his. Good chance he can provide us with some critical information about him."

Erika had agreed, with the proviso that if Greg couldn't be reached early in the day, she would drop by Laszlo's regardless. "You don't have a class until two this afternoon, so let's not tax Grace with the job of baby-sitting just yet. You can watch Luc, yes?" Inflected as a question, but he recognized it for what it was.

As it happened, there would be no need for Erika to contrive an excuse to get her foot in the door. Shortly after breakfast, while she was donning her pantsuit and Harrison was dressing Lucas for an impromptu walk in the park, she received a call on her cell phone from Min Cho herself. After the call, she zipped up her pants and hurried off to Lucas's room to inform Harrison of the revised plan.

Lucas was raising his arms to allow Harrison to pull on his sweatshirt. "We're going for a walk," the boy said, as his face was hidden by the garment. "No carriage," he added, as his delicate features emerged. He pushed his tousled hair away from his eyes. "We're taking Jake. Wanna come, Mommy?" Jake, in attendance, wagged his tail.

"I'd love to, sweetie, but I've got to go to a meeting. Later, when I come back, I'll take you and Jake for a walk again, okay?" Another wag.

Harrison shot her a questioning look.

"Okay," Lucas agreed and came to her for a kiss goodbye.

"I love you," she said, bending to his level for their huggy kiss. Rising, she asked, "Can I talk to Daddy before I go? You want to pet Jake for a minute? He's looking like he'd really appreciate a good petting." To Jake, "Right, boy?"

Jake rolled onto his back. *Right!*

They left Lucas's door open and walked to the end of the hallway.

Harrison rested his hand on her shoulder. "What's up? You can't be thinking of going to Laszlo's yet. I left a voice message for Greg. At least give him a chance to call back!"

"Min Cho just called me from her office. On her *cell* phone. She wants to talk to me. I suggested we meet for lunch, maybe at Docks, the seafood place a couple of blocks from Laszlo's, but she says she always has her lunch in the staff's break room. She said it would look suspicious if she went out."

"You're kidding. What's she hiding?"

"I have no idea. She referred to our involvement in solving art crimes, so obviously that's what it's about."

"Ivan Brooks's murder."

"What else could it be?"

Already, that familiar twinge in his belly. "I don't like the sound of this. I'm going with you."

"I'll be fine. Anyway, she wants me to come alone. Keep the visit low profile."

"*That* makes sense," he scoffed.

"Actually, it does, sweetheart." She kissed him on his mouth and gently removed his hand from her shoulder. It dropped limply to his side. "Have fun with Lucas. See you soon!" Overdoing the lilt in her attempt to ease his mind.

* * *

Min Cho was waiting for her beside the receptionist's station, a simple white marble circular desk to the right of the entrance, the structure dwarfed by the vast open space of the building's ground floor. "And here's my guest, Cecily," she announced to the tailored young woman sitting behind the desk. Min presented her hand to Erika. Erika noticed its tremor and clasped it firmly in hers before Min guessed she'd noticed it. "I've signed you in," Min said. Her smile couldn't have been tighter. "Come, follow me."

"I'm still amazed by the size of this hall," Erika remarked, small talk always a safe opening, as she trotted after her host.

"It was planned to accommodate larger-than-life sculptures and assemblages," Min said, straining to put her heart into it. "An auction of Pop artists is scheduled for July. Claes Oldenburg's soft sculptures—giant fan, typewriter eraser, clothespin—will be featured." They'd reached the staircase leading up to her office. "We also plan to hold community-oriented events, like silent auctions featuring our highly respected, but lesser-known artists, many on display in our gallery."

"Innovative ideas for an auction house," Erika commented, stepping onto the landing after Min. "Getting the community involved."

Without answering, Min hurried past the *assets & finance* office and ducked into her own, encouraging, with a snappy wave, Erika to be quick about it.

What was up with her?

Min planted herself in her desk chair and gestured at the one across from her. "I haven't thanked you for coming," she said, sounding out of breath.

Erika took her seat, jamming her tote bag at her side. "No need. I was going to initiate a meeting. You beat me to it. So thank *you*."

Min cocked her head. "To discuss your piece for *Art News*?"

"Not really. Well, not now, anyway."

Min sat forward. "We're on the same page, then. Yes?"

Why so cryptic? "I wanted to talk about Ivan Brooks's murder." Coming right out with it. "I thought if we had more details about—"

"'*We*,' meaning you and your husband?"

"Yes. If we had more details about Ivan's work at Laszlo's, and about the painting that was whisked off the market so unexpectedly, and about its owner—about its provenance in general—we could do some probing. If you approved, that is."

"I heard something," Min said, indirectly answering Erika's implied question. "It's been weighing on my mind. I can't think of anyone else to tell."

Stabbing at a response, "Your colleagues? The police?"

"No, no. I promised Ben—Mr. Laszlo—I'd keep my mouth shut. Anybody but you, it would have gotten back to him."

"Why didn't you call me from home, keep it private?" *What the hell are we talking about?*

Min heaved a sigh of exasperation, either at herself, or at Erika for not having guessed what was on her mind. "This is my safe place. All my friends are here. I have no one close on the outside. Mr. Laszlo took me in, not exactly off the streets, but in this business, it amounts to as much. I had a low-level job and not much of a reference, but he told me at my interview that he had a gut feeling about me and hired me on the spot. That's the way he is: impetuous. But it comes with a price. He can just as impetuously fire you as hire you."

"Labile," Erika said, just to register a reply.

"I'm sticking my neck out, but I have no choice."

"Conscience over loyalty," Erika returned, with another on-point non sequitur.

"Exactly right." Min pinned her with a direct gaze, sustained, for the first time, longer than a hummingbird's. "And you know something? What I heard has probably nothing at all to do with Ivan's murder."

"I understand," Erika said. "You're not willing to take that chance." She locked onto Min's gaze with equal determination, as if they were playing a children's staring game.

"Yes." Min glanced down at her lap, then back up at Erika, though with diminished intensity. Game over.

Erika waited for Min to come out with it. After the build-up, she was expecting an anti-climax.

"A call came in the day before yesterday," Min said. "I pick up Ben's calls if he's not at his desk." She checked the closure of the white silk blouse, visible between the lapels of her suit jacket. All was in order. "It was around two in the afternoon. Mr. Laszlo was in conference with the head of finance. The person on the phone sounded extremely agitated; said he needed to speak with Mr. Laszlo at once. I told him to wait a moment and went to fetch Ben from down the hall. As a rule, I dare not interrupt a meeting in progress, but I believed the situation warranted it."

"What made you think it couldn't wait until Mr. Laszlo was free?"

"Don't laugh, but the person had a very distinguished British accent. I assumed he was a distinguished *person*. My bias, but there it is."

"Do you remember his name? Did he give you a hint about the reason for his call?"

"The caller ID registered as 'name unavailable,' but he announced himself as 'Professor Blethmore,' no first name. I remember only the first part of the phone number: forty-four, the country code for the United Kingdom, and twenty, the area code for Greater London. And no, Professor Blethmore did not mention the subject of his call. Worse, I failed to inquire about it. A lapse on my part."

Erika cocked her head. "With no information, how are you associating this call with Ivan Brooks's murder?"

"Good question. For one thing, because of its proximity to the event. That, and its apparent urgency. Maybe more important, Ben's—Mr. Laszlo's—reaction to the call. How eager he was to keep it from becoming known. Even to the point of wiping its origin from existence."

Why was Min struggling to keep Laszlo's first name from escaping her lips? "Are you saying Mr. Laszlo deleted the phone number from the digital records?"

"He did, yes." Min lowered her gaze. "I tried to find it. I couldn't." Her remorse was palpable, either because she'd attempted to betray her boss, or because the effort had failed.

"It's okay," Erika assured her. "It won't be that difficult to track down the professor."

"You're not expecting me to, I hope."

"Not at all. I can see this is making you uncomfortable."

"I can trust your confidentiality? That's why I reached out to you."

"You can, absolutely." Erika adjusted the position of the bag pressed against her hip. "If you're able to, it would be a help if you could provide us—me and my husband—with any information about the withdrawn Monet painting. Its present owner, provenance, anything you have on record or you've, well, *overheard*, that you think might be of use in helping unravel this case."

Min nodded. "I imagine you two are able to draw people out more readily than the police."

"Sometimes, yes."

Min smiled. "More likely *often*, I suspect." She rose from her chair and stepped over to the bookcase on the wall adjacent to her desk. The bookcase, in matching ebony, contained art monographs and legal tomes in separate blocks on the shelves, their segregation absolute. On top of the bookcase, an assortment of auction catalogues lay in a series of neat horizontal piles.

Min stood on tip-toe in her stylish blue and white spectator pumps and removed a catalogue from one of the piles. "Here we go," she said, handing it to Erika. "It contains the Monet provenance. I'll give you the addresses of the consignor and also Ivan Brooks." She returned to her seat. "Although I wouldn't disturb Mrs. Brooks just yet."

"Of course not. And thanks for the catalogue." Erika gazed at the still life gracing its cover. It was a beautiful reproduction, the colors about as vibrant as the original, she imagined. The Impressionist technique of capturing objects as ephemeral constructs of light had not fully evolved, and the objects in the painting were clearly outlined. She was touched by the portrayal centered on the Wedgewood vase of a woman—a Greek goddess, she supposed—playing the lyre; the act, it seemed to Erika, as transient and timeless as the flowers tumbling from the vase, partially obscuring the musician's left forearm. She flipped open the catalogue to search for the painting's provenance.

Min opened a side drawer of her desk. As she did so, Erika heard the door to the office swing open. She looked up from the catalogue to see Min stiffen at the sight of the person who'd opened the door. The door was directly behind Erika, and she decided it might be rude to swivel around to see who it was.

"Well, well, Cecily tells me you have a visitor," trumpeted the entrant as Min noiselessly shut her desk drawer. "Am I wrong, or is it the better half of our crime-solving duo." The question a declaration.

"The distaff half," Erika corrected, rude or not. She lifted her bag to make room to turn around in her seat. Changed her mind and stood up instead. The bag fell to the floor. She was still holding the catalogue. She recognized the man because she'd seen photographs of him. He looked coarser-featured and older in person. She imagined a tattoo on his forearm. His graying brown hair was pulled back in a man bun, and he had on a cashmere turtleneck and a designer suit. A retired wrestler spiffed up by Armani, she thought. "Mr. Laszlo," she said, extending her hand.

"Erika Shawn Wheatley," he barked, giving her hand a vigorous pump. He bent to pick up her bag.

"Thanks." She reached out to take it from him, but he was not ready to give it up. Instead, he stood there, weight on one hip, as if allowing her the pleasure of giving him the once-over.

"You're here to quiz us about the murder," he said.

Another question auto-answered. She guessed he did this a lot. Meant to instill the idea that he knew all the answers; that he could not be played. She recognized the technique. Her father had used it, among others, to subjugate her mother. Erika had realized this only after he'd run out on them, and she'd had time to reflect. Until then, she'd been his pet and his ally.

"Actually, I've come for *this*," she said, holding up the catalogue.

"Quick thinking," he said.

"Ivan introduced me to Erika last night," Min said, finding her voice. "She's writing an article for her magazine on the state of the art market. I told her I'd talk to her any time." She folded her hands on the desktop. "She has a deadline to make," she added for credibility. Her knuckles had turned white.

"Of course, we also talked about last night's tragedy," Erika said, in the hopes of winning Laszlo's trust—not so much for herself, but for Min. Min, who had looked so confident last night. "How could we *not*? But I didn't come here with the intention of *quizzing* anyone. If I'd wanted to, I would have come to you first."

"Appreciate that." He handed her the tote bag.

"Thank you."

"Glad I got to meet you in person." He cupped her elbow. "We'll let Min get back to work. I'll walk you downstairs."

She slipped out of his reach. "That's okay. I can see myself out."

"Your loss," he said half-jokingly. He wagged a finger at her. "Next time you want to scope us out, ask to speak directly to me."

"Will do." She tapped the catalogue to her forehead by way of a salute and headed out the door.

** * **

Erika found Harrison in his study on the first floor, cramming graded essays into his briefcase. He paused to hear her out. She gave him a brief account of what had occurred at the auction house.

"I wish you hadn't been confrontational with Laszlo," he commented afterward.

"What gives you the idea I was confrontational?"

"I can read the room."

"You weren't *in* the room."

"By your tone of voice. Your summary had a bite to it. I could tell you were annoyed with him. I figured he parried."

"*I* was the parrier," she objected.

"Is that even a word?"

"*What?*"

"Parrier."

"I don't know. Probably. Yes!"

"What I'm proposing, Erika, is that this individual is clearly hiding something and, therefore, not the sort of person you want to antagonize."

Generally, she found his occasional professorial turns of phrase quite endearing. Now, not so much. "You saying I should suck up because he's a potential source of information or for my protection?"

"Both. But come on, I'm not really suggesting you suck up."

Didn't she know that? "I know that," she said, her snit vanquished by his rueful look. She held out the catalogue. "You have time to look?"

"Sure." He packed the remaining essays into his briefcase and snapped it shut.

"By the way, you hear back from Greg?" she asked en route to the couch, which was surprisingly free of papers and books.

"Not yet." They sat down beside each other. "I meant to ask, did Min tell you the name of the professor who called Ben Laszlo the day before the auction? The call Laszlo's so eager to keep under wraps?"

Erika lay the Laszlo catalogue and her cell phone on the coffee table, next to a pile of books, one of them Harrison's monograph on the artist Theodore Gericault. "I didn't say? Sorry—Blethmore. Professor Blethmore. From somewhere in London."

He looked surprised. "*Norman* Blethmore?"

She shrugged. "He didn't give his first name. You know him?"

"Norman Blethmore's an art history professor at the Courtauld Institute of Art in London. How many Professor Blethmores can there be in London?"

She awakened her cell phone. In a minute, Google had filled her in. "There's a Jane C. Blethmore, taught life drawing at Central St. Martins. Died three years ago. Then there's Louis Blethmore, a *histologist*, office in Kensington. Short answer, one: Norman Blethmore, at the Courtauld. How do you know him?"

"He gave a talk at a conference at N.Y.U., must be at least seven years ago. We spoke a bit after his talk. Brilliant guy, couldn't have been more than thirty-five years old. Hard to forget. His field, the Impressionists; his specialty within the field was—still is— Camille Pissarro and everything in his orbit. Tremendous insight."

"Pissarro knew Monet. Didn't they meet at the Académie Suisse in Paris?"

"Yes, in 1860. Did you know the godmother of Monet's son, Jean, was Julie Vellay?"

"Pissarro's wife?"

"At Jean's christening in 1868, she was still his mistress, but yes."

"Interesting. Hmm."

"You're thinking, what's the relevance of all this to a Monet still life and the murder of its sales rep."

She nodded.

"So am I."

"Maybe none. I don't know. Maybe Blethmore was calling Laszlo about the Pissarro scheduled to be on the block at yesterday's auction."

He smiled. "You really don't think that, do you?"

"No, not really."

"The confluence of events tells you otherwise," he suggested.

"Tells my gut. Yes."

"Mine, too."

"You're usually not that quick to rely on instinct," she half-teased.

"You're a bad influence." He stroked her thigh.

She laid her hand over his. "I'm calling Min on her cell phone after hours in a day or two. Give her time to recuperate from my visit. Maybe she'll have more to say."

"Just be careful."

"I'll be diplomatic," she edited. "Why are you so obsessed with my safety?" Without allowing him time to deny or justify the accusation, she asked, "When's a good time for you to call Professor Blethmore, given the five-hour time difference?"

"Depends if I'm calling him at his home or at Courtauld's. Did you see a home listing for him? Home would give us more privacy."

"I didn't see one, but I'll look again." She re-awakened her Google search. No luck. Harrison would have to wait until tomorrow; try reaching Blethmore at the institute. "Shall we have a go at Monet's still life?" She picked up the catalogue, rifled through to the page devoted to the Monet. "I'm hoping the provenance will suggest something in the past that might have impacted the present." She sighed. "As if the due-diligence people at Laszlo's wouldn't have picked up anything fishy without our help."

"You underestimate our skills," he jested. "Especially your own."

"Our objectivity, maybe," she replied in all seriousness. "That might be a deciding factor here. Let's look." She slid closer to him, resting the open catalogue on his lap. Printed below the sharp reproduction of a Wedgewood vase overflowing with colorful blooms, the provenance:

Oscar-Claude Monet (1840-1926), Wedgewood Vase with Flow-ers, executed May 1870, oil on canvas, 20"x 17"; until January

3, 1871: purchased by James and Abigail Scott of Greenwich, Connecticut; until May 2, 1908: transferred by inheritance to Elizabeth Barden née Scott, Greenwich; until January 5, 1927: purchased by Lewis Keller of New York City; until June 7, 2015: transferred by inheritance to Morris Keller, New York City.

Original (1871) and in-house certificates of authentication may be examined upon request.

Erika tapped the page, as if that would help commit it to memory. "Morris Keller, present owner, as of 2015." Stating the obvious to get the ball rolling.

Harrison rescanned the summary. "What are we looking for?"

"Could it be that some associate or relative believes he or she is the rightful owner of the painting?" Erika grabbed out of a hat. "In which case, an in-depth probe of its history would be in order."

"Why murder someone over such a claim?" Harrison objected. "Ownership disputes are brought to court almost on a regular basis."

"Who knows. Maybe the transaction was made over a handshake. Maybe the critical documentation was lost or destroyed."

"But *murder*?"

She shrugged. "Passion a possible factor?"

"Passion aimed at the putative owner's account executive?"

"I'm spinning my wheels. Let them spin."

He leaned toward her, touching his head to hers. Pulling away to face her directly, he said, "After we speak to Greg, possibly Min Cho, possibly Norman Blethmore, we'll have a better grasp of what avenues to pursue."

"What if the Monet was stolen?" she asked, on to other scenarios. "What if this trail of ownership is a fraud and someone was threatening to expose Morris Keller?" Her comeback to his reactive smile: "What do we know about the mysterious Mr. Keller, anyway?"

"Oh, I'm sure you're itching to dig your heels into *that* one!" The merry words no sooner out of his mouth than he was fretting about the risks she'd be willing to take for the cause.

She noticed his double-take. "Spinning the wheels," she reminded him.

"Going nowhere."

* * *

As he was about to head off to his 2:00 p.m. class, Harrison got a call back from Greg on his cell phone. Erika was on her way up to her study on the third floor. He requested she come back down. He wanted her in on it. "Greg, hello." He activated Speakerphone. "How are you doing today?"

"Glumly. Just hitting me today, to be honest. Ivan was an excellent fellow and too damn young to be cut down. Did you know he had two children? Little ones, pushing two and three. Think they'll even remember their dad? Do *you* remember anything from that age?"

My father, blowing his nose into an enormous white handkerchief. "Bits." By this time, Erika was at his side. "I've got you on speakerphone. Erika's here."

"Hi, Greg," she checked in. "I heard what you were saying. No adequate response to it, is there? I'm sorry."

"Thanks, love."

Harrison winced inwardly despite himself.

"How's his wife doing?" Erika asked.

"Robin's doing as well as can be expected. That is, dreadfully."

"Stupid question," Erika chided herself.

"No, reflexive. You ever hear it *not* asked?"

The purpose of the call was threatening to become the elephant in the room. Harrison segued: "As a colleague—a friend, even—you must know things about Ivan—traits, associations, his *past*—that may have a bearing on this tragic event. I mean to say, *do* you?" He waited for an answer. There was none. "Greg, have I offended you in some way? If so, I apologize." He glanced at Erika. He took her who-knows? shrug as moral support. "Greg?"

"No offense. I was thinking, is all. I saw Robin this morning; visited her in New Jersey. She wanted to see me. Alone. I'd never met her, but apparently, Ivan had sung my praises, gotten it into his head that I was a splendid, trustworthy chap. I suppose she's a malleable sort and was convinced. This morning she disclosed something to me and swore me to secrecy. I decided no harm in telling you people, whose trustworthiness surpasses mine, and I was just about to do so."

The silently chorused *And?* hung in the air.

"I decided otherwise. Perhaps I'm more trustworthy than I thought."

"I'm not sure how to react," Harrison replied. "Obviously, we're curious."

"What you were told must be related to the murder investigation," Erika said, more to the point. "Otherwise, you wouldn't have considered divulging it."

"Why else, indeed." After a pause: "I'm thinking I should ask Robin if I might bring you two over to meet her. I think she could be persuaded to take you into her confidence."

"If she wanted to see you alone, why would she welcome two strangers?" Erika asked.

"She might not. I'm hopeful that after I share a bit of your sleuthing history and attest to your sterling characters, she might. I'll give her a call. Would tomorrow—Friday—work for you? Marcia and I have postponed our flight back to London to Monday, early, so Sunday would be the very latest. Good chance the poor woman may be inundated with relatives on the weekend."

Erika's hours at *Art News* were flexible, and Harrison could arrange for his T.A. to take over his Friday seminar. They would await Robin's decision.

Chapter Three

At 5:15 a.m., in the faint light just before the sun was about to break the horizon, Harrison crept out of bed. He slipped on the jockey shorts, sweatpants, and T-shirt crumpled at the foot of the bed and grabbed the cell phone from his night table. He tried not to rest his gaze on his sleeping wife, guilelessly splayed in bare-breasted grace, as if arranged in that position by a besotted artist—himself, as he was occasionally given to fantasizing.

Once in his study, he scooted around his desk and pulled out his chair to allow Jake, aroused from drowsy guardianship just outside Lucas's room, to take occupancy in the kneehole of the desk: his favorite spot, but only when he was sharing it with Harrison's lower legs. "Good boy," Harrison said, when Jake was properly tucked in and he himself had taken his seat.

A ballpoint pen and an open spiral pad lay on the desktop at the ready. The name "Norman Blethmore" and the phone number for the Courtauld Institute headed the page. Harrison reawakened his cell phone. The time registered on its screen was 5:21. 10:21 in London, British Summer Time. Should be good. He punched in the number. After choosing "main desk" as the safest prompt, a crisp female voice greeted him and inquired after his reason for calling. He identified himself and asked to speak with Professor Norman Blethmore. After a troublesome pause reminiscent of Greg's, she required a more specific motive for the call.

"It's a personal matter," he said reactively, instantly remembering the more compelling answer up his sleeve.

"I'm afraid the professor has passed away."

"*What?*" As if he hadn't heard her!

"Professor Blethmore has—"

"Yes, yes. Sorry." An image of a young man, slightly round-shouldered—a stance of humbleness, he remembered thinking—yet speaking with authority and brilliance despite himself. "May I ask the circumstances…" he began.

"I'm going to put you through to the art department's acting chair, Professor Meagan Dunne," the gatekeeper politely replied, cutting him off. "She's in Professor Blethmore's office now, I believe. Please hold while I try the extension."

Shortly, the professor announced herself. "Meagan Dunne here," she said, sounding like she wished it was elsewhere. There was a rich tone to her voice. He imagined it was generally more melodious. He introduced himself.

She recognized his name; had read his book on Gericault and was familiar with his and his wife's forays into the world of art crime. Instantly legitimized, he dove right into the subject of his inquiry, aiming for the middle ground between forthcoming and circumspect. He touched on three closely occurring events: Norman Blethmore's call to Laszlo's, the removal of a Monet still life from the auction block, and the murder of Ivan Brooks. "I don't know why Professor Blethmore called Laszlo's. The call's proximity to the other two events is all we have at the moment. Erika and I, that is. There's a good chance the detectives investigating Ivan's murder are unaware of the professor's call."

"I understand," Meagan said. "The active players in this case—*any* case—are more likely to take you into their confidence than those more forbidding authorities—in or out of uniform."

"Exactly."

"And in order to determine its relevancy to Mr. Brooks's murder, you're hoping to find out from us, here at Courtauld's, why Norman called the auction house in New York City."

"Actually, I was hoping to speak to the professor himself. I was just told that he had passed away." He balked at the euphemism. "To be honest, I can't believe it. He was so young, so…*thriving*. When did it happen? His call to Laszlo's took place only three days ago!"

"That's the day he died—Tuesday—late Tuesday night!"

"Meagan, has it been determined what he died *from*?"

"His death is still under investigation. He was found in his office, slumped over his desk. There's talk of suicide—a drug overdose. I don't believe it for a second."

"Oh?"

"I have no idea why he made that call to the auction house, so I can't help you there. I do know he was working on a book, his second on Camille Pissarro, and was of sound mind and body. No spurning lover or terminal illness in sight. I'm just now packing up papers, photos, plants, remnants left behind by the police. I've looked them over, and I can assure you there's nothing here of possible interest to you."

"You think he was murdered," Harrison declared. He hadn't meant to sound so certain.

"I'm not prepared to say," Meagan replied, suddenly evasive. "You should speak to Darien. He might be of help."

"Darien?"

"Darien Roth. A colleague. Teaches a comprehensive course on art history, but his area of expertise, the Surrealists—in particular, Dali and De Chirico. Darien and Norm are close friends—*were*. He's not in today, but I'll send you back to the operator, and she'll connect you to his line at our residence facility. Sorry, but I'm not at liberty to give you his cell phone number."

Harrison thanked her and waited for the gatekeeper to come on the line. When she did, he advised her that at Professor Dunne's behest, he was to be connected to Darien Roth's residence number. This time, no further explaining was required.

Darien's voice message was a buoyant but brief request to "leave your name, reason for your call, and a contact number." Harrison stated his "reason" as "an urgent matter concerning Professor Blethmore" and hoped he'd hear back.

There was no way of getting back to the operator except to hang up and redial the institute's number. Before reconnecting, he glanced down at the four names of faculty members he'd gotten from Courtauld's online catalogue and had entered in his notepad below Norman Blethmore's: instructors whose courses, hence interests, might possibly dovetail with Blethmore's. A shot in the dark, but he had to start somewhere. Darien Roth's name was not on his list, proving the inaccuracy of his aim.

A male's voice greeted him the second time he opted for the "main desk" prompt. Again, after reciting the name of the individual he wished to speak to—randomly selected from his list, Professor Matt Henley—he was asked to explain himself. This time, he was ready with the answer he'd forgotten to use the first time around: another digitalized bit of information he'd picked up on Google. "It's in regard to your upcoming conference on Cubism and Abstract Art. I've received an invitation to be one of your guest speakers." He was put through immediately.

Professor Matt Henley was on a break between classes, "grabbing a bite to eat in the discomfort of my office," as he cheerfully reported. "An egg sandwich and green tea—a play on Dr. Seuss, sounds like." Right off the bat, setting a receptive tone.

Harrison had put Matt Henley on his list at least partly because his field of expertise was, as one of his courses indicated, "Art as Business," pertinent to the article Erika was writing and a possible resource for it. He was not expecting to strike gold here. After presenting Henley with more or less the same exposition he'd given Meagan Dunne, he waited to hear an amiable but dead-end answer.

"My God, of *course* the call is relevant!" he heard instead.

"The call Ivan made to *Laszlo's*?"

"Yes, yes, wait while I gather my thoughts," Henley rapid-fired. "Where do I begin?"

"Wherever! Take as long as you like!" Considering Henley was on a break between classes, he added, "Although if it's inconvenient, we can talk another time." Hoping the offer would be declined.

"It's fine, this won't take long." Henley took two distinctly audible breaths and began. "My field is the art market. I study its fluctuations and their determinants, such matters as the cause-effect relationship between concurrent tastes and political climate. As such, I keep up with the goings-on in the avenues of exchange. Art auctions being one. I'm on the mailing list of all the major houses of the world. Laszlo's is a relatively new addition to my list. In most cases, I receive the online version of catalogues of auctions scheduled for the near future, and subsequently, outcomes of the the events themselves. Laszlo's is one of the few houses that sends me its hard-copy catalogues.

"Two weeks ago, I received the Laszlo catalogue for its upcoming auction. When I finally got around to looking it over, maybe two days before the event itself, I saw there was a lovely Pissarro up for auction, and thought I'd give Norm a heads-up, Norm being the undisputed authority on the artist." He paused. Harrison pictured him shaking his head at his misuse of the present tense.

"I brought the catalogue to his office and handed it to him," Henley went on. "I was about to reference the page number where he'd find the Pissarro, but he was staring at the *cover* of the catalogue with what I can only describe as alarm."

"The Monet still life of a vase and flowers," Harrison prompted. He had to be absolutely certain.

"Yes. I asked him what had caught his attention, but he put me off; asked if he could borrow the catalogue. Now, it makes sense. I have no idea *what* sense, but after hearing you talk of the proximity of his phone call to Laszlo's and the Monet being pulled from the auction, I'd venture to say that Norman's phone call is, one way or another, related to the tragic turn of events. You must agree!"

"I do now."

"I don't understand. The fellow was obsessed with Pissarro, practically living at the Ashmolean Museum, poring over the latest personal documents of the artist's that had been gifted to the institution. Documents that had apparently turned up pursuant to the sale of his son Lucien's London home. Norm was working on another book on Pissarro, you know."

"I wasn't aware the Ashmolean Museum had received an addition to their Pissarro archives," Harrison said, already planning ahead on how to frame his inquiry to the institution.

"Not exactly headline material… Say, before we end this call—and we really must end this call, I've got about four minutes to finish my grub and get to class—I wonder if you might tell me under whose aegis you and your wife are investigating the murder of this Ivan Brooks fellow?"

Did Harrison detect a sudden note of wariness? "Our personal aegis, to be honest."

"May I ask why?"

"As I told you, my wife was there. She met Ivan Brooks that night; he showed her around; later, she saw him lying in the courtyard, dead. In the rain. She feels a certain obligation. Because of her, so do I. This is the first time we're acting on our own initiative. In the past, we've been asked to participate."

"Well, then, you're bona fide sleuths."

"In a sense."

After a near-explosive exhalation: "Aha—the Nigerian case! I *knew* your name sounded familiar! I was so intrigued by the circumstances of the case, your name dropped by the wayside!"

"Good. We try to keep a low profile."

"It's working."

They shared a laugh. Harrison's first of the day.

They were signing off as Erika knocked on the door and entered the room. Barefoot and clad only in her clingy floral silk robe, her sleep-rumpled hair framing her face as it had done earlier, as she lay sprawled on her back, dead to the world and her husband's scrutiny. "Getting the jump on me, are you?" She cocked her head. "Why are you looking at me like that?"

"As if you didn't know."

"Focus. What have you been up to?" She wrapped herself more securely in her robe, as if a play on modesty would do the trick.

He summed up his interactions with the Courtauld staff, beginning—and ending— with the shocker.

Erika sank down onto the couch. Blethmore was *murdered?*"

"No official call—suicide is presently under consideration—but from what

I heard, homicide seems the more likely cause of death. He was apparently in good health and preoccupied with researching his second book on Camille Pissarro, deep diving into the Ashmolean archives. Not a likely candidate for suicide."

"Agreed. There's no proof, but I think we should assume that his death is a homicide and related to what transpired at Laszlo's."

"It won't hurt to make that assumption if it moves us forward." He rose from his desk chair and headed for the couch. Jake stirred, but decided to hold his ground.

Harrison sat down beside Erika, careful not to come into contact just yet. "I'd like to look through the material Blethmore found so engrossing," he put forth.

"You'd like to visit the Ashmolean," she phrased more directly. "I'm guessing you'd also like to follow up your phone conversations with face-to-face interviews," she added, throwing her arm across the back of the couch and unintentionally baring more of her décolletage.

"With you, of course," he proposed. "You can get away for a few days, can't you?"

She shook her head. "I think at this point we'll cover more ground if we went in different directions. Besides, who knows how much new material has been added to the Pissarro archives? Maybe tons. You don't need me hanging around looking over your shoulder." She returned her arm to her side, which caused a sizable gap to form at the robe's now more relaxed closure. This she noticed, but did nothing about, her teasing in mischievous counterpoint with their sober conversation. "Plus, the professors will feel more at ease if they're able to speak to you one-on-one."

"You think?" He was trying to maintain eye contact.

"I do. And meanwhile, I'll be making inquiries of my own, stateside."

No point in asking Erika to stay out of trouble. She'd accuse him of being an alarmist and do what she liked, anyway. "John might be of some help to you," he suggested—subtly, he thought.

"You mean as my bodyguard," she came back, flashing a wry smile. "But seriously, I was thinking he might be our go-between with the detectives on the Ivan Brooks murder case."

"Translation, our informer."

"Yes." John Mitchell was their cop-turned-private-detective cohort and, informally, on standby as their partner in crime-solving. "You know," she said, "he's gotten his deputy status with New York's FBI Art Crime division renewed; should be good for another year."

"Useful. Greg, too, is always up for probing the data files of Art Loss Register for us, as well as gaining access to sources we're not privy to."

"Agreed." She crossed her legs, causing the sides of her robe to part, just enough to suggest the shape of her thigh. "Since we're virtually trespassers on this case, our association with Greg gives us a certain legitimacy." She reached over and gave his knee a chummy rub. "So, I guess you'll be wanting to give a call to the Ashmolean around about now."

She was drawing him in, wasn't she? He lay his hand over hers. He was unable to suppress a smile. "You're evil, you know that?"

She mugged an innocent shrug.

He rose from the couch.

"Where are you going?" she asked, clearly disappointed.

"Where do you think?" he shot back, reveling in her dismay. "To lock the door!"

When he returned, she was lying on the couch, robe untied and fallen open, the natural pose reminding him of the one he'd pretended to have arranged earlier, bedside. Only now the artist's subject was awake, aware of his gaze, and ready for him.

* * *

Jake emerged from beneath the desk and padded over to the couch. Who knows what olfactory and auditory stimuli had led him to believe the lovers' closed session had concluded? Erika, her robe aligned and belted only seconds ago, rose from her seated position. Still flushed from their lovemaking, she offered, "I'll make coffee. You call the Ashmolean?" Responding to Harrison's contented "Yeah," she headed for the door.

Jake, torn between which of them he should choose to be with, finally chose the passive, more tactful option and plopped down where he stood.

* * *

By early evening, neither the Courtauld Professor, Darien Roth, nor the Ashmolean archives conservator had responded to Harrison's voice message. Owing to the five-hour time difference, he no longer expected to be hearing from either one today. It was also disheartening that Greg had never called back with a response from Ivan's widow, Robin, regarding her willingness to see him and Erika on this or any other day. There had been no need for Harrison to call on his Teaching Assistant to take over his seminar. He'd led it himself.

Still, psychologically, the Wheatleys were on alert, waiting for the calls they were certain would not come. They were sitting at the kitchen table, busying themselves by peeling tangerines for a pre-prandial snack neither particularly wanted. Lucas had already eaten his dinner and was seated at his play table pretending to read a Winnie the Pooh book.

Erika collected the peels from both their tangerines and rose from the table. "I'll give Lucas his bath and read to him for a while. Let's watch a movie tonight, okay, babe?" She dropped the peels in the garbage disposal.

"Sure," Harrison replied. "Classic or crap?"

"Definitely crap." She kissed the top of his head. "Lucas, sweetie, time for a bath. Afterwards, you want to read that book with me?"

Ten minutes after Erika and Lucas had gone off together and Harrison was poking around the refrigerator looking for another distracting snack, his cell phone rang. He kneed the refrigerator door shut and dug for the device in his pants pocket.

"You're on," Greg opened. "Tonight."

"*Now?*"

"Now. Robin just called. Been waffling all day. Might change her mind again."

"Erika is giving Lucas a bath."

"Dry him off. It'll keep."

"I'll see if Bill can drive us. Otherwise, we'll take a car service. Either case, we'll swing by the Park Lane. Give us a half hour."

Fifteen minutes later, after having completed the bath routine, Grace was helping Lucas climb into his pajamas while they discussed what book they were going to take on together. Meanwhile, his parents were heading west up 59th Street on their way to the Park Lane, Bill at the helm.

Chapter Four

The terminus, after a little over an hour's drive along a relatively un-scenic but serviceable interstate highway looping into a more colorful network of local byways, was a modest clapboard house at the corner of South Avenue, a road that ran parallel to the shoreline of Atlantic Highlands and a hop and a skip away from it. Ivan and Robin must have taken that short stroll to the beach on many a sunny day or balmy evening, and Erika wondered if they would have grown to miss it had they moved to Manhattan at Ben Laszlo's urging. The house was on a small lot, but the oak trees surrounding it—the largest in the area, as far as she could tell—were thick-trunked and densely crowned and lent a kind of majesty to the property.

Bill parked in front of the house, and his passengers stepped onto the sidewalk. Three stone steps and a short pathway led to the entrance of the house, the approach minimally bathed in the half-moon light and a rustic lantern sconce mounted above the door. Greg took the initiative and knocked on the door. It was opened at once.

"I was looking out for you," their greeter announced awkwardly, as if it were a line she had just learned. A tall, slender woman, she was wearing wide-legged, severely pleated blue jeans, a tucked-in white shirt buttoned up to the neck, and brown lace-up Oxfords. Her chestnut brown hair was tightly drawn back into a serviceable bun. All in order, except for the swollen eyelids and smudged eyeliner, which may have been applied to counteract them. "Please come in." She stepped aside to allow them entry.

The interior of the old house had clearly been renovated to meet the "open concept" design in popular demand. There was no place to hide. The living room opened into the dining room, which in turn flowed into the kitchen. Erika wondered if the work had been done to raise the value of the home in preparation for the move to Manhattan. A large painting featuring broad strokes of blue, yellow, and coral hung above the sleek stone fireplace. The colors were echoed by the sofa's carefully aligned throw pillows. They were the only accents of color in an otherwise neutral expanse. The staged environment was brought to life by the savory smells emanating from the kitchen. Erika tried not to breathe them in too deeply and give herself away. She, like her companions, had postponed dinner in order to make it to Robin's without delay.

Greg handled the introductions, after which the guests were ushered into the kitchen, where they were asked to make themselves comfortable on the tall chairs along the edge of a toppled granite monolith, or "island," while Robin checked whatever was cooking in the oven. "Forgive me," she said, gently closing the oven door and returning to her posture-perfect stance. "I'm preparing Ivan's favorite dinner. Chicken Marsala and buttered noodles. It keeps me grounded." She stepped closer to her guests and tightly folded her arms against her chest. Every movement she made appeared to be considered before undertaken, as if she were bracing herself for the unexpected—or preventing it from occurring. "Yesterday, I made shepherd's pie. Another favorite. Ivan had a sensuous connection to food. We both did. We never missed a meal together when he was with Art Loss Register. When he began working at Laszlo's his hours became more irregular. He missed dinner sometimes." She hugged herself more tightly. "*Often*," she amended. She turned back to the oven. "The noodles are ready." She took the oven mitts from the counter and slipped them on, then removed a large casserole dish from the oven and placed it on the stovetop. "Give the chicken five minutes more. I'm sorry. I haven't asked if you wanted something to drink." She removed the mitts and stacked them neatly on the counter. "Anything."

Her guests declined, but she poured each of them a glass of sparkling water. "You'll stay for dinner. Don't turn me down. I don't want to be alone tonight. My babies are with my parents in Philadelphia for the weekend. I never should have let them take them away." There was a sudden desperation in her voice.

How could they protest? Moreover, when the casserole dish containing the Chicken Marsala emerged from the oven, accompanied by its enticing aroma, it was no longer possible to do so.

The dish could easily have served a ravenous party of ten.

To her guests' wide-eyed response, Robin said, "This is what I do. Call it therapy. What isn't eaten, I freeze. *Ivan* understood." She looked as if she was about to cry.

"If I could cook like this," Erika jumped in, "I'd do the same."

"Thank you. Let's move to the dining room."

"You really don't have to—" Greg began.

"Humor me."

"—go to the trouble of—"

"Greg!" Robin warned. "Don't you want me to feel comfortable with your friends? Don't you want me to"—her focus shot to Erika then Harrison—"*open up* to them?"

The three were visibly taken aback.

Robin blanched. "I didn't mean to take that tone. I tend to do that. Even under normal circumstances. Ivan would call me out on it." Her glance again flitted between the Wheatleys. "Don't misunderstand. I have absolute faith in Greg's judgment, and he's assured me your motivations are pure. After all, I did *summon* you here, didn't I? I *want* you to help." She flipped open the door to a cabinet, revealing her dinnerware.

Greg spoke as all three rose to help Robin. "Robin doesn't believe the detectives in charge are inclined to show the same, shall we say *discretion*, as you two. Isn't that true, Robin?" He snatched the plates from her hand.

She snatched them back. "Yes. It's true. Now go seat yourselves at the dining room table and I'll see to everything else. I'm working myself up to telling you what I know. This is part of the process."

Greg threw up his hands. "Who are we to argue with the process?" The threesome obediently withdrew to the dining room, leaving Robin to her own devices.

When all the accouterments of dinner had been properly laid out on the dining room table, Robin finally joined them. "Thank you for not interfering," she said. Dead serious.

"It wasn't easy," Erika replied, her minimalist smile meant to coax one from Robin.

Unreactive, Robin flipped open her cloth napkin and laid it neatly across her lap. "I should have had you come earlier in the day. We might have walked to Ocean Boulevard, stood atop Mount Mitchell, where you would have seen a panoramic view of New York City."

"Another day," Harrison gently suggested. "Right now, it's good to be here, where we are." Not so subtly encouraging her to focus on what good there *is*, rather than on what might have been.

For a short while they ate in a silence broken only by the soft clatter of utensils and restrained exclamations of praise, the meal more than living up to its aromatic overture. Yet, beneath the silence there was an insensate hum of anticipation, like an underlying spice that defines a dish, but can't quite be identified.

Erika was slicing into a tender fragment of chicken; Harrison, scooping up a forkful of buttered noodles; Greg, wiping his lips with his napkin—when Robin, staring down at her plate, suddenly blurted, "Ivan and I—we were having a squabble." She looked up. "It wasn't much of anything at the start, but it escalated. We were having dinner. Right where we are now, at this table." She seemed to marvel at the coincidence. "I complained, not very adamantly, that he was spending a lot of time in Manhattan—too much time. He said he was 'learning the ropes.' I remember thinking, how odd, I've never heard him use that phrase." She studied her plate again. "I told him he didn't share things with me. What was he doing at Laszlo's? Who were his colleagues? I became agitated. I asked him if he was having an affair." She sucked in her breath, as if someone other than herself had surprised her with that statement.

"He was stunned by my accusation. At a loss. For a minute, he was silent, and then he said, 'An *affair*? You want to know what I haven't *shared* with you? Something personal? All right, I'll let you in on my secret, my *only* secret, but you have to swear you'll keep it to yourself. It concerns the contract between me and one of my clients. I'm going against my word here, you understand. I gave Mr. Keller my word I'd keep it between us.' It was essential, Ivan said. *Essential.*"

Robin picked up her fork and began pushing a morsel of chicken around on her plate, poking at it, as if to get a response out of it. "What was I *thinking?*" She let the fork drop onto the plate and looked up. "I can't talk about this. I swore not to. There was a reason not to tell. A danger in telling." She shook her head. "Greg, Greg, I was drunk with grief when I shared this with you. I know you'll keep your word. Erika, Harrison, I'm sorry. I'll give you anything else but this. Not this."

Erika was sitting next to Robin. She laid her hand on hers. Robin placed her free hand on Erika's and kept it there. Erika nodded her understanding, inwardly begging Robin to recant. The plea went unanswered.

A short time later, after acceding to Robin's remorseful insistence they partake of her apple pie à la mode and coffee, the sated visitors were back on the road, heading toward Manhattan.

All three were seated in the back of the car, Erika between the men. Bill had taken it upon himself to shut the partition separating him and his passengers so that they could converse in private.

For a while, silence ruled. Then, not quite breaking it, Erika turned to Greg on her left and, cocking her head ever-so-slightly, fixed him with an imploring look.

"No," Greg said.

"Just thought I'd ask," she answered. "I understand." She rested her head on Harrison's shoulder and tried to distance herself from the double-edged guilt of having pressed Greg to break his oath and disappointment for not having succeeded at it.

Chapter Five

The Wheatleys were activists, fired up when confronted by anything resembling stonewalling.

The countdown to a figurative liftoff continued the following day, Saturday. Erika, hoping to counter Robin's reticence with a lead from Min Cho, had called Min on her cell phone. To her dismay, Min had been militantly polite and tight-lipped, as if Laszlo were holding her at gunpoint. Meanwhile, Darien Roth, the collegial close friend of the fallen Norman Blethmore of the Courtauld Institute, had returned Harrison's call and was equally unforthcoming, but at least he had not been averse to meeting Harrison in person. Moments later, Harrison had encountered the same resistance from Aubrey Devan, assistant chief of archives at the Ashmolean. Aubrey was constrained by the museum's rules governing security, though he would be willing to review the Camille Pissarro documents on-site with Harrison, provided he appeared with the required credentials.

"We've got to strike while the iron is hot," Harrison prompted, slapping his thigh, although there was no need to rev up Erika; she was already in high gear. "I've set up appointments with Roth and Devan. "Now, to book my flight."

They were sitting on the edge of the couch in Harrison's study. It was 10:30 p.m. Grace and Lucas were asleep. A useful lull. Time to solidify plans. First thing, Harrison booked a round-trip from JFK to London Heathrow, Delta's flight schedule, the most convenient. He would leave at 11:05 p.m. on Monday, two days hence, and arrive Tuesday, 10:55 a.m. in London. He'd leave London Friday evening and arrive home in time for dinner. As for booking a room, he opted for the Old Bank Hotel because it was a short walk to the Ashmolean, where his first meeting was to take place, and the comments were favorable on Yelp. The drive from the airport to the hotel was estimated at forty-eight minutes. If his grade-school math still served, allowing for a modest flight delay, baggage pick-up, Uber connection, hotel check-in, and washing-up, he figured he'd be on time for his meeting at 1:45 p.m. He wished he could have talked with Darien Roth about his friend, the late Norman Blethmore, before diving more or less cold into the Pissarro documents that had so interested the deceased professor, but Roth wasn't available until mid-Wednesday. Enlightenment would have to be postponed.

Erika's plans were next on the adrenalin-driven agenda. Up to now she'd been waiting on the sidelines, on occasion putting in her two cents while Harrison did his thing. When her turn came, she expected the concern for her safety to arise, but not quite in the manner with which it would be expressed.

"I'm not totally secure leaving you on your own," Harrison said.

"That may be the most patriarchal sentence I've ever heard you utter," Erika replied.

"I'm sorry."

"No, you're not. Be that as it may, here's what will happen. John will escort me wherever I go. His renewed deputization from the FBI's Art Theft squad will lend authority to my interview requests. That's *my* motivation. For *yours*, he'll serve as my bodyguard."

"Armed bodyguard," Harrison edited. "He's got a license to carry."

"I'm not anticipating a shootout."

"Nor am I. My primary concern is that you'll give him the slip. You may recall having gone that route."

"I recall."

"And?"

"And what? I used my judgment. You'll have to trust it."

He sighed. "I will, but you have to promise to—"

"Drop it, Harrison. Be happy I'm no daredevil and wish me Godspeed or whatever. Agreed?"

He could not help but smile at her feistiness. "You drive a hard bargain, but yes, I—"

"About my plans," she cut in, eager to get on with it. "I've spoken to Min Cho—if you can call it speaking—and got nowhere. I might give her a break, then try again. I'm thinking that with Greg's help I'll have an easier time connecting with Laszlo's principal players. I'd love to have a word or two with a couple of those big-game hunters at the auction. Maybe they'll be willing to reveal something useful about the dynamics of the Laszlo organization—or the man himself. Also, I'll ask John to get in touch with the detectives on the case. He's got connections all over town from his tenure as a police officer."

"Now moonlighting as our snitch," Harrison bluntly acknowledged. "You've got a lot of potential balls in the air," he observed.

"That's for starters. I'm waiting to get a call back from Morris Keller, owner of the Monet pulled from the auction. I left him a phone message this morning."

"I thought you were a persona non grata at Laszlo's," Harrison said, marveling. "There must be more than one Morris Keller in New York City. Who gave you his number?"

"I searched online for Morris Keller and also his father, Lewis. Remember the provenance summary in Laszlo's catalogue? Morris inherited the Monet from Lewis in June 2015. I found a *New York Times* obituary for a Lewis Keller, died June 7, 2015. It makes reference to his son, Morris, and several other relatives. I tracked down the telephone numbers for multiple Morris Kellers in the five boroughs of New York City. As you probably know, each internet listing notes household or family members that are or have been associated with the name in question. I called the Morris Keller associated with the names in the obituary. I took a chance, but not a big one. Don't worry, I left Morris a tame message, mentioned nothing about the murder, only that I'd been at the Laszlo auction and would like to talk to him about it. Used my association with *Art News* as an excuse."

Harrison sat back. "You're a wonder, Erika."

She smiled. "Maybe, but this exercise doesn't prove it. It was an easy hunch to follow."

"If you say so, darling. What else have you got up your sleeve?"

She shrugged. "If Morris Keller calls back and allows me to interview him, I'll see where it takes me. This mystery has gotten ahold of me, Harrison. Two deaths, linked in a manner so..." She looked for the word.

"Unintuitive?" Harrison suggested.

"Exactly!"

"You really want to get your teeth into it, don't you?"

"Don't *you*?" she shot back.

"*Hell*, yes!"

Chapter Six

Tuesday, 2:00 a.m. Harrison was well on his way in every sense of the word: halfway across the Atlantic Ocean and with at least two appointments booked in digital stone in his schedule app. Erika, on the other hand, had made no headway and was chomping at the bit. Her putative Monet owner, Morris Keller, had not returned her call. Given the feeble message she'd left in his voicemail, she would not have returned the call herself. It left her with two options: drop the idea of meeting him or upping the initiative.

Make that *one* option. She would get John Mitchell in on the case. Together, they'd surveille the townhouse she'd digitally located in Brooklyn Heights associated with her Morris Keller. When it looked like what was most probably her mark entering the home, she and John would give him a minute to settle in, maybe mix himself a martini, before giving his hospitality the acid test. For the four days Harrison was in London, John had cleared his schedule in order to be at Erika's beck and call. He was committed wholeheartedly to his dual role of detective and bodyguard. He'd played it before, not always to rave reviews.

For her part, Erika was relatively free to slink around on the prowl. First, most of her work for *Art News* could be done at home on Microsoft Word. Her immediate superior, Sara Masden, was good with that, though when it came to staff meetings and the critical one-on-ones, she preferred her attendees to present themselves on site "three-dimensionally and pelvically clad." Luckily, no on-site meeting had been scheduled until the following week. Second, Lucas's nanny, Kate, had returned from her family visit earlier in the day, leaving Erika to rest easy, knowing that in her periodic absences from home, Lucas would be impeccably cared for by Kate and Grace, ever in friendly competition for the boy's greater affection.

Erika would text John now, asking him to give her a call ASAP. If he was the night owl he had once casually claimed to be, she'd hear from him immediately. If not, she'd try to get some sleep.

Disappointed, she tried to get some sleep.

* * *

Erika awakened at exactly 6:00 a.m. Last time she'd looked, her bedside clock had registered 2:46 a.m. The interval of three-plus hours had been taunted by resurfaced dreams of loss and abandonment.

She reached for her cell phone. Harrison was scheduled to arrive at Heathrow in five minutes, and she was eager to see if he'd texted her. Yes, only minutes ago! His plane had landed ten minutes early, and he was on his way to Baggage Claim. He planned to give her a call at a more reasonable Eastern Seaboard hour. She heaved a sigh of relief on his having arrived safely and moved on to John's text, received an hour after she'd contacted him. John apologized for his delayed response, but his mother-in-law had taken ill and he'd been driving his wife to LaGuardia Airport to catch a flight to Boston when Erika's text had been recorded. He told her to feel free to call him at any hour, 24/7.

She punched in John's cell phone number.

"I didn't want to disturb you in case you were sleeping," John spouted before Erika had a chance to say a word. "I figured if it was an emergency, you'd be awake and would answer my text. Oh Lord, *was* it an emergency?"

"No, John, it wasn't," she assured him. "How's your mother-in-law doing?"

"She's fine now. She had severe chest pain and was rushed to the hospital. Turns out she experienced what they call an esophageal spasm, which can mask as a heart attack, since the esophagus runs right behind the heart. They'll try to prevent another occurrence with some changes in her diet. Worst comes to worst, she'll undergo what they say is minimally invasive surgery, but that's down the line and hopefully to be avoided." He let out a whistle. "You learn something new every day."

"Yes," Erika agreed. "And how's your wife taking it all?"

"She had quite a scare, but she's okay. Staying with her folks for a couple of days, though. Thanks for asking. I want to know what's up with you, Erika. Harrison should be arriving in London about now. You hear from him?"

"Yes, just. His flight arrived early."

"Good. So, what's up, and how can I help?"

With hardly an explanation, she sailed straight to her plan for the day.

"So, you want us to stalk this gentleman from Brooklyn Heights—on Pineapple Street, did you say?"

"There are a couple of fruit names in Brooklyn Heights. Yes. Not quite stalk. Surveille."

"Excuse me—*surveille?*"

"Yes, we're going to sit in front of his townhouse and—"

"Wait. How do you know the address is a townhouse?"

"I saw a street view on the internet."

"Ah, of course." A bit of mockery in his voice. He was a frequent visitor on the internet, but not a big fan. "Okay, so you want to wait for a time that you figure your mark is at home, and then we move in on him."

"We're not going to arrest him," she said, the words sprinkled with a nervous laugh. "You'll bring along your FBI document to flash in front of him." She paused. "And I think I'll take along one of those big fold-out maps we can hold in front of us."

"I suspect to make us look touristy, should any passerby stop to wonder about our presence. I know you, Erika."

She laughed. "Too well, it seems."

He echoed her laugh. "I love you anyway. When do you want me to pick you up? You can explain the details of our exploit while we're driving."

"We want to see Keller as he's entering his home, so in all probability, it's too early in the day for that to occur. Still, if he works from home, maybe he'll step out for a roll and coffee. Can you pick me up in an hour? I'll put together a picnic basket for a party of six. That should hold us for the day."

"Sure. By the way, I'm allergic to stuffed goose."

She laughed. "I love you, anyway, too," she said. "Thanks, John."

Chapter Seven

The vigil began curbside, two doors down from the Kellers' townhouse on a quiet, copiously tree-lined street that looked like it had remained stuck in an earlier time, when lives were shorter, yet ironically more leisurely-paced. In these environs the stakeout was an anachronism, which made Erika feel her presence was particularly glaring. "We stick out like a couple of sore thumbs," she said, pretending to study her fold-out map.

"Maybe not so much if you weren't holding the thing upside down," John said. He took the map from her and tossed it over his shoulder into the back of the car. "Forget the props. Pretend to be relaxed, and you'll trick yourself into believing it." He checked his rear-view mirror and cocked his head toward the right. "Take a look out your window. There's a couple about to pass us by. There. See how integrated they are with their surroundings? Try to think like that." The couple had slowed down to glance curiously, but unintrusively, into the car. John cracked a friendly smile, but not too friendly, and the woman twaddled her fingers in greeting and moved on with her mate. John gave Erika's knee a paternal pat. "Like that. Try to integrate. You're fidgeting. Try not to." He sighed. "Do it for me. We might be here all day."

"You're good," Erika said.

"Second nature to me. You'll get the hang of it. Take in the scene. What do you think of these houses, for instance? Describe them to me."

"Well, the one next to the Kellers' looks kind of formal, with those slender columns flanking the door…"

"Colonnettes."

She raised a brow and went on. "The house is three stories, the third of which is fitted with two dormer windows cutting into the front and rear slopes of the roof. I believe its architectural style is Federal, but I may be wrong."

"No, you're correct. What about the Keller house itself?"

"I'd say its style is a little more embellished, but it still retains that basic classic look. It has three floors, and its construction is brownstone. I can't tell from here what carved ornamentation surrounds the cornice and windows. Garlands, maybe."

"Possibly acanthus leaves," John suggested. "They've been a popular motif in Grecian art since 500 BCE. They symbolize rebirth. What else?"

She smiled at his harmless flaunting. "Its fence is more or less a duplicate of the one belonging to the house directly opposite us. Interesting feature, those interlacing curved bands filling the rectangles of the basic form."

"Guilloches."

"Aha. Would you call the style Renaissance Revival?"

"I would. Built maybe around 1880, give or take."

Erika shook her head in amazement. "I knew you were a math whiz. Now I discover you're a *polymath*."

"If I take an interest in things, I learn about them."

She remembered how industriously he'd applied himself to learning about the Benin Bronzes. "Yes, you do."

"Kind of insulting, your surprise. You suppose all gumshoes are ignoramuses?"

"Of course not! I'm sorry."

He smiled. "No problem. The exercise worked, anyhow. You're more..."

"Integrated," she finished, returning his smile.

"It's only ten o'clock, but I'm hungry—you?" he asked.

"More excited than hungry, but yes, I could eat something." The food and beverage parcel she'd prepared was perched on the back seat. She turned around in the passenger seat and got on her knees to reach for it. "Ham and Swiss, turkey, or tuna?"

"Ham and Swiss, thanks—Wait!"

The cry, surely her cue to glance out the window. "Got to be Keller!" she exclaimed, with unwarranted certainty, spotting the man as he descended the stone steps of their targeted townhouse. She turned back around in her seat. "He was in the house all the time. We might have knocked on the door."

"If he wasn't there and someone else was, he might very well have been forewarned. Best way to handle this is to take him by surprise, when we're right up beside him, with a foot in the door, and I mean that literally."

She hadn't gotten a clear view of his face, since his head was lowered as he came down the steps, and then he had turned away to walk up the street, hands in the pockets of his jeans, corduroy jacket fanning out behind him. All she'd observed about his physical appearance was that he was on the tall side, bean-pole slim and balding. She had the urge to jump out of the car and accost him on the spot, but restrained herself. John was right. Best to have that literal foot in the door. "I hope he's not out for the day."

"My instincts say no," John remarked. "He's wearing a shirt, no tie. Not carrying a thing—no briefcase, nothing. Walking with an undetermined step, decidedly not on a tight schedule. I'm betting he's gone out on a local errand and that he'll be back within thirty-five minutes." His eyes narrowed. "Do I have any takers?"

She grinned. "I want you to be right. No way I'm betting against you."

"An automatic win. My prize, a ham and Swiss."

"Coming right up," she said, once more turning in her seat.

* * *

"Lucky you didn't bet against me," John crowed, thirty-two minutes later, when their alleged Morris Keller approached the staircase leading to the door to his townhouse. In one hand, he was gripping the handles of a medium-sized plastic bag, a folded newspaper visible at its opening. In the other, a large Starbucks paperboard cup, lidded. When he reached the door, he gave it a couple of non-aggressive kicks, and it was opened by someone within. The door was closed behind him.

"Perfect," John said, brushing away any residual bread crumbs from his Windbreaker before hopping out of the car. "Get him while it's hot."

Hard to juggle hot coffee while staving off intruders, Erika figured John meant, as she jumped out on her side, tote bag in tow. She smoothed down her pantsuit, and together, she and John took off.

John ran his hand along the fencing as they sprinted up the steps. "Acanthus motif, as suspected," he remarked. Arriving at the door, he gave it four hard raps with his knuckles. "Get in closer," he urged Erika. "Not an inch to spare." She edged in.

The door opened the chain's length. "Yes?" their alleged mark on the other side clipped. Not quite hostile. A promising start. From what they could see, he must have set down the plastic bag, but was still holding the cup—a Starbucks Grande, the twelve-ouncer. The lid had been removed and steam was rising from the piping hot brew. A potential hazard another point in their favor.

"I'm Erika Shawn Wheatley," Erika announced, leaning in. "I left a phone message for you. I thought I'd come by." Not exactly the opening she'd planned.

"The magazine writer."

"Art magazine, yes." His slender face was dominated by a Roman nose, which gave him a magisterial look.

"You're writing a piece on the financial state of the art market, and you got my name from Laszlo's because you thought I might contribute an interesting point or two for your article."

"Yes."

"Bullshit."

"Which part?" John challenged, nostrils flaring. He had his foot planted against the door in a manner he'd tested and refined in the field. The door would remain ajar.

"All of it," the now self-confirmed Morris Keller, owner of the auction's withdrawn painting, replied.

John pulled out his FBI Art Crime Team's document from the inner pocket of his jacket and held it up to the opening, making sure Keller would get a good look at the impressive logo, a colorful montage of bits of famous paintings—Vincent van Gogh's brushstrokes the only ones John could identify for sure.

"This is by no means an official visit," Erika submitted, hoping to ease what must be Keller's escalating tension. "Please allow us to come in and talk. I know this all seems quite odd, but if you let us explain, I promise it'll all become clear to you. We only want to be of help."

"Open the door, Morris," a woman's strident voice demanded from somewhere to his rear. I want to hear what these people have to say."

The man glanced over his shoulder. "I've been shielding you."

"Nonsense. Let them in." Suddenly, she came into view, a woman half his age but equal in stature. "Here, I'll do it. Watch the coffee, Morris." With a swoosh, she released the chain and opened the door. "Let's not stand on ceremony," she advised the petitioners. "Come on in."

"Thank you…Naomi?" Erika inquired, somewhat tentatively, as she stepped inside.

"You've been doing your research," the woman commended, giving Morris a sideways glance. "Yes, I'm Naomi. Grab a seat."

Morris, still clutching the coffee container, holding it away from himself as if it were a baby needing a diaper change, looked totally out of his element, a foreigner in his own home.

Erika was at a loss where to sit. The room looked like the kind showcased at a museum you view from behind a velvet rope. Somewhere in the home, there was a kitchen—in townhouses like this, traditionally on the floor below—and she imagined it was fitted with the most advanced appliances available to the modern consumer. But the room in which they stood either had been preserved from an earlier time—perhaps from Morris's grandparents' day—or had been designed to give the appearance of having been so. In either case, the intent had been to create a jaw-dropping verisimilitude with the Italian Renaissance.

The layout was done to a T in the Renaissance style, with a central focal point flanked by symmetrical arrangements of furniture. The eye-catcher was a life-size marble statue of a Roman Patrician set on a column plinth in a dedicated arched niche at the far end of the room. On each side of him was an arrangement of two brocade-upholstered lounge chairs and a small pedestal table. Closer to where Erika, John, and their hosts stood were matching sofas upholstered in burgundy velvet, each paired with two occasional chairs upholstered in a floral pattern of burgundy and emerald green. Each grouping shared a decoratively carved coffee table of sorts, upon which rested a sculptural bust of what may have been one ancient Greek goddess or another. A large area rug adorned with a complicated leaf pattern covered most of the dark wood floor paneling, and on the walls hung a number of ornately framed moody seascapes and senatorial gatherings, adding to the room's dark and brooding aura. No sign of an Impressionist's gift of light anywhere in sight.

Naomi moved toward one of the nearby seating arrangements and sat down at one end of the sofa, crossing her legs in that pretzel-like manner that only long-legged women can comfortably attain. Her slender form was clad in black tights and a sweatshirt with a full-frontal Versace logo. Erika and John each took one of the flanking chairs. Morris chose to stand over them.

"Find a place for the coffee, Morris," Naomi suggested, challenging his lordly position.

"I'll hold onto it, thanks," Morris replied, refusing to yield. "What's on your mind, Erika—I assume I may call you Erika?" He was acting like the person in charge, but his eyes betrayed an underlying tension—*fear*, in fact, Erika decided.

She folded her hands on the tote bag slumped in her lap. "Of course, you may. First, I should tell you that neither John nor I are here on official business, but that we *are* here with the blessings of the executive board at the Art Loss Register organization and with the tacit approval of the FBI. Second, my interest in the financial status of the art market is not bullshit, as you suggested, although ever since I came close to witnessing your account executive, Ivan Brooks's murder last Wednesday, it's become less of a motivation for my wanting to interview you. You see, my husband

and I—"

"This man your husband?" Naomi interrupted.

"Friend of the family and working detective," John said, opting to replace the adjective "private" with "working" to give the title more heft.

Erika launched into an explanation of her own, and Harrison's well-established presence in the art crime world, and John bolstered her résumé by touting the Wheatleys' reputation for being models of discretion. Not one to dilly-dally, he then abruptly asked to be shown the painting that had been withdrawn from the prior week's auction. "It may be of significance," he added, rising to his feet.

Morris stiffened. "The painting isn't on the premises."

The conversation had taken a sharp turn away from where Erika was heading, which was to an inquiry into Morris's relationship with Ivan Brooks and any insider information he might have on the man himself; same line of questioning to be applied to Morris's association with Ben Laszlo. Actually, John's spontaneous request might prove to be more fruitful. "Yes, where *is* the painting?" she chorused, visibly stripping Morris of what was left of his composure. His hands shook; the untouched coffee was on the verge of spilling. Gingerly, he set the cup down on a decorative plate sitting next to the bust of what Erika guessed was the goddess Aphrodite. Before pressing again for an answer to the question that hung in the air, Erika thought she'd go for one that was possibly more conducive to opening up a friendly exchange, namely, *who's the subject of the lovely sculpted bust?* She opened her mouth to speak, just as a thunderous pounding on the front door shook the room.

"What the hell!" Naomi exclaimed, untwisting her legs and popping up from the sofa. Without an instant's hesitation, she headed for the door.

"Don't open it!" Morris cried without moving a muscle to prevent her from doing so.

"Why? Who'd you think it is?" John shot back, following Naomi. He patted his hip, and Erika guessed he was instinctively checking his revolver. She knew he'd gotten a permit to carry from the Bureau of Security and Investigative Services—BSIS—as well as a concealed weapons permit. He beat Naomi to the door and stood by her as she barked, "Who is it?"

"Lois effing Keller! Let me in at once!"

Naomi glanced over her shoulder at her husband. "You expecting your ex?"

"No, of course not," Morris replied uncertainly, suddenly ashen-faced. "Don't let her in. Tell her I'll call her later."

"This should be good," Naomi remarked, ignoring him and opening the door. "Hello, Lois. To what do we owe the pleasure?" she sniped.

"Pleasure, my ass," Lois returned, pushing past her and colliding with John. She gave him the once over, followed by a dismissive sniff, and strode straight toward Morris. She was holding a document of some kind, and as she approached him, she began waving it on high franticly, as if she were warding off a swarm of bees.

Erika was not sure how to respond to this agitated visitor. Lois was a slight, frail-looking middle-aged woman in a Chanel or Chanel knock-off suit and sneakers. She did not look capable of landing a solid blow, but on the other hand, her thunderous fist-pounding on the front door boded otherwise. John drew near, on silent guard. Naomi pulled up alongside her husband. The glint in her eye indicated she was itching for a showdown.

"You know what this is?" Lois shouted, waving the paper in front of Morris's face.

"How can I? You're not letting me see it."

He's stalling, Erika thought. *He knows.*

"It's from Galaxy Fine Arts Insurance Company. Did you forget they send me duplicate notices? I don't think so!" She held the paper out in front of her and, like the town crier of yore, began her proclamation: "'Dear Mr. Keller. As per your recent request that we terminate your policy, number—'"

Morris snatched the letter from her. "Stop!"

"Why stop?" Naomi challenged. "You want to keep me out of the loop, that it?"

Still focused on Lois, he implored, "It's for your own safety!" He ventured a glance at Erika and John, and his tension rose.

Lois followed his eyes, taking in Erika and John. Her expression tautened, mirroring her ex's. "What are these people doing here? To execute another scheme of yours?"

"Calm down," Morris implored, failing to take his own advice. "They're here to inquire about…recent events."

"Who *are* you?" Lois barked at them.

Erika and John reported their identities without embellishment, as if responding to a roll call.

"You two aware of this fiasco?" Lois asked, grabbing back the letter from Morris and fluttering it at them. Reacting to Morris's warning look, she folded it up and shoved it into her skirt pocket.

"Has this anything to do with the withdrawal of the Monet?" Erika boldly inquired. "Are you contesting the ownership of the painting?"

Lois guffawed. "The blue vase with the flowers? Heavens, no! What I'm talking about is—"

"No!" Morris bellowed, cutting her off.

"Go on, Lois!" Naomi vehemently urged. "I want to hear what you have to say!"

"Come to think of it, it's actually none of your damn business," Lois clipped.

Lois uttered not a word more about the issue. Meanwhile, whatever fragments of thought had managed to escape her lips were causing Erika's curiosity to run rampant. Maybe in a calmer setting, Lois would be willing to open up to her, she dared contemplate. She glanced at John. Without John, of course. Lois would feel less threatened without the big guy hovering over her. In any event, whatever the future held, there was nothing more to be gained at this meeting.

Without fanfare, Morris ushered the three unwelcome guests to the door. When he reached for the doorknob, his hand was trembling. Except for his promise to contact his ex, no further communication was suggested by him, not even to put up an agreeable front.

When the trio had descended the stone steps and were standing on the sidewalk and about to go their separate ways, Erika addressed Lois. "We're parked right here. Can we give you a lift somewhere?"

John's look of surprise was barely suppressed. Lois's was staged with a dramatic rise of her eyebrows. "That's thoughtful of you, but my apartment's nearby, and I need to walk off that dreadful encounter." With that, she turned on her heel and walked off in the opposite direction from where John's car was parked.

It was John's turn for a purposeful brow-raise.

"I thought it would be a nice gesture," Erika said.

"I'll bet. Good job, though. It took me a second to spot your ulterior motive. Should take you about the same amount of time to come up with her address, despite her lack of cooperation." Bypassing her feigned look of innocence, he added, "Just so you know, I'm tagging along with you when you visit the lady."

"If I do go that route, of course, you'll come with me," Erika assured him, adding sub-vocally, *Not if I can help it.*

Chapter Eight

To Harrison, the vast complex of Oxford University, founded over nine-hundred years ago and expanding ever since—twenty-eight libraries at the last count—was both exhilarating and daunting. Something like looking up at the night sky and feeling both chosen and inconsequential. To think of the centuries of recorded wisdom housed in these fortresses of knowledge! How blessed to have been able to contribute his scholarly works to these storehouses of learning—and yet how meager his share. Still, it was a beautiful day, and he was alive and well, and his outlook quickly plateaued to its set-point of well-being.

His meeting was scheduled for 2:00 p.m. at the Ashmolean, Oxford University's museum of art and archaeology founded in 1683, housing a collection of art and artifacts from ancient Egypt to modern times, and just one more repository of creative works banded together in central Oxford. From the Old Bank Hotel, yet another imposing edifice in town, he'd headed north from High Street to Broad Street and had been milling around the magnificent, over-four-centuries-old Bodleian Library, the University's main library before walking on to Beaumont Street, the path to the Ashmolean. It was 1:35. He figured he'd be about fifteen minutes early.

Aubrey Devan, Ashmolean's assistant chief of archives, had told Harrison to meet him in the Western Art Print Room. "Take the staircase off Gallery fifty-three, European Goldsmiths' Work," he'd advised in a text message Harrison had received as he was checking into the hotel. "There's an intercom to the left of the door. I or another staff member will let you in after you identify yourself."

Harrison's estimate was on the mark. He was indeed fifteen minutes early—to the *museum*. It took him at least another five to find his way to the Western Art Print Room.

The staff member who would hear his thumbnail résumé and bear witness to his testimony that he was not in possession of food, drink, or chewing gum, had been on alert for his arrival and, after a brief inquisition, let him in. It turned out the disembodied voice belonged to a pleasant young woman, who escorted him to the seat at the head of a long communal table. At the other end of the table, a diverse, multi-generational group of a dozen or so white-gloved guests were bunched together, most sitting, a few choosing to stand. Across the table from them stood a man in a tweed jacket with elbow patches. He was gesturing with a white-gloved hand toward an open folder resting on a large felt mat, which prevented the folder from coming into direct contact with the wood tabletop. From what Harrison could make out from his end of the table, it looked like the two artworks on display were charcoal drawings of ballet dancers by Edgar Degas.

"Works on paper," the man was saying, "must be treated with tender loving care. They tend to fade and therefore cannot—certainly *ought* not—be on permanent display." As one of the visitors pulled a notepad from her shoulder bag, he warned, "As I've already said, pencils only!" The woman tossed him a knowing smile and drew forth a pencil from her bag and held it on high.

The man offered a brisk nod of approval before instructing the group to spread out a bit to ensure each of them had an optimal view. As they were doing so, Harrison heard a barely audible creak. He reflexively turned toward the origin of the sound and beheld a stocky, middle-aged man in a perfectly cut three-piece suit standing at the open door to the print room. In one hand, he held a small leather portfolio; with the other, he gestured for Harrison to approach.

Once Harrison and his beckoner had stepped foot outside the room, the young woman who'd cleared Harrison for access shut the door gently behind them. "Bright girl, Emily," the man said, grabbing Harrison's hand from his side and initiating a mutual shake. "An Oxford art history grad student, doing time as an intern." He smiled, releasing Harrison's hand. "Emily informed me who you were. Sorry. I'm Aubrey—Aubrey Devan."

"I was counting on it," Harrison said, grinning.

"You must have realized this is not the ideal place for a private meeting. Especially with a tour party in attendance."

"It crossed my mind."

"I thought it was as good as any place to meet before taking you to my office. My room is nearby, but hard to find if you're not a resident of these parts. Follow me."

Harrison got the point of Aubrey's remark after following him up a staircase and around one L-turn, then another, before coming upon a door bearing the screw holes of a missing plaque. "The old sign's being replaced," Aubrey said, unlocking the door with a key from his jacket pocket. "To match the font of the other doors on this floor, if you can believe it. I was unsuccessful in getting the board of directors to grandfather mine in. "Enter."

Aubrey's office was bright and commodious, but with no sense of interior design. The furnishings seemed to have been added as needed, with function rather than harmony their selling point. The main piece was a big old oak desk that reminded Harrison of the one in his teacher Miss O'Malley's fifth-grade classroom. Aubrey's desk chair was a modern barrel-type, sculpted in sleek leather with a chrome base. The bookcases and cabinets were of diverse heights, widths, and material components, no doubt to accommodate various dimensions of books, folios, files, drawings.

Aubrey placed the leather portfolio he was holding on the desk and took his seat, indicating with a wave that Harrison should choose one of the two unmatched straight-back chairs opposite.

Harrison randomly went for the one without arms.

Aubrey waited for Harrison to settle in before speaking. "Before we begin, Dr. Wheatley__"

"Harrison, please!"

Aubrey acknowledged the edit with a collegial smile. "Harrison, it is. Now, then, we'll have to take a glance at a couple of your credentials. You have an

Enhanced driver's license? A faculty ID?" He smoothed his hand over the portfolio, as if it were a pet that required attention. "In your case, a mere formality, because now that I've seen you, I recognize your face from the newspaper."

"The case of the Benin Bronzes," Harrison said. Hardly a wild guess. He'd asked the photographer from *The Guardian* to refrain from taking his photograph at the conclusion of the Benin case, but he had been ignored. He reached for the wallet in his pants pocket.

"You look unhappy," Aubrey said.

"I like to avoid publicity." Harrison plucked his license and faculty ID from his wallet and handed them to Aubrey.

"The entire drama took place on our doorstep," Aubrey said. "You can hardly have expected it to have gone unnoticed." He took a cursory glance at Harrison's cards and handed them back. He flashed a sly grin. "You were pretty hard on us Brits, as I recall," he added.

"Well, in a sense," Harrison said.

"Now, *there's* a cryptic comment for you." With a friendly guffaw, Aubrey slid the portfolio closer to himself. "We better get on with it before we come to blows." Carefully, he unzipped the portfolio and withdrew a large transparent plastic envelope with a snap closure. The envelope contained an assortment of papers, the nature of which was yet to be revealed. He set aside the envelope and removed the only remaining item in the portfolio: a leather-bound ledger book. He placed it alongside the envelope, then stowed the portfolio in one of the desk's roomy side drawers. His next step was to fetch two pairs of pristine white cotton gloves from the drawer above. "Now then," he said, handing one of the plastic-encased pairs to Harrison. "One more thing before we commence, and it might determine how we approach the material. We spoke briefly—*very* briefly— about your reasons for wanting to examine these documents, but I hope you won't mind reviewing and perhaps expanding on those reasons. Also, if you wouldn't mind telling me what individual or organization encouraged or subsidized your investigation in general."

"Certainly," Harrison said. He began with the prequel to his London visit, starting with the auction at Laszlo's, during which the catalogue lot, Monet's *Wedgewood Vase with Flowers*, had been abruptly removed from the group of paintings offered, and the consignor's executive, Ivan Brooks, had been summarily murdered. Next, he spoke of the part played by Professor Norman Blethmore of the Courtauld Institute of Art. First, to the professor's reported look of alarm on seeing a photograph of Monet's *Wedgewood Vase with Flowers* on the cover of the auction's catalogue. Second, to his mysterious phone call to Ben Laszlo shortly before the auction took place.

"As for my reasons for getting involved in this investigation," Harrison went on, "I must first make it clear that my wife, Erika, and I are equal partners—trouble-makers, if you will—in this side-line of sleuthing that we've been engaged in for the past several years. We were initially brought together in a kind of academic match-making, at the request of an art magazine bigwig and a private individual who wanted her investigation to take place under the radar." Beneath his spoken words, memory flooded into focus, of their first encounter, his and Erika's, at the Hotel Pierre's gala, the images kaleidoscoping with fragments of Michelangelo's bathers, the parting of terrycloth robes, and Erika's bared hips.

Seemingly not diverted, he continued. "Contrary to what you may have been led to believe, my wife and I are not paid or sponsored by any individual or organization. We have, though, been called upon—encouraged, if you will—by highly respected agencies to help track down crimes that have taken place in the art world, past and present. For *this* particular case, we virtually set out on our own, since Erika felt personally involved—I should say *obligated*—to play a part in solving it. She was, after all, the one who discovered the body of Ivan Brooks, a man she had just met and who had been willing to put himself out for her.

"That said, we have since been aided and abetted by the FBI Art Crime division and the Art Loss Register organization." (*An overstatement, but surely harmless*, he reasoned.) "This should give us the legitimacy I suspect you're looking for."

"It does, indeed," Aubrey said.

"I should add that our reputation of discretion has engendered a good deal of trust."

Aubrey slapped his hands on the desktop. "You're either one upstanding citizen or one helluva salesman. In any case, I'm convinced. I'll help you in any way I can. Tapping the unopened parcel, he said, "Are you aware of how these documents came into our possession?"

"Superficially. I believe they were found in the former London home of Camille Pissarro's son, Lucien, when it was sold some years ago."

Yes, the eighteenth-century house, located in the Stamford Brook Conservation Area, was sold in 2019 to an investment banker. Lucien died in 1944, as you probably know, and the home had remained in the ownership of his descendants up until its sale. The house has since required extensive repairs, inside and out, and has been recently undergoing major interior beautification to boot." Aubrey's look turned reflective. "The Pissarro family has turned out to be an international treasure, hasn't it?" he mused. Five generations of artists they've given us. The latest, Lyora, has already been exhibited all over the world. Lovely people as well, the lot of them. Take after their tribe's progenitor, Camille, known to have been a most kind, generous man. Artistic talent and moral grit—in the genes, I'd say!

"But I digress," he confessed, smiling. "I was considering how Camille Pissarro's latest documents found their way to us, and I could not help citing the remarkable quality of the Pissarro family. You see, these documents were found in a sealed envelope tucked away in Lucien's artist's workroom in the rear of the kitchen. On the envelope, the words 'Camille Pissarro, Correspondence, etc.' had been written in Lucien's handwriting."

"Is it assumed that Camille either forgot or intentionally left the documents behind?" Harrison asked. "I mean, in the 1890s, on one of his many trips from France to his son's home."

"Precisely," Aubrey replied. "At any rate, one of the renovators came upon the parcel and handed it over to the owner, who in turn passed it on to the Pissarro family member with whom he'd transacted the purchase of the house. The envelope, you understand, had remained sealed all those years." Aubrey paused again to shake his head in wonder. "Hear this. The envelope was given to the Ashmolean with its seal unbroken. I myself was its immediate recipient, and I spoke directly with the Pissarro family member who'd been entrusted to transfer it to our safekeeping.

"To be frank, I was bewildered. 'Why didn't your family examine the contents of the envelope?' I asked this individual. And the answer? 'We consulted among ourselves and decided that if we looked over the letters, we might be tempted to withhold one or more for any number of reasons—sentimental, political, who can predict? In the end, we felt the contents of the envelope by rights belong to the public, the final arbiters of Camille's work, and must remain intact.'" Aubrey reverently lay his hand on the envelope as if he were about to take an oath on it. "There was a moral imperative to that decision. It amazes me still." He looked to Harrison for an amen.

"I don't know how they resisted the temptation to review the letters," Harrison remarked, more surprised than awed. "I know I wouldn't have been able to." From Aubrey's barely audible "hmph," he realized it was not quite the affirmation the archivist had been seeking.

"Well, then, my good fellow!" Aubrey declared with a sudden spurt of goodwill, perhaps, on reflection, realizing his buildup had been too worshipful, "Let's get on with it, shall we?" He slipped his white gloves from their plastic sleeve and pulled them on. Harrison followed his lead. After disposing of the plastic casings in the bin near his chair, Aubrey set the ledger before him, opened it to the first page, and turned the book 180 degrees so that it faced Harrison. Holding it open with the tips of his fingers, he said, "This page records the name of the parcel's donor, the date of its receipt, and the text written on the original envelope." He turned the page. "Here we have an informal listing of the documents." Harrison perused the list:

- letters to Camille Pissarro, 1867-71: 17
- letters (drafts) from C. P., 1869-72: 3
- receipts from sales of C. P.'s paintings, 1869: 5
- invoices for art supplies, 1868: 3

"May I photograph this—and possibly the items themselves?" Harrison asked, assuming the answer was no.

"No photos, no exceptions. But you can copy anything you like. Looks like you need writing material."

Harrison drew a notepad and pen from his breast pocket; realized his error at once, even before Aubrey's reprimanding headshake. "Sorry, I'll need a pencil."

Aubrey took one hand away from the ledger and drew forth a pencil from his middle drawer, a legal pad from one of the side drawers, and placed them at Harrison's elbow. Tapping on the legal pad, he commented, "You can use the upgrade."

Harrison tucked his supplies back into his pocket. "Thanks."

Aubrey returned his attention to the ledger. "Here's where individuals reviewing the documents sign in." He turned the page. "You'll be the third." He removed a ballpoint pen from the middle drawer. "The only time you'll be using this," he added with a grin.

Harrison signed the page, adding the name of his workplace, email, and cell phone number where indicated. Norman Blethmore's signature had been entered on June 8; a Yale professor's, on June 20—coincidentally or significantly, the day before the Laszlo auction. Harrison delivered the ballpoint to Aubrey's extended palm, and Aubrey snapped the drawer shut on it like he was trapping a poisonous snake.

Harrison jotted down the information in the legal pad he'd been provided, then turned to the previous page and hastily recorded the types of documents in the collection and the number of each. "Has this collection been kept segregated from the balance of the Pissarro archive?" he asked, eyeing the unopened envelope.

"Yes. We've got a countless number of documents yet to be digitalized, and these are among them. They're being segregated until we get to them. They're also in line for translation. Most of the material is in French. How's your French?"

"Lurchingly fluent."

"I can help. Mine's impeccable." He set the ledger off to the side and snapped open the envelope. About to remove the contents, he asked, "Where would you like to begin? I can just sit here and keep my mouth shut. Selections from our archives are routinely examined in our study room, the visitor silently watched over by a security guard and video camera. In this situation, you've got a potential collaborator. So, what'll it be? Buckingham guard or chatty Prince Harry?"

"The latter, if there's no other choice," Harrison replied with a chuckle, turning serious, seeing the material suddenly laid out before him. "I'd like to start by counting the items," he decided on instinct.

"You think I dropped some on the way over?" Aubrey asked, taken aback.

"Don't take offense. It's more than likely that this material is associated with one murder, possibly two. I have to approach the subject with suspicion."

"Or paranoia."

"Or paranoia," Harrison readily agreed, to Aubrey's surprise. On a blank page in the legal pad, he wrote the headings:

- letters to P
- letters from P (drafts)
- receipts
- invoices

He then picked up the topmost document with a gloved hand. It began "*Mon cher* Pissarro." He put it aside. "Letters to P," he said, and put a vertical stroke next to the first heading. Next came a receipt from an art store, garnering a stroke next to "receipts" and a pile of its own.

After he'd gone through all the documents, two out of the four heading counts matched with those recorded in the archive's ledger. There were, however, only thirteen letters written to Pissarro among the documents on hand and two drafts penned by Pissarro himself. "There are five letters missing," Harrison announced, as if Aubrey hadn't been watching his every move and needed to be told.

"Count the documents," Aubrey whispered hoarsely. "There should be twenty-eight in all."

Harrison did so without objection. The count was, predictably, twenty-three. "Are there video recordings of both Norman Blethmore's and the Yale professor's visits to the study room?" he asked.

Aubrey shook his head, as if clearing it of cobwebs. "What? Oh. Yes, there are digital video recordings."

"Let's look at them after we've examined what we've got," Harrison said. "Maybe there's a clue hidden here."

"What sort of clue?"

"No idea." Harrison picked up the first of the two remaining letters in the "drafts" group. After the date, "17 June '71," Pissarro had written "*Mon cher* Ludovic." Harrison read the salutation aloud, then haltingly delivered his translation of the letter proper. In it, Pissarro was announcing that he and Julie, his long-time companion and mother of his children, had finally wed, three days prior, in the City Hall of Croyden, South London. A rather acerbic remark about his mother's refusal to come to England to witness the event had been crossed out and presumably excluded from the final draft.

"After the Franco-Prussian war broke out in July of 1870, Pissarro and his family left Paris and retreated for a number of months to the safety of his dear friend Ludovic Piette's home in the village of Montfoucault, Brittany," Aubrey elaborated. "It was some time thereafter, you see, that Camille Pissarro and Julie Vellay were married—in South London, where they resided for less than a year before moving back to Paris. Pissarro's mother was a disapproving elitist bitch, hence the negative reference to her, graciously deleted. The woman had previously given the pair her reluctant blessing, but rescinded it at the last minute."

Harrison was aware of Pissarro's upheavals during the war and perennial problems with his mother, but nodded attentively as Aubrey went on about the artist's life, figuring the archivist needed to deflect from his immediate problem: the loss of irreplaceable documents for which he himself would be held accountable.

When Aubrey had finally spent himself on his review of Pissarro's travails, Harrison no longer felt it impolite to return his attention to the letters. One by one, he read the letters to himself, occasionally asking Aubrey to verify his translation of a word or phrase; other times, to read aloud a passage of human interest or historical note, such as the artist Paul Cézanne's moving expression of grief on hearing of the death of Pissarro and Julie's three-week-old daughter, Adèle-Emma, who, in November of 1870, had contracted a fatal intestinal infection from her wet nurse.

Despite the letters' inherent importance, none were striking Harrison as relevant to the questions weighing on his mind: Why had the Pissarro authority, Norman Blethmore, been visibly alarmed at seeing Monet's painting on the cover of Laszlo's auction catalogue? Why had he called Ben Laszlo the day before that fateful auction—moreover, about a subject Mr. Laszlo was determined to keep to himself?

With his gloved hands, Harrison delicately picked up the next to last letter in the letters-to-Pissarro pile. It was dated "9 *Janvier* 1871" and began, "*Mon cher* Pissarro." He glanced down at its closing. It was signed "*Veuillez agréer*"—Faithfully yours— "Durand-Ruel." He began reading the letter, expecting to be interested, but not avidly. He suddenly stiffened.

"What now?" Aubrey asked resignedly.

"This is a letter to Pissarro from the noted art dealer, Paul Durand-Ruel. It's dated January the ninth, 1871, when both men were temporarily living in London to escape war-torn Paris. Let me read some of it to you. Quote. 'That was a brilliant idea of yours—which I put to use in my transaction of Tuesday last! Not a soul was hurt. There were no losers, and but for a harmless white lie, no misdeeds. Above all, Monet was delighted when I told him his paintings had sold for more than five times the amount they generally fetch these days. When he asked me who had bought his paintings, I told him the couple preferred to remain anonymous. When he asked why, I said I dared not press them for details and chance a change of heart. From one white lie, others follow. If this is not an adage, it should be.'" Harrison put the letter down; waited for a reaction from Aubrey.

"And?" Aubrey responded.

"And this may very well have a bearing on the recent tragedies! Here, we've got a sale of Monet paintings directly linked to Pissarro's *brilliant idea* and a bunch of little white lies!"

"Granted," Aubrey admitted, "the names Monet and Pissarro coming up in the same breath and under questionable circumstances, does make one wonder, especially since they're again puzzlingly linked, present-day. But does the date referred to ring a bell? It doesn't for me."

"That's just the thing," Harrison said, shaking his head. "It's ringing, but faintly." He dug for his phone in his jacket pocket. After a minute's research, he reported, "January the ninth, 1871 fell on a Monday. Durand-Ruel's reference to a transaction taking place on 'Tuesday past,' turns out to be January third."

Hear any chimes yet?"

Harrison shook his head. "Something is eluding me, but just." Whatever it was, it was tingling on the brink of recovery, like an arm that's been slept on too long. "It'll come to me."

"Or not," Aubrey replied with a touch of cynicism.

"I can't help but think that the missing letters would shed a whole lot of light on what transpired on January third, 1871," Harrison said, more to himself than to Aubrey, who was obviously still stuck in a turmoil of a different order. "I think someone swiped those letters for some devious reason of his own and either overlooked this one or left it behind in a rush to get away."

"Speculation," Aubrey scoffed.

"Yes, but based on facts. Can we look at the security camera's digital records of the two visits—Norman Blethmore's and the Yale professor's?"—he glanced at his legal pad— "Nadine Lowery's?"

"Yes, sure," Aubrey replied, starting to gather up the Pissarro material. When Harrison tried to help him, "I got it!" Aubrey objected, his aggressive scowl in direct opposition to the delicacy with which he was handling the documents.

* * *

Aubrey's mood hadn't improved when, a half hour later, the Pissarro documents had been locked away and he and Harrison, along with the museum's security technician, were huddled together in an out-of-the-way windowless room lined with screens displaying different sections of the museum's traversable space, while two unintrusive security guards silently panned the monitors like spotlights in a prison yard.

Harrison, legal pad in hand, and Aubrey stood closely behind the technician, a young man barely past pubescence, and leaned over his shoulders as he tapped inscrutable commands on a computer keyboard.

"You headed for the Blethmore visit, Jerry?" Aubrey interrupted.

Jerry struck the letter "q" as if it were the last note of a piano concerto. "Done!" He leaned back, causing his swivel chair to roll backwards and nearly knock over the men like bowling pins. "Oh, sorry! You good?"

"We're good," Harrison replied, letting go of the shoulder he'd grabbed onto, and focusing on the image that had just filled the screen. He recognized Norman Blethmore at once. If he'd aged a day, the image wasn't sharp enough to show it. The caption had recorded the date as June 8; the time, 11:32, the number changing as the seconds had passed. "It's Norman Blethmore," Harrison said, his voice unexpectedly somber.

"Yes, sir, that's him walking into the Western Art Print Room."

In his right hand, Norman held the precious envelope loosely against his chest, as if it were a frail lover. His left hand gripped the handle of a slim briefcase. The fingers of a pair of plastic-encased white gloves peeked out of a trouser pocket. His step had the barest spring to it as he approached the seat he'd decided to occupy at the long table. All this touched Harrison, but not as deeply as the eager expression on the man's face. The image on the monitor did not catch the glint in his eyes, but Harrison knew it was there. *This is not a man contemplating suicide.*

Norman positioned himself so that the security camera happened to capture a head-on frontal perspective. His hands were in full view, except as he reached into his briefcase to remove a hardcover notebook and pencil.

Mid-act, Jerry put the recording on pause and fetched a couple of folded metal bridge chairs from a corner of the room. He set them up on either side of his helmsman's post and waited for the tourists to settle in before unpausing the action.

For the first ten minutes after the recording had resumed, Harrison and Aubrey closely watched Norman's movements as he meticulously entered into his notebook each of the items in the Pissarro collection. This was an unexpected bonus for his observers since it provided clear evidence that all twenty-eight documents given to the Ashmolean by the Pissarro family could be accounted for, at least up to the morning of June 8. They watched the tape run at normal speed for another five minutes, then asked Jerry to pick up the speed a notch. When the session was over, the Pissarro material had been put back in the envelope, and the envelope snapped shut; the time registered on the screen was 4:21. Norman's study period had lasted close to five hours, during which time he had pored over each document, sometimes appearing to be more completely absorbed than others, when he'd lay his pencil aside and lower his face so close to the reading matter that it seemed as if he meant to devour rather than merely read it. Several times during the run-through, Harrison asked Jerry to return to normal speed so he could study those moments. They fascinated him as an academician quite apart from the investigation at hand. At one point, it looked like Norman may have been copying a letter in its entirety. In any event, it would be the longest period of time he would spend on a specific item.

Even with the occasional stops and starts, it took under forty-five minutes to review Norman's study time with the Pissarro documents. It was mutually agreed upon that all activity had been aboveboard.

Jerry's next task was to set up the digital recording of Nadine Lowery's June 20 interaction with the Pissarro documents. Unlike Norman Blethmore's clip, which had begun with his entrance into the print room with the Pissarro documents parcel in hand, the recording of the Yale professor's parallel experience showed only a medium-sized shoulder bag in her possession. The only other feature that set her apart was her startling beauty, impossible to hold in check, if that was her aim, by a prim countenance and a buttoned-to-the-neck shirt under a boxy jacket.

"Pause the tape, Jerry," Harrison requested.

Aubrey cracked a smirk. "Going in for a snapshot?"

Harrison appreciated the woman's beauty, but his interest was elsewhere.

"Why was Blethmore given the documents before he got to the study room, but Lowery is obviously going to have to wait for them to be presented to her?"

Aubrey took a second to recalibrate. "The way Lowery receives the material is the usual procedure. Blethmore was a special case. He'd been researching the Pissarro archive for years. The man even did some of its collating for us. What did you think? Of course, he enjoyed special privileges. He was given the documents directly from archival storage." Aubrey nodded to Jerry to continue.

Harrison threw up his hand. "One second, Jerry!" To Aubrey he directed, "By whom?"

"What?"

"By whom was Norman given the material?"

Aubrey glared at him. "By me! Is this an accusation?"

"Of course not. I don't recall you mentioning you knew Blethmore, but I suppose I should have guessed. I'm just trying to determine the chain of custody."

"'Chain of custody,'" Aubrey mimicked. "Our amateur detective turns pro."

"Come on, Aubrey, let's not revert to the schoolyard comeback."

"I thought I was being accused. Or about to be."

"You weren't."

Jerry slumped down in his seat.

Aubrey feigned a remorseful pout. "Look here, we're embarrassing the lad," he said in an obvious attempt to restore civility.

Jerry sat up. "I'm not embarrassed," he said. "I'm tired."

The declaration came off as a punchline. "Then, for God's sake, get on with it," Aubrey prompted with an exaggerated smile, glancing at Harrison for confirmation.

Nadine Lowery sprang to life, continuing her walk to the table Norman Blethmore had headed to just twelve days prior. The chair she chose was cattycorner to the one Norman had occupied, and Harrison could not help but imagine him sitting there, absorbed, stirring at the unexpected movement beside him, looking up from the document he was studying to see Nadine slipping the strap of her bag from her shoulder, placing the bag on the table, draping her jacket over her chair, and then, with one hand smoothing the skirt over her bottom, the other pulling the chair closer to the table, lower herself into the chair. How much of that twenty seconds worth of settling in would Norman have allowed himself to observe? Would he have turned away upon the placement of the bag? Would he have seen it through to the end, perhaps dwelling on the hand smoothing over the rear, slipping down the thigh, even as his eyes glazed over the written words? *Do I even know how long* my *focus would have strayed, or with what tenacity withdrawn?*

"Who was that actress again?" Jerry wondered, as a gloved gentleman holding the prized envelope like a serving tray approached Nadine. Jerry put the recording on pause. "You know, the one in that old movie, not the remake, about the—"

"Grace Kelly," Harrison said.

"This woman looks exactly like her—like her…what's it called, again?"

"Doppelganger. Can we resume, Jerry? Thank you."

The gloved gentleman waited for Nadine to remove a black-and-white composition book and a pencil from her shoulder bag, set them on the table, then hang the bag on the back of her chair. She folded her hands at the edge of the table like a schoolgirl as, with a sheepish grin, he removed the documents from the transparent plastic envelope and carefully placed them before her, as if he were serving her dinner. The envelope he laid beside them—the side dish. From his breast pocket, he removed a pair of white gloves and handed them to her. She said something to him that prompted a nervous smile and slipped on the gloves. With a slight bow, he backed off a few steps before turning to walk out of camera range.

"Does he stay in the room?" Harrison asked Aubrey while Nadine delicately plucked a document from the pile.

"He may or may not. There's always at least one staff member in the room, so it's not required."

Nadine seemed to be reviewing what was on the page. Harrison assumed she was able to read French, although he was not about to take anything for granted. After a minute or two, she placed the document at her left elbow, entered a quick note in her composition book, and picked up the second document. "Please pause, Jerry," Harrison directed. Jerry paused. "You happen to know the running time of the Lowery segment?"

"Thirty-five, forty minutes. Not long."

Harrison was surprised at its relative brevity, but not unhappily so, since it made reviewing Nadine's actions at normal speed, or even in slow motion, that much more feasible. He opened the legal pad to a fresh page and grabbed his ballpoint from his breast pocket. Mid-page, he drew a rectangle to signify the pile of documents still to be examined. To its left, another rectangle, this one to represent the document or documents set aside. Within it he inserted a short vertical line; one document accounted for. "Okay, go, Jerry."

Nadine examined two more of the documents and placed them on top of the one already reviewed. Harrison added two more vertical lines to the corresponding rectangle.

Nadine withdrew the fourth document from the pile. After ten seconds, she raised it slightly, as if to see it from a better angle. When she had scrutinized it to her satisfaction, she slid the transparent envelope away from her right elbow and placed the document in the space newly created. Harrison drew another rectangle to record the action, and entered its first vertical stroke.

Nadine methodically reviewed the remainder of the material. When she was done, there were twenty-three vertical lines in Harrison's left-of-center rectangle, five in his right.

Nadine removed the white gloves and placed them neatly on top of the plastic envelope. Then, as if realizing she was running late for an appointment, she hopped to her feet, hooked the strap of her shoulder bag over her wrist, grabbed her jacket from the back of the chair, slung it over her arm, and lastly, scooped her composition book from the table and slapped it on top of the jacket. Holding the book in place with her free hand, her shoulder bag swinging mid-calf, she gave a little self-deprecating shrug aimed at someone out of camera range, then spoke a few words—

"okay" and "thank you" lip-readable—as she cocked her head at the pile of documents left on the table. Her parting gesture, directed at the individual off-camera, was a breathtaking smile.

"Incredible!" Harrison exclaimed.

"She is, isn't she?" Jerry said, stopping action as Nadine stepped out of camera range.

"Aubrey, did you see what just happened?" Harrison asked, following Jerry's remark.

"Pardon?"

"What sleight of hand! And flashing that smile to put the poor man off-guard—that is, if he was ever *on*! I'm assuming Nadine was directing her closing scene to the fellow who was to collect the documents. No matter, it could have been anyone on duty."

"Not sure I'm following you," Aubrey said.

Harrison had Jerry replay the last few minutes at half-speed. "Watch carefully," he advised.

This time Aubrey understood the sequence for what it was. "There were five documents in the pile she swiped, weren't there?" he cried.

"The number that went missing, yes. You saw what she did, I take it."

"There were two piles left in the end," Jerry said, electing to reply. "On the left were the rejects. On the right, the five that were important to her—not that I know the reason why. When she was getting her stuff together, doing a couple of things all at once, seems like, she put her notebook on top of the five-pile and, at the same time, with her other hand slid a couple of docs off the pile on the left, giving her two piles. Made it look like nothing had been changed—same two piles all along, right?"

There was something endearing about the young man relishing the spotlight. "Right, Jerry, what next?" Harrison encouraged.

"She threw her jacket over her arm and then picked up her notebook—along with the five papers underneath it! —and placed it on top of her jacket. It all went very quickly, and if you weren't paying close attention, which would have been easy, what with her looks and everything, you would have missed it."

"You got it," Harrison said. "Exactly what happened."

"Something amiss here," Aubrey submitted. "Anyone studying the tape, as we have, would have caught her in the act. Wham. She's nabbed."

Harrison shook his head. "Doesn't matter. All she needs is time to scurry off, and she's home free." He gestured toward the two staffers scanning the feed from the museum's many monitors. "Unless one of them is staring at the critical screen at the critical moment, the trick will go undetected until way after it's committed—if ever. As for anybody watching Lowery in the flesh, forget it."

"It seems beauty has its merits," Jerry offered, punctuating his powers of observation with a pearl of wisdom.

Aubrey was not yet convinced. "Hold on. We know where she teaches; we can…"—the light dawned—oh."

"Exactly," Harrison said. "What college instructor in her right mind would brazenly purloin a bunch of important papers knowing she'd be caught on video, with the possibility, however remote, of her crime being detected?"

"We have no idea who she is, do we," Aubrey said.

"As the saying goes, 'trust, but verify,'" Harrison said, digging for his cell phone. Before long, he was posing the obvious question to someone in an administrative position at Yale University.

"Nadine Lowery," the administrator repeated. "Yes, the professor was a faculty member here at Yale. How can I help you?"

"I'm sorry, *was*?"

"Emeritus, yes. She retired last year, moved to Wyoming to be near her children and grandchildren. I can put you in touch, if you like."

Harrison politely declined the offer, and the call was terminated.

"I suppose this means our counterfeit professor might just as well have fallen off the face of the earth," Aubrey sullenly concluded. "I'll transmit her image to the authorities, see if they can find her in their database, but I'm not hopeful."

"I agree," Harrison said. "Whoever's running the show, they're not about to hire a recruit with a rap sheet to pull off a caper like this. But I'd follow through, of course."

"The National Crime Agency—NCA— covers the United Kingdom, with connections worldwide."

"Right," Harrison acknowledged. "In fact, they were helpful to me and my wife in the Benin case." He shrugged. "Even if they get a bead on her, my gut says they won't track her down." Another thought coming to him, he said, "I bet her fake credentials were near perfect, like the rest of her performance."

Aubrey nodded. "Credentials are always carefully scrutinized." He spread his arms, referencing the universe. "You think she might be the mastermind behind it all? My gut, like yours, it appears, says she's a cog in the machine. Too much going on—the murder in New York, the probable murder on my own turf, the Monet slash Pissarro slash Durand-Ruel business. You think I'm not giving her credit because she's a woman? You think I'm biased?"

"If so, you're not alone. You ever hear of a *queen*pin?"

Aubrey uttered a half-hearted guffaw and looked at his watch. "I don't mean to be abrupt, but I've got a board meeting to attend. I've been asked to speak on my department's progress on archival digitalization. I'm going to have to bring up the theft. I hope I'm not sacked."

Harrison rose to his feet. "If you need a character reference, just say the word." Realizing, from the crestfallen response, that his humor could use some brushing up. "Just kidding," he amended as Aubrey stood up beside him.

Too late, the damage had been done.

Chapter Nine

As Harrison was walking back to the Old Bank Hotel and wishing he could undo the flippant remark that had bruised an ego already sensitized by unfortunate events, across the ocean Erika was, ironically, on the receiving end of a barbed statement delivered by Lois Keller, Morris Keller's feisty ex wife.

"I can't say you were *resourceful* in finding my telephone number," Lois came at her right out of the gate. "It's listed. All you had to do was look it up. I'll give you *tenacious*, though. How's that?"

"I'll take anything I can get," Erika replied, rolling with the punches. In the same agreeable tone, she pressed on. "I'm trying to make some headway in a murder investigation," she said, her gaze wandering aimlessly about her study, settling on a David Hockney poster transplanted from her old apartment. "I think you might be of some help—very indirectly, of course. Is there a convenient time we could get together?"

"A face-to-face chat is uncalled for," Lois said, the snappishness at least abated. "I can't add much to what you heard at the house today, and frankly, Morris's abject fear of my leaking information, even in the presence of his twit of a wife, had me quite unnerved."

"I never give away my sources," Erika said. "You can take that as an absolute."

After a pause, Lois asked, "What does a collection of eight perfectly lovely Monet paintings kept under wraps—*lawful* wraps—have to do with a homicide?"

"Maybe nothing," Erika hedged. "Anyway, I'm not at liberty to discuss details for the same reason my lips are sealed in regard to *your* possible disclosures."

For a moment, Lois was silent. True, the fact that there was more than one Monet painting in Morris Keller's collection had been inadvertently disclosed earlier in the day, at his home in Brooklyn. However, Erika wondered if Lois realized that she'd just revealed the exact *number* of paintings. *Thank you, Lois.*

"Even if I wanted to, there's nothing much I can tell you," Lois pouted. "I was to get one of the paintings as part of the divorce settlement, but it was a handshake agreement Morris has yet to honor. In the meantime, I have no idea where *any* of the paintings are, and if you're thinking of contacting the Galaxy Fine Arts insurance company, don't waste your time. They have no idea where the paintings are either."

Whatever her state of mind, Lois did not appear to be on the verge of cutting Erika off. No harm in carrying on. "I'm wondering why, after all these years, Mr. Keller had put one of the paintings up for sale," she mused, inviting Lois to reply, but only if she chose to.

"I suppose he needed the money to invigorate one of his building projects. He's never been satisfied with the status quo. What passes as wealth to most does not foot the bill in Morris's world."

"He aims high," Erika encouraged.

"Let's say he's the kind of person who can afford a Mercedes, but craves an Aston Martin. There now, I've said enough. No thanks to your marketing skills. I have a tendency to shoot my mouth off."

"I appreciate your generosity, whatever the cause."

"You can't be ruffled, can you? I believe this conversation is over."

The call ended with an air of finality. As in the case of Min Cho, Erika suspected Lois Keller would be unavailable for future questioning. Still, she would write off neither one of them as future informers.

* * *

After her call to Lois, Erika got back to her article on the evolution of the art market. Her plan was to hand in a polished piece within two weeks. She'd just about gotten back into the rhythm of it when her cell phone rang from behind her computer screen. She reached for it.

"Hey, Greg!" she greeted, clicking the "save" prompt. (No matter how adept she'd become on Microsoft Word, she hadn't totally eradicated the fear of a document going AWOL.)

Greg had called her on FaceTime. "I'm interrupting something," he said.

"Not at all." She recognized the wall of books behind him. He was in his den in his London home. "When did you get back?"

"Late last night. I've got news. Harrison around? He should be in on this."

She told him where Harrison was and why. "Only for a couple of days. If you want to see him while he's still in Oxford or thereabouts, act fast. What's the news?"

"I convinced Ivan Brooks's widow, Robin, to allow me to divulge the secret she'd shared with me in a moment of weakness. I found a tactful way to tell her that now Ivan was dead, nothing much worse could come of it. That, in fact,would more likely be a help in tracking down his killer. I reminded her of the Wheatley code of discretion that you two would never blow your source."

"Basically what I assured Lois Keller."

"Say, what?"

"Lois is the ex-wife of Morris Keller, the owner of Monet's still life," Erika said. "The one pulled from the Laszlo auction. Looks like she's got some sort of iffy stake in things. Based on a handshake with the ex."

"Good luck with that. What else did she tell you?"

"Probably what you're about to tell *me*—that Morris Keller is in possession of a total of eight paintings by Monet. Am I right? That the secret?"

"*Half* the secret," Greg replied. He cocked his head; waited for her reaction.

Her wide-eyed look expressed her bewilderment.

His look of satisfaction conveyed his manly pleasure in relieving it. "It's a bit complicated," he began. "Let's start with the contract between seller and agent on file at Laszlo's. It contains all the usual conditions pursuant to the auction of a single work of art, in this case, Monet's *Wedgewood Vase with*

Flowers. This contract is accessible to the account executives at Laszlo's, and to others at their discretion, I would think. You follow?"

A cat—fat, or maybe just long-haired—jumped onto Greg's shoulder and, from there, to the top of the bookcase behind him. "I follow," she said.

"Listen carefully. That contract is invalid. It's for show only. There's another contract, dated and signed a day later. *That* version is the one in force. *That* document is for the signatories' eyes only, and each of them has a fully executed copy stashed away someplace deemed safe. You still with me?"

"Yes, Greg. How do the contracts differ, and what's up with the subterfuge? By the way, I think your cat is about to jump onto your head."

"I'll be fine," Greg said, as the cat jumped to his shoulder and from there to parts unknown. "This is how it goes. The in-force contract lists the eight Monet oil paintings and stipulates that they are to be auctioned off over time. Laszlo's Auction House is listed as Morris Keller's consignee; Ivan, his account executive. Now, the standard commission the owner is obliged to pay the auction house is generally ten percent of the painting's hammer price. In this case, because Keller is guaranteeing that Laszlo's will be handling the sale of all eight of his Monet paintings, the commission he'll be obliged to pay on each of the transactions is substantially lower, that is, six point five percent. Ben Laszlo and Ivan Brooks were to share the commission, Ben, of course, receiving the lion's share. Not clear? Why are you frowning?"

"I understand the terms of the contract, Greg. What gets me is the cloak-and-dagger routine. Why all the secrecy?"

"I'm getting to that." The cat was back, jumping onto Greg's lap. One stroke from Greg's broad palm down the length of his body seemed to settle him in. "There you go," Greg soothed, continuing his ministrations. "First off," he declared, returning his attention to Erika, "if Ivan's on-staff colleagues—that is, the more *senior* execs—had ever gotten wind of the exclusive deal Ivan had landed, there would have been hell to pay."

Well, hadn't *there been hell to pay?* Erika asked herself. "Why did Ben Laszlo choose Ivan to handle the deal in the first place?" she asked aloud.

"He didn't. Morris Keller insisted Ivan be his man. Keller would have brought his business to one of the more established houses, like Sotheby's or Christie's, were it not for Ivan's presence at Laszlo's."

"What am I missing?" Erika asked.

"Ah, you probably didn't hear the story. It made the back page of your newspapers right after one of those horrendous school shootings of yours. The art-marketing hounds didn't miss it, of that I'm sure!" Greg continued to stroke the cat in the same easy manner while his voice became more energetic. "About a year ago, Ivan came across a pleasant landscape painting at a yard sale in his hometown. The price tag read two hundred dollars. The artist's signature was indistinct. Ivan silently scrutinized the painting, which encouraged its owner, eager to seal the deal, to reduce the price to one-hundred-fifty dollars. "'I believe you have a very valuable painting here,' Ivan was overheard saying. 'Thomas Cole painted New England landscapes in the 1830s and 40s, and this may very well be one of them.' To cut to the chase, Ivan walked the owner through the process of attribution and consignment, and the Cole was sold at auction for six hundred thousand dollars." The cat, as if in response, uttered a purr as loud as a car engine.

"What a story," Erika said. "I can see why Keller would want to have someone like Ivan Brooks watching out for him."

"You bet. After that, his reputation was unassailable. Could have robbed a bank, gotten away with it. Say, did you happen to see any of the Monets in question when you were at Keller's house?"

"No. In fact, Lois—his ex—claims that neither she nor the company that had until recently been insuring them have any clue where they are."

"Odd. Who was the insurer?"

"Galaxy Fine Arts."

"Good, I'll find an excuse to look into it. Meantime, what was Keller's demeanor through all of this? Was he confrontational? Cautious? Conniving? What?"

"Scared shitless," her unedited reply.

* * *

By the time Harrison reached Erika from his hotel room via FaceTime later in the day—4:00 for her, 9:00 for him—she'd heard from John Mitchell. John had taken it upon himself to use his connections with the local police department stateside and the National Crime Agency abroad—"across the pond," as he put it—to probe, respectively, the murder of Ivan Brooks and the suspicious death of Norman Blethmore.

The first order of business had been Lucas and Harrison's chat. Lucas had been explosively joyous to connect with his father, and although it had been at least five minutes since Kate had whisked him off for a play date with Jake, Harrison was still on a high, strangely at odds with the lead item on the agenda: homicide.

There was a lot to cover. Erika started off by reporting John's findings. The cop-turned-private-eye had been told by the lead detective in the Ivan Brooks case that a senior account executive at Laszlo's, one Sheldon Adams, was, to date, their only person of interest. "He had a weak alibi," Erika elaborated, "and three witnesses had overheard him and Ivan having a row the day before the murder. Since the dynamic of the incident had allegedly been Ivan defending himself against a curse-laden ad hominem attack, none of the witnesses could say what exactly the conflict had been all about." Erika went on to explain how this turn of events dove-tailed with Greg's account of Morris Keller's secret contract with Laszlo's, in which Ivan was named broker. It was tempting, she suggested, to hypothesize that Sheldon Adams had gotten wind of this under-the-radar contract and had become furious over it. In fact, she proposed, after Ivan's demise, wasn't it possible that Morris might be persuaded to work with Sheldon? In which case, Sheldon would stand to rake in a couple of million dollars on the staggered sale of Morris's eight Monet paintings. Motivation served on a platter!

Nope. She and Harrison weren't buying it. As far as they were concerned, the complexity of events, entangling incidents in the United States and England, past and present, couldn't hinge on a single individual with a personal gripe—at least not exclusively. Their conclusion was bolstered by two factors. First, John's earful from the NCA regarding Professor Blethmore's death. Yes, it was true that an overturned empty bottle that had contained barbiturates had been found next to the professor's body, but only a trace was detected at autopsy. The cause of death was determined to have been a poison similar to ricin and delivered by injection. A pinpoint of blood under the decedent's left shoulder blade indicated the injection site. The second factor was the century-hopping montage of mysterious and criminal activity surrounding the Pissarro-Monet connection, as narrated by Harrison.

Erika listened in silence, studying Harrison's animated facial expressions as he delivered his account of his Ashmolean experience. At the end of it, in the professorial manner that occasionally emerged unintentionally and which she found sexy and endearing, he asked for her observations.

"The cluster of events occurring between June twenty and twenty-one are clearly related," she declared. "The circumstantial evidence is overwhelming. On the heels of Blethmore's alarm at seeing Monet's still life on the cover of Laszlo's auction catalogue, we've got his urgent call to Ben Laszlo on June twentieth. Same day, we've got the beauteous counterfeit, Nadine Lowery's theft of five of Pissarro's archived letters. Later that same day, Blethmore is murdered. And the very *next* day—*across the pond!* —the Monet still life is pulled from the Laszlo auction, and Ivan Brooks, its broker, is shot to death! It's a tangled web. Question is, who the hell's the spider?"

"Well put," Harrison said. "You think the spider is an individual?"

"No, an entity. Too much going on stateside and abroad."

"Agreed." He paused.

She waited for an apropos remark.

"I wish you were here," he put forward instead. "We could order up room service. Let's eat together, anyway. You hungry?"

"Matter of fact, yes," she said, smiling. How she loved him! "I'll slap together a sandwich, bring it up here to my study."

"Sounds good. I'll grab something from the room fridge. It's pretty well stocked, I noticed. Talk a little more first?"

"What I was about to suggest." She filled him in on the details of her visit to Morris Keller's townhouse and on the information gleaned from his ex-wife, Lois. "Greg is going to see if he can find out anything about the whereabouts of the eight Monet paintings from Galaxy Fine Arts, the company that had previously insured the paintings. Lois claims they have no idea, but that may be a cover-up, Lois's or the company's."

"Okay. Keep me up to date on that. Back to the Pissarro-Monet connection. Remember, I mentioned the date in the art dealer Durand-Ruel's letter to Pissarro?"

"The one that mentions the tantalizing reference to his sale of Monet paintings to an un-named couple, with the little white lie surrounding the transaction? How could I forget?"

"The letter is dated January the ninth, 1871."

"Yes, you told me."

"You remember the date of the sale?"

"Yes. 'Tuesday past,'" she quoted. "January third, you determined it to be. Is this a test?"

He laughed. "It may be. The date, January third, 1871. It's ringing a bell, but I can't place it. Can you? The answer might be on my laptop, but I left it at home. I've got a lot of sensitive information on it, and I was afraid of losing the thing or having it swiped. Call me paranoid." He watched as her expression turned pensive. "Erika?"

"Wait a minute." She pulled open the bottom drawer of her desk and pulled out the auction catalogue Min Cho had given her. Faced the cover toward him.

It took him a second. "Yes, of course. Don't keep me in suspense!"

She turned to the page that listed the provenance of *Wedgewood Vase with Flowers*. Without saying a word, she smiled and faced it to her cell's screen.

It was as if the significant words had been highlighted.

...oil on canvas, 20" x 17"; until January 3, 1871: purchased by James and Abigail Scott of Greenwich, Connecticut...

"Looks like I have my next assignment cut out for me," Erika said.

"Greenwich, Connecticut, here I come," Harrison supplied. "By the way, we've got to remember that all we've spoken about, my end and yours, is not yet in the public domain. No sharing outside our little circle."

"Absolutely not." Erika put the catalogue back in the drawer. "This is gratifying and maddening at the same time. It's like fitting together pieces of a jigsaw puzzle without seeing the big picture. Damn, if we only knew what was written in those letters swiped from the Pissarro archives!"

"We may never."

"On that optimistic note, shall we eat?"

Chapter Ten

Harrison awoke the next morning invigorated, his circadian rhythm miraculously in sync with the British Summer Time zone. Maybe due to the hotel mattress's ideal balance between plush and firm; maybe illusory due to his hyper-eagerness to get the ball rolling. He was meeting Darien Roth later in the day, and he had high hopes that Norman Blethmore's close friend would be providing some needed insight into his and Erika's investigation. Darien had made last-minute plans to meet with a prospective summer student at 10:30 a.m., after which he'd promised Harrison, "I'm yours for as long as you want me." He'd suggested they meet at the Courtauld Institute's Art Café at 11:30 for a casual brunch, then head over to the suburb of Wembley, a twenty-minute drive from London, for a get-together with Meagan Dunne, the Courtauld professor who'd initially suggested Harrison reach out to him. "You won't regret it," Darien had assured him. "Meagan is a vessel of institutional gossip. A *porous* vessel."

The drive from Oxford to the Courtauld Institute in London was an estimated one hour and twenty minutes. Harrison planned to call for an Uber at 9:45, but it was only 6:00, and he was raring to go. True, he hadn't brought along his laptop this trip, but he had packed a pair of sneakers and sweatsuit with the intention of jogging around Christ Church Meadow, a vast green expanse about three minutes from the hotel. Erika, a seasoned jogger, had done the research on jogging paths in Oxford before his trip and had encouraged him to "go for it."

Actually, he no longer needed encouragement to go for it. At the beginning—must be at least a year ago—he did need some prodding. Shaming, more accurate. "Just because you're built like a gym rat without ever having lifted a barbell doesn't mean you should rest on your laurels," Erika had teased, making him feel like a slug endowed with good genes. It hadn't taken long for the activity to grow on him. Jogging in Central Park gave him a new perspective on city life, on nature, on well-being, and, when he and Erika jogged side by side, on the pure physicality of moving through space with a partner.

After downing a buttered roll and a shot of coffee, Harrison took off for the appointed grounds at a run, slowing down to a jog only after he'd reached the tree-lined path circling the vast green expanse of Christ Church Meadow. The path was bounded by the Rivers Thames and Cherwell, and reminiscent of the jog around the Jacqueline Kennedy Onassis Reservoir in Central Park. It was a clear day, about seventy degrees, and windless. Harrison expected to see a number of like-minded individuals along the trail, but surprisingly, he came across only two—an elderly couple walking briskly hand-in-hand, who waved at him as he jogged by. He waved back, then pushed off the hood of his sweat jacket. It was too beautiful a day to be covered up. Across the meadow, he could see the spires of Christ Church and, in the middle distance, two Longhorn cows languidly grazing. Erika had told him he would come across a few footbridges and boathouses along the way, and he anticipated coming upon them with an unusual keenness. The jogging tour was estimated to take about an hour. He picked up the pace. Not because he wanted to save time, but because he felt tireless and chose to challenge himself. On this particular morning, in this moment of time, he felt invincible.

* * *

At 11:25 a.m., Harrison arrived at the Art Café— "a relatively new addition to the Courtauld Institute," as Darien had described it. What *isn't* "relatively new" when you're talking about a complex of palatial structures built in the eighteenth century? Harrison wondered, stepping foot inside the contemporary-style restaurant and bar. The bar area itself, an exclamatory red from head to toe, seemed to be an in-your-face rejection of its staid neo-classical exterior. Like a rebellious teenager, came to mind, only there was nothing hateful in this example of gleeful self-expression. Eventually, the styles, like parent and child, would come to terms and live together in lovingly disruptive harmony.

The dining section consisted mainly of a row of small round tables-for-two backed up on one side by a long leather banquette; on the other, a line-up of chairs. Most of the tables were occupied by solos. Harrison scanned those faces in plain view for one resembling the headshot of Darien Roth he'd seen on Courtauld's website, hoping not to find it. The tables were placed so close together, even a whispered conversation would be shared by neighbors.

From the rear of the room, a voice rising just above the ambient hum of chatter hailed, "Professor Wheatley!" Harrison spotted its source in a red cardigan—*got* to be Darien Roth—in the far corner, standing by one of two stools placed at a round table exactly like the others, only higher. Two more out-of-the-way seating arrangements of this kind were up against the back wall, and although the nearer one was occupied by a party of two, the tables were separated by at least six feet, so privacy would not be an issue. As Harrison approached, Darien waved in a slow, broad arc, as if he were guiding a lost ship to shore.

The wave lowered for a handshake as Harrison pulled into harbor. "Darien Roth," his greeter announced. "I recognized you from your photo on the New York University Fine Arts online faculty roster."

"Same here—from *your* website. Drop the 'professor.' It's Harrison."

"As you wish. Shall we sit?"

"Sure," Harrison said as he tried to merge his anticipated image of Darien to the one before him. The headshot on the Courtauld roster captured a plump round face covered with a short, scruffy beard and a haircut that continued the pattern, putting Harrison in mind of a teddy bear. The man before him seemed much diminished. Same teddy bear, but after the cat had eaten its stuffing. As for his slender body, Harrison imagined it had been pudgy as well, and not that long ago, since in both the photo and real life, Darien looked to be in his mid-thirties. He wondered if the weight loss had been intentional.

"It must have been a terrible shock," Harrison said as they took their places on the sleek wood stools.

"What? Oh—that was abrupt, Harrison. You mean when I heard my friend, Norman, was gone. Yes, it was a shock. I couldn't accept it. The very idea of *suicide!*" Darien fingered one of the menus lying on the table, then shoved it aside. "Norm was such a robust individual—physically, emotionally, academically. It was like I'd been thrust into an alternate universe."

"When I spoke briefly on the phone to Meagan Dunne, that's basically what she told me," Harrison said. "She didn't believe it was a case of suicide either."

Darien shifted around in his seat. "It's understandable to feel this way— especially for someone as close as I was. To be honest, it felt rather like a betrayal." He shook his head slowly. "I suppose one never can be sure. In the end, even the closest of friends don't fully know one another."

It was tempting to jolt Darien out of his epistemological reverie and tell him the autopsy had confirmed that Norman Blethmore had been murdered, but Harrison was bound to keep this privileged information to himself. He nodded his head in sad acknowledgment and applied his directness elsewhere: "Did Norman ever discuss his most recent research on Camille Pissarro? I mean, he *must* have!" To soften what sounded like an accusatory tone, he gave a slightly bewildered shrug. "Right?"

"He did mention it, yes," Darien replied. "We often spoke about what we were working on. Norman was not quite as forthcoming as I was. He talked more about the process than the content of his work—the ups and downs of working with an editor, his obsession with accuracy. He was superstitious about discussing the *meat* of his work before his article or book was on the cusp of being released. Not for fear that his ideas would be stolen, but that they'd become less…"

"Newsworthy?" Harrison suggested. "I know the feeling."

"I don't feel that way myself in the least," Darien said. "Give us a minute," he said, addressing a waitress arriving tableside. He picked up a menu and gave it a token glance. "I recommend the poached salmon salad."

"Sounds good," Harrison said without checking the menu. "So, did Norman refer in particular to his research of the Pissarro archives housed at the Ashmolean?"

"Of course. He was always rooting around those archives. As I recall, he was intending to look—actually *did* look, come to think of it—at the latest collection of letters and such that Pissarro, or his son, Lucien, had stowed in Lucien's London home. What they're about, I wasn't told." Darien hailed the waitress, at the ready a courteous distance away.

Without further ado, each ordered a poached salmon salad and a cup of Earl Grey tea. Harrison continued to prod Darien for information, hoping he'd drop in an anecdote or observation that might hint at Norman's state of mind, or more pointedly what was *on* it, at the time of his death. He waited until they were halfway through the meal, and Darien seemed to be about as relaxed as he was going to get before slipping in the question at the heart of his inquiry. "I'm wondering," he said, "did Norman ever tell you why he was so alarmed at the sight of Monet's still life on the cover of Laszlo's auction catalogue?" He pushed around a shred of lettuce with his fork to give Darien a moment to gather his thoughts.

"What are you talking about? What catalogue? What still life?"

Harrison tried not to show his surprise at Darien's ignorance—or feigned ignorance—of the matter. "When I spoke to Professor Matt Henley, he mentioned he'd shown Norman the auction catalogue. He said he'd thought Norman would be interested in the Pissarro painting that was going up for auction June twenty-first. He was taken aback when Norman reacted so strongly to the *Monet* painting featured on the cover."

Darien frowned and shaded his eyes, as if from the sun. "I have no idea what you're talking about."

"Here it is in a nutshell," Harrison began. "Norman called Laszlo's the day before the auction. It remains a mystery why. The Monet still life was pulled from the auction during the event itself. Its broker was murdered that same night."

"Wait! You said Norm called the auction house on June twentieth?"

"Yes."

"That was the day he took his own life!"

"Or *did* he?" Harrison took a sip of his tea; granted Darien another moment of reflection.

Darien blanched. "No, no, it can't be." He flapped away the thought as if it were a circling fly. "We'll visit Meagan. She'll throw some light on this."

Wishful thinking. Harrison pulled out his wallet from his pants pocket. "Shall we get a move-on then?" He looked for the waitress. She was within hailing distance. He caught her eye.

Darien reached for his wallet in the pocket of his cardigan. Harrison threw up his hand to signal stop. Pretty clear he meant business. "Thank you," Darien said. His color had not yet completely returned. "My car's a short walk away, on John Adam Street." He attempted a light-hearted smile. "It was not easy finding a reserved spot close to home. Almost impossible in Central London. I should put it in my will; leave it to my next of kin, should I ever acquire one."

* * *

"One moment." Darien stopped in front of the gaping maw of the underground garage and pulled his cell phone from his pants back pocket. "Reception's iffy inside. I'll text Meagan, give her an estimated time of arrival." Harrison stood by as he sent the message. "Okay, we're good. Let's go. We're one level below ground."

A narrow pedestrian walk rimmed the drivers' path that sloped down to the lower level, to where Darien had Harrison follow him. As they approached the bank of cars, Darien plucked his car key out of his side pocket and aimed it at a point about forty-five degrees to their left. The ensuing chirp was followed by the blinking rear lights of a blue sedan some twelve yards away.

As they got closer to Darien's car, they could see a big bruiser of a motorcycle tucked into the parking slot next to it. Its owner—or someone dressed for the part, complete with helmet—was crouched beside it, palpating the rear tire, his back to the newcomers. Harrison gave Darien a questioning look. "No idea," Darien muttered under his breath.

On arrival, "Just ride into town?—Nice hog!" Darien lilted, addressing the biker, his strained falsetto about as far a cry from hipness as his Mr. Rogers red cardigan was to the biker's black leather getup.

Without turning, the biker raised a gloved hand in acknowledgment and rose to his feet. The motorcycle was parked on the driver's side of Darien's sedan, and Harrison was about to walk around to the passenger side, but the man uttered the words "Yeah, well I …" as he unzipped the macho gear bag hugging the gas tank, and Harrison stuck around to hear the rest of the sentence. Darien stood in place as well, ignition key at the ready.

The biker removed a metal bar from the bag—a tool of some kind, maybe twenty inches long, Harrison figured, as he waited for the thought to continue. "Like I came here to…" the biker restarted as he zipped closed the tool bag. Then, in one continuous movement, he snapped down his helmet's visor—*is he going to fix his bike or ride off?* flashed in Harrison's brain as he stood there, rigid with disbelief—and spun around, drawing back the rod-like instrument and swinging it forward, dead-ending its path against Darien's ribcage. Darien uttered an explosive grunt and fell sideways, his head just missing the fender of his car and striking, with a crack, the unforgiving cement floor. To Harrison, time froze for all things except for himself, and as fear-generated adrenalin crested into fearlessness, he seized the opportunity to leap into action.

Time resumed as the biker, seeing Harrison was coming at him, took a wild swing with his weapon, but missed his mark as Harrison, untrained in the art of combat, hurled himself forward in an unpredictable manner, making contact in a powerful high-five chest bump while grabbing hold of his opponent's forearms. Finding it impossible to secure his grip on bulky limbs sheathed in thick leather, he used the inertia of his forward thrust to push the brute past Darien's motionless form. Once outside the parking grid, he tried to body-slam him to the floor, hearing in advance the thwack of Darth Vader's helmet as it hit the cement, his entire being wordlessly affirming *I can do this*!

Like the flip of a switch, the advantage was suddenly the biker's, and Harrison was on his back, pinned to the floor by a massive boot pressing down on his upper chest. His hands flew up to shield himself from the oncoming weapon, but its arc was so wide it was impossible to know where it was headed until his left knee exploded in pain, and he heard himself howl like an animal who's been shot and again, when it struck again, lower down the leg. "Slow you down for a while, yeah?" the hunter asked softly, below Harrison's groans. "You and your friend, keep out of what's none of your business. You get me?" Another blow, this one to the right knee, expanding the universe of pain, already boundless.

Buried in agony: a voice—no, voices, and footsteps—nearing.

The clink of the dropped weapon. The repeated thrust of the engine revving. The steady roar, echoing in the enclosed chamber. Backing up, tire crushing bone. Again, in forward gear. On the move now. The roar of the engine receding to utter silence.

* * *

His legs were on fire. A face was inches away from his. "*Who?*" he heard himself say, as if from another planet, pain devouring all that was near.

"I'm a security guard. Help is on the way. You were out for a couple of minutes."

"Darien?"

"Your friend? He's right here. Being seen to."

"Left leg, is it…?"

"The medics, they'll be looking after you."

Harrison let out a yelp. "Excruciating!"

"You'll get help with the pain. Try to hold on."

"Biker…" He felt himself growing faint again; didn't allow it. "You get him?"

"The police are on it."

"He was wearing a visor. Tinted. I couldn't…"

"It's okay, sir. You'll talk to the police." The face turned away. "Move on! Thank you!" Back to Harrison, with a passing grip on his upper arm. "People are curious. Don't let it bother you."

He hadn't noticed the onlookers, burrowed in his pain. But immediately after the guard spoke, he heard a siren's wail in the distance growing nearer, and he lifted his head to the sound. The guard gently cupped his head and instructed him to keep it still, adding the worrisome "You never know…," which motivated Harrison to heed the sinister warning and allow the guard to support his return to unbearable passivity. *In the new world*, the thought erupted: *will I be running only in my dreams?*

The ambulance pulled up at an angle close by and its siren fell silent, although its lights remained active, casting an eerie blue glow on the ceiling of the garage. The vehicle itself looked like an enlarged toy—painted yellow, with red chevron stripes at the rear and neon yellow and green checkerboard on the side, partially in Harrison's view. Seconds later, a cacophony of sirens filled the silence, and as a gurney laden with equipment was being hauled from the rear of the parked ambulance, another ambulance pulled up behind it, followed by a police car, then another.

Suddenly, the space was filled with movement. Paramedics and EMTs coming his way and Darien's, each team pushing a gurney loaded with gear. Behind them two—no, four—police officers loped toward the victims, passing the medical personnel, certain to arrive ahead of them.

Harrison was already thinking ahead despite the pain. Deciding what he would share with the police. More precisely, what he would *not*. His gut told him the broader the law enforcement presence, the more methodically the organization behind the crimes would cover its tracks. Yes, *organization*. If anything, the biker's warning attack, in conjunction with all the rest, was once and for all proof, the related crimes that had taken place in the US and the UK had not been committed by some ocean-hopping chameleon.

The security guard crouching by Harrison's hip yielded his position to one of the two officers coming to a halt at his feet—*don't touch, don't touch!* He felt the slightest contact with the big toe of his left foot would cause his leg to fold up like an accordion. "You're going to be taken care of, sir," the officer said, getting down on one knee beside him. "I'll be asking you more questions in good time, but for now, just one: did you know your assailant?" To Harrison's resigned headshake, he replied, "Okay then, let's let the medical team set you up for transport. If you'd just let me see some form of identification? I'll give it right back after I get a photo on my cell phone."

Harrison's gurney had pulled into place. One of the caregivers, a burly young woman with the face of an angel, was squatting by his feet, scissors in hand. "My name is Jamie. My partner Steve and I will be taking care of you." Steve, removing equipment from the gurney, turned to nod a casual greeting, as if they were being introduced at a local bar. "And what's *your* name?" Jamie asked.

"Harrison Wheatley." Jamie helped him withdraw his wallet from his pants pocket and handed it to the police officer. Harrison noticed the officer's partner was off to the side in a huddle with the security guard who'd watched over him. The partner was holding a large plastic bag containing the weapon the biker had left behind.

"Harrison," Jamie said, "I'm going to cut away your pants legs, okay?"

"Please be careful!"

"I usually am," Jamie said affably, lifting the cuff of his left pants leg.

"Sorry."

"Don't be." She began to slice open his pants leg. "I can see you're in a lot of pain and trying to tough it out. On a scale of one to ten, ten being the worst, how bad would you say it is?"

The officer, having finished recording what he was after, gently placed the wallet in Harrison's jacket pocket and got out of the caregivers' workspace.

"Nine," Harrison said, answering Jamie. He supposed sawing off his leg might hurt more. Had he just heard Jamie expel the tiniest grunt at the sight of it? Wasn't it his manly obligation to take a look at the damage? Gratefully, the rigid brace with which Steve was now immobilizing his neck, prevented him from following through. "It looks bad, doesn't it?" he asked Jamie, who had begun slicing open the second pants leg.

"I've seen worse," Jamie said.

He should have anticipated that answer.

"We'll be stabilizing your legs with pneumatic splints," Jamie said. "Do you have any allergies to cocaine or morphine?"

"I do not want opioids or any controlled substances," Harrison expelled, grimacing as Jamie and Steve began removing his shoes and socks. "Oh God!"

"Sorry, man," Jamie said. "This won't take long. You seem adamant—about the drugs, I mean. You're not a recovering addict, are you? Sorry, I have to ask."

"No. I just want to have all my senses about me. I want to be alert."

"I understand. Are you fine with acetaminophen—like Tylenol?"

"Yes."

As Jamie fetched the pills from a plastic container atop the gurney, Steve took a reading from each of Harrison's legs, apologizing all the while for adding to his discomfort. "Left leg pulse distinctly weaker," he reported to Jamie on her return. "No notable pallor." To Harrison, he said, "Can you wiggle a toe on your left foot?" Harrison reluctantly complied.

"Good job," Jamie said. "Mild ischemia is caused by pressure on blood vessels, but it must be reversed ASAP, before swelling and tension progress, okay?"

As if he had a say in the matter. "Okay."

Jamie was at the ready with the Tylenol, along with a bottle of water and a straw. "Don't try to move," she said. "I'll help you."

After two pills had been administered, the work began in earnest. Together, Jamie and Steve moved Harrison's left leg a torturous hair's breadth. "We're aligning it for the pneumatic splint," Jamie crooned apologetically as Harrison clenched his jaw to stifle a scream. They repeated the process on the right leg, then removed what looked like two thick plastic mats from the gurney. He guessed they were about to wrap these things around his legs, then pump air into them. This was confirmed when Steve removed an air pump from the gurney.

Darien, lying motionless on his assigned gurney, entered Harrison's line of vision on the way toward the bank of emergency vehicles. "Will he be okay?" Harrison asked as he prepared himself for an escalation of pain.

"I hope so," Jamie said.

"What hospital is he being transported to?"

"I think Blackheath."

"That where you're taking me?"

"I don't know yet. I'll be contacting Guy's Hospital in the borough of Great Maze Pond, no more than ten minutes away. It's Ajay Singh's primary location. Mr. Singh is one of our top orthopedic surgeons. If we're in luck, he'll be there—or able to get there quickly." She started to raise his left leg to allow Steve to slip the mat-like device under it.

Harrison clenched his fists to combat the pain caused by her efforts.

"You're doing great, Harrison," Jamie said. "Hang in there."

Chapter Eleven

id-afternoon, London, and Harrison was on his way to Guy's Hospital, sirens blaring. At that same moment in Manhattan, Erika was returning home from her morning jog.

"Hi, all!" she sang, taking the steps to the second landing three at a time, hearing the sound of voices coming from the living room, with Luc's breathlessly giggled "Oh, no, Jake!" overriding the playful chidings of Kate and Grace. "Okay, what have you done *now*, you naughty dog?" Erika asked, with mock sternness, on entering the room. Jake answered by leaping at her with as much joyful vigor as his old shoulders would allow.

In the center of the room, a mass of Lego bricks, many in connected clusters, lay scattered about. Surrounding the ruins: Grace, in her starched black and white uniform, perched on the ottoman of the easy chair; Kate, barefoot, in black tights and red tank top, sitting in a lotus position, flaxen ponytail styled to fall to one side of her head like a mortarboard tassel; and Lucas, in blue jeans, plaid shirt and light-up sneakers, sitting with his legs splayed, hands waving.

"We had a castle—with horses and people and a..."—he checked with Kate— "a..."

"A moat!" Kate supplied.

"A moat, Mommy! And Jake crashed it all down with his feet, and it made him scared!" He started to laugh again. "Wanna build it over, Mommy?"

"Sure. Let me take a quick shower first. Can you start without me?"

Her plan accepted, Erika trotted up to the master bedroom to make good on her word with a one-minute shower, then threw on a sweatsuit. Later, she planned to change into something more formal, like jeans and a blazer, and run over to the office. Sara hadn't called a staff meeting or summoned her for a one-on-one, so there was no need to drop by, but she wanted to discuss in what direction her article on the state of the art market was headed, that is, to an in-depth study of specialized and diversified art funds. Her interest in the subject had been sparked by Ivan Brooks, and she was going to give him credit for it in her essay.

The day's schedule was pretty much chock full. After her impromptu Lego playdate, she was all set to call the Chamber of Commerce in Greenwich, Connecticut. It was a long shot, but she was hoping they'd be able to come up with a lead on James and Abigail Scott, residents of Greenwich at the time of their purchase of the Monet still life pulled from the Laszlo auction. The sale date listed in the work's provenance was January 3, 1871, and, coincidentally, the very sale date alluded to in art dealer, Durand-Ruel's tantalizing letter to Pissarro. Erika suspected that the sale Durand-Ruel wryly commented on in his letter and the Scotts' transaction might very well be one and the same. The event may, in fact, be at the root of the present-day morass of crimes, including murder, under scrutiny by Harrison and herself. Erika thought of the Lego blocks scattered on the floor of the living room—the seeming chaos made up of parts of a coherent whole: a castle with horses and a moat! There was also coherence to be found in the time-scattered fragments of the mystery she and Harrison were immersed in. This self-evident fact was in itself enough to ramp up her resolve to find it.

She took a moment to review her prospective timeline. After her play period with Lucas and call to Greenwich, Connecticut, she would head off to *Art News* headquarters. She estimated her chat with Sara would run about a half hour. While on-site, she planned to touch base with the advertising director. She had a bone to pick with him about his placement of ads in the last issue. Fifteen minutes, give or take. Add ten minutes to change her clothes and a half-hour round trip by bus—a conservative estimate. All told, just over two and a half hours, three, to be on the safe side. According to her calculations, she'd be back home in time to collect Lucas and head down to the Mommy-and-Me converted warehouse downtown in Soho, where

Lucas was registered in a class called "pre-competitive sports."

"Ready or not!" she called to her playmates as she scooted down the steps to the living room.

* * *

Phase two of the morning was off to a promising start. Erika sat at her desk in her study, waiting on hold while the president of Greenwich, Connecticut's Chamber of Commerce, Sharon Resnik looked up the phone number of the town's Historical Society's secretary. "If Libby Newcomb can't give you a bead on your James and Abigail Scott, nobody can," Sharon said, before breaking contact.

Ten seconds into a swath of New Age music, Erika was alerted to a call waiting. She recognized the opening numbers, 020, but none that followed. Her breath quickened. Who could be calling from London? Her hand trembled as she went to hit the "accept" option.

"Yes?" she detonated, not meaning to.

"This is Ajay Singh. I'm calling from Guy's Hospital in London. I'd like to speak with Erika Wheatley."

"Speaking! Is my husband hurt? Can I talk to him?"

"Mrs. Wheatley, there's been an incident, and your husband was brought here. I'm the orthopedic surgeon looking after him. I promised him I'd let him talk to you before I explained the situation—yes, yes, Harrison, here she is! I'm handing him the phone now, Mrs. Wheatley. Here you go."

"Is he in pain?" she cried.

"Yes, darling, I'm in pain," Harrison answered weakly. "But hearing your voice—"

"What happened to you? Oh, sweetheart!"

"I was meeting with Darien Roth. Details later. There was an attack. My legs were injured. Mr. Singh will explain. I'm putting him back on. I love you. I'll call you on my cell phone as soon as I can. I'm being prepped for surgery."

"Wait! I want to see you. Tell Singh to put you on FaceTime!"

"It's okay, darling, I'll see you later."

"I'm catching the first flight out of New York!"

"No, no, don't want you around danger. Can't go into surgery worried about you. Promise me you won't come!"

Terrified, frustrated, she promised.

"I'll explain what's going on, Mrs. Wheatley." Singh was back on the phone. "We'll have to make this brief."

She hadn't told Harrison she loved him! "Yes, but put the phone to his ear for a second—please!" The surgeon complied. "I love you," she said, her voice quivering. "I love you."

"I know," Harrison said, his voice barely audible. "Talk soon."

"Soon, very soon," she said, before the world turned quiet. "Mr. Singh, you there?" She noticed Sharon Resnik had terminated the call. It could wait. Everything could wait.

"Here I am."

"I want to know everything. Don't hold anything back."

"I'll be brutally honest."

"Please."

"All right. Your husband was brought to the hospital after being struck in the legs with a heavy metal pipe. With great force, judging from the severity of the injuries. Two blows to the left leg, one to the right. The left leg suffered additional damage by being crushed under the wheel of a motorcycle. Understandably, the left leg will require more complicated, limb-saving care. Harrison's bone density is good, which is an advantage when it comes to repair and reconstruction, but the more time we lose, the less guaranteed the outcome. I'm performing the surgery after this call. First and foremost, we've got to release the pressure on the blood vessels of the left leg."

Must keep it together. *Deep breath. Deep breath.* "What surgery exactly?"

"I'm getting to that. You're doing great. Listening. Forcing yourself to keep calm. I can hear it in your voice."

This is not about me, she snapped back internally, embarrassed to have felt praised. "What surgery, doctor?"

"We've got to restore a normal pulse in the left leg. This will be accomplished by repairing the fractured tibia and fibula—shinbone and calf bone. Because of the multiple traumas to the limb, we will be using hardware to reconnect the displaced bone fragments. For the tibia, a plate may be the best option.

"As for the patellae, or kneecaps, there will be more work required to repair the left, where the inner side of the knee caught the brunt of the blow, causing serious tears to the knee ligament. Here, we will perform an autograft by replacing the ligament with a piece of healthy tendon from your husband's hamstring and grafting it into place to hold the knee joint together.

Both patellae were broken, and the bone fragments will be fixated with cannulated screws and k-wire, which may or may not be prudent to remove after about a year. This is a lot to process, but you wanted to be fully informed. I or someone from my surgical team will call you right after the surgery is completed. Don't ask me to approximate the number of hours this will take. Be assured that you'll be notified promptly." He paused. "Are we good?"

"Thank you," Erika said, rather than lie. Her questions, about everything from surgical complications to rehabilitation, were clamoring to be heard. If she uttered one, there'd be no stopping her. She was trying and not trying to picture Harrison being moved from bed to gurney.

In accepting the call's ending, she felt like she was being made to sever ties with him. In the natural course of things, she would be beside him, holding his hand, comforting him. Mr. Singh had given her both his cell phone number and the number of the nurses' station in the intensive care unit ward where Harrison would be transferred after his surgery. She clung to these scraps of information like his life depended on it.

* * *

Out of Lucas's hearing in the kitchen, Erika gave Kate and Grace a revised version of what had befallen Harrison. The less they knew, the less they could disseminate. "He was mugged on the way to a lecture," she said. She could hardly fudge the truth about the injuries he'd suffered, or the surgery he was about to undergo.

After expressing her well-modulated alarm, Kate went off to tend to Lucas, in his room "reading" a Dr. Seuss book to Jake. Grace remained seated at the kitchen table with Erika, who was planning on aborting all plans in order to wait at home for the promised call from the hospital.

"You've got to carry on with your day," Grace insisted. Not getting a response, she added, "It won't do anyone any good to sit around and work yourself up."

"I know you're right, Grace, but how can I go off to the office, then to a Mommy-and-Me sports class while Harrison is under the knife?"

"You're capable of doing two things at once, worrying and playing catch," Grace said, reaching for humor for the first time in Erika's recollection, maybe even Grace's.

"What if they call me during the class?" Erika asked.

"Will they be calling your cell phone number?

"Yes."

"So you'll answer it," Grace said. "What are your plans?"

"I should make a call to Connecticut, apologize to someone for abandoning her on the line. Then stop by the office, for maybe half the time I'd allotted. Then come back for Lucas."

"So get going, Miss Erika. You and I both know our Mr. Harry would approve." She leaned toward Erika; hesitated, unsure a hug was called for.

Erika completed the action for her.

* * *

The call from Guy's Hospital came just as the Mommy-and-Me class was wrapping up, the mommies gathered around the instructor, praising her creativity and warm-heartedness; the unmonitored kids batting around a colorful plastic orb the size of a basketball on steroids.

Erika hastened to the far corner of the warehouse's re-imagined space.

115

"Hello! Is my husband okay?" she whispered hoarsely, on the run.

"This is Ajay Singh," the caller declared. It seemed to take a lifetime for him to get to the next sentence. "Your husband did very well, Mrs. Wheatley."

"Ah!" she exhaled. "Thank you! Can he talk to me? His legs—the left leg—is the pulse back to normal?"

"Yes, the pulse is normal. All procedures on both legs were performed. I thought we might have to postpone the right patella repair because of the time factor, but we decided the patient was hardy enough for us to carry on. I want to keep an eye on him for at least a day or so before we allow him to be flown home, but we can leave the discussion of logistics for another time. Right now, he's in the ICU and not yet fully awake, so not ready to talk to you. His cell phone is fully charged, and you have my number and the number for the nurses' station, so I'd say we're all set in the communications department."

"What about his care during the night and for the rest of his stay?" Erika asked. "Will he be having s special nurse assigned to him? Can I hire a private nurse?"

"The hospital provides excellent care, but yes, one can hire a private nurse. Prior to surgery, your husband did, in fact, arrange for this service. He said you'd insist on it. The nurses' station can give you the agency's name and number. Before I go, do you have any questions?"

Hundreds. "No," she said. "Thank you for taking care of Harrison. You don't know how grateful I am."

When she returned to the mommies, she was given a few questioning looks, but no one asked why she'd suddenly taken off. To the one woman who asked the generic "You okay?" she responded in kind: "I'm fine, thanks."

Your husband did very well, Mrs. Wheatley. Singh's reassuring words would be her comfort until she was allowed to speak to Harrison.

As the mommies were collecting their children, she asked Lucas, "You have a good time, sweetie?" Singh's words looping into hers.

The FaceTime call from Harrison would be received an interminable hour and a half later. Thank God for the earworm.

* * *

Harrison's long-awaited FaceTime call was more a torrent of gratitude and relief than a conversation. Harrison was alive and in one piece, and was coming back to her, and all Erika could do was marvel at this stroke of luck.

Ten minutes later, she had to reconnect. She couldn't help herself. There were questions she'd forgotten to ask, concerns she'd stifled in order to preserve the spirit of optimism. She had to see if the pained expression he'd almost succeeded in suppressing—she, in observing—had passed.

"Hello, there," she said as his face appeared on her laptop screen. "It's been too long."

"Ages," he said, smiling, his eyes giving him away.

"You're in pain."

"Yeah, but I've finally allowed myself the dubious luxury of a controlled painkiller. A low dose, at least. I'm afraid of it from every angle, but it was time."

"You don't have to prove anything, darling. It's okay to want to ease the pain."

"I suppose." Another smile. This one more genuine. "I was going to call you back, by the way."

"How come?"

"Probably for the same reason you called."

"Phone sex?"

His laugh, more genuine still. "Because all we did was celebrate my survival. Besides, my nurse just stepped out for a cup of coffee. She'll be back soon. Come on, distract me. Tell me what you've been up to. You were going to look into the original sale of the Monet still life, most probably part of the transaction the dealer Durand-Ruel referred to in his letter to Pissarro. The dates match. January third, 1871."

Erika nodded. "Right. In the still life's provenance, the purchasers are listed as James and Abigail Scott of Greenwich, Connecticut. I reached out to the Greenwich Chamber of Commerce in the hopes of digging up some records on the couple and was given the name of the secretary of the

Greenwich Historical Society, and apparently its maven."

"Every town has one. And?"

"Something more important took precedence."

"Me."

The little syllable, so little boyish, made her breath catch.

"I need you to be tough, sweetheart," he said, noticing.

"I have to be. It's personal now—*more* personal. I have to get to the bottom of all this…" She flung up her hands, the gesture more expressive than the word she was floundering for.

"*We* have to get to the bottom of *all this*!" Harrison protested. "I may be an invalid for now—or for life, who the hell knows—but my brain's still working and—"

"Oh no, I'm sorry. Yes, of course, I got caught up in the feeling of helplessness—with the investigation—with *you*!" She felt the tears come. Damn it, she wanted to stay strong for him.

"No, *I'm* sorry for taking my frustrations out on you. Don't cry. It's killing me to see you cry."

The urge to collapse into her grief was not as powerful as her determination to rally. "Okay, Harrison, okay." She wiped her wet cheeks with the back of her hand.

"Look, I'm worried more about you than I am about my sorry ass," he said. "I haven't told you what happened, have I? Let me try, before the nurse comes back or one of the doctors decides to drop in. Darien and I were attacked in a parking garage by a man obviously out to whack us. He wasn't just some random mugger. He knew what we were about. Threatened us accordingly. I'm worried about how far this threat extends—literally, figuratively. I mean, it's okay for you to call Greenwich, as long as you couch your inquiry in a misleading story, you know? But you can't be making calls and running around town giving away our primary objective. Not outside our inner circle, anyway—Greg, John, Robin Brooks—maybe not Robin Brooks."

Erika could see his passionate outburst had taken its toll on him. He looked drained of color, of energy. She'd assumed the attack on the two men had been pre-meditated. She wished he had not felt compelled to talk about it just now. She wondered how Darien was doing, but would not burden him with another subject to tackle. "I'll be careful," she said. "I won't go anywhere."

"Not like your usual practice," he quipped—grinning; with effort, she could tell.

Playing along with him, she parried, "Exactly." Making sure he understood her sincerity, adding, "Truly, Harrison. I get it."

"I believe you. By the way, Greg is insisting on accompanying me on the plane ride home. I accepted because I knew it would make you feel more secure about the trip."

"Yes, that *is* a relief." Suddenly, she could hear voices, the speakers out of camera range.

"Here are Mr. Singh and my nurse, Wendy," Harrison announced. "My wife, Erika." He turned his cell phone to bring the newcomers into eye contact with her. Polite, but brief, greetings followed; Wendy, a pleasant matron who'd not yet met Erika, becoming the featured party. Circumstances demanded that, without delay, Erika bid Harrison goodbye and yield her place to his caretakers. She did so graciously and, to her credit, with barely a twinge of jealousy.

Chapter Twelve

Because of his messed up ribs, Darien was stabbed in the chest every time he took a breath. They'd drilled a hole in his skull to clear out the intracranial hemorrhage, but they hadn't touched his brain. Still, it felt like a botched transplant.

"The nurse said you were out of it yesterday, but now you're back. Told me to make it a short visit, though."

Darien's vision was still a little off, but he recognized at once the figure hunched over him—the bulbous nose, the drooping eyelids. His breathing quickened—agonizing. "Why was I attacked?" he asked, his voice huskier than he'd ever heard it, as if an alien had taken over his body.

"For your own protection," Chauncey Gladstone said, bringing his face closer to Darien's. "To make certain you'd be seen as a victim. Who could predict you'd crack your head open?" Spoken without a trace of sympathy.

How could he have been so naïve about Gladstone's nature? Or had he been deceiving himself all along in order to overlook his own tainted character? He was afraid to respond. Anything he said might be taken as evasive or confrontational. He was afraid *not* to respond and appear dismissive. If only he knew what expectations were idling behind those curtained eyes. He settled on a faint smile, meant to be interpreted as an acknowledgment of both the man's sound reasoning and humor.

"You're very valuable to us," Gladstone said, lightly patting Darien's cheek, the tips of his fingers coming into contact with the edge of the bandages encasing Darien's head. "But keep in mind, a *talkative* asset becomes a deficit faster than you can say Jack Robinson."

Darien envisioned the padded fingertips drumming directly on his brain. "I understand."

"I know you do." Gladstone straightened up and stepped away from the bed. "I love you, my boy. You'll be up and running before you know it." Heading for the door, his back toward Darien, he raised his hand in a two-fingered victory gesture.

As if Darien's cell phone had eyes and ears, it rang just as his unwanted visitor was out of sight and hearing. The device lay beneath the light cover and sheet, by his left side—his good side, where his ribs were intact. His physical discomfort had been aggravated by the visit, and he was in no state to receive calls. But curiosity is a powerful drive, and his hand, acting independently from what he thought were his intentions, brought the cell phone out from under and held it up in front of his face.

He was unable to move with any degree of ease, which made the act of initiating the connection awkward, but holding the phone loosely in his left hand, he managed to press the "accept" and "speaker" options with his thumb.

He dumped the phone onto his lower torso. "Hello, Harrison. I've been thinking about reaching you—I mean, not for that long; I wasn't myself until today. Not that I'm altogether with it yet, although the nurse did say she was amazed at my communication skills." He hoped the tremor in his voice did not sound as wretched to Harrison as it sounded to himself. *So why am I talking so much?*

"They told me yesterday you weren't up to a phone call, but they didn't say much else," Harrison said. "Last time I saw you, you were unconscious. Fill me in."

"I had an intracranial hemorrhage, which had to be drained," Darien said, unable to put on the brakes. "They tell me they're going to be measuring the pressure inside my head by giving me repeated head scans. I'm on various drugs to prevent an artery spasm and also on painkillers, which aren't doing much good, or so it seems. The ribs that were hit had to be repaired. A fragment punctured my lung, or I should say, came close to. A rib had to be held in place with steel plating; very thin plating, they said." *What's wrong with me?* He sounded like a drunk on a prison break, slurring his words yet racing ahead. *Shut up, goddamn it!* He was out of breath. Took a deep one, and cried out in pain. "What happened to *you?*" he finally thought to ask.

Harrison told him.

The nausea Darien had felt as a result of his head injury returned. "Oh my God," he murmured, the words escaping him.

"What's wrong—you okay?" Harrison asked

"Have you spoken to anyone?" Darien asked, no longer able to mask his underlying fear with a run-away account of his injuries and repairs.

"You mean the authorities?"

"I mean *anyone!* That attack had to have been a *threat!*"

"It was, I heard it. And yes, I was questioned by a police officer."

"Did you tell them anything about the situation—I mean about Norman's death—I mean *any* of it?"

"I didn't, actually. I believe the more people in law enforcement are seen to be on the prowl, the deeper underground the bastards will burrow."

"When are you being discharged?" Darien asked, plowing ahead. "You *are* going back home!" Meant to be a question, came out a demand. "*Aren't* you?" he pressed, unable to control his nerves.

"I'm counting on tomorrow," Harrison said. "Assuming there are no complications—undue infection, swelling, fever. How about you?"

"You've got to back off, Harrison. What I'm afraid of is, you've got the drive to be some kind of hero. For your own good, curb it!"

"Thanks, Darien, but I think I can take care of myself." With a self-derogatory chuckle: "Most of the time."

Another wave of nausea; this one tidal. "Got to go, nurse here," Darien lied. A U-shaped basin had been placed beside his pillow. As he twisted his body to aim for it, his cell phone fell to the floor. The call was over. Had he made his point?

Until he was done heaving and they'd cleaned him up, nothing mattered.

Chapter Thirteen

Bright and early next morning—noontime in London—Erika received a FaceTime call from Harrison. "I didn't wake you, did I?" he asked.

"No," she assured him, rising in bed to a seated position. She was not about to admit she hadn't slept and worry him. "How are you feeling today? No problems, I hope." The debilitating dread of *problems* was what had kept her awake all night.

"Feeling sorry for myself, but no complications. They're discharging me tomorrow."

The dread fell from her like dead weight. "Really? For sure?"

"Unless the flight's canceled, for sure."

"Let me grab a pencil and paper." She dove for the items in the night table drawer. "Go!"

He relayed the details, including contact numbers. A private jet would be transporting him, along with an orthopedic nurse practitioner, all needed and potentially needed medical equipment, and Greg Smith, morale booster. A private ambulance, hired through RCA Ambulance Services, would be meeting their plane at JFK Airport and driving them to the Wheatley residence. Arrival home was estimated at 8:00 p.m.

"I'll meet you at the airport," Erika said, stating what in her mind was a given.

"I asked about that, darling. I'm afraid there won't be room in the ambulance for all of us. Unless we jettison Greg."

"No, of course you can't do that," she said, hiding her disappointment.

"Where will Greg be staying in New York? His usual hangout, or with us? I'm hoping with us."

"With us. I took the liberty of inviting him. I knew you'd approve. I made sure he understands I won't be accepting his help, only his scintillating company. Says he's due for one of his shuttle trips to Art Loss Register's New York City headquarters, anyway. He was in town just a few days ago, so I don't believe him. Damn nice of him to want to come along for the ride. By the way, I gave my medical team carte blanche on my credit card to purchase items that'll make my—our—life easier to navigate until I'm back on my feet—hah! You should be receiving a busload from Amazon sometime tomorrow."

"Okay. I can't wait to see you, Harrison." Her heartbeat accelerated at the sound of it.

"Same here."

"It seems like years."

"*Hasn't* it been?" he asked, a poignant undertone to the jest.

* * *

Despite her lack of sleep, Erika was hyped up, even before her morning jolt of caffeine. After spending some precious one-on-one time with Lucas—breakfast, reading aloud, building Lego towers specifically for Jake to knock down—she delivered Lucas to the loving hands of Kate and Grace and sequestered herself in her study to work on her art and economics piece until she deemed it a reasonable hour to contact Libby Newcomb, secretary of the Greenwich Historical Society.

The call was made at 10:00 and went straight to Voicemail. Ten minutes later, she got a call back. "Whew, sorry, I was breastfeeding Maggie," Libby opened familiarly, like they were old friends. "How's it going?"

Erika was prepared to relate her concocted story to an elderly woman with rimless spectacles, not someone she'd been hanging out with since First Grade. "Going okay. With you, too, I hope. How old is Maggie?"

"Six months. A handful, but we love her to death. Your message was intriguing. You say you write for an art magazine; interested in doing an article on the Cos Cob art colony. This was a group of artists who gathered in that section of Greenwich roughly from 1890 to 1920. Impressionists, mainly, like Ernest Lawson, John Henry Twachtman, Childe Hassam, Theodore Robinson. The dawn of American Impressionism began right here, in Greenwich, you know—but of course, you know."

"It looks like you're more informed than I am."

"My wheelhouse is American History," Libby offered by way of an excuse—or apology. "I fell in love with this town when we moved here eight years ago and have been steeping myself in its history ever since. I'd just earned my doctorate and had landed a job teaching at Franklin College in New Haven, Yale's residence college, established less than ten years ago. Right now, I'm on a leave of absence. Loving it, but missing the hustle of academia. Ready for anything that approximates it. What can I do for you?"

"Well, I'm especially interested in the times leading up to the art colony's creation. You know, the 1860s, 1870s."

"Ah, yes indeed," Libby said, clearly warming up to the assignment. "After the Civil War, there was a longing for the days of innocence, and Greenwich offered a pastoral setting and a lovely coastline for artists wanting to paint en plein air. At the same time, to answer the call of the city's bright lights or to acquire instruction in the arts, Greenwich was a mere hop, skip, and a jump from metropolises like New York City." She chortled. "Did I mention the rent was cheap?"

"Funny," Erika said with a collaborative chuckle. She was walking a fine line. She needed to make sure Libby understood what she was after without giving herself away. "So, I'm wondering if your historical society has preserved any written accounts covering the decades leading up to the establishment of the Cos Cob art colony. I'm looking for stories of human interest. Personal goings-on."

"Gossip."

"That's it. Untapped anecdotal accounts of everyday life are often more compelling than those found in history books."

"Right on," Libby agreed. "We've got just the vehicle for you. I should tell you that when I moved to Greenwich, I headed straight for the historical society. To my delight, I found a treasure trove of artifacts from the town's history, dating back to the 1680s. Attractively displayed, but not organized up to my standards. I took it upon myself to record and date all archived material. Among the gems, a series of bound journals dating from 1862 through 1885, started by Marylou Jackson and continued by her daughter, Tess. It begins with an account of Marylou's son's induction into the Tenth Connecticut Infantry Regiment and ends with Mrs. Murphy's cat urinating in Tess's shoe. Believe me, there is much you will find of interest within these pages."

Erika was elated by the mere possibility of turning up a tidbit about James and Abigail Scott. "This is great! Does the organization have regular hours, or do you suggest I make an appointment?"

"No need for a visit," Libby said. "That is, unless you want to come say hello. I've had all twenty-three years' worth digitalized into five PDFs. That is, I outsourced the job to a professional scanning bureau. Say the word, I'll email you the docs."

Erika said the word. She was emailed the five PDF installments within minutes, while she and Libby were still on the phone. "How can I repay you?" she asked, upon verifying the receipt of the documents.

"That's kind of you," Libby said, "but no need to thank me. Your interest is thanks enough. But if you feel so inclined, you can go to the society's website, greenwichconn dash history dot org and make a donation. Or you can buy a mug."

After the call, she did both.

Chapter Fourteen

ccording to Heathrow Airport's posting, Harrison's flight had left moments ago, right on schedule; the 8:00 p.m. estimated time of arrival home, still in effect. Erika wondered what she was going to do for the next ten hours—more, if there was a hitch in transit. Her nervous excitement seemed to be way more than it should be. Then again, maybe it wasn't. Who cared? The answer would have no effect on her state of mind.

She might have spent a good chunk of wait time poring over Marylou and Tess's commentary on Greenwich life, but yesterday, after receiving Libby's emailed attachments, she suddenly caught Harrison in her mind's eye, propped up in bed and looking as dejected as a scorned lover. She exited the site. Examining the documents must be a fresh experience for both of them. At no point during their criminal investigation would Harrison be allowed to feel side-lined.

She thought she might take a stab at wrapping up her article on the state of the art market, but found herself skittering in her wayward imagination to the interior of the plane, where Harrison was strapped to a gurney, the strap too tight, tugging with every flop caused by the violent turbulence, nobody paying attention to him, and he too embarrassed to call out for assistance.

She shut down her computer and fled to the living room, where Lucas and Jake rescued her from her dreaded premonitions, drawing her into the immediacy of their world. With Lego blocks—Lucas was obsessed with Legos—she and Lucas built castles and crazy towers and laughed as Jake knocked them down. Seemingly encouraged by the reaction he got with every destructive success, Jake became more buoyantly aggressive with each targeted strike.

A long walk in the park took the Tigger out of both Jake and Lucas and by the time they got back home, each was ready for a snack and a nap. Erika read Lucas to sleep with a few poems from A. A. Milne's *When We Were Very Young*, quitting in the middle of "The Four Friends," around about when "George found a pen, but I think it was the wrong one," and she was sure, by the rhythm of his breathing, that he had slipped into his own magical realm. Jake, snuggled at Lucas's feet, had gone out like a light after the first word.

Mid-afternoon the anticipated barrage of cartons arrived from Amazon. Seeing to it occupied another block of time Erika might otherwise have spent on an untargeted expenditure of nervous energy. There were twelve cartons in all. They contained, among other things: an elevated toilet seat, a commode, bathroom bars, a transfer board, a wedge-shaped pillow to keep the legs raised in bed, two plastic male urinals. Laying hands on these objects solidified Harrison's imminent return and the reality of his injuries, producing a tumult of emotions.

In their en suite bathroom, as she was wiggling the new toilet seat to test its stability, she burst out crying. *Let it all out now*, she ordered herself. *You cannot do this when he's back*!

* * *

The call came at 7:05 p.m. "Hi, luv, we're just about on our way." It was not Harrison's voice.

"Hello, Greg. Where's Harrison?"

"He's run off to the duty-free shops."

"Greg!"

"Ease up. He's being loaded into the ambulance. It takes some doing."

"Sorry, I'm a bit on edge."

"I never would have guessed."

"How did you two do on the flight?" she asked.

He chuckled at his inclusion in her concern. "We did great. Seriously,

Harrison is one hell of a trooper."

"Yes," she said. The thought of Harrison grinning and bearing it brought her to the edge of tears. *No!* she warned herself, although she had no idea what punishment she'd dole out if the tears should roll.

"Say, did the Amazon order arrive?" Greg asked.

"It did, yes."

"Good. We'll be adding to the gear. Wheelchair, the star of the show. She's a real beauty. You may be jealous."

"I'll try to control myself," she said, warming up to his humor. "I'm glad you came along, Greg. I know you had to be great company for him."

"Have to admit, I kept him in stitches." He groaned at the pun. "Must run now. Our boy's strapped in and ready to roll."

"Safe trip," Erika said. "Give Harrison—"

"Don't say a kiss."

"—my love," she finished. But Greg had already punched out.

* * *

It was raining when Erika's vigil was over, the ambulance pulling up curbside. The rain had started ten minutes earlier, so she was prepared. Even before the engine was shut off, she was poised by the ambulance's rear exit with her oversized doorman's umbrella held on high.

"Jesus, you could have been killed!" Greg shouted, after emerging from the passenger side and spotting her as he came around to the rear. "What if the driver had decided to back up?"

"Well, he didn't, did he?" Erika replied as Greg took the umbrella from her.

"Get under here," he said, pulling her closer in. "Good to see you." He gave her a peck on the cheek.

"You, too." What was happening behind those doors? "What's happening?" she asked.

"The orthopedic nurse—Raymond—is wrapping Harrison's legs in plastic to protect the cast and knee braces from the rain. First, he had to remove his clownishly baggy sweatpants and slide him into a stylish pair of basketball shorts. Didn't think to bring along the easy-to-wear one-piece waterproof cast coverings, which I hear were part of your Amazon purchase. By the way, don't be alarmed at the big reveal. The gizmo on the left leg looks like something Rube Goldberg might have dreamt up."

"I want to see him already. Can I get in?"

A door up front slammed shut.

"Here comes the driver," Greg said. "Tony," he announced as a big guy in a hooded Windbreaker appeared. "This is Erika, Harrison's wife."

"Hello, Erika," Tony said, waving off Greg's gestured invitation to take cover under the umbrella. "Step out of the way, please." When they did so, he pulled open the double doors.

For a split second, all Erika took in was his face. "Harrison," she said, almost in a whisper, as her focus widened, and there he was, sitting in a wheelchair, legs stuck out in front of him like a wooden doll's, propped up by the chair's elevated leg rests. She could not properly make out the equipment he'd been fitted with because the plastic wrapping was nearly opaque. Behind the wheelchair and grasping its side handles, a heavily bearded man of indeterminate age waited for Tony to complete the ramp's manual release.

Harrison spread his hands and gave a little shrug. "Take it or leave it," he said, referring to himself. Not quite a joke.

The words stung. "I'll take it," she said, the answer awkward and inadequate.

Greg held the umbrella over Harrison as he was wheeled down the ramp, at the same time introducing Raymond, the specialty nurse to Erika. Erika waited until they were on level ground, then bent to embrace Harrison. "At last," she said. Harrison wrapped his arms around her, pressing his face more forcefully against her neck. She felt his shoulders heave, and on her neck, a dampness she told herself was rain. He said nothing, and when they let each other go, she could no longer deceive herself. She wiped away his tears with her fingertips, and, despite her resolve, failed to keep her own in check.

"Okay, let's get our boy inside," Raymond gently admonished, taking matters in hand by pushing the wheelchair forward, with Greg walking briskly alongside, umbrella held aloft.

Erika ran ahead to open the front door, but when she was halfway there, it seemed to open of its own accord until Grace came out from behind it.

"He's back!" Erika reported, as if his approach weren't proof enough.

"Oh dear, oh dear!"

"We've got to show him we're tough, Grace."

"I'm perfectly capable. I need a second, is all."

Living up to her word, after a pat on Harrison's shoulder and an almost authentically chipper "Welcome home, Mr. Harry!" Grace ushered Harrison and his attendant into the lobby, scooting aside with the agility of a toreador in order to avoid being struck by Harrison's rigid limbs. Erika and Greg followed them in.

"Do we need to take our shoes off?" Raymond directed to the Botero nude, as if expecting the statue to answer.

"It will suffice to wipe your shoes on the mat," Grace answered. "Thank you."

Tony, the driver, bringing up the rear, was last to enter the lobby. He was carrying Harrison's and Greg's small suitcases, one in each hand, Raymond's backpack slung on his shoulder, and under his arm, a pair of crutches. "Be right back with the extras," he said, releasing his cargo to the floor. A minute later, he returned with two stuffed-to-the-brim totes emblazoned with Guy's Hospital imprint.

"Swag bags," Greg said.

Harrison grimaced. "Easy, Raymond!" he cautioned the nurse, who had already begun peeling off the plastic layers encasing his legs. He reached for Erika's hand.

"Done in a minute," Raymond said.

"Lucas sleeping?" Harrison asked Erika. "Or hiding from me."

"Sleeping," she said, squeezing his hand. "Come on—*hiding*?"

"Joking. Well, mostly. I hate this; what I'm about to put you through." He waved at his legs, now fully unwrapped. "Ta-da! Am I beautiful or what?" His right knee was fitted with a long rigid brace that went from mid-thigh to mid-calf. The left knee was stabilized by a brace that was shorter, ending where the cast holding together his shattered and crushed lower leg began. The left knee brace, Harrison explained, had been jerry-rigged "by the versatile Mr. Singh," with two side-bars that were connected to a metal ring at the head of the cast. This would keep the leg rigid until the patella was "released from bondage."

"I'm going to leave now," the driver announced. "We all set?"

"Thanks for putting up with me, Tony," Harrison said. Unwilling to let go of Erika's hand, he raised his left for a handshake. "Couldn't have done it without you."

Greg pulled out his wallet. "Here, let me—"

Tony put up his hand. "All taken care of, sir." He headed for the door, Grace formally escorting him to it.

A high-pitched whine sounded from another room.

"Jake hears your voice," Erika informed Harrison. "I put him in your study. I was afraid he'd pounce."

"He'd be fine, but we can wait a while until we're all settled in."

Raymond brought the Wheatleys to attention with a token cough. "Since I'll be flying back early tomorrow," he said, glancing from one to the other, "I'd like to talk to you sooner rather than later about what to expect during the healing period, plus a few pointers on self-care."

"Please give us a half hour," Harrison said. "I'd like some alone time with my wife."

"As long as you get those legs raised. Is there a reclining chair on this floor?"

"We're going up to our bedroom. There's one in our room."

"You're thinking of going *upstairs?*

"No, we're not thinking about it. We're *doing* it!"

Overriding Raymond's protests, plans were made for Grace to show the guests to their rooms during the couple's half-hour respite. Raymond, to Harrison's study, where the sofa bed had already been made up and from which Jake would soon be freed; Greg, to the spare room next to Erika's study, also ready for occupancy. Although they'd had dinner on the plane, Grace insisted on being permitted to whip up a light meal for them; she'd be insulted if they turned her down. They were to meet in the kitchen after they'd freshened up.

"I've been betting on there being room for me in the elevator," Harrison confided to Erika, still holding onto her hand. "I don't want to think about an alternative."

"Whatever has to be, we'll make it work." She slipped out of his grip and positioned herself at the back of the wheelchair. "Here we go."

She swirled the wheelchair around so it would be facing out and pressed the elevator button.

"Hey, you're a natural at this," Harrison said, again the humor edging on pathos.

The elevator lived up to his expectations, but barely. "Good thing I didn't eat that second Oreo this afternoon," Erika said, squeezing in beside him in the oak-paneled compartment, quite serviceable under normal conditions.

Once Erika had managed to maneuver the wheelchair out of the elevator, down the hall, and into the haven of their bedroom, Harrison's entire being seemed to breathe a sigh of relief. She parked him alongside the bed and hugged him from behind, wrapping her arms around his chest and kissing the top of his head, his nose, his mouth; he, reaching up to cup her face in his hands. "Thank goodness," he said, and she didn't ask what he was thankful for because it could have been anything and everything, and why not leave it at that?

Except after coming around to face him and seeing the look on his face and realizing that the gratitude had been meant for *her*, she suddenly felt undeserving, incapable of living up to the task. "I wasn't able to mount the bathroom grab bars," she confessed. "Actually, I *could* have mounted them, I mean, they came with the screws and all, but I didn't know *where* to mount them."

"It's okay. Raymond will help us out."

"And now that I'm looking at the height of the wheelchair seat compared to the height of our mattress, I'm thinking, how can the transfer board possibly work?" She glanced over at the board, propped up against the recliner chair, a well-worn relic from his beloved grandmother. "The mattress is so much higher than the seat!"

"I won't need the board. I'll be able to hoist myself onto the bed."

"If you say so," she said, hardly convinced.

"We'll be okay," Harrison said, reassuring them both. "Kiss me again."

She complied. From the front this time and more deeply.

"Careful, my love," he cautioned. "I won't be able to control myself, and we can't have sex."

"Are you doubting my creativity?" she asked in jokey confusion.

"No, I'm fearing it. Raymond tells me we should hold off for at least a month. Seems at the time of ejaculation, all the body systems change, including at the site of the fracture. Makes it take longer to heal."

"You're saying ecstasy prolongs the healing process? Okay, then." She wished she could refer to an article in the AMA journal to dispute the claim, but it did sound valid—valid and unreasonable.

He pressed down on his groin. "Talk about something else."

"What can I do for you? You want me to bring up something to eat?"

"Later, maybe."

"Want to take off that sweatshirt? Can I get you something lighter?"

"Before we go to bed—Erika?"

"What is it, sweetheart?"

"I have to pee."

Her confidence went up a notch. This she could do. "I'll just grab one of the portable urinals."

"I'm sorry."

"For having a bladder? Right back. They're in the bathroom." On her return, she said, "We'll keep it bedside. I'll set up a tray table." She handed him the plastic receptacle.

A precedent was about to be set. Should she turn her back? Would the very notion of propriety embarrass him by defining the act as improper? They knew each other's bodies like the backs of their hands. She'd seen him pee. Shouldn't the new staging of the act be taken in stride? Otherwise, wouldn't awkwardness be bound to creep into the management of any number of bodily functions requiring help of an intimate nature? But wait. What was she thinking? Hadn't Harrison gotten a head-on view of an eight-pound individual bullying its way out of her vagina stretched fifteen times its normal size? What could be more intimately jarring and yet tolerable? More than tolerable—celebrated!

"Need any help?" she asked, planting herself on the edge of the bed and watching him try to yank down his basketball shorts while lining up his penis with the opening of a urinal about two-and-a-half inches in diameter. Reminded her of a plane refueling mid-air.

"Sure," he said. "Hold down the shorts. Great. Thanks. Aah."

The precedent had been set.

Erika was emptying the urinal into the toilet when she heard a knock on the door to the room. No response from Harrison, but she heard the door open anyway. She flushed the toilet and laid the urinal on the tank lid. As she exited the bathroom, Harrison was saying, "What's up, Raymond? You were giving us thirty minutes. What's it been, ten?"

Grace, standing at the door, responded. "He demanded I show him to your room, Mr. Harry. I could only assume it was for your own good." With something approximating a curtsy, she tip-toed off.

"I'm sorry, Harrison," Raymond began, sounding nowhere near apologetic, "I could not in good conscience sit idly by and watch you reverse the excellent progress you've made since your surgery."

"I take it I'm about to be read the riot act."

"Call it what you like. I wish I could stay with you for a week and set you on the right track, but even if I didn't have other commitments, the UK doesn't have reciprocity with the medical governing boards in the USA, so I'm unable to practice here without acquiring the proper credentials. Officially, I'm a friend on an overnight visit.

"Look at you. Your legs are supposed to be elevated as much as possible. In anticipation of undue swelling after surgery, your left limb was stabilized by a posterior tibia splint rather than a cast. Your swelling actually manifested at the low end of the spectrum, and the surgeon was encouraged to put the leg in a cast—the more restrictive mode of stabilization—before you left for home. You must not push your luck. You need full-time professional help for at least the first week."

"I want to be as independent as possible," Harrison declared. "Now that the pain has abated some and I'm back with my wife and on familiar turf, I feel confident I can handle it—*we* can handle it."

"If you could possibly install the toilet bars, or tell me where to place them," Erika inserted, "that would be a big help. Maybe give us some instruction how to use to transfer board..."

Raymond shifted his weight to one hip and set his arms akimbo. Ready to rumble. "I'll install the toilet bars, but Harrison is not ready to use the toilet, not until he can bear some weight on his right leg without causing much pain. Maybe in a few days, maybe more. That is, when he can safely get from here to there with crutches."

The commode, standing boldly at the bedside, instantly became the elephant in the room. Harrison glared at it, as if about to challenge it to hand-to-hand combat.

"As for the transfer board, "Raymond went on, "forget it. I'm guessing there's about an eight-inch difference in height between the wheelchair seat and the mattress. You'll need a ski tow. Furthermore, without being able to bear some weight on the right leg, even if the heights matched, you'd have difficulty. You need a trained healthcare worker to transfer you properly without your injuring yourself further."

"I can hoist myself onto the bed right now," Harrison said, throwing down the gauntlet.

Raymond smiled. "No chance in hell, but challenge accepted. Providing I can stand by you, in case you need my assistance."

"Granted." Harrison took stock of his immediate surroundings. "Would you be good enough to move the night table out of the way, so the back of the wheelchair can be more or less flush with the wall? The commode, too, please." He groped around, looking for something on the left armrest. "Where can I find the button to flip back this armrest?"

When his prerequisites had been met, he took a moment to reassess the situation, then, with jaw set in determination—*I cannot fail at this!*—he latched onto the top of the headboard with his left hand, the right armrest with his right hand, and pushed down hard, lifting himself up off the chair seat, the feat accomplished through his upper body and arm muscles working at newfound capacity. Since he could not rely on his thigh muscles to keep his battered legs aloft, he asked Erika to support them as he swung himself onto the bed. "Was that too much of a strain?" he asked her afterward. "We'll hire someone to help if it was."

"No strain at all," Erika said, grateful to have been of service. She helped him adjust to a more comfortable position, then tucked the large wedge cushion, which had been sitting on the other side of the bed, under his legs. "There you go. Elevated. Need a drink of water?"

"That would be great. Can we spice it up with a couple of Tylenol?" Addressing Raymond, who hadn't moved an inch throughout the entire stunt, Harrison asked, "How'd I do?"

It would take a moment for Raymond to find the words.

Chapter Fifteen

"It's very quiet around here," Harrison said. "Where is everybody?" He was lying on top of the covers, three firm bed pillows tucked beneath his head and shoulders, one large wedge-shaped support pillow keeping his legs, clad in the oversized sweatpants, elevated above the level of his heart. Jake was lying beside him, his head resting on Harrison's belly. Last night, when Jake had been released from confinement and allowed to scamper upstairs to greet his beloved master, returned from parts unknown, he'd been careful not to pounce. Instead, he'd delicately sniffed at Harrison's legs, then nudged his hand with his nose—in a reassuring manner, Harrison had decided. Earlier this morning, when Kate had brought Lucas into the bedroom to say hi to his dad, the boy knew not to touch Harrison's legs only because he'd been told not to. Jake just *knew*.

"Kate and Lucas are out for a walk," Erika informed him. "Greg went along with them. Greg's very restless, you know, itching to do something, either for you personally, or to progress the investigation. Raymond is getting ready to leave. Grace is cooking our favorite dish, beef bourguignon."

"If Raymond smells it, he'll miss his flight. Thoughtful of Kate to keep to herself last night."

"She had a date with her boyfriend. You going to live up to your promise to rest today, or are you going to attempt another Cirque de Soleil stunt?"

"Rest." He plucked a strip of bacon from the breakfast tray Erika had prepared for him and studied it as if it were telling him something. "I don't want to languish," he said, returning the bacon strip to the tray. "I'm now officially on a three-month leave of absence, and my T.A. will be taking over my summer courses and launching the fall semester. I'll be guiding him from behind the scenes, but still, I feel *out* of it. Am I putting you in that spot as well? I can't allow that to happen."

"Absolutely not," Erika stated firmly, helping herself to the rejected bacon strip. "You do know I work mostly from home, and when I've got to show up at the office, Kate and Grace are here to help out. In fact, in a pinch, Kate can fill in as my surrogate at the Mommy-and-Me sessions I've enrolled Lucas and me in. With either one of us, he'll have a blast." She chomped down on the bacon to underline her point.

"That's a comfort." He paused. "You won't leave me out of the loop, will you? I've got to stay active in the criminal investigation. I know I've got to lay low and all that, but…you understand?"

"What do you think? I held off unveiling the Greenwich journals so we could look through them together. You know what discipline that took?"

He laughed. "I can only imagine. Thank you. Let's begin—now. While the Tylenol's still working. In general, I'm experiencing a lot less pain, by the way. Tomorrow, I'm going to test out my right leg, see how well it tolerates a little weight-bearing."

"That's fine, as long as you don't push yourself."

"That's *exactly* what I'm going to do."

She smiled. "I asked for that, didn't I?" She reached for the breakfast tray. "You done?" He indicated he was, and she moved it to the recliner's side table. Grabbing her cell phone from her night table, she said, "I'm going to forward you the email from Libby Newcomb with the five PDFs attached. We can decide what sections each of us will review. Sound like a plan?"

Her question was answered by the ringtone of his cell phone lying beside him. "It's John Mitchell," he said, glancing at the caller ID. "Does he"—gesturing toward his legs— "*know*?"

"He doesn't."

John was looking for a heads-up on how their investigation was going. He was predictably shocked when it was granted him. As a member of the Wheatleys' inner circle, he was given an un-redacted account of Harrison's experience. He was furious, both for the fact that such an event had occurred and, less so, for his not having been notified about it. Ready or not, he was on his way over. "You don't expect me to lie around waiting for you to ask for my help, do you? I've got to do *something!*"

"That makes two of you," Harrison said. "Greg Smith accompanied me back to the states and he's equally anxious to move ahead on this case. He's staying with us a couple of days before he heads back to London. He's out for a walk with Lucas and his nanny, Kate. They should be back soon. Are you up for a brainstorming session?"

"Are you serious? I'm out the door!"

"I'll round up a couple of extra chairs," Erika said, when the call had ended. It was understood the Greenwich research was to be put on hold. She picked up the breakfast tray and headed for the door.

Jake raised his head from its warm resting place, assessed the pros and cons of following Erika or staying put, and chose the path of least resistance.

* * *

Greg was the first to come up with a plan of action after the group had settled in, and Grace had come and gone, leaving behind a tea cart of beverages and assorted pastries and rolls. "I'll be dropping by the offices of Galaxy Fine Arts," he said. "Since they were the insurers of all eight of Morris Keller's Monet paintings before they were spirited away, they're bound to have some useful data on file, including photographs." Greg was ensconced in the recliner chair; Erika and John, spaced out beside him in lightweight chairs swiped from other rooms. Harrison faced them, like a king graced by his attendants, the royal canine, sleeping by his side. Greg checked the room for approval, his gaze holding on Harrison.

"I don't want to thwart you," Harrison said, suddenly remembering to wiggle his toes, as Raymond had said he should do every now and then, "but you, as well as John and Erika, have to steer clear of people associated directly with the case. No doubt about it, we're dealing with a network of criminals spanning at least two continents. That's the first reason. The second is that I'm already on their enemy list and, by default, so might anyone I associate with. Galaxy Fine Arts is too close to the epicenter of the storm, so I have to discourage you from questioning them."

"It was a great idea," Erika jumped in, seeing Greg's look of disappointment, "but after spending some time in Morris Keller's company with John, and afterwards having a private word with Keller's ex-wife, Lois, I'm pretty sure calling Galaxy would be a wasted effort."

"Keller shat himself," John bluntly summed up. "On himself and on behalf of the wives. Being that he terminated the insurance coverage for those paintings—judging by his demeanor, he was coerced into doing so—there's no doubt the insurance agents would have been forewarned to keep their mouths shut." He plucked a cherry tart from the tea cart. "You would have exposed yourself for no good reason, Greg, and we want to have you around for a while; you've got a cool accent."

Greg responded with a confirmatory nod. "Got it. The Galaxy's a no-go. So, let's discuss where we're allowed to tread and what's taboo. I was also going to approach Ben Laszlo, but I suppose that's too risky as well."

"Believe me," Erika replied, "after my experience with Laszlo, I'm sure he's not about to share any useful information. Min Cho told me he swore her to secrecy regarding the urgent phone call from Norman Blethmore. She was terrified Laszlo would fire her if he found out she'd mentioned it to me. For all we know, Laszlo's in on the criminal goings-on."

"Point taken," Greg said. To review. We're to stay away from any situation that'll arouse the suspicion Harrison's still on the hunt."

"Exactly," Harrison concurred. "This is to protect your necks as well as mine. In some cases, the danger is two-fold. As in contacting Ivan's wife, Robin, which would put her in danger as well as us. We don't want these bastards accusing our allies of consorting with the enemy."

"So where does that leave us?" John asked. "Looks like everyone but Jake, here"—Jake raised his head— "is off limits." He took a bite of the cherry tart.

"Offhand, I can think of two resources I can safely pursue," Greg said. "One is easily accessible—for me, that is—the catalogue raisonné of Monet's art works, including those works still under consideration. Actually, there are several such catalogues, but by far the most authoritative and diligently revised and edited is the one compiled by the Wildenstein Plattner Institute."

"Catalogue *what-was-that?*" John asked.

"Raisonné—translation, 'received.' It's an annotated listing of an artist's known works or those in a particular medium. For many collectors, it's the ultimate stamp of approval authenticating a work of art, although its compilers do not guarantee absolute certainty of authorship. Works are submitted to a committee of experts, and acceptance into the holy ranks is predicated on its vote. I would like to look for a Monet painting entitled *Wedgewood Vase with Flowers* associated with the data found in the Laszlo June twenty-first auction catalogue, and see if it comes up. If it does, there's a chance I'll find details about the painting and its history that are new to us. I'm going to assume there are no moles from the underworld planted on the Wildenstein selection committee. If you're not willing to agree to this, we might as well pack it in."

"I'm for it," John said. Can't let paranoia hog-tie us. What do you say, Harrison? You're at the top of the hit list. You ought to decide."

"Of course, I'm for it. Erika?"

"Same. Any other proposals, Greg?"

"Yes, and this one's just as unlikely to put me in direct contact with one of the potential suspects. As you may know, the art dealer Paul Durand-Ruel, kept detailed accounts of his sales over the years. His many letters, papers, records are archived at various sites—the National Gallery of Art, the Frick Collection, University of San Francisco, Yale, et cetera. I'm going to see if I can find the one stock ledger among Durand-Ruel's many, that records the sale of Monet's *Wedgewood Vase with Flowers...*remind me, folks, to whom and on what date?"

"James and Abigail Scott, January third, 1871," Harrison recited. He smiled. "Thanks to Erika, a date etched in memory. Isn't anyone going to have something to drink? Greg, have a roll or something."

The urging seemed to stimulate the guests' hunger. Greg decided on a buttered roll. John indulged in a second tart—lemon this time around—and each poured himself a cup of coffee. Plates and cups were parked on the end-of-bed bench, designated as a table for the occasion.

"This one's even better," John remarked after sampling the tart. "So, what assignment have you people chosen for me?"

"You think you can find out what's happening stateside with the Ivan Brooks case?" Greg asked.

"I've already had another go at the locals in charge. Morris Keller, for one, was ruled out. His alibi is airtight. He was home with his wife at the time of the murder. There's a record of his call from their landline to one of his business associates—verified by the business associate. Sheldon Adams, one of Laszlo's senior account executives, is still the only person of interest. I know what you're thinking. You're thinking maybe we should tell these homeboys what we know about a couple of crimes abroad, the crimes we're ninety-nine percent sure are connected with the one they're wanting to pin on Sheldon. You're thinking maybe an international connection would take the heat off Sheldon. My opinion? For security's sake, I say we lay low about sharing information at this time. All they've got on the guy is that he had a noisy dispute with Ivan and that he may be resentful Ivan leap-frogged over him to gain brokership of that Monet still life you've been talking about."

"Good point, John," Greg praised. "The less we share, the better. For instance, if I leak the fact that Laszlo's in-force contract with Morris Keller states that the named broker will be in on not one but *eight* Monet sales, Sheldon Adams's motivation to eliminate Ivan would skyrocket, and so would pressure to indict him."

John did a visible double-take on that bit of information, but let it lie. "Whatever. Right now, Sheldon's not been charged, so I'll keep out of it. Want me to poke around the London police or the National Crime Agency—NCA—for any reason?"

"It would be great to know what the authorities found on Norman Blethmore's computer," Erika said. "He may have recorded details about the archived Pissarro letters before they went missing. How valuable would a discovery like *that* be in solving these interrelated crimes?"

"Priceless," Harrison offered.

"And risky," Erika qualified. "For one of us to openly seek information on the most vital issue in our investigation, and probably the most vigorously guarded by the criminals? I don't think so."

"I'll see what I can do," John said. "I can be stealthy if push comes to shove." He polished off the lemon tart. "What else do you have in mind for me?"

Erika hesitated. "Well…"

"What's up, luv?" Greg encouraged.

Erika addressed herself to Harrison. "Are you up to talking about what happened the morning you spent with Darien? I don't want to spring it on you."

"The lass said, as she sprang it on him," Greg appended—his way of lightening the mood.

"We've got to talk about that morning," Harrison said. "It's the only way we'll know what steps to take in cornering the guy who attacked Darien and me—more so, the party or parties who ordered him to. Fire away—*all* of you. I'm dealing with physical discomfort and rage, not PTSD." He fumbled with the pillows supporting his head, trying to find a more comfortable position.

Erika jumped up to help him. "Better?" He nodded. She sat down at the edge of the bed, facing him, her back to the others. "We haven't really talked about it, not in detail. I'm assuming the biker knew which reserved parking space was Darien's. I thought maybe he'd been stalking Darien, waiting for an opportune moment to strike, but I realized that couldn't have been the case."

"Why not?" Greg piped up.

Erika directed her answer to Harrison. "Because you were not collateral damage, you were a target—maybe *the* target—of the attack. From what you said, the biker issued a threat to you specifically. He must have gotten wind that you were meeting Darien that morning and were planning to drive somewhere at a certain hour. He was ready for you—both of you."

"I believe that's a given," Harrison said.

"Think, Harrison," Erika went on. "Do you remember entering the garage and approaching Darien's parking spot?"

"Vividly."

"What did you see? Exactly."

"I saw the path in front of me as we walked down to the level where Darien's car was parked. When we arrived, Darien unlocked the car door remotely and I saw the rear lights of his blue sedan blink. As we got nearer, I saw a figure clad in leather head to toe crouched by the back wheel of his motorcycle. Checking something out, I figured."

"Did he turn around at your approach?"

"No."

"What happened next?"

"Darien made a friendly comment about the guy's motorcycle—what a 'nice hog' it was—and the guy raised his arm in acknowledgment."

"Did he turn around to take a look at you *then*?"

Harrison shook his head. "He got something from his gear bag, started to say something, snapped down his visor, and only then did he turn around."

"Turned around swinging, did he?" Erika pressed.

"Yes. Clearly, he knew whom he was about to whack."

"The *two* people he was about to whack."

"Yes. He had to know beforehand who was standing by him. Might have been an elderly aunt tagging along. Had to be *damn* sure."

"Damn sure at precisely that *moment*," Erika reminded him. "How long do you think he was poised in that crouched position, pretending to check out the rear of his bike?"

Harrison stared solemnly at Erika. "Is it possible?" he asked, directing the question more at himself than at her. In contemplating ways of smoking out the criminals, had he unconsciously steered clear of the incident for fear of reliving it? The idea appalled him. "Of course," he said ruefully. "There's no other explanation. Someone alerted the biker of our imminent arrival."

"Who's the most likely informer?" Greg asked.

"I've got someone in mind," John offered. "You won't like it."

"Darien himself?" Erika asked cautiously, turning toward John. She knew Harrison well enough to know he was quietly berating himself for what he'd consider an oversight.

"Yes," John replied. "You know I always go for the simplest answer."

"We were supposed to be heading out to Meagan Dunne's place in

Wembley," Harrison reflected, addressing John, but again, more to himself. "A twenty-minute drive, Darien said." He felt a sudden throb in his left leg, spiking the plateau of pain he'd gotten used to. He concealed it with a cough.

"Who's Meagan Dunne?" John asked.

"What—oh, Darien's colleague at the Courtauld Institute. Darien implied she knew all about the goings on at the institute and that she'd be a good person to interview. I'd already spoken to her briefly, and she'd been very forthcoming—oh."

"What is it?" Erika asked.

"I remember, right before we stepped into the garage, Darien texted Meagan to tell her we were about to leave town and when to expect us."

"You look over his shoulder?" Greg asked wryly.

"No, I didn't. It's hard to believe he may have been giving our attacker a heads-up."

"Not so hard for a cynic," John countered. "My take is he alerted the fellow. In order to come across as looking like victim number two, he expected to receive a glancing blow. Didn't expect such a convincing one. I heard he suffered a severe head injury."

Harrison winced. "That's because after he was struck on his side, he had the bad luck to fall and hit his head on the cement floor."

"What I wouldn't give to see Darien's cell phone," Erika said. "Or the chance to call Meagan Dunne to check if she got the alleged text from Darien."

"No can do," John forbade. "You call Meagan, and Harrison's pretense at having quit the investigation is dead in the water. If you like, though, I can do a background check on Darien. I'll be discreet. Very slim chance it'll get back to him."

"Do it!" Harrison stated emphatically, confidence returning. The sharpness of his delivery woke Jake up, and he looked at Harrison questioningly: *Was that a rebuke?* "It's okay, boy," Harrison answered. Returning his attention to John, he confessed, "I'm hoping you'll find something shady in Darien's background. It would be our first hook in the narrative."

"I second the motion," Greg said. He gulped down the remainder of his coffee. "What do you say we call it a day?" He rose to his feet, making the call for the rest of them. "Harrison will never admit he's uncomfortable as hell, so we've got to assume he is."

"Sure thing," John said, popping up as well.

Harrison smiled. "Is it that obvious?"

"Yes," Erika said. "Thanks for taking the initiative, Greg."

John approached the bed. "Call you tomorrow or sooner." He hugged Erika and clasped Harrison's hand. To Harrison: "No need to walk me to the door, buddy." To Erika: "Stay right where you are!" To the group at large: "Let's stay coordinated."

Greg gave a stab at being of service—one of many: "What can I do for you, Harrison? Can I help move you to the recliner? How about I help get you downstairs?"

Harrison responded with his stock refusal. He did not need Greg's immediate help, but he'd let him know when he did.

"How are you holding up?" Erika asked, bending over him after the door had closed behind their guests. "I want an honest answer."

Harrison finger-combed the hair that had fallen across her cheek and tucked it behind her ear. "Honestly? I haven't done a damn thing, but I'm beat. I wanted to get started on the Greenwich journals, but..."

"It can wait," she finished for him. "Close your eyes." She lay her head down next to his and stretched out as close to him as possible without suffocating Jake. "We'll work on the journals this afternoon," she said softly.

He was asleep before the end of her sentence.

Chapter Sixteen

After his nap, Harrison was raring to go. With another one of his challenging transition maneuvers, he'd gotten himself, via wheelchair, over to the recliner chair and then into it, and had adjusted its angle so that neither his comfortable reading position nor the proper elevation of his legs had been more than minimally compromised for the task at hand. Erika, equally keen to get a move on, sat beside him in one of the chairs pulled from another room. Meantime, the rest of the household was humming along on its own, leaving the couple to its own devices. Kate, Grace and Jake were keeping Lucas entertained, and Greg was in text conference with his connection at the Wildenstein Plattner Institute in the hopes of determining the status of Monet's critical still life, *Wedgewood Vase with Flowers* vis-à-vis the artist's catalogue raisonné.

Harrison's laptop was sitting on his chest, opened to his email account. He tapped on the email Erika had forwarded to him containing the five PDFs commenting on local life in Greenwich, Connecticut, from 1862 through 1885 and scrolled down to their lineup. "Let's see what we've got here," he said.

Erika, whose laptop was resting befittingly on her lap, homed in on the same grouping. The headings under each file short-handed the authorship, dates covered, and size in megabytes. "MJ" and "TJ" clearly stood for Marylou Jackson and her daughter, Tess. The century number "18," was understood, therefore omitted in all headings. The first file was identified as "MJ 62-64 10MB. "A big one," Erika remarked. "About a thousand pages."

"Looks like all the docs are at capacity," Harrison observed, "except maybe file number five, a mere seven megabytes, and the only one attributed to Tess Jackson, who covered the final years, 1877 through 1885. How do you propose we navigate this extravaganza?"

Erika contemplated the regiment of files. I say we start off by doing a search for key words in each of the documents, then, if we're successful, hone in on the surrounding text. After that, we can discuss what we think bears further scrutiny."

"Agree on all of the above," Harrison said. "I was thinking we should concentrate on and around 1871, the year Abigail and James Scott transacted their Monet purchase, possibly with the dealer Durand-Ruel, as the dealer's intriguing letter to Pissarro leads us to believe, perhaps wishfully."

"Sure, but I don't want to skip over the outlying years altogether," Erika said. "You never know what enlightening premonition or flashback we might chance upon in the years before and after the Scott's encounter with Monet's Wedgewood vase." She reached for the legal pad and ballpoint pen, at the ready on the recliner's side table.

"I hear you," Harrison said. "No file will be overlooked." He nodded toward the writing materials. "You ready to jot down reference words?"

She nodded. "Shoot."

"Abigail, James, Scott, art, Monet. Durand-Ruel," he began.

"Elizabeth and her married name, Barden," she added. "Elizabeth inherited the Monet from her parents in 1908, but who knows, maybe she's mentioned somewhere along the way."

"Wide-eyed optimists, aren't we?" Harrison said.

"What have we got to lose? You want to start with 1862 through '64? I'll take a look at '65 through '67?"

With that, their search was launched. "Fascinating," Harrison commented a minute into it. "Marylou's first entry describes her conflicting emotions of pride and fear at her son, Edward's induction into the Tenth Connecticut Infantry Regiment. Her only son, it seems. I hope the hell he survived. I've got to find out if he did. I'm searching his name."

"I'm trying not to get involved," Erika said. "Although it's hard. Marylou begins 1865 with a list of local births first week of the new year. 'George P.

Morgan,' she recited. 'January six, eight pounds two ounces. Delivered by Postmaster Dan Gerity on the floor of the post office. Dan was awarded the Good Samaritan award by the mayor.' End quote."

"Nice," Harrison commented distractedly. "Wait. A letter from Edward is received November twentieth, 1864. You want to look him up in your document, see if his name comes up after the war ends?"

She did so. "Here he is!" she exclaimed after her 'Edward' search resulted in an immediate highlight on Marylou's April 20, 1865 entry. "Seems the Tenth Infantry Regiment was on scene when Robert E. Lee surrendered to Ulysses S. Grant at Appomattox Courthouse on April ninth. Edward was there. Got home intact. There you go."

"Good," Harrison said. He cracked a helpless smile. "At this rate, we'll never get through this, will we?"

"Not a chance," she said, ricocheting his grin. "Let's try to stick with the assignment. We can get back to it at our leisure."

"I'm hoping not to have much of that," he said, dead serious. "I plan to be working my ass off." He glanced at the pair of crutches propped up against his closet door; a silent challenge—or reproach: had he actually needed that nap?

"Don't get down on yourself," Erika ordered, reading his face. "It won't be tolerated."

He answered with a military salute. "Sorry I'm unable to stand at attention." Mock formality melting into a smile, he returned his focus to his open file. "Right. Let's get on with it."

Despite their meandering start, seconds after resuming their word search, they hit pay dirt.

"Found her!" Erika proclaimed. "September fourth, 1865."

Harrison's fingers froze mid-word. "Who? Abigail Scott?"

"Yes—well, Scott née Peterson, it appears. Listen to this. Marylou worked at the local library. On this day, her friend—and I quote—'Abigail Peterson, came by to ask me to recommend a book on Renaissance painters. Well, I have to start *somewhere!* she said. Abby recently told me that it is her intention to fill the gaps in her education. I dearly love the girl, but I suspect her goal is not quite as noble as it appears. It does not take a detective to observe her keenness for one James Scott, our most eligible bachelor, newly blown into town. James is an optometrist and fine arts enthusiast, and at thirty-four, ten years Abby's senior. From the way I caught him looking at her at the county fair last Saturday, her study of art will not be a determining factor in their courtship.' End quote. How's that for starters? Let's go on to the next reference. I predict wedding bells."

Harrison mugged a dubious look. "How do we know it's *our* Abigail and James?" he pretended to question.

"Killjoy," she shot back, simultaneous with a rap on the room door. Followed by a greeting.

"Greg here. You decent?"

"No, but come in," Harrison answered.

"Grab a chair," Erika said when he appeared. "You look excited. What have you got there?" she asked, referring to the paper he was waving in the air.

"A list." He pulled up a chair—the mate to the one Erika was sitting in—and plunked down in it. He paused to take stock of their tableau. "The disciples before their leader. Anyone got a sketchpad?"

Harrison grinned. "Don't keep us in suspense."

"Yes, yes." With another flourish of his mysterious document, he said, "Well, I must have been expecting my search to come to a dead end. That must have been the reason I was so taken aback."

Are we talking about Monet's catalogue raisonné or Durand-Ruel's critical stock ledger?" Erika asked.

"The catalogue. I must tell you, things did not go as planned. I found no mention of Monet's *Wedgewood Vase with Flowers* in the Wildenstein records, either public, rejected, or in review, so I decided to look elsewhere. Namely, the Global Arts Research Corporation. You know of it?"

"I know it has an active corporate giving program," Harrison said. "Funding a museum dedicated exclusively to the display of children's artwork comes to mind. A center for performance arts, another project. I'm aware their main source of revenue is in attribution and conservation, but I've never had direct contact with them."

"Brief history. The Wildenstein family has been in the art business for generations. Any organization associated with the name has gravitas among serious art collectors. Compared to the Wildenstein domain, Global is an upstart. Something like Laszlo's auction house vis-à-vis Christie's or Sotheby's. They've been around for roughly ten years, cultivating relationships worldwide with companies, institutions, and individuals noted for their marketable expertise in the field. Many of these entities have become affiliated with Global, which serves as a networking agent. The corporation has generated its own catalogues raisonnés in various genres, and for a growing number of collectors, they've become the final word in those areas. To be sure, Guy Wildenstein's having to face charges of tax fraud and money laundering back in 2016 did wonders for Global's reputation."

"Wasn't Wildenstein cleared of the charges?" Harrison asked.

"Yes, but accusations do have a tendency to stick, don't they? Besides, the presiding judge did off-handedly remark that the defendant had"—air quotes— "'a will to dissimulate.' Hard to un-remember that, I'd say."

"True," Erika politely agreed. "But getting back to the issue at hand..."

Greg laughed. "When I'm excited, I tend to ramble. Of course. Monet. The *Wedgewood Vase* still life."

Erika smiled. "Yes."

"Well, then. I decided to give it a shot. I knew Global affiliates have challenged Wildenstein rejections of ostensibly well-documented submissions, so what could I lose? Turns out the corporation has a digitalized catalogue raisonné of what they've entitled 'Claude Monet, the Early Years, 1850-1875.' Starting at age ten! Scheduled to release in hardcover within the year. Is this a deus ex machina, or what?" He held up his document as if it were a signed copy of the Ten Commandments.

"I'm guessing the still life in question is listed in the catalogue," Erika said. "From your elation, I'm assuming you learned a few more details about its provenance. What we've got is pretty scant. No galleries or dealers named in the sales transactions. No private or public venues in which it was shown. Nothing."

Without saying a word, Greg handed her the paper. Erika rose from the chair and perched on the arm of the recliner in order to share Greg's discovery with Harrison. Together, they read a series of lines written in Greg's neat cursive:

June 26: on the authority of Global Arts Research Corporation, 8 Monets, oil on canvas, included in its catalogue raisonné, Claude Monet, the Early Years, 1850-75

    Girl at the Piano, March 1869, H. 32" x W. 20"

    Wedgewood Vase with Flowers, May 1870, 20 x 17

    Woman Reading, April 1870, 24 x18

    Seaside, ?1866, 38 x 50

    Picnic on the Lawn, May 1867, 32 x 40

    At the Shore, ?1866, 38 x 50

    Woman in the Garden, ?1867, 24 x18

    Luncheon Party, July 1865, 32 x 40

All of the above sold to James and Abigail Scott of Greenwich Connecticut, January 3, 1871. By inheritance, passed to Elizabeth Barden née Scott of Greenwich, May 2, 1908. Sold to Lewis Keller of New York City, January 5, 1927. By inheritance, passed to Morris Keller, New York City, June 7, 2015.

"When do you two practice making identical facial expressions in the mirror?" Greg asked when they looked up from his notations. "When you brush your teeth in the morning?"

"What?" they asked in unison.

"Quizzical expressions. Exactly the same." He shook his head. "Never mind. This is a group of Monet works Global Arts have accepted into their catalogue raisonné of Monet's 'early years.' I thought you'd be pleased."

"Of course we're pleased," Harrison replied. "Thank you, Greg!" He turned toward Erika. "I was taken aback by the date of inclusion, that's all. You?"

"Yes," Erika said. "I realize now it was an understandable oversight."

Greg stiffened. "What are you talking about? What did I omit?"

"The *year* the eight paintings were admitted into the catalogue raisonné. Omitting the year implies it's the present year. Since, as you say, the organization has been around for about a decade, I'm assuming the paintings' inclusion occurred either just before or soon after Morris Keller gained possession of the works in 2015."

Greg slapped his head. "I'm gobsmacked. Truly. Why did you think I was elated, mates? Because we *are* talking about the present year. The eight oil paintings were admitted into the holy fold on June twenty-sixth of this year. Eleven days ago. Five days after the Laszlo auction!"

Erika and Harrison's brows rose simultaneously.

Greg laughed. "You people really do practice in front of the mirror. Blimey, the sex must be incredible. Yes, this is crazy, and for just that reason, it means we're getting somewhere in this investigation. Let me pose a question. Why would a Monet painting be snatched from the auction block, only to be spirited away with seven of its cohorts to be, en masse and posthaste, slipped into a reputable organization's catalogue raisonné? You have one guess—*between* you."

Erika and Harrison traded revelatory glances. "Go ahead," Harrison prompted.

"The paintings were removed to parts unknown and promptly entered into an esteemed catalogue raisonné for one reason," Erika began. "To be sold, either on the black market or by some other unscrupulous means. Any obstacles standing in the way were eliminated. I can't see it any other way." To Harrison: "You agree?"

"With every word. What I'm wondering is, aside from the date of the certification—which smells of foul play on its own—how the hell were eight paintings analyzed and certified in five days, tops? Specifically, who scrutinized these paintings, Greg?"

"Whoever they are, if they have the imprimatur of Global Arts Research Corporation, their reputation is more or less indisputable."

"I'm thinking less."

"More likely a bad seed in the organization."

"I'll give you that," Harrison said. "Where do we go from here?"

"You mean, where do *I* go?" Greg corrected. "You're going nowhere near the source of potential risk, either by text, phone, carrier pigeon, or any other means of communication." He glanced at Erika. "That goes for you, too."

"Got it."

"In my line of work, prowling around art hang-outs, from galleries to museums to the underworld, is de rigueur. My goals here have not yet been fully met." He paused abruptly. "Time out. The list came with photos of the corresponding paintings. Of no real use except general reference, since they're black-and-white postage-stamp sized repros. Still. I need you to introduce me to your printer, so I can make copies for us. Where was I? Yes. I want to see names. Names of administrators. Names of the art experts who played a hand in authenticating the Monets. I want to know where this race-to-the-finish took place. And where the hell the paintings are now!" He smiled at their expressions of mild consternation. "Don't worry. My aggression is contained within these walls. My approach will be smooth as silk."

"I know it will," Erika said, clearly relieved. "Where is Global headquarters, by the way?"

"Cincinnati, Ohio, but I believe I can proceed with this business remotely. So far, it's worked out fine, thanks in part to my one-off encounter in the past with Global; brief, but notable. A while back, I recommended them to a prominent art collector whose Egon Schiele painting had been stolen and held for ransom. My Art Loss Register posse guided her through the process of pay-and-recover, but when the painting was returned to her after she'd paid the ransom, she insisted the original had been replaced by a counterfeit. One of Global's affiliates confirmed her claim, and she received a handsome settlement from her insurance company. Now she's a big fan of Global, and, needless to say, I'm on excellent terms with them as well. No problem obtaining the list of Monets. I had a great cover story, but hardly needed it. In fact, my contact was thrilled to share the news. If there's a bad apple in the bunch, you can bet it's not this chap. In any case, rest assured, I'll come up with a strategy that's both risk-free and clever as hell." He gestured to their open laptops. "And what are *you* two up to?"

They clued him in. Hearing the names of the individuals who'd purchased the eight Monets in 1871 piqued Greg's interest, and he asked if they'd mind if he sat in on their word-search session. "Abigail and James…where the trouble all started," he mused, not without a grain of cynicism.

Erika forwarded to Greg's email the five PDFs containing the personal accounts of the Jackson women. "Why don't you open Marylou's account from 1868 through 1876," she suggested. "That should be the most revealing period for our purposes. I'd start with a search for the art dealer, Paul Durand-Ruel."

"Done," Greg said, followed by "No dice," seconds later.

Erika overrode her disappointment by going for her next highlighted *Abigail.* "As predicted," she said, coming upon it on June 11, 1867, at her and James's wedding. "Marylou was Abigail's matron of honor," she announced. "If you're interested in hearing what food was served, let me know. Otherwise, we move on."

"Wish I had something to move on *to*," Harrison complained. "I'm batting zero here. Think I'll join Greg in what promises to be the more fruitful years." He closed his document and tapped open the PDF covering 1868 through 1876.

"Try searching the words 'Scotts' and 'London,'" she suggested to both Harrison and Greg. "It's possible Marylou mentioned the Scotts' visit to an art dealership in London without referencing the dealer's name."

"Say, *here's* something of note!" Greg declared. "I took the slow route via the word 'Abigail.' Come join us in 1870, Erika. December twentieth, to be precise. Prompt the words 'Cunard Line.' Take you right to it; no local stops."

Erika took his advice, and in a moment, all three were scanning the same passage.

You know how some folks set out to do something, but never get around to doing it? Not so with the Scotts. No sooner does James Scott take it into his head to travel across the Atlantic than passage is booked for him and Abigail on a Cunard Line iron screw steamer bound for London. They leave tomorrow. The ocean voyage is expected to take a week to ten days, and passage home is booked for January 15. I've told Abigail she needn't write me every day, but if I receive no news from her at all I shall be sorely disappointed.

"How's that for a lead?" Greg applauded himself. "This couple will be well ensconced in London and over their New Year's Eve debauchery by January the third, 1871, the day of their Monet purchase. Does this dovetail with Durand-Ruel's letter to Pissarro or what?"

"It does," Harrison agreed. "Though what would place the Scotts at Durand-Ruel's gallery with absolute certainty would be to find a specific reference to Durand-Ruel himself."

"Which there isn't." Greg shook his head in disbelief. "The evidence placing the Scotts at Durand-Ruel's London gallery is overwhelming, Harrison. If I ever murder someone, I want you on my jury."

"Touché. At any rate, we haven't checked the 1877 through 1885 file. Unlikely there'll be an entry mentioning the Durand-Ruel sale in retrospect, but no harm trying."

"I just tried, sweetheart," Erika said. "No luck."

Greg smiled. "Great minds think alike. Now then, playtime's over. The word 'Abigail' is working for us. Let's check its next appearance."

The name Abigail came up again on February 8th, the day Marylou received what she referred to as "my friend Abigail's one and only letter postmarked from London, arriving two weeks after she was back in Greenwich, no less!" Marylou's summary of the letter's contents focused on the newest trend in fashion, the bustle dress, with its multiple layers of ruffles and gathers planted primarily in the back, with, according to Abigail, "all interest residing in the lady's departing figure as opposed to its approaching." The readers moved on.

The next entry highlighting the word "Abigail" appeared three weeks later, on February 29th, and was as perplexing as it was confirmatory. It described a chat Marylou had had with her friend over "coffee and," as Marylou put it, at the "darling little café around the corner from the library." Under review, the Scotts' trip to London. The three readers fixated their attention on the crucial lines.

> By chance, the Scotts stepped into an art gallery of a dealer who'd fled Paris to escape the turmoil of war, more for the safety of his pictures than himself, or so Abigail surmised.
>
> While they were looking around, a man entered the place carrying a stack of what turned out to be eight unframed canvasses. As it happened, this was an artist delivering his oil paintings to the dealer, who was representing him. Before the canvasses changed hands, the Scotts asked to see them. They were quite taken by the paintings (James the more fervent of the two), and offered to buy them then and there. The dealer, a perfect gentleman, ceded his right to a commission. Claiming superstition to be the reason, Abigail did not reveal the name of the artist to me. Nor did she invite me to see his work. (Fearing rejection, I did not have the gumption to invite myself.) I am comforted by the fact that Abigail, by nature, is not at all forthcoming. When I ask where she purchased a particularly appealing hat, for example, she inevitably says, "I forgot."

Greg was the first to comment. "Well, I *say!*"

"Ditto," Harrison tagged.

"Abigail's story totally contradicts the one alluded to in Durand-Ruel's letter to Pissarro," Erika said, spelling out her concurrence. "Judging from Durand's reference to the event, he orchestrated what went down and quite slyly at that! Furthermore, I think he implied that Monet was not present at the time."

"I'm putting my euros on Durand-Ruel," Greg said.

"Good bet," Harrison agreed. "He was known as an honest and above-board dealer. In fact, when he refers in his letter to his little ploy, he can't help raising his concern for moral correctness."

"The Scotts were up to no good," Greg bluntly concluded. "I believe they, not the Kellers, omitted Durand-Ruel from the provenance of Monet's still life."

Harrison nodded. "I agree, but maybe not so confidently. If the Scotts were hiding something, what was it?"

"If I can get ahold of Durand-Ruel's stock ledger of that period, we may be able to come up with an answer to that. Incidentally, although you'll probably tell me I'm jumping the gun, I think the quote, 'stack of what turned out to be eight unframed canvasses' refers to the eight Monet paintings that eventually found their way to the Keller family. The number eight, not a coincidence. Something unsavory about that initial transaction—or more likely what occurred subsequent to it, if we're taking for granted Durand-Ruel's upstanding reputation. And it was that deed— that X factor!—that set off a butterfly effect resulting in a couple of murders, not to mention"—gesturing toward Harrison—"your messed up limbs."

"If you're jumping the gun, I'm right along with you, Greg."

"Good. You, Erika?"

Erika nodded. "Occam's razor wins again."

The word search continued, but with the exception of learning of the birth date of the Scotts' daughter, Elizabeth, in March of 1880, their luck seemed to have run out. Deciding a page-by-page scan of the journals might be worth the effort, each of them committed to reading an assigned portion of the files and reporting anything of possible relevance to their investigation.

"To end on a positive note," Erika said, "at least we can eliminate Elizabeth Barden née Scott as the perpetrator of the alleged misdeed. She was born eight years after it occurred."

Harrison was beginning to feel restless, perhaps solely for not having the option to just get up and *go*. "Greg," he said reluctantly, "I'm going to take you up on your offer."

"At last!"

"Can you help haul my ass into the wheelchair? I'm sick of this recliner, and I don't know if I have it in me for another heave-ho."

"My pleasure." Greg rose from his seat to bring the wheelchair into optimum transfer position. As he was swiveling it into place, a cell phone rang. He locked the brakes and shoved his hand into his pants pocket.

"Mine," Harrison said, recovering his cell phone from the pocket of his sweat jacket. An unfamiliar number registered on its screen. The idea of treating it as a scam call was overruled by a touch of curiosity. "Hello, who is this?" he answered warily. His eyes opened wide on hearing the response. He placed a cautionary finger to his lips and tapped on the speakerphone. "Hello, Meagan."

"*Dunne?*" Erika mouthed.

He nodded.

"I'm on a burner phone," Meagan said, her voice cracking on the word "burner." "Are you alone?"

"Yes," he lied on impulse.

"I would feel more comfortable if I could see you, Harrison, but burners have only basic features, apparently, and Darien insisted I use a burner—not even the burner app. He would not trust me managing the app."

So much tension in her voice. Harrison pictured her vocal cords as guitar strings about to snap. "Darien had you call me?"

"I wish we had met while you were here," Meagan went on, hurt creeping into her voice. "I'd have more of an idea who you are. I'm surprised Darien didn't think to introduce us. I live just outside London. I would gladly have come into town."

Harrison locked focus with Erika and Greg in turn. Their wide eyes indicated comprehension: *Darien's text to Meagan outside the parking garage? Never happened!* "How is Darien doing?" Harrison asked in an attempt to steer Meagan into a substantive exchange.

"Darien will be discharged from the hospital in two, tops three, days, he says. I don't know how. He seems totally…*unlike* himself. He should be given a comprehensive psychological evaluation. He hardly spoke to me, and all the while, his eyes were darting everywhere, as if he expected a monster about to spring from the wall or ceiling. What really happened in that garage, Harrison? Darien says you were mugged, but he doesn't know why. Is this true?"

For Meagan's safety, the truth was off the table. "Yes, Meagan, you must take Darien's word for it. We were attacked by a stranger for no apparent reason. The police are assuming it was a case of mistaken identity. I'm sure you can understand how paranoia can arise from having experienced such a brutal assault coming from out of nowhere. I have nightmares myself," he bluffed, to emphasize the point.

"Oh no, how could I?" Meagan cried. "I'm so involved in what's happening over here, I forgot! Believe me, Darien was not so thoughtless. He was very clear about having me ask after you. How *are* you doing, Harrison?"

"Doing better. I've got a great support system. To get right to the point, Meagan, why didn't Darien call me himself?"

"He says the hospital is not a secure place. I tell you, his fear was palpable. Harrison, are we on speakerphone? There's a bit of an echo in your voice."

Startled, but answering on the spot, he said, "Yes, we are. I needed it to hear you better. Our connection is not as good as it was the last time we spoke. Maybe it's the reception from your burner phone."

"Sorry, I had no choice."

"Nothing to apologize for, Meagan. I hear you just fine. You were saying?" He waited for Meagan to deliver Darien's message—or had she already?

"Darien wanted me to tell you to expect a call from him as soon as he's back in his apartment. He said to answer all phone calls. One of those suspected cold callers will actually be him on a burner phone. Thank you for picking up *my* call," Meagan added, the guitar strings slightly less taut. "We had no plan B."

Harrison wondered if Meagan had any idea why Darien was anxious to connect with him. He suspected not, nor was he about to ask.

"You'll be sure to pick up?" Meagan asked.

"Absolutely. And send Darien my best, will you?"

"I've instructions not to call him any time soon, but I will when I can," Meagan said, clearly relieved the call was about to terminate. "At any rate, I *do* hope we'll meet one day," she added enthusiastically, relief spilling into her parting declaration.

"What just happened here?" Greg asked after the call ended.

Harrison shoved his cell phone back into his pocket. "You want to know what I think?"

"Please!"

"For one thing, I think Darien wanted to let me know that he'd lied to me—that he hadn't texted Meagan outside the parking garage."

Greg shook his head. "What am I missing?"

"First, are we agreed that Meagan was not given the full story on either the assault or Darien's cock and bull story preceding it?"

"Yes. I believe Meagan's ignorance was genuine."

"You with me?" Harrison asked Erika.

"Yes, and I think I know where you're going with this—and I'm with you there, too."

Greg issued a disgruntled sigh. "And the spoiler alert is…?"

"That Darien knew his lie to me would be blown, one way or another," Harrison said. "Either Meagan would innocently out it the way she had, or, more likely, that I'd express my regrets that Darien and I had never made it to Wembley according to plan, only to hear Meagan's confused reply that this was all news to her."

"Are you implying what I think you're implying?"

"That Darien is coming in from the cold? Yes."

"Doesn't *this* put a spin on things! You positive about this?"

"No."

Greg grinned. "Sorry, dumb question, knowing you. What do you think Darien wants to talk to you about on the sly? A confession? A quid pro quo of some sort?"

"Maybe. I'm hoping."

"I'll text John," Erika pitched in. "Ask him to prioritize his background check on Darien." She had already begun messaging him on her laptop.

"Good idea," Greg commended, after the fact. "Now, let's get going, lad," he directed at Harrison, while double-checking the wheelchair's brakes had been secured.

It was not easy for Harrison to yield governance of his physical being, and he had no intention of getting used to it. "Sure, thanks," he said, his need to proclaim his virility manifesting as gruffness. "You're a big help," he added remorsefully.

"My pleasure. Just remember, when I get whacked in the legs, I expect payback." Without missing a beat, he scooped Harrison out of the recliner and planted him in the wheelchair, Harrison's laptop going along for the ride. "What else is needed? I want to be useful."

Harrison grabbed his hand. "Your friendship is needed, Greg. That's all the 'useful' I need from you."

"You get maudlin, I'm gone." He clasped Harrison's hand in both of his. "Seriously, I can start digging around for Durand-Ruel's 1871 sales records if you have nothing for me to do up here."

Harrison seized on the idea for reasons he did not care to divulge. The group planned to meet later for dinner, which Grace had planned to bring up to the bedroom. One parting squeeze of Harrison's hand, and Greg took his leave.

"Where to?" Erika asked after the door shut behind Greg.

"I have to use the commode," Harrison said, pronounced as if it were a death sentence. He released the wheelchair's brake and swiveled the device into the direction of the freestanding toilet, then reluctantly allowed Erika to steer him to it. "I can manage from here," he said on arrival.

Erika understood he had not meant to sound brusque, merely efficient. It was a way of objectifying the deed he was about to perform. She knew it must have been easier for him yesterday, when Raymond, a professional witness to embarrassing acts and thus inured to them, had helped him through the exercise. But Raymond had flown back to England. It was she, his non-medical *wife*, who must now deal with what he surely viewed as an adult potty, different only in its unwieldiness from the one on which Lucas was presently in training. She must squelch the maternal instinct to croon some comforting words, which under the circumstances he would find intolerable. "I'll be right back with the supplies," she said crisply. "Need some help getting the pants down, or you want to scoot over first?" *Scoot? Damn!*

He could not help smiling over her attempt at casualness. "It would be a help, yes." He pushed down on the armrests and lifted himself off the seat a bit so Erika could pull down his baggy sweatpants and shorts. "There. Thank you." Curt again.

Erika paced her stride to the bathroom as if it were a walk in the park. There, she overturned the wooden wastebasket and dumped its contents onto the tile floor. She removed two rolls of toilet paper and a packet of wet wipes from the cabinet under the sink and brought all needed items to the commode site.

The wheelchair and commode seats were each about eighteen inches from the floor, so Harrison had not found it difficult to *scoot* his way from one to the other. He did not look comfortable, physically or spiritually. Erika placed the wastebasket upside down within his reach and set the toilet paper and wet wipes on the small table that had been created.

"Let's just slip one leg out of the pants, don't you think?" she asked.

"Sure."

She gently pulled his pants off his right leg—the less damaged one—which enabled him to part his feet. "I'll wait in the bathroom if you like. Call me when you need me. Take all the time you like."

"Good. Would you lock the bedroom door first, please?"

"Of course."

They were over the first hurdle. The more difficult one—for him, not her—was yet to come.

It took a while for him to feel free enough to relieve himself. Another few minutes to clean himself up—to the bone, if he could! —and wet-wipe his hands. Only after he had slid back into the wheelchair and slapped down the lid of the commode—*what's the use, she'll have to see what I've done*—did he call her back.

"Tomorrow, I'll be weight-bearing on my right leg," he said as she approached. "I'll get myself to the bathroom."

"Only if it doesn't cause undue pain," she said firmly. "We're dealing with bodily functions. News flash. Everybody's got them." She'd adopted a tone somewhere between a dental hygienist and a nun.

"I appreciate your stoicism, but I find this humiliating," he said.

"I love you," she said, maintaining a firm demeanor. "This is another level of knowing, of sharing the indignities of life. Think of it as a dry run for old age, when we will be helping each other manage such challenges as hip replacements and incontinence. Think of it as a new facet of devotedness."

"Only you could wax philosophical over a pile of shit," he said through his laughter.

"Made you laugh; don't knock it," she said as she flipped open the commode lid.

Chapter Seventeen

ood a time as any, Harrison thought, grabbing the crutches propped against the wall, his side of the bed. Erika was performing her morning ablutions in their en suite bathroom and in no position to try to talk him out of it. He smiled, thinking that he could hear everything going on in there. Erika had taken to leaving the door open—wide open—"in case you need me for some reason," her professed reason, although he knew, somehow, primarily to assure him that her bodily functions were every bit as open to scrutiny as his own. He would have done the same for her had the tables been reversed, but that did not detract from the fact that he was deeply touched by the gesture.

He jiggled his ass into a stable position and set the crutches under his arms. He could hear Erika peeing. Gingerly, he tapped his right heel on the carpeted floor, as lightly as if he were establishing the location of an ant without harming it. No pain. A little harder. A bare minimum of pain. Because the hinge of the knee brace was in lock position, in order to set his foot flat on the floor, he must rise to his full height. He pressed down on the axilla bars of the crutches and lifted himself from the bed until he was upright, the casted left leg raised slightly, its foot poised no more than two inches from the floor, the right foot in full contact, bearing the weight of his body.

With a reverberating bellow of pain, he fell back, arms flailing out to stabilize his position on the bed, crutches falling outward from his armpits in unison, plunging to the floor like a pair of synchronized swimmers.

"Harrison!" Erika screamed, running from the bathroom in bra and hastily pulled up underpants riding askew on her hips. "Are you okay?" There was a danger of him slipping off the bed, and she straddled his thighs and slammed herself against his pelvis as he secured his purchase. "You tried bearing weight—without waiting for me!"

"We would have argued about it. I might have been convinced. I'm glad I tried. I'll do it again tomorrow."

No use in arguing. She thought about asking if he needed a painkiller. Decided against it. "You want to get ready to go down for breakfast?"

"Sure. Unless you want to stay in this position all day." Cute. Another second and he'd start sliding again, end up on the floor. He clawed at the bedding, managed to snag a patch of the fitted sheet in his left fist, enough to enable him to tug himself back a couple more inches, from which point he could sit up without bobsledding off the edge.

Perched near the edge of the bed, uncomfortably, but in little danger of crashing, he brushed his teeth, wet-wiped his hands and face, and combed his untamable hair. He slipped on a white T-shirt over his bare chest, and Erika helped him change into clean underpants and a second pair of baggy sweatpants found among the supplies Raymond, the orthopedic nurse, had left him. A clean pair of socks came last. He passed on the sneakers. "Who am I kidding?" he asked.

"I'm giving you a sponge bath tonight," Erika said, climbing into her jeans. "Why? Do I stink?"

"You know I have a weakness for the smell of your sweat, but no. I just thought you'd enjoy it." She reached for her white shirt and slipped her arms into the sleeves.

"I would," he said. "It's a date."

"Great." She finished buttoning up her blouse. "Let's go." She drew the wheelchair up to the side of the bed, and he hoisted himself into it.

The elevator maneuver was easier this time around because of their confidence in having already accomplished it. As the doors opened onto the second level, they could hear a pleasant murmuring of voices coming from the kitchen.

The balance of the household was well along in the breakfast ritual when

Erika and Harrison wheeled in on them. The group formed quite a domestic scene. Kate was leaning toward Lucas in his booster seat, cutting up his pancakes while he drowned them in maple syrup. Greg was standing at Kate's shoulder, refilling her coffee cup and asking if she'd like another helping of pancakes. Grace was standing at the stove, flipping them. Jake sat by her, waiting for one to miss the pan.

"Room for us in your Normal Rockwell?" Harrison asked, with a dig at America's beloved illustrator.

"Make yourself at home," Greg said, one-upping him.

"I'm having pancakes, Daddy!" Lucas broke in. "Can I sit on your lap?"

"Nuts, I wanted to sit on *your* lap!"

Gales of laughter were followed by a brief, amazingly mindful, stint in Daddy's lap, after which breakfast resumed, with Erika and Harrison joining in.

No reference to the ongoing criminal investigation was made until the party broke up.

"I learned a thing or two last evening," Greg mentioned in the hallway after Kate and Lucas had taken off—end goal, the park—and Grace was tidying up in the kitchen. "Shall we retire to your bedroom where you can get those legs up, old chap? I'd like to check in with John, too, see if he's made any inroads."

"Let's do it," Harrison said.

The Wheatleys took the elevator; Greg, the stairs. They met at the door to the bedroom, Greg revealing his classic breeding by not having dared enter another adult's vacant bedroom unescorted.

"What have you got for us?" Erika asked after Harrison had been helped into the recliner-throne and his acolytes were sitting at his feet in their armless chairs.

"Well, if you're thinking I've located the eight Monets and know all about them, I haven't. I made a stab at it, but my source seems to have clammed up. I'll carry on when I'm back on my stomping grounds. Besides, it's the weekend. Weekends are a bad time to curry favor. However, I made up for the lack with something that will make your heads spin. You recall that I was going to try my luck at tracking down Paul Durand-Ruel's stock ledger from 1871, yes?"

"To definitively pin down the sale of the Monets to Abigail and James Scott on January third," Erika said. "Yes, of course."

Greg sat forward. "So, I jumped through hoops, looking for the ledger. I researched every institution housing Durand-Ruel's archived material—the Frick Museum. The Getty, the National Gallery, you name it. Nada. It finally dawned on me to reach out to either of the co-editors of Durand-Ruel's memoir, his great-grandson and great-*great*-granddaughter—Paul-Louis and Flavie. I couldn't locate Paul-Louis, but found Flavie in Brussels. I called her at three a.m.—there's a six-hour time difference—and she was remarkably forthcoming, given the fact that she doesn't know me from a hole in the wall. Well, Flavie informed me that the transactions Durand-Ruel made while he was leasing gallery space on New Bond Street during the Franco-Prussian War were not recorded in a stock ledger until he returned to Paris. And there lay the crux of my wild goose chase!" Greg sat back and folded his arms.

This is it? Erika thought. *This can't be it.*

"What's the upshot?" Harrison asked, voicing her thought.

"Patience," Greg admonished. "Bombshell ahead. After Flavie dropped this bit of news, she advised me that Caroline Durand-Ruel Godfroy, another member of the clan, is in possession of the stock ledgers relevant to our inquiry and that, furthermore, she herself would contact Caroline and get back to me with the information I'm after." He slapped his knee. "And would you believe it? She got back to me within the hour. Drum roll, please."

They waited while he took a folded paper from his pants pocket and unfolded it.

"The ledger entry on February tenth, 1873 reads: 'January three, 1871, London. Two Monet pictures plus x's six. 7,500 francs. J. and A. Scott, US.'" He refolded the paper and shoved it back into his pocket. "Need I say more?"

Dead silence.

Finally, from Harrison: "The still life withdrawn from the Laszlo auction was not a Monet. It was one of the six being passed off *as* Monets."

"Of course," Erika returned without hesitation. "That explains why Norman Blethmore was so shocked seeing the still life IDed as a Monet on the cover of the auction catalogue. Why else would he have called Ben Laszlo in such an agitated state? To warn him!"

"But why didn't Laszlo respond by immediately removing the painting from the works scheduled for auction?" Harrison asked. "Something underhanded there."

"That's for sure," Erika agreed. "Let's start from the beginning. Blethmore discovered the truth about the eight paintings in the archives at the Ashmolean—in the Pissarro letters that were subsequently stolen. The question is, how did Blethmore's discovery find its way to a network of criminals coordinating their efforts between the United States and England?"

"The missing link," Greg offered, up to now bobbing his head from one to the other.

Erika nodded. "I'm pinning my hopes on Darien."

"Speaking of which," Harrison said, "I'm hoping John will be getting back to us soon with a background check on him. What do you say we give him a call?"

"Can't hurt." She pulled her cell phone from her jean's side pocket and punched in John's number.

"Mitchell," he answered mid-ring. "Ah, it's you. Can it wait, Erika? I'm on a case."

"No problem, John. Give us a call when you can."

"Will it hold 'til five?"

"Sure."

"Gracias." The call was terminated.

"We wait," Erika said.

"Why don't I take you for a walk?" Greg asked Harrison. "My last day with you, and I'll be leaving tomorrow morning before the sun rises." Addressing Erika: "You, too, luv."

"You two enjoy yourselves," Erika said. "I'll catch up on some editing."

"You'll accompany the old boy down in the elevator, yes? I'm afraid I won't fit."

"Of course."

"Will someone put on my sneakers?" Harrison asked. He hadn't yet consented to be taken *anywhere*, but he kept his mouth shut about that. The last thing he wanted to be taken for was a grumpy invalid.

* * *

At exactly 5:10, John called. Erika, Harrison, Greg, and Lucas were in the living-room at the time, having a pre-prandial go at building with Legos, Lucas's passion. Jake had been lying despondently on the sidelines ever since Greg had asked him not to interfere. Lucas might have objected to Jake's dismissal, but Harrison's clowning around with such antics as constructing a giraffe and balancing it on his head until it fell into his lap was enough to distract the child from the injustices of life.

The call came in on Erika's cell phone. She moved to the corner of the room to take it out of Lucas's earshot, as if his innocence would be lost if he overheard so much as a fragment of their crime-related conversation, even though it would be incomprehensible to him.

"Do you have a pen and paper?" John asked. "I'd prefer not to text this."

"Hang on a minute, John. It's John," she directed to the men as she ran by them.

"Don't go, Mommy!" Lucas hurled at her as she whizzed by.

"Be right back, sweetie-pie!"

Grace and Kate were in the kitchen preparing dinner. She raced past the kitchen and up the stairs to the master bedroom, where she recovered a pad and pen from her night table drawer. "Ready, John. What's it about?"

"For my first news item, you don't need writing tools. You wanted to know if any useful information had turned up on Norman Blethmore's computer. For this inquiry, I contacted the Thames Valley Police, whose jurisdiction includes Oxford. Never mind what story I gave them. It sounded legitimate. Unfortunately, my story-telling amounted to naught. The computer that Blethmore, according to his partner, brought to his office at the Courtauld every day was never recovered. Vanished. The computer recovered from the couple's residence contains nothing but household accounting matters and non-professional communications and searches."

"That's disappointing," Erika said. "But thanks all the same."

"No trouble. Now you can click open the pen. For my second task, I decided to exchange my cop's hat for my more impressive FBI deputy's hat and reach out to the UK's NCA—National Crime Agency. Spoke to the fellow I met when we were in London on the Benin Bronzes case."

"This is where you initiated the Darien Roth background check."

"Yes. Well, they came up with everything about the guy, from his mother's maiden name to a traffic ticket from years ago. I've saved it all, but here's the information of possible relevance. Aside from being on the staff at the Courtauld and the author of a bunch of papers about the Surrealists, he's a consultant at Richardson Gallery and Conservation Studio located in London."

Erika recited the title as she jotted it down.

"Right," John said. "And here's what they do—the subtitle, if you will." He spoke slowly so Erika could get it all down without his having to repeat himself. "'Attribution, conservation, restoration, consignment, specializing in nineteenth and twentieth-century painting and statuary.' Wait, I'm not done."

"There's *more*?"

"Just the company's affiliation. As written: 'a business division of Global Arts Research Corporation.' Which. I should add, is based in Cincinnati, Ohio."

"Oh!"

"'Oh'?"

Erika informed him of Greg's eye-opening discovery that the eight paintings originally purchased by the Scotts in 1871 were classified as bona fide Monets and entered in the artist's catalogue raisonné less than two weeks ago by none other than an affiliate of Global Arts Research Corporation!

"Interesting," John said. "And?"

Erika had forgotten that John had also not been in attendance when Greg had delivered his second mic drop on the subject. "The eight Monet paintings?" she began. "There are apparently only *two* Monets in the lot. The rest are…well, *not!*"

"And how did Greg happen to come by *that* nugget of information?"

Erika told him about how Greg had been directed to the art dealer, Durand-Ruel's stock ledger recording the sale in 1871. "'Two Monet pictures plus x's six,'" she quoted from it.

"*There's* a head-scratcher for you," John marveled. "Well, I've got one more bit on Darien, which may be useless as hell, but here it is. His kid brother, Richard, is serving time in prison for a homicide he claims he did not commit. A lawyer is actively working on his appeal."

"Really?"

"Really. Listen, I'm available anytime—*almost* anytime—you guys want to get together or hand me another assignment. Right now, I've got to run. I promised my wife I'd cook dinner tonight, and I have to pick up a couple of items at the supermarket. How's *your* other half doing, by the way?"

"Not bad, John, given the circumstances. I won't keep you. Thanks for the update. Good luck with dinner."

She'd told Lucas she'd be 'right back.' In Lucas-time, the five minutes she'd been gone would be perceived as an eternity.

"Where *were* you, Mommy?" he complained on her return. "You missed *everything!*"

* * *

"Are you ready?" Erika asked, returning from the linen closet with an armload of plastic items and towels needed for the sponge bath. After dinner, they'd had a meeting with Greg, at which Erika had reported the substance of John's call, and the three had discussed where they were in the investigation. Later, Erika had given Greg instructions on how to use the printer in Harrison's study, and Greg had made copies of the digitalized page of titles and postage-stamp sized photos of the eight paintings recently thrust into Monet's catalogue raisonné. Now, they were officially done for the day.

Harrison, seated in the wheelchair, shed the clothing above his waist and tossed it halfway across the room. "I yield myself to your charge. Do what you will."

Erika grinned. "Don't think I won't." She dropped her haul on the recliner chair, locked the door, and returned to draw the plastic sheet from the heap. "First, let's get this on the bed. Then you can do your gymnastic feat and get yourself on top of it."

After Harrison had managed to plant himself on top of the plastic sheet, the next step, Erika spontaneously decided, was to set up the sponge bath itself. She would remove the rest of Harrison's clothing after everything was in place, figuring that the less time spent sprawled in naked passivity watching her puttering about, the less time to feel totally vulnerable and useless.

From the recliner chair, she retrieved the assortment of towels and the plastic sleeves to pull up over Harrison's legs. After laying them neatly on the bed, she fetched one of the chairs that earlier had been swiped from another room and placed it next to the bed. This would serve as a stand for the basin. She was about to set up the basin of soapy water, but realized the water would get cold while she was preparing Harrison for the bath. "I'm going to take off your sneakers and your pants as gently as possible. Before we start, are you hurting at all?" She rolled up the sleeves of her blouse.

"Feeling okay."

Living up to her word, with utmost care, she removed everything from his body except his cast and braces. "Now for the leg shields." With the same deliberation, she fitted him with the waterproof garments.

He put a hand over his private parts. "This calls for a fig leaf," he said.

They laughed a little over his newfound shyness. "I suppose because it's a unique situation," he explained, as much to himself as Erika.

There was a hand towel in the pile. "How's this?" She covered him with the towel, an act which elicited another joint chuckle, although neither considered it amusing enough to reverse the act.

When the basin of hot, sudsy water with bobbing sponge orb was at last in place, Erika played out the opening sequence in her mind. "Let's start with your back," she said, retrieving the sponge from the water and squeezing it just enough so it wouldn't drip, at least not excessively, on its way to its recipient. "Can you lift up on your elbows a bit? I'll brace you."

He obliged. With one arm around his shoulders steadying him, she ran the soapy sponge all over his back in random swirls, shifting about her supportive arm in order to include his neck and shoulders in the operation. "I should have thought to put a towel under your back," she said. "It'll be uncomfortable if you lie back down on a plastic surface." She lay the sponge on his belly and reached for one of the bath towels. "Can you hold yourself up another second while I spread this out?"

"Sure. Are you okay with this, Erika?"

"I'm loving this," she said, as she smoothed out the bath towel. "You can lie back down now."

He did so.

Next, she asked him to tilt to one side, then the other, so she could soap down his buttocks. When this had been accomplished, she said, "Now you can just lie still and relax. Close your eyes and don't think about a thing." The hand towel had fallen away during the tilting exercise, and she replaced it.

"Not sure that's possible, darling. Not thinking about anything, that is. I'll give it a shot, though." He closed his eyes. His vision of her standing over him remained. The hand towel would be tenting about now. How ludicrous it must look.

She tried not to look. With the newly sudsed sponge, she cleansed first his arms, underarms, and hands, then proceeded to his chest and torso, and onward to his upper thighs. She wondered if she should remove the hand towel in order to be more thorough in her ministrations. What decision would be least cruel? She postponed the decision, moving on to attend to his feet instead. Decided to massage them while she was there. Thought, mistakenly, it might sedate or sublimate the erotic surge.

Harrison lay his hand on his lower torso. "Jesus," he said.

It was as if his hand had slid under her clothing to find the equivalent region. The ache was sudden and insistent. All imagery turned corporeal, even the engorged sponge she let fall by his side. Filmed with lathery water his skin was slippery smooth, and she could anticipate the feel of it before her palm made contact.

"Whatever you're thinking, the answer is yes," he said, opening his eyes.

"But you were told…" she faltered.

"It was a caution, not an order. One slip-up, and then we'll comply. I'm in agony."

"It's just that I need to…"

"What, love?"

"Feel you under me"—she put her free hand between her legs— "here."

His breath came in small bursts, as if he were underwater, trying to keep from breathing. "Please."

"Okay. Thank you."

His laugh came out as a gasp, as if he were drowning. "You're welcome."

She removed what she had on below her waist; no time for anything above. When she climbed onto the bed and straddled him, her legs as wide apart as her anatomy would allow, she experienced an exquisite comingling of relief and incompletion, and when he slid his hand beneath her, raising the heel of his palm to form a speed bump in her travels up and down his body, she could bear it no longer. She reached behind her to throw aside the hand towel, and when she touched him—the merest touch—he uttered a low, but heart-piercing cry, and there was no other course but to raise her pelvis and sink down onto him. He lay still, in painfully exquisite anticipation, and allowed her to transport him to their rapturous union.

Afterward—after she'd rinsed away the soap and returned the environment and their attire to a semblance of normalcy—they lay side by side. Harrison shifted his legs, finding a more comfortable position for them atop the replaced wedge pillow. He turned to Erika and, with a look of feigned innocence, asked, "You up for a shampoo tomorrow?"

She smiled. "Make that a dry shampoo and you're on."

Chapter Eighteen

Darien downed two painkillers with a slug of vodka; the pills to dull the migraine—his new normal—the liquor to steady his nerves. Last minute the doctors had turned conservative on him, urging him to remain under observation in the hospital a day or two longer. He had refused.

He might have felt safe and sound back in his tidy little flat in Courtauld's residence hall, but as a realist, he knew any notion of impregnability was as porous as cheesecloth.

First thing on his checklist: see that his papers were in order—*now* there's *a phrase that makes death as hackneyed as* it *is*, he thought, even as he opened his desk drawer to run through the useless exercise. Of course, the documents were in the drawer. Where would they have walked off to?

What next? He took the burner phone out of his pants pocket. Punched in a number. As usual, it took a while to run the obstacle course. Finally, the voice: "Dar? How the hell are you? You get sprung?"

"Yes, Richie, I was discharged. I'm good. Never mind about me. You coping?"

"If you mean is Kayo still harassing me about the chocolate bar he claims I stole from him, the answer is no. Freddie saw to it."

"I won't ask you how. About your case—things are moving along, Rich. You've been granted the right to appeal. That's a big hurdle you're over. Have you spoken to your criminal defense solicitor about what's next? Has he instructed a barrister to represent you in court? You've got to be thinking ahead."

"I told you, Darien, I don't want you blowing your life savings on me. I can just as easily go through the Public Defender Service as saddle you with the expense of a solicitor-barrister combo. Go live your life, brother."

"You're going to be asked to end this call in a minute. Don't waste time. A witness has come forward who was never asked to testify. She must be handled with kid gloves. Then, there are the trial mismanagement issues. This is not up for debate. You are to have the best representation straight through to the end, and you are going to allow me to see to it. You've got to promise me you will."

"But, I—"

"Promise!"

"Shit, okay!"

After they were cut off, Darien convinced himself that Richie could be trusted with the promise. There was no alternative. His kid brother was as good as a son to him. He had taken care of him all through his life while their birth parents were catering to their addictions. He was responsible for him. Not legally, but intrinsically, which was the stronger bond.

The call to Harrison Wheatley would be more of a challenge because it was not as straightforward. He took another swig of vodka.

Wheatley answered the phone before Darien had a chance to prepare an opening line. "It's Darien," he said in response to Wheatley's "Hello?"

"How are you doing, Darien?" Wheatley asked.

Wheatley sounded cautious, which was how Darien had expected him to sound. After Meagan's call, Wheatley had to have realized the text supposedly sent to Meagan outside the parking garage had been pure fiction. If he hadn't set up Meagan to innocently blow his cover, he probably would not have had the courage to say what he was about to. "It's my fault," he heard himself say. There was no turning back now. He thought he'd be feeling something on the order of panic or, at a minimum, regret. Instead, he felt weightless. "Harrison?"

"I'm here, Darien. What's your fault?"

Darien heard voices in the background. Stupid, his forgetting to have checked. "You're not alone," he said.

"We've just had breakfast. I've left the kitchen. I'm in a wheelchair. Give me a minute to get myself to another room. No one's heard a thing."

"Tell me when you get there. Can you lock the door?"

"Yes," Wheatley said. After a good three minutes, adding, "Here I am." Darien heard a click—of the lock, he assumed. "You hear that?" Wheatley followed up. "We have complete privacy now. What's your fault, Darien?"

"Everything."

There was a pause; again, no surprise. "Can you be specific? Tell me everything on your mind. I've got all day."

"I'll start at the beginning. I'm not an evil person. I want you to understand that."

"I'm a pretty good judge of character, Darien. I consider you a decent person. Whatever you tell me, I doubt my opinion's going to change."

Darien pretended he believed him. It made it easier to open up to him, although the degree of ease was irrelevant. One way or the other, he was going to excise the guilt. It was eating him alive. Where to begin. He could start with his dysfunctional childhood, garner sympathy, but that would be self-indulgent. "I'm a consultant at Richardson Gallery and Conservation Studio," he said. "The firm's in London. You know of it?" He thought he heard Wheatley's intake of breath. Might have been his own.

"No, I don't," Wheatley said.

Darien gave him a rundown on the company's functions, finishing with, "It's affiliated with Global Arts Research Corporation, a very prestigious entity."

"I'm familiar with it," Wheatley said. "They've sponsored a number of admirable projects."

"Yes, well, about two years ago, I was approached by someone in Richardson's attribution department. A client had brought in a Giorgio de Chirico he was anxious to sell, but he had encountered controversy over its authenticity. A decisive finding by Richardson's would put its authorship in solid standing. I was told that my reputation as an authority on the painter had prompted Richardson's to seek out my help. I was flattered." A self-derogatory grunt escaped his lips. "No doubt they did a background check, saw I was strapped for cash. What a naive fool I was."

"Whatever you in all innocence were drawn into," Wheatley began, "how the hell could you have known?"

Darien was impressed. Wheatley was either genuinely sympathetic or a damn good actor. It hardly mattered. As long as he heard him out and, in the end, accepted the challenge. "Don't waste your breath, Harrison. I'm way past the need for sympathy. Redemption, maybe."

"Above my pay grade," Wheatley said, a smile in his voice.

Poor chap, Darien reflected. *Trying to lift my spirits, keep me talking—as if there was a chance I'd shut up.* "You probably know what's coming," he said. "I found the purported de Chirico to be a forgery, albeit a competent one. I was bribed into thinking otherwise. Later on, I was told that my consent to having committed this crime had been recorded. Another incentive, besides the cash rewards, to retain my loyalty—and compliance. I performed a number of *favors* of this sort over time, and though the remuneration was high, I was told it would be at least doubled if I was the one initiating the *transaction,* as my handler called it."

"Handler?"

"For lack of a better word, yes."

"You said this person was in the attribution department."

"Yes, but he was the only person from the company I answered to. I got my instructions—and payments—from him. It was to him I passed on the information Norm Blethmore had given—*confided* to me."

"What exactly did Norman tell you, Darien?"

A little breathless, that last question, Darien felt, but for the most part, Wheatley was doing a good job camouflaging his nervous excitement. He was sorry he didn't have more to give him. "I withheld this from you when we met at the café, but Norm told me he'd come across some eye-opening news in the Ashmolean archives—the latest addition to the Camille Pissarro collection, that is. I was able to pry only this one piece of information from him." He paused to give it prominence. "The Monet still life on the cover of Laszlo's auction catalogue is not a bona fide Monet."

"Aha," Wheatley commented. It sounded like he was waiting for more.

"On whose authority?" he finally posed.

"That's all the information I could get from him. I took it to my Richardson contact and—"

"Excuse me—the *name* of your contact?"

"Chauncey Gladstone, but for all I know, it's an alias. Nothing's certain to me now except my sinful behavior." Darien shook his head. Stated so flatly his admission sounded disingenuous. Should he explain to Wheatley how, in some visceral sense, objectifying his crimes released him from them? No, he decided, skirting another temptation to self-indulge. "I thought Gladstone—or whomever *he* answered to—was going to inform the owner, Morris Keller, that he'd expose his painting as a fraud if he didn't turn over the handling of its sale to him. His argument would be that with the Richardson imprimatur, the counterfeit would easily be accepted as the real thing."

"You didn't follow your reasoning to its logical conclusion," Wheatley suggested—gently, as if he were a doctor delivering unpleasant news. Kind of him.

"Exactly right," Darien said. "If Gladstone planned to pass the counterfeit off as a Monet, all evidence proving otherwise had to be eliminated—the documents themselves, as well as the scholar whose intention was to publicize their content."

"The individual's computer as well, I'd imagine," Wheatley said—again, with the doctor's touch.

"Yes, but my mind wouldn't go there. Not even after Norm was found dead in his office. There were the pills, weren't there? And the initial report of suicide? It was only when you hinted at the possibility...but I swept it out of my thoughts...even then. It was only after that brutal attack—my God, Harrison, I was told you'd be shaken up by maybe a slap or two, but that a verbal warning in the form of a serious threat would be the weapon to scare you off. When I heard what had been done to you, I at last faced the truth. I was like an amnesiac, the memories flooding back, only this time, undisguised."

"So, you only know about the one painting, the still life withdrawn from the auction," Harrison slowly pronounced.

"Why? Are there *more*?" He had lied before. Would Wheatley believe his ignorance when it was legitimate?

"I was hypothesizing," Wheatley said.

Was he? Darien couldn't be sure. It wasn't important. "I see," he said. *Spit it out*, he prodded himself. *Tell the man what you've got in mind!*

"What do you know about the murder of Ivan Brooks?" Wheatley asked—a little less gently, Darien detected.

"I don't know anything about the murder of Ivan Brooks. I don't know *of* an Ivan Brooks." He didn't.

"Never mind, then," Wheatley said. "Are you reporting what you know to the police? Are you expecting *me* to?"

Here I go! Darien inwardly yawped, whipping himself up. "And what would the police do with this information? Do they have the tools to deal convincingly with the experts, moguls, and hucksters in the art world? Talk in their jargon, name-drop with conviction, win them over?"

"You're suggesting we set up a sting," Wheatley said evenly.

"Not we—you. You have the resources—human and strategic—to draw from. Above all, without exposing yourself. I am adamant about your staying safe. You think I want another death on my conscience?" He emitted a nervous laugh, which alarmingly sounded like Count Dracula's. "Above all, you've had experience along these lines." He was not sure how he was coming across. He had another swig of vodka, emptying the glass, and waited.

As did Wheatley.

Darien yielded. "I have two pieces of information to help jump-start your thinking process."

"Go on," Wheatley said, in that newly acquired neutral tone Darien found disconcerting.

"I can give you the name of a major client who passed away three months ago. I heard Gladstone talking about him on his cell phone. Manuel Garcia; billionaire in textiles and fashion; family estate in Salamanca, Spain. If the right person familiarizes him- or herself with the man and from there is able to invent personal anecdotes, quirks, things that are shared with close associates—they should be able to worm their way into Gladstone's good graces, set up a spurious deal, catch him in the act."

"Interesting," Wheatley commented. Still non-committal, but the old warmth on the rise.

"I've another bit to add," Darien said, wincing from the coyness in his tone. "The company keeps the bulk of its artworks warehoused in the Geneva Freeport, where it conducts most of its business transactions. I suspect that's where your counterfeit still life is being held."

"Unless it's been sold," Wheatley said.

"Correct. Although oftentimes new owners will choose to keep their precious new commodities in the freeport for nigh on forever, visiting them every now and then either for aesthetic pleasure or self-aggrandizement."

"You've grown cynical," Wheatley said.

"I think perhaps I always was." Darien felt a startling wave of sadness, seeming to come out of nowhere, but in all likelihood out of loneliness, made indelible by his irreversible acts. "We may not be talking again, Harrison."

"Do you plan to turn yourself in, Darien?"

"You mean *ever?*"

"Yes."

"After the maneuver. Too soon, it'll blow your cover." The words drew a weary smile. *Too soon, too late—either way, a moot point.* He was tempted to think it aloud, but didn't.

Chapter Nineteen

Erika had followed Harrison into the spare room at his beckoning wave. It was actually she who had locked the door while Harrison angled his cell phone to best transmit the decisive click to Darien.

She was the first to speak after the call had been terminated. "I sensed there was a confession of sorts, but not much else. Too bad you weren't on speakerphone."

"I couldn't take the chance. Not after Meagan's keen observation."

"I know. So fill me in. I'm on tenterhooks."

"First, what you sensed was correct. There was a confession." Harrison spelled it out for her, from Darien's commission of unethical acts at the behest of Chauncey Gladstone of Richardson Gallery and Conservation Studio, to sharing Norman Blethmore's findings with that person. "It was his guilt over having been the cause of Blethmore's murder that prompted the catharsis."

"You think he was on the level?"

"What motivation would there be to fake it?"

"None, I suppose. I take it having you play surrogate priest was not the only purpose of his call. I heard you say something about his suggesting you set up a sting?"

"Right. For justice—or, more accurately, revenge. He'd like me to coordinate it."

"Remotely."

"Very."

"Did he supply you with a bit of inside information to give you a head start?"

"He gave me the name and a detail or two of a recently deceased client of Richardson's—Manuel Garcia. Using him as a reference could give us an in. Plus, he said Richardson's keeps a major portion of its artworks in the Geneva Freeport, where the company also conducts most of its sales transactions. This is another piece of useful information."

"Backup for review. My understanding is that a freeport is where art works as well as other commodities can be held to defer payment of taxes or customs duties until they're transported elsewhere."

"Yes. It's meant to encourage trade. The commodities are considered in transit at these locations."

"What if a collector wants to keep his art—or at least some of his most precious pieces—warehoused indefinitely?"

"Many do. In fact, Darien made a point of that. By the way, the word 'warehouse' is a little misleading. It conjures up an image of a dreary place with stacks and stacks of crates filled with unseen art works, but although many works are stored in such a fashion, there are beautiful showrooms where all forms of art are brought out of hiding and admired—also bought and sold. And, of course, both the security and climate control of the facility are top-of-the-line.

"Admired, you said. But not by the public."

"Exactly. Geneva Freeport has been called the largest private museum in the world, with well over one million works of art."

"It hardly seems fair. But right now, I'm concentrating on a total of eight paintings. Does Darien think they're housed in the Geneva Freeport?"

"Darien is aware only of the existence of the counterfeit still life. And yes, he believes it's being housed in Geneva—if it hasn't yet been sold. If that's so, I'm guessing we can assume the other seven paintings went along for the ride."

"Is this where he imagines the sting should take place?"

"We didn't get that far."

"Guess we're due for another brainstorming session with Greg and John. We know the primary object of the sting—to get our hands on the paintings and the culprits to incriminate themselves—but what we need help with is finding a reasonable cast of characters to execute it, none of whom traceable to you. Adventurousness a requirement all around."

Harrison smiled. "You're probably cooking up plots as we speak."

"Multiple." She leaned over the side of the wheelchair and gave him a hug—slightly awkward, her nose bumping into the top of his head, producing a yelp of pain from her.

"Oh, no!" he cried. "Are you okay? Let me look at you!"

She jiggled her nose. "I'm okay. What an idiot." She stood before him, let him get a good look at her. "See?"

"Being around me is a dicey business," he said, on the edge of meaning it. "But I'm getting there. I tried bearing weight on the right leg again—this morning when you weren't looking. Not the most pleasant experience, but I didn't sound any alarms this time. By tomorrow, I'll be hobbling to the bathroom."

"As long as you'll let me accompany you."

"You have my word. I'm looking forward to being challenged. Physical therapy on the right leg begins in a couple of days. I've made arrangements with the ortho team to whom the Brits sent my records over at Langone Medical Center. Home visits, twice a week for six weeks."

He patted the cast on his more seriously damaged left leg. "Physio on this one begins in about five weeks."

"You amaze me. You have such a positive attitude."

"Don't make me blush. Let's shoot a couple of emails to Greg and John, arrange a secure Zoom meeting ASAP—well, we'll give Greg a chance to catch his breath; after all, he just left for home at dawn this morning. Alright. Then, we should get back to the Greenwich journals. Remember, we were going to have another go at them. The Laszlo auction catalogue references an anonymous certificate of authenticity issued in 1871, and the data Greg picked up from Global Arts Research, invaluable though it is, is missing any reference to an original authenticator."

"Wow. You're actually hoping we'll find something in the Jackson women's journals that'll give us a clue as to who that person might be."

"Why the quizzical look? Didn't you just commend me for my positive attitude?"

* * *

Fifteen minutes later they were settled in Harrison's study, each of them with the five unopened PDF documents on their laptop screens.

"First, let's get oriented," Harrison said. "Can we assume that the Scotts, the original purchasers of the eight paintings from Paul Durand-Ruel in 1871, are the perpetrators of the deception? That this couple conspired to pass off—or pass *on* to their daughter—two Monet paintings and 'x's six' as the dealer referred to them, as a set of *eight* Monet paintings?"

"We can assume that, yes," Erika said. "The notes in Marylou Jackson's journal certainly point to that. Not only did the couple apparently hide the paintings from view, but their story about what took place at Durand-Ruel's gallery in London is so different from the trustworthy dealer's reference to the event, there's really no rational choice but to conclude that they're the culprits."

"Agreed."

"One other thing—something obvious, but easy to lose sight of..."

"Don't leave me hanging."

"The six paintings by 'x' Durand-Ruel refers to are not forgeries. They're the works of a painter for one reason or another he chose not to identify. They did not bear Monet's forged signature at their inception. The dealer, Durand-Ruel, distinguishes the paintings from the two Monets. He never would have sold counterfeit Monets. His reputation was as untarnished as—well, as Ivan Brooks's. It was only the *signatures* on those six other paintings that were tampered with, most likely by the Scotts, or by an expert hired by them!"

"Sharp observation," Harrison praised. "'Something obvious,' as you say, but I, for one, needed reminding."

"Are we ready then?"

"We are. I propose we embark on a serious read-through rather than try to come up with more off-beat words to search. Let's start with document number three, Marylou's account from 1868 through 1876. If we're going to find anything of relevance, it's probably going to be within that time period. Granted, it begins three years before the octet's sale and certification, but we might as well start there. I'll read from 1868 through 1872; you, from 1873 through 1876. If we come up empty-handed, we can read through Marylou's earlier entries and her daughter, Tess's, later ones. Are you in agreement?"

"Yes."

Harrison pretended to raise a glass in the manner of a toast, and they dug in.

* * *

The eureka moment—or what irresistibly felt like one—came twenty minutes later, with Harrison's whooped "Yes!"

Up to that moment the only sounds in the room had been their breathing and reflective hmms and ahs, and Jake's occasional grunts as he shifted around in the knee-hole of Harrison's desk. Harrison's exclamation made Erika jump.

"Search the word 'Renaissance,'" he directed. "It'll take you right there. Only beware, my excitement may have been premature."

Erika's search time-warped her back to Wednesday, August 14, 1872. She read the text in which the word "Renaissance" was embedded. Then, read it again. "Your excitement was definitely not premature," she concluded. "It was mature as hell!"

He smiled. "We probably never would have hit on this passage if we had stuck to the hunt-and-peck system of research."

"I realize that, yes." She scanned Marylou's commentary once again.

What a tragedy! Dr. Ryan Jacobs, one of our regular sojourners during the summer months, has perished in a boating accident early this morning. RJ was the Associate Dean of a most prestigious Academy (PAFA) in Philadelphia. Although his field of expertise was the Renaissance, during his summers with us he taught classes in life drawing and portraiture, both of which were filled to capacity months in advance. He and my friends, A and JS, had grown quite fond of each other over time, and frequently sailed together on Long Island Sound in the couple's boat. Today, only RJ and JS were aboard the small vessel, when, according to the distraught JS, the wind suddenly changed and the mainsail swung to starboard, its boom striking RJ in the head, causing him to fall overboard. In desperation, JS dove underwater repeatedly as the boat sailed out of reach, finally seizing hold of his friend and swimming to shore with his limp body in tow. He was still trying to resuscitate the man when the emergency team arrived. I spoke to my friend earlier this evening. Despite her husband's valiant attempt to save poor Dr. J, he is apparently wracked with guilt, blaming himself for setting forth in questionable weather and not being "agile enough"—his very words—for effecting a rescue.

"We're assuming 'A and JS' are Abigail and James Scott," Erika said.

"We are. And I've come across this shorthand several times in the text, where it's unquestionably the couple Marylou is referring to—referencing their London trip and James's optometry practice."

"And 'PAFA' refers to an art academy."

"Pennsylvania Academy of Fine Arts, the oldest art museum and art school in the country. It was founded in 1805 by the painter Charles Wilson Peale and the sculptor William Rush, among others. Am I lecturing?"

"No, but I don't mind when you do. You have an unpatronizing way about you. I find it comforting."

"Not an especially feminist reflection, but I'm flattered."

She smiled. "Let's not lose the thread. I'm wondering if your scenario gibes with mine, or if I'm the only one pushing the reality envelope."

"Let's check. The first thing that comes to mind is that Dr. Ryan Jacobs doctored the signatures on six of the paintings the Scotts purchased in London, and the following year, maybe because his conscience was beginning to bother him and he was ready to spill the beans, he was conveniently eliminated in a boating accident."

"Yeah, we jibe."

"Which means we're both fantasists." He shook his head. "Greenwich, Connecticut, was a haven for artists. We find one artist associated with the Scotts, and we demonize him? What were we thinking?"

"One artist who dies in Mr. Scott's company, let's not forget."

"So you're suggesting we throw caution to the wind."

"I'm curious to see where it blows us. Yes."

"I love your audacity. Never fails to energize me."

"Good to hear. Now, if we could find out the name of the expert on record who certified the authorship of the eight paintings purchased by the Scotts, we'd be getting somewhere. Seems like it should be the easiest thing to do, except that we'd be sticking our necks out if we approach any of the people who know the answer."

"Yes, exactly." He noticed Erika had begun wrinkling her brow in consternation or contemplation. He wasn't sure which. "Tell me."

"I think I know the person I can approach," she replied tentatively.

He tried to guess what was coming.

"Lois Keller, Morris Keller's ex-wife."

"Are you serious?"

"Yes, but hold that thought. Don't you want to spend a little more time going through the journals before we log out? At least search the records for another mention of Dr. Ryan Jacobs?"

"You want to keep me dangling, I see. Sure. Let's do it."

One other reference to Jacobs was found in the journal: a brief notice of the memorial service in his honor hosted by the yacht club. Nothing about him the Wheatleys didn't already know.

"What about Lois Keller?" Harrison asked as he punched out of his email app. He wasn't about to "hold that thought" a moment longer, especially since it was bound to be the harbinger of another of Erika's risky schemes.

"I've already had a conversation with Lois," she said, "and I can assure you, she's got one goal, and that is to get her hands on the painting her ex promised he'd give her. If she thinks I can in any way facilitate this, she'll divulge the name of the 1871 authenticator on record. That is, if she knows it."

"You have the physical advantage. I'm in no position to duct tape you to the chair. Promise me you won't be meeting this woman face to face."

"You have my promise. "I'll phone her. I'll put the call on speakerphone. You can stay by my side, see that I don't arrange to meet her in the dark alley of her choice. How's that?"

"What are my options?"

"None, as far as I can tell." She shot him a sly smile. "Although duct-taping me to a chair sounds interesting."

He was preparing for a comeback when he was alerted to a FaceTime call coming in on his laptop. It was from Madame Denise Fontaine, their nonagenarian Parisian friend, who bore a remarkable likeness to his beloved grandmother, or was, in fact, her embodiment. As was the case with his grandmother, he was incapable of withholding information, however sensitive, from Madame D—Denise, as she demanded to be addressed by him and Erika. Unfortunately, Denise had not yet been informed of his recently sustained injuries. *I'm in for it now!* his last thought before greeting her nicely sculpted chin: "Hi, there, Denise! You want to adjust the screen so we can see your lovely face?"

"Hey, Denise!" Erika chimed in, shutting her laptop and moving her face close to Harrison's in order to be in Denise's eyeshot.

"Hold it, my dears…that better?" Her face now in full view, she turned to address the visible denim-clad hip to her right. "You can leave now, Gretchen. I'll let you know when we're done here." The hip vanished. "*Now* then! How is my precious *famille américaine?*"

"We're doing well," Erika said, seeing that Harrison was struggling for an answer. "And how are *you,* Denise?"

"Fit as the proverbial fiddle, provided no one dares pluck it. And how is my great-godson, the little charmer? Available for an audience?"

"Lucas was to go for a walk in the park with his nanny, Kate, after breakfast.

Maybe they haven't left yet. I'll go check." Erika placed her laptop on the chair seat and hurried out of the room.

"You're silent as a clam, Harry," Madame D remarked. "What are you keeping from me?"

The woman was a bloodhound. "Well, I…"

"*Mon Dieu*, I see the side handles! Remove your arms from the armrests at once, Harry. Thank you! Yes, as I suspected, you're in a wheelchair! Hold the lap device so I can see your lower half. Oh, *mon cher fils*, what happened to you?"

Erika stepped back into the room to hear Harrison's lame reply: "An accident, Denise. Don't trouble yourself. I'm on the mend."

"That was the most disingenuous answer I've ever heard come out of your mouth, dear boy. Where is Erika? Perhaps she'll be more forthcoming. Ah, here she is," she said as Erika took her seat. "Empty-handed, I see. No matter, I'll catch up with Lucas another time. What in heaven's name happened to Harrison? He's being most evasive."

"I suggest you inquire no further, Denise. He's not being coy; he's being protective of you."

"Unacceptable. At my age, risk is a stimulant. I demand an explanation."

Harrison could no longer keep the truth to himself. "I'll tell you everything, but only if you promise not to take action in any way, shape or form."

Madame D uttered a staged chuckle. "You know better than that, Harry. When have you known me to play a passive role?"

Never, Harrison thought, as he recollected her active participation in several of his and Erika's sleuthing ventures. "Never," he repeated aloud, before dutifully reviewing in detail the events leading up to the biker's assault, along with the relevant encounters that followed. Erika, while smitten by the relationship between these two, worried about what dangerous business Denise would be cooking up for herself after hearing Harrison's exposition.

"I must get to know all about Manuel Garcia," were Denise's first words at its conclusion. Ignoring Erika's fretful sigh, she added, "This will be very useful when I apply for an interview with Mr. Chauncey Gladstone of

Richardson Gallery and—what was it? —Conservation Studio."

"You're not planning to travel to London," Erika inquired, omitting the inflection in her voice to communicate the ludicrousness of the question. She looked toward Harrison for support.

"Of course she isn't," Harrison said.

"Of course I *am*!" Denise objected. "Did you think I was going to execute my scheme via one of your infernal remote applications rather than in the flesh? No, indeed. It is a tête-a-tête encounter where I shall perform my mischief. Mr. Gladstone will be put off guard by my frailty, which serves as a disguise without my need to dress up. To boot, my establishment is a tattoo parlor with a long history of having been a fine prints shop. What better front for an eccentric old woman in the business of shady art dealing?

"Which is, my friends, exactly how I intend to present myself. And if you are concerned that the journey itself will be unduly taxing, put the thought out of your collective mind. Unlike you, my dear Harry, the wheelchair is my natural habitat." She slapped her delicate hands on the armrests of her wheelchair. "It befits me, does it not? In addition, with Gretchen, my receptionist, coming along as my assistant—my *aide*, I shall call her—my guise of helplessness will be complete. People—men especially, I believe— have a habit of conflating physical frailty with witlessness." She threw up her hands, and the loose sleeves of her blouse dropped to her elbows, revealing her bony arms. "I am exhilarated by the very thought of it all!" she sang.

"Denise, dear, no," Harrison pleaded, and Erika caught her breath at the overtones of regret and guilt. "You must not."

"Don't be mawkish, Harry. It does not become you. With Erika's and your help, I intend to get Mr. Gladstone to incriminate himself and put us in contact with the eight absconded paintings. Which brings to mind the necessity of my being wired for the occasion—or occasions. How shall we facilitate this?"

Harrison did not adhere to the philosophy of determinism. He believed one's fate is not written in the stars, and the exertion of free will has an effect on how things turn out. The exception to the rule was Madame D, a force of nature not to be crossed. In order to have any influence on the force, he must first concede to it. "Wiretapping isn't the same as it used to be," he said, stifling all signs of *mawkishness*. "Or as it's still sometimes portrayed in movies. No longer is the transmitter fitted with a device with straggly wires taped to his or her chest, only to be revealed in a dramatic moment when his or her shirt is ripped open. These days a tiny recorder can be camouflaged by as small an item as a pen or a key fob, virtually unnoticeable."

"Excellent," Madame D remarked. "Although it might be wiser to stick with the outdated method. After the shock of ripping open my blouse and seeing my bare chest, with or without wires, our target will be ready to confess to anything."

"Ah, Denise, we've missed you," Erika responded, mid-laugh.

"I miss you, too. It's your turn to visit me, you know."

After the close of their last case, the Wheatleys had had the pleasure of entertaining Madame D as their guest for a time during the summer. "It'll be a while," Erika said. "Harrison will be undergoing physical therapy— recovering. But, yes, that sounds great—for all of us, Lucas included. We'd love to visit you in Paris. Harrison?"

"Wonderful idea," Harrison said, somewhat tentatively. "It will be something to look forward to."

"I caught your trepidation," Madame D said. "Relax, my dear, I will survive the event. Now, let's give ourselves a little time to think on it and refine our plans. Can I count on you or one of your cohorts to secure on loan one or two valuable oil paintings to use as bait, should it be deemed useful?"

"I...believe so," Harrison said.

"Well, put on your thinking caps. Meanwhile, I'll do my research on the deceased Spaniard, Manuel Garcia. Gretchen will serve as my docent on the computer. Are we ready to call it a day? I don't like protracted goodbyes. They depress me."

"Let's talk again in a day or two," Erika suggested.

"Excellent," Madame D replied. "Gretchen?" she shouted.

Gretchen—or a segment of Gretchen—appeared on Harrison's screen.

"Would you be so good as to turn me off? Thank you, dear."

Harrison's screen went dark.

"It's what she wants to do," Erika said afterward, responding to Harrison's anxious look. "She thrives on it. Let her be."

"That's the outlook I try to maintain, but it's not easy."

"Taking your mind off Denise's daredevilry may help. I'm about to call Keller's ex, Lois, to see if she can come up with the person who certified the eight paintings the Scotts purchased from Durand-Ruel."

"Don't jump the gun. Focus on the still life removed from the Laszlo auction."

"I'll keep that in mind; see what feels comfortable."

"It's helping, by the way."

"What's helping?"

"My angst about Denise's recklessness is easing up."

"Transferring to your concern for my safety, you're trying to say."

He nodded. "But go ahead, get it over with. However, reminding you of your word, I am not leaving this room. I want to hear everything you two are saying."

"As agreed." Avoiding further badgering, she promptly tapped "L Keller" in her cell phone's contacts file and punched in the number. *C'mon, answer!* she silently pled, activating the speakerphone.

"What do you know, the one person I didn't try to reach, and here you are!"

The couple exchanged looks of disbelief.

"To what do I owe this unexpected, but welcome, greeting?" Erika asked.

"Took the words right out of my mouth. As for myself, I have been trying to make contact with anyone who can give me a lead on the Monet painting Morris promised me. An incomplete list includes the formerly friendly agent at Galaxy Fine Arts Insurance. Also Mr. Ben Laszlo, Morris himself, our mutual estate lawyer, Morris's divorce lawyer, even his preferred picture framer. I have been stonewalled by everyone. It never dawned on me to call you. My word! To what do I owe the pleasure of your—wait, *is* it a pleasure?"

"I'd keep the word 'pleasure' on hold," Erika said. Our goals are different, but we're in perfect alignment. We can help each other."

"CONFIDENTIALITY," Harrison mouthed. "GIVE NOTHING AWAY." Funny to see his lips moving as if he were yelling to someone at the other end of a football field.

"Our conversation must be kept between ourselves, Lois. I remember you saying you had a tendency to shoot your mouth off—your words—and this has me worried. This is a scary case, and we want to stay clear of any unsavory characters involved in it. Do you understand the seriousness of my request—I'm sorry, my *order*?"

"Completely. I know how to keep my mouth shut, too, I assure you. What exactly is the nature of the case?"

"For your own safety, I'm not going to discuss it," Erika said as she watched Harrison's shoulders relax. "Would you like to tell me the name of the painting you were promised? I can keep a special eye out for it."

"Of course. *Picnic on the Lawn.* It was love at first sight."

"I'll remember that. I have only one question. Do you know the name of the individual who verified the authorship of the painting—or any of the eight paintings you yourself alluded to?"

"Not offhand."

Erika's heart sank.

"But it must be noted somewhere in the papers I have on file. I made copies of all the documents associated with the paintings, from Morris's father's purchase to all the insurance data. Do you want to hold on while I look through them, or shall I call you back?"

"Oh, I'll wait," Erika said, hope soaring.

"You sure? This may take up to fifteen minutes. Maybe more."

"I'm sure."

The Wheatleys waited in silence, afraid to make a sound lest it be overheard by Lois. Of course, it was understood that Erika was not working on the case in a vacuum, but the sound of them talking would break the illusion that she did, even encourage Lois to share their interchange with others. To connect, they held hands. Like children, Erika thought. She wondered if Harrison felt the same way. Neither looked at the time, but it must have been at least twenty minutes before Lois came back on the line.

"How long did I take?" she asked. "I didn't look."

"Neither did I," Erika said. "Any luck?"

"I came across the expert's name in the papers Lewis Keller received when he bought the group of Monet paintings in 1927. From the woman listed as Elizabeth Barden née Scott," she added—languidly, Erika perceived, as her heart raced. "The name given is Ryan P. Jacobs, Ph.D."

"Aha!" Erika whooped unwittingly, grateful Harrison had maintained control over his vocal cords.

"Are you surprised?" Lois asked, sounding perplexed.

"Only that you were able to come up with the name. I was wary of approaching anyone else but you for the answer. I'm trying not to draw attention to myself. You must do the same. This is for your safety, Lois. I'm dead serious."

"I got the message earlier on, Erika. I'm not a slow learner. May I ask how your knowing this name will help locate my painting?"

"Lois, no. I'm sorry. I—"

"Never mind, I get it. It's difficult, but I will hold my curiosity in check. I do thank you. You must understand that and forgive my impatience. I'm counting on you to get to the bottom of this, Erika."

"I'll do my best, Lois."

When the call ended, Harrison breathed a very audible sigh of relief. "You know how difficult it was not to make a sound?"

Erika smiled. "I could tell how badly you wanted to engage. Thank you for not. So, now we know for sure the Scotts are responsible for the fraudulent signatures on the six paintings created by another artist."

"True. And also that Lewis Keller and his son, Morris, were in all likelihood unaware of the fraud."

"Until recently," Erika qualified. "I think at the least Morris Keller was informed of the fraud by Chauncey Gladstone, who coerced him into dealing with him as a broker or be ratted out."

"Or suffer even more dire consequences," Harrison suggested, "judging from your description of his state of mind when you and John dropped in on him."

"True. And now we need to touch base with Greg and see if he can come up with a couple of paintings Denise can use in her dealings with Gladstone, although she should be in on the conversation. I can only guess what plot she's brewing." Seeing his features tense, she added, "Try not to beat yourself up with worry. Denise is going to do what she's going to do, with or without your blessings."

"Easy to say, sweetheart."

"I know." She paused for a second or two. "Harrison?"

"Yes?" What was coming?

"I'd like to brush up on my knowledge of Monet. It's been a while. What books do you recommend?"

"May I ask why?"

"Isn't it obvious? He's at the center of our investigation. C'mon."

"I've got two books in my study you might want to look through. *Monet by Himself*, edited by Richard Kendall. It contains many of Monet's letters, if you want to get a subjective take on the man. Also *Claude Monet, the Truth of Nature*, a book produced by the Denver Art Museum."

"Thanks!"

The incisiveness of her tone elicited a frisson of fear. He tried to talk himself into believing his suspicion she was up to something was a product of his imagination, already taxed by his worrying over Denise. He almost succeeded.

Chapter Twenty

On Tuesday, July 11th, eight days after her original exchange with the Wheatleys and subsequently, with their obliging friend, Greg Smith, Madame Denise Fontaine rolled into the plush workspace of Chauncey Gladstone of Richardson's Gallery and Conservation Studio, Lombard Street, London. She was accompanied by Gretchen, playing the role of her aide.

Assessing Gladstone as an unattractive man, at least in his late fifties, Madame D chose to jump right in with a sternly flattering, "You're too young to be in charge here. Are you filling in for Mr. Gladstone? I made it clear I would speak only to him." Judging from the wisp of a grin, she suspected that under the droopy lids, the eyes briefly sparkled.

Gladstone rose slightly from his chair and extended his hand across the desktop. "The man himself, Madame Fontaine." He shook her hand as if it were a brittle leaf. "Please call me Chauncey. May I call you Denise?" He sat back down.

"As you wish." She turned her head. "Gretchen, dear," she said, as Gretchen stepped to the side of the wheelchair so her purported charge could see her. "Why don't you have that nice receptionist show you the way to a comfortable place where you can sit and wait? Perhaps there's a tearoom nearby, where you can have a *spot* of it, as they say."

"I'll alert Vivien," Chauncey said. "We have a tearoom on the premises. Vivien will show her the way."

The moment Gretchen was out the door, Madame D leaned forward in her wheelchair. "Now then," she said, "before we get down to business, I must be absolutely certain that we're not being recorded. I have to trust you about this, but I'm willing to do so. As I told you when we spoke on the phone, I have been assured that your reputation is beyond reproach. You keep your word, and confidentiality is your trademark. At least according to my client, who heard it from the horse's mouth."

Chauncey nodded. "Manuel Garcia. You said your client knew him."

"Yes, indeed." Madame D had decided not to take any chances. Garcia, as it turned out, had been a very private individual with essentially nothing written about him except his obituary. Rather than grabbing a name from the obit and inventing an anecdote around it that would sound forced at best, spurious at worst, she'd decided to casually drop the name into her introductory phone call with Gladstone and hope it would serve as an entrée into his good graces. It had worked. Or maybe her charm had been the sole catalyst, she'd teased herself.

"Manuel was a stellar individual and client," Chauncey said, running a pudgy hand through his unnaturally raven hair.

Someone should tell him to go a shade lighter, Madame D thought. "I can speak with certainty only about my own client, whose stellar character I will attest to without question," she said, leaning back in her wheelchair. "Before we go any further, you have not given me your word that our conversation is not being recorded."

Chauncey offered a mea culpa, palms up. "Sorry, I thought that was understood. We are not being recorded." He cocked his head. "By the way, I like your drop earrings. My wife loves black pearl. May I ask where you purchased them?"

The question, juxtaposed with the subject of the audio recording, startled Madame D. The drop earrings had been given to her by the Prefecture of Police of Paris, more specifically by one of its members who'd bought her concocted tale of an employee planning to lodge a sexual harassment complaint against one of the tattoo parlor's regular patrons, and needing proof of it. One of the earrings was an innocent by-stander; the other, a voice-activated recording device. Startled, to be sure, but one of Madame D's strong points was spontaneity under fire. Her recovery was instantaneous.

"I'm afraid I don't know their origin," she said. "They were a gift from a cousin of mine, now deceased. Your wife and I have similar taste. I have a weakness for onyx as well. She, too, perhaps?"

"I don't know, come to think of it, but meanwhile, I would like to hear the full story of what brings you here, Denise. We spoke in generalities over the phone. It is my understanding that you've brought photographs of two Fernand Léger paintings with you, which your client would like me to authenticate. In addition, this client is interested in purchasing paintings by Monet and Renoir. There's more to it, I'm sure." He paused about ten seconds without moving a muscle, presumably to allow her to reflect on this. "Be specific—and blunt. As I said, we're not being recorded. It may ease your mind to know that I regularly check my office for bugs. I did so this morning. Enlighten me."

Madame D reached for the satchel bag tucked at her side and laid it across her lap. "Thank you for the reassurance. I will be blunt. My client is in possession of two formidable works, allegedly by Fernand Léger from his famous *Contraste de formes* series, which, as I'm sure you're aware, pressed art beyond Cubism into pure abstraction of shape and color."

"Momentous for the art world. Continue."

"The date on each of the paintings is 1913."

"So far so good," Chauncey commented.

Madame D raised a finger. "You speak too soon. These paintings have not been seen in public since 1967, when my client purchased them from an art dealer in Sweden, where they were certified by the dealer himself. It is only recently that their legitimacy has become an issue for him."

"He wants to sell them," Chauncey said.

"Yes, but he's afraid to take them to a run-of-the-mill authenticator ever since the controversy over a Léger painting of the same era ended badly."

Chauncey's nod was accompanied by a disdainful chuckle. "You're referring to the painting that had been hanging for decades under false pretenses at the Guggenheim Museum. They took a sample from the canvas's clean edge and had a particle accelerator measure its radiocarbon level. After the nuclear bomb tests in the 1950s and 1960s, the level rose, you see, in the environment and in all living things. The conclusion was that the cotton content of the canvas sample proved that the canvas was made in 1959, four years after Léger's death." He uttered another chuckle. "My guess is your client had samples of his canvasses put through the wringer, and they suffered the same fate."

Excellent! Madame D silently praised, the kudos aimed at both Chauncey's knowledge, which made it easier for her to reel him in, and also Greg Smith, for his clever choice of bait: authentic Légers, on loan for the duration of the sting from a venturesome collector. "Absolutely correct," she said, with a little clap of her hands. She smiled impishly. "Do I detect a note of cynicism in your reaction? Are we of the same mind, then? For myself, as long as the lovable mutt comes with an impeccable pedigree, my conscience is clear."

"One hundred percent, Denise. If its owner feels pleasure, even fulfillment, from a well-executed doppelganger, what does it matter whose hand produced the treasure?" He pointed at her satchel. "Let's see what you've got. If the photographs are of high quality, I'll know at a glance if the paintings are likely to meet my high standards or not. I won't put the name of the firm at risk for anything but the best of the best. Am I understood?"

"Loud and clear, my lad." *Battery, don't fail me now*! she silently commanded the pendant suspended from her left earlobe. She slipped a manila envelope from her satchel and handed it to him.

Chauncey reacted as she suspected he would. After all, the paintings were authentic and, as the dimensions written below each of the photographs attested to, quite large. He took a deep breath as if he were inhaling some paradisiacal aroma. "Excellent. I can move them within twenty-four hours, if your client is amenable."

"I'm acting as my client's proxy," Madame D said. "I dare say he trusts my judgment"—she grinned— "well, *nearly* as much as your clients trust yours. I must point out that he is insisting the paintings be entered in Léger's catalogue raisonné before I entrust them to you to pass them on. Knowing the paintings were executed after Léger's death, are you willing to accommodate us?" She smiled slyly. "Remember, you advised me to be blunt, Chauncey. I am being blunt."

He smiled in kind. "Of course, I will see to it the paintings are authenticated by an expert and become part of the catalogue raisonné. What did you think? This will increase my commission and, let us say, *accommodation* fees tenfold. Yours as well, I imagine. As a pair, I predict they'll bring in around a hundred million."

"My client will be pleased. This will enable him to fund—*begin* to fund—his lofty ambition to enlarge his collection of Impressionists; most lacking in the persons of Monet and Renoir, most particularly Monet. Do you have the wherewithal to launch his journey, sir?"

"I do. But be aware, all plans are in the wishful thinking phase. Until I see the Léger impersonations in the flesh—"

"And I, your proclaimed Impressionists—"

"To be sure. Until then, there will be no negotiations. Are you able to make a trip to the Geneva Freeport? It's where we hold our assets and those of a number of our clients."

Madame D gave her armrest an affectionate slap. "Give me a chance to oil my wheels, and I'm on my way."

Chauncey gave a hearty laugh, causing his bulbous nose to flush. "We need to agree on a date and who is to be present on site."

"This will require some thought. May we postpone this discussion to, say, two days from now—Thursday afternoon?"

"I'm good with that, but not much later. I'm willing to keep the paintings I have in mind on hold for up to six days."

"Make that tomorrow afternoon, four o'clock my time; three, yours."

"Much appreciated. And what can I do for you at the present moment?" He glanced at his watch. "I believe you have two and a half hours before your train leaves for Paris."

"I could do with a spot of tea," Madame D answered at once. "If possible, spiked."

Chapter Twenty-One

Wednesday, July 12th. Madame D had just ended her conference call with the Wheatleys, Greg Smith and John Mitchell in preparation for her scheduled plan-finalizing call to Chauncey Gladstone, coming up in fifteen minutes. It was exactly 3:45 p.m. in Paris. 9:45 a.m. in New York.

* * *

At that very moment, Hilda Huebner, the Kellers' housekeeper, was climbing the staircase to the door to her employers' townhouse on Pineapple Street, Brooklyn Heights. She felt a bit winded from the modest climb, but blamed it on the extra slice of apple pie she'd had for breakfast. She was sixty-eight years old and nowhere near meeting her savings for retirement goal. Slowing down was inconceivable.

Hilda fetched her key holder from the inner pocket of her tapestry handbag, out of character for her simple tastes, but a cherished gift from her late husband, who, if he were watching over her, God willing, would be pleased to see it put to daily use. As she was selecting the key to the Keller residence amongst her own, she noticed the door was an inch or two ajar. She had been coming to work three days a week at this location for the past ten years, a stint that spanned the changing of the guard, as she privately referred to the marital shift, and this was the first time she'd been faced with this particular circumstance. She reviewed her options and chose the one that did not make her out to be a fool or a coward.

"Hello, there!" she called as she pushed the door open and stepped inside. Silence greeted her.

"It's me, Hilda. Hello?" She shut the door behind her. Immediately, she felt trapped. *Grow up!* she mutely scolded herself. Mr. Keller had probably rushed off without seeing the door had been properly shut. Between him and Naomi, he was the more careless of the two.

Be that as it may, Naomi Keller had always met Hilda near the entryway with a scrawled list of assigned chores for her to complete before the end of her workday at 2:00 p.m. Where *was* she?

Perhaps below, in the kitchen, fixing herself a late breakfast. Hilda headed for the staircase. With her keys still clutched in one hand, the strap of her handbag in the other, she started down the rather steep flight of steps without holding onto the railing on either side. Her heart was still aflutter from her precarious descent when she turned left at the bottom of the staircase and entered the kitchen proper.

She opened her mouth to scream, but only a deep-throated grunt emerged, as if from an imposter. Morris Keller lay sprawled on the floor, arms splayed out at his sides, one seeming to stretch for the broken coffee cup just out of reach. Her heart raced as time stood still. Morris was wearing a linen suit she had never seen—brand new, never worn? —its jacket flung open, as if to avoid becoming stained by the blood pooled on the right side of his chest, ruining for good the eggshell white shirt she herself had no doubt washed and ironed. Was he breathing? She snapped out of her paralytic state and dove for the cell phone in her bag. As she let the keys drop into the bag, she noticed the red puncture marks they had made in her palm.

She punched in the numbers 9-1-1 robotically. It was either that, or neuronal chaos. Her voice, when she recited her name, the reason for her call, and the address to where an ambulance was to be sent, maintained that same dissociative control. When the agent asked her if Mr. Keller was breathing, she said she didn't know and that she was afraid to go near him and contaminate the crime scene, which she said she was certain it was. When asked if there was anybody else in the house, she said she didn't know. Only after the call ended did the full impact of the agent's question hit her.

She might have bolted then, but she was a woman who, once committed, saw the situation through. "Help is on the way, Mr. Keller!" she assured the inert figure in the powerful voice she used to communicate with her deaf aunt. Did she see his closed eyelids twitch in response, or was it her imagination?

Hilda trundled up the steps to the main floor, then up another flight to the bedrooms, all the way calling out Naomi's name. Finally, as she was about to try the door to the first of the two hallway bathrooms, she heard a tremulous voice from within. "Hilda, are you alone? Is he gone?"

"Is who gone? Open the door, dear." She assumed it was locked.

The lock clicked and Naomi opened the door a crack. "Is my husband okay? *Morris.* Is he okay?" she whispered hoarsely, still unseen, from behind the door. "Come in, come in." She opened the door wider, grabbed hold of Hilda's forearm, and pulled at it. "Hurry!" When Hilda was fully inside, Naomi re-locked the door. "Be careful. The floor is wet. Morris. Did you see him? *Answer* me!"

"I saw him, yes. He is in the kitchen. He's been…injured. I've called an ambulance. They should be here in a few minutes." Hilda had never seen Naomi without makeup, uncoiffed, and unattired. With only a bath towel wrapped around her wet, shivering form and water dripping from her hair onto her bony shoulders, she may not have looked like a drowned rat (although the image came to mind), but she did look—what was the word? —diminished. "You must dry yourself off and put on some clothes, Miss Naomi. You must be *ready*."

"I was taking a shower," Naomi said, unheeding. "When I shut off the water, I heard Morris yelling at someone, and then I heard a shot!"

"You'll explain all that to the police. Come, I will walk with you to your room. Then I will go downstairs and wait for the ambulance. I assure you, whoever was here is gone." *Was he?*

"I have to see Morris!" Naomi cried, as she fumbled with the lock, at the same time holding the bath towel in place. "Is he dead? He can't be dead!" When the door opened, she started toward the staircase, Hilda huffing after her. "He can't be dead!" Naomi repeated. "I won't allow it!"

Hilda caught up with Naomi before she reached the landing and took hold of one of the hands clamped onto the bath towel. "Go to your room, please. You can't go dripping water on the scene. There may be a shoeprint or a drop of the assailant's blood. Evidence must remain intact!" She sounded to herself like a detective from one of the TV murder mystery series she was hooked on, but it got Naomi's attention.

The sound of sirens was heard as Naomi decided to act on Hilda's directive. "Don't let them take him away without me!" she cried, as she took off down the hall.

"Then hurry up, Miss," Hilda urged as she scurried to the staircase. She was itching to add *never mind the fake lashes*, and hoped God hadn't read her mind.

* * *

"You said this happened earlier this morning?" Harrison asked in disbelief when John broke the news to him and Erika—who was standing beside his wheelchair and listening to the words amplified by the speakerphone.

"Knocks your socks off, doesn't it? Maybe ten, ten-thirty this morning I was checking in with my guy working the Murray Hill precinct; seeing how the Brooks homicide case was progressing. Told me the Brooklyn Heights crew had just dropped a bomb on him."

"You said Keller had emergency surgery to repair the lung, but not how he fared. Is he expected to live?"

"Touch and go. The bullet was removed, and he's got a tube suctioning out air, fluids, and blood from the lung and heart area. The trauma was compounded by a heart attack, which sent him into a coma. As of a half hour ago, he hadn't come out of it. He's at NYU Langone-Brooklyn, in a private room in the Intensive Care Unit; intubated, IVed, monitored—the works. They've got a security guard posted outside the room. Nobody's allowed in except select staff and the wife, who I hear hasn't left his side. Refusing food and water and won't take something to calm her nerves. Going to need an IV herself if she keeps this up." He paused. "I don't mean to sound heartless, but how's this going to affect the Geneva Freeport operation? I would assume Morris Keller would have wanted to be on hand."

"I imagine his wife—Naomi—might consider going in his stead if his condition improves, and he wishes her to represent their interests," Harrison said. He glanced at Erika. She was being uncharacteristically quiet. It had him worried.

"Doubt she'd be willing to leave his side," John said. "Besides, sounds like she's in no shape to travel or make decisions. Guess they can have a proxy act on their behalf."

Still, not a word from Erika. "You'll keep us up to date on the situation, yes?" Harrison checked with John.

"Will do. Ciao, my man."

The call ended without a peep out of Erika, and Erika was not one to drift off. "What the hell!"

"What?" she replied, all innocence.

"You didn't say a word."

"You were handling things beautifully," she said, the words dripping with pretense.

"Cringe-worthy," he said.

"I know. I should have just come out with what was on my mind, but I was dreading your reaction."

"You make me sound like a tyrant."

"I don't mean to make you feel like a tyrant."

"I don't. I said you make me *sound* like one. I'm in no mood to parry, Erika. Out with it."

She took a deep breath. "I've decided to accompany Denise to Geneva."

He held his emotions in check—*tried* to—by extracting his thoughts and enunciating them clearly and succinctly. "You were rehearsing for this role all along. That is why you chose to *brush up*, I believe you said, on Monet."

"You're wrong, but not entirely," she said.

Maddening!

"My main purpose was to learn as much as I could about Monet—about the stages of his painting, the highlights of his life—in order to help you and others piece together the criminal activity centered on him. I didn't think I'd wind up participating in the sting because I assumed Morris Keller would be in attendance and he would give away my identity, which would put you in jeopardy. But I wanted to be prepared." She sighed. "So I prepared."

"Prepared to be an understudy," he suggested, trying to avoid a wry—or *any*—tone. "The hangdog look is out of character, Erika. Just state your mind without the dramatics."

"Certainly," she said, as business-like as possible. Her mood was gravitating toward resentment. Harrison's lecturer's approach she found charming. This was crossing the line to gratingly patriarchal. "Ease up, Harrison. I understand how you feel, but don't push it. Try to be objective. Now that Morris Keller will not be coming along and, from the sound of it, his wife, Naomi, will not be up to the task, it seems an opportune time for me to step in. Think of how helpful it might be if I could lay eyes on those eight paintings."

"I am against it wholeheartedly," Harrison said. He realized his attempt to eliminate passion from his tone was producing one equally untenable. "I'm afraid for your safety. It's as simple as that. At least, by your logic, John would be able to accompany you as your bodyguard—no matter what role he's given to play."

Erika cocked her head. "Well, you're right about the logic of it—I mean, John wouldn't be recognized by any of Chauncey's crew either, but I don't think so. What role would he play? Lawyer? Art expert?"

"And what role would *you* be playing?" Harrison retorted. "Remember, Chauncey is in the attribution department at Richardson's. He knows his stuff. If you say you're an expert, he's apt to throw all kinds of scientific jargon at you regarding the latest methods of testing the authenticity of paintings, just to see if you squirm."

"No problem. I can take over Gretchen's role. Denise and I can invent a good story. All I'll need is a fake ID. We'll be fine." As Harrison threw up his hands, she grew suddenly pensive. "Only one thing is holding me back."

"Thank God."

"I don't want to leave you alone. Kate will be busy with Lucas, and Grace is too frail to help you out physically. And I already know you'll never consent to having a professional come in to stay with you, even during the day."

"True."

"But wait. Kate's fiancé is in town. He's a nice, big guy. I'm sure he'd love to hang out here a couple of days, and you can't very well refuse to have him as a guest. His presence in the house will make me feel secure." She lit up. "And oh, yes, the physical therapist will be coming several times a week to begin therapy on your right leg. We'll make sure the first visit coincides with my absence."

"Who would be watching over you in Geneva, Erika?" he asked resignedly, not yet giving in, but foreseeing it in the future—the near future.

"I know with their connections Greg or John will see to it an agent from the Swiss Customs and Border Security is present under one guise or another. You know, since 2022, there's been a big push for increased cooperation between the US and Switzerland in the prevention of money laundering."

"You've been cramming for this event. Admit it."

"I thought I already had. How about we make a deal. I promise I won't embark on this journey unless we're assured someone in law enforcement is right there on the scene. Deal?"

"I wish the hell I could be with you," he complained bitterly.

He watched Erika beam. Well, of course. That answer was as good as a yes.

Chapter Twenty-Two

One more time, Madame D checked that her recorder earring was securely attached to her earlobe. *"Es tu prêt?"* she directed at Erika, who was emerging from the rear of the tattoo parlor's tight living quarters, where she'd spent the night. The rationale for Erika's sleepover was that flying together on a morning flight from Paris to Geneva would best support the bare-boned cover story they'd concocted for the operation.

"Yes, I'm ready," Erika said. She spread her arms. "How do I look? Too much?"

"You look like a Bohemian. Is that what you were going for?"

"More or less. The clip-on nose ring was an afterthought. I bought it online." She had swept her hair up into a tortoiseshell clip and was wearing John Lennon-type round glasses, a loose-fitting long-sleeved coral knit sweater, black maxi-skirt, and black high-top sneakers.

Madame D had on her go-to black mourning attire, reminiscent of Whistler's mother.

"Votre taxi est arrive!" Gretchen called from the establishment's reception area. She had insisted on coming in early to see off her boss. Erika wondered if she'd felt a smidgeon of jealousy toward her for having usurped her role as escort.

Ten minutes later, Madame D's folded wheelchair had been installed in the trunk of the taxi; she and Erika, in the vehicle's back seat. The driver's GPS had been set on Charles de Gaulle Airport. Estimated time of arrival: 8:12 a.m.

* * *

After an hour and ten-minute flight, the Air France Airbus carrying Erika and Madame D touched down at Geneva Airport. The limo driver Chauncey Gladstone had hired to collect them was waiting at the gate, holding a sign that read "D. Fontaine." Erika pointed the wheelchair in his direction.

"Here I am," Madame D announced on arrival. "This is my wheelchair, if you're wondering, not the airline's. It is manually driven and may be legally stowed in the cabin portion of the aircraft, unlike its more cumbersome, electrically-run brethren. We may, therefore, be on our way at once. This young woman is my house guest, Ellie Silverman. What is your name, my good man?"

"Joshua, Madam. Good day to you both." Apparently acting on Madame D's bid for haste, he led them off at a trot to his awaiting vehicle.

* * *

Joshua must have called ahead, because fifteen minutes later, when they pulled into the industrial stretch monopolized by the Geneva Freeport, two uniformed female guards were waiting for them in the cordoned-off parking area reserved for individuals with special permits. Erika was expecting to undergo a thorough security check, complete with metal detector wand and pat down. Instead, after Joshua had set up Madame D's wheelchair and helped her into it, the duo delicately probed the contents of her satchel and Erika's own slouchy Hobo and apologized for the inconvenience. Joshua, his job done, bid the women "a pleasant day" and drove off.

The day did seem to be aiming to please, Erika thought. The temperature must have been around eighty degrees, and though the sunlight reigned supreme, unobstructed by natural growth on this sprawling terrain, its sole purpose appeared to be sacrificial—to spend itself on melting these fortress walls and freeing the treasures within to public view. The dull gray and tan façades of the sprawling complex glowed with the sun's gallant attempt to warm the compound's cold heart, but the mica particles or whatever caused the persuasive glow and inspired Erika's errant thoughts did nothing, in the end, to change reality. This was an unwelcoming fortress meant to keep the public out. How different from the temples of art, with their exterior displays designed to draw the public in—the Louvre, with its grand colonnade; the Metropolitan, with its sculpture-adorned niches, the changing display now on annual commission; the Prado, with its bronze statue of the artist Diego Velázquez greeting visitors at the main gate.

Erika was already harboring resentment for the place as she followed behind the guards and steered Madame D toward one of its drab entrances. The mood only deepened as they entered the facility and were led through pristine halls lined with either rows and rows of wooden crates or long metal drawers containing who-knows-what imprisoned creations. The sheer quantity was staggering. To think that forty percent of this monument to secrecy was comprised of over a million artworks estimated at around 100 billion dollars. Kudos to Madame D for managing to keep to herself the florid protests Erika could only imagine were at the tip of her tongue.

An elevator ride to the third floor, a turn to the left, and halfway down another hall of anonymous gray storage units, they arrived at a wide metal door in keeping with the character of the warehouse—unmarked, unwelcoming. One of the guards tapped something on her cell phone—a text, a code? —and the door was opened several inches by someone behind it. "All good?" a man's voice clipped.

"Yes, Mr. Gladstone," the guard answered.

"Thank you. You are free to go."

The pair marched off.

"And here we are!" Chauncey Gladstone greeted, swinging open the door to its full extent. "You complete our party, Denise—and Ellie, I believe? Come, come!" He waved in the wheelchair driver like an impatient garage attendant.

Erika's breath caught at the sudden presence of color after the bleakness of what had preceded it. It was like coming upon a hidden garden. The cut pile carpeting, the color of mown grass; the plush chairs in soft rose and lavender; the walls a deep gray-green, from which the magnificent paintings beamed forth in competitive glory. Four men other than Gladstone were standing about, hardly detracting from the effect. She recognized none of them.

"At last—how lovely!" Madame D cried, capturing Erika's sentiment. "And yes, this beautiful young woman is indeed Ellie—Ellie Silverman. I mentioned she was coming along."

"Only briefly. What is your connection exactly?" He looked Erika up and down. "Chauncey Gladstone," he added, honoring her with his identity. He touched the door with his forefinger, and it slowly swung shut.

"Ellie's great-grandmother, an American studying abroad, and I were classmates at King's College, London," Madame D said. "We never lost touch over the years. When I heard Ellie was coming to Paris to scope out the art schools—"

"Let's allow Ellie to continue," Gladstone suggested with a slow-motion blink of his reptilian lids.

"I'm looking to apply for an advanced degree in fine arts," Erika said, winging it, wishing she hadn't gone along with Madame Denise's maxim, "spontaneity is the best means to deception," and had been more thoroughly prepared. "I'm looking around for the best fit. I thought being on the spot would be ideal. Madame Denise was kind enough to offer me a place to stay." She smiled broadly—gave it her all. "I'm also thrilled she brought me along today." Her smile narrowed. "Although I think Gretchen might have been a little jealous."

"I take it you're impressed with the venue," Gladstone tossed out, more and more acting her superior.

"I'm literally blown away," Erika enthused. "Reading about the Geneva Freeport is one thing. Seeing it in person, quite another!" She set her features in what she hoped was an otherwise sophisticated adult's star-struck look— lips slightly lax, gaze unwavering.

Gladstone granted her a stingy smile. "Let me introduce you ladies to the present company."

The men who up to this point had not deigned—or dared—to open their mouths simultaneously offered the women a hodge-podge of hellos and fell into line before Madame D. Gladstone posted himself at one end of it. "First, let me properly introduce *you*, dear lady. Madame Denise Fontaine is the owner of an elite tattoo establishment in Paris. She represents the anonymous individual who is seeking to purchase the eight Monet oil paintings you see hanging on the wall to your left. The said individual's decision will depend, in good measure, on this good lady's discerning eye. In addition to his role as an aspiring buyer, Denise's client is the owner of the two Fernand Léger oils hanging on the wall adjacent and is anxious to sell them. In the latter transaction, if it should come to pass, Denise and I will serve as co-brokers, and our respective commissions will be deducted, according to convention, from the sale price. As for the sale of the eight Monet paintings presently owned by one Morris Keller, I alone shall be serving as broker. Whatever Denise is to receive from her client as a finder's fee is between her client and herself and is both none of my concern and"—humble chuckle— "none of my business."

"Well put," Madame D stated, folding her hands in her lap. "Now, who are these patient gentlemen standing before us?" Addressing the group, she inquired, "Am I to assume one of this fine quartet is my client's legal advisor, Mr. Leon Boucher?"

A tall, fit-looking middle-aged man in a beige, unstructured suit raised his hand. "Guilty as charged!" he replied.

Unexpected jauntiness from a man in his position, Erika thought. The pseudonymous Leon Boucher was, in reality, an agent in the Swiss Federal Office for Customs and Border Security (FOCBS). John Mitchell, using his deputy agent status on the FBI's Art Theft team, had approached the FOCBS in the hopes of stirring up interest in the Geneva Freeport sting. The fact that Switzerland and the United States had been forming ever-deepening ties in their attempts to fight such crimes as money laundering, theft, and fraud in the art market had helped John's argument for joint participation. "That, and my engaging personality," he'd jested.

"Happy to meet you, Mr. Boucher," Madame D said, extending her hand. "I hope you're as smart as you look."

"Oh, at *least*, Madame." He smiled, bending to shake her hand. "Call me

Leon."

"And you may *all* call me Denise," Madame D grandly bade, releasing her hand to sweep it in front of her.

Gladstone gestured toward the next attendee in line, a lean, smooth-faced man who looked to be in his early forties and who wore a double-breasted power suit and his hair flat against his head with a severe part in order to look either tougher or more earnest. "Victor Simms is Morris Keller's legal representative," Gladstone said. "I know I speak for all of us when I express my sincerest hope for Mr. Keller's speedy recovery."

Nods and yeses all around. Erika wondered if all present actually knew what had befallen Mr. Keller.

"Victor is here to keep me on my toes," Gladstone went on. "Next, we have Police Officer Marcel Meyer of the canton of Geneva." He moved in front of the man in question. "*He's* here to keep me *honest!*"

The remark was greeted by an obligatory chorus of chortles, including from the officer himself, a hulking young man with a grim resting face that made a one-eighty when he smiled. "Officer Meyer has been good enough to appear in casual wear since he is even *more* formidable in full regalia," Gladstone said.

So there are two, *not* one, *crime stoppers among us*, Erika thought. How she wished she could update her anxious husband!

"For those of you who might not know," Gladstone said, looking directly at Madame D, then at Erika, still gripping the handles of the wheelchair, "there are twenty-six regions, or cantons, in Switzerland. Each has its own police agency, independent from federal authority. The Geneva canton is the Freeport's major shareholder and leases it to a private company that runs it. As you can imagine, the canton has a major financial interest in the facility." He wagged his finger impishly at Madame D. "We must, therefore, be on our best behavior."

"I hardly have the resources to behave otherwise," Madame D replied, shaking her finger back at him. Focusing on the gentleman as yet unannounced, she asked, "And who may *you* be, young man? You look as impatient as I feel. Are the paintings calling to you as they are to me?"

"You're observant," the man said, not quite at ease. He ran his hand over his shaved head and down a scruffy cheek. "I should like to get down to business. I am here to answer any questions you may have regarding the authenticity of the Monet paintings and also, at the request of Mr. Gladstone, to give my final judgment on the… legitimacy of the Léger paintings. The pair arrived late yesterday afternoon, and I, only this morning, so I have not had time to issue a definitive answer."

Oh, they're authentic, all right, Erika voicelessly responded. Ever-dependable Greg Smith, with his highly respected position at Art Loss Register, had come through again, this time successfully courting Max Rayburn, the wealthy art collector who'd attended Laszlo's fateful auction a month ago. Rayburn had left in a huff after Monet's still life had been eliminated from the event, and Greg thought that if he were promised first dibs on the painting after it had been recovered, he might be willing to cooperate in the sting. There was no need for Greg to drum up excuses for keeping him in the dark about the nature of the operation because Rayburn under no circumstances wanted to hear a word about it, only that his Léger paintings would be returned to him unscathed. Harrison, always eager to mete out, for a worthy cause, the unearned wealth he'd inherited from his grandmother, had offered to foot the bill for shipping and insuring the paintings' transport to and from Geneva, but Rayburn had insisted on remaining in control of this critical phase of his artworks' adventure.

"I say we stop dawdling and get down to business, as this sensible man has suggested," Madame D stated. "No need to push me, Ellie. I'm fine on my own in limited quarters. Your goal is to explore the art. Go take it in." She placed her hands on the wheels to propel herself forward, but stopped herself. Addressing the man she'd just been talking to, she said, "I haven't gotten your name. What is it?"

The man heaved a sigh of resignation, as if he thought he'd gotten away with not having to reveal it. "Darien Roth," he mumbled.

Erika's heart skipped a beat.

"Your place of business?" Madame D inquired.

"I teach at the Courtauld Institute in London."

What is he doing *here?* Erika wondered. Had Gladstone made it impossible for him to leave the fold? Would that explain his pained look? Where did his allegiance lie? Did he even *know?* She rummaged for answers. "The Courtauld was one of my choices before I settled on Paris," she said, forcing herself to say something bland in case she'd gone ashen.

Madame D apparently had had her fill of preliminaries. "Onward!" she sang, giving her wheels a push to set her chair in motion. "Out of the way, gents!"

There was no choice but to roll with the punches, Erika decided. She'd react to whatever transpired as best she could. Meanwhile, she was determined to study the eight paintings—entered in Durand-Ruel's ledger as "two Monet pictures plus x's six"—as undistractedly as possible in order to retain as many details as she could. Notes and thumbnail sketches would have been of service, but there were clearly unspoken protocols in place. As she and Madame D approached the paintings, Gladstone had deftly swiped both their bags from them—Madame D's satchel from her lap, Erika's Hobo from her shoulder—and delivered them to the hardwood table desk set against the blank wall, where comparable items belonging to the other attendees shared space with a bronze statue of a discus thrower, along with an assortment of writing materials and documents. To boot, there was not a cell phone in use or in sight.

Madame D drew up to one of the two seascapes.

Erika began her study with the painting at the start of the turmoil: *Wedgewood Vase with Flowers.* The wave of sensory delight instantly swept aside, at least for the moment, her tension over how the day would play out. When she'd first seen the painting in crisp reproduction on the cover of the Laszlo auction catalogue, she'd thought that its colors were probably as vibrant as they were in their original form. And maybe in the strictest sense, they were, but when seen in three-dimension, the texture of the brush strokes affecting the reception—the *play*—of light, they came alive. The gladioli, with their variations of purples and mauves; the pinks and reds of the lilies…she imagined fingers gripping a brush, the delicate application of paint…what was it about the painting that touched her so deeply? She focused on the goddess strumming a lyre in the center of the vase. Here, too, a delicacy of touch—the artist's as well as the goddess's—see the tentative tilt of her head—such a minor detail, but significant somehow. A youthfulness about it. That was it.

"Heads up!" Madame D alerted Erika as she moved to the next painting—to her right and right beside Erika. She began maneuvering her wheelchair into the proper viewing angle. Erika made an attempt to help her, but she shooed her off. The men, who were sitting about waiting for the transactions to begin in earnest—all but Darien Roth, who was exploring the two Léger paintings with a magnifying glass—rose to their feet en masse to come to her aid.

"I can manage on my own, thank you!" Madame D balked, swinging the wheelchair around, forcing Erika to leap out of the way. "Sorry, dear. I was distracted."

The men retreated and the preparatory study continued, Erika concentrating next on the painting she assumed must be the one titled, on the list provided by Greg, *Picnic on the Lawn*. This was the painting Lois claimed had been promised to her by her ex-husband. It was an impressive painting, both in size and subject matter. Erika wondered how the individuals casually sitting, reclining, and standing about on the picnic grounds were related to either Monet or the mystery artist. Friends? Relatives? Models? She tried quite literally to take a mental snapshot of the canvas, refining her gaze as if it were a camera lens, going so far as to inwardly utter the word "click" when the image became crystal clear. She had never tried anything remotely akin to this trick, *but who knows*, she mused, *maybe this is how the brains of people with photographic memories work without their being aware of it.*

While Erika was attempting to commit, one by one, all eight paintings to memory, Madame D was touring the display in a more haphazard manner, studying one or two paintings at length, others briefly; returning to look again at those she'd paused opposite for the longest time.

"May I have a word, Chauncey?" Madame D blurted without warning, backing off from the painting undoubtedly titled *Girl at the Piano*. "In private," she added as he approached.

Erika deliberately kept her eyes glued to the painting in front of her to avoid drawing attention to herself. "Over here," she heard Madame D quietly instruct him. After an extended interval, during which a low-voiced exchange must have been going on, Madame D praised, in her normal voice, "You're absolutely right, Chauncey. I yield."

Darien, who, like Erika, had been totally unheeding of the exchange—and maybe for the same reason—removed one of the Léger paintings from the wall, turned it over to take a look at the reverse side of the canvas, and hung it back on its hook. "I've concluded my examination," he said, his voice a dull monotone. "In my opinion, these oil paintings are those of Fernand Léger." Erika watched him walk over to the table desk, lay the magnifying glass on it, and lower himself into the nearest vacant chair. He appeared to have aged ten years.

"You may steer me to the congregation, Ellie," Madame D advised. "Maneuvering on this dense carpet has been more of a workout than I thought it would be."

"Of course." Erika pushed the wheelchair toward the men, stopping it alongside Gladstone, who stood facing the seated foursome. Thrusting out his chest, he announced, "I believe we are ready to begin our negotiations. Denise has indicated to me that based on the recent acceptance of the eight Monet paintings into the artist's catalogue raisonné, as well as her in-person examination of the paintings today, she is ready to open the negotiations with an offer on behalf of her client for the lot of them. I, in turn, after Darien's positive assessment of the Léger oils, am ready to reach out to a Léger enthusiast of my acquaintance who is certain to snap them up—I suspect by day's end."

Marcel Meyer, introduced as a canton of Geneva Police Officer, sat forward in his chair. "Are the respective financial institutions on standby, ready to execute the deals expected to go down?" he asked, the naturally down-turned corners of his mouth curling upward in a cheerful grin, coming across as an unexpected elevation of mood. Erika caught herself smiling.

"The New York branch of Morris Keller's financial institution is closed at this hour," Gladstone said, "but its branch in England has been open since early this morning, and my personal account executive has left her day open for us. She will deposit to his account the funds received from Denise's client, less my commission, which she has been instructed to deposit to my account." Turning to Denise, he said, "When we have agreed on a price for your client's Léger paintings, I will transfer the amount, less our commissions, to his account. How does that suit you?"

The pseudonymous Leon Boucher, stand-in for Madame D's client's lawyer, gave a grand nod, as if he were playing it to the balcony. "Should suit you to a T, Denise. What do…*you* say?"

"I say that sounds like my cue. Well done, sir." She carefully unsnapped the clasp of her left pearl drop earring and removed the earring from her lobe. "Very heavy, this one."

Her cohort rose from his chair and extended his hand. "Here you go, Mr. *Boucher*," she said, handing him the earring. Wincing, she rubbed her ear lobe. "And none too soon, I might add."

Gladstone spun around to face Madame D. "What the hell's going on?" he asked, his anger sounding more tentative than aggressive, as if he was not ready to believe what he already knew.

"Have you found the button?" Madame D asked her compadre.

"Right beside the USB connecting interface," he said. "Here we go."

"That was a yes-no question, Chauncey," Madame D's taped voice uttered— softly, yet surprisingly distinct and true to the real thing, given the size of the recording device. "Don't confuse me."

"*What?*" Gladstone shouted, no longer in denial.

"Again. What do you think of the Léger look-alikes?" Madame D's taped voice sounded.

"Close to authentic as it gets," Gladstone's taped voice responded, just above a whisper, but clear as a bell. "Pretty damn flawless."

Gladstone's rage seemed to have turned him to stone.

"Are you able to pre-date their entry into Léger's catalogue raisonné?" Madame D's recorded voice gently rose. "I think it will appear to be more genuine."

"Yes," came the assured answer. "And what do you think of our Monets?"

"Lovely." After a second's pause: "Tell me, Chauncey, which ones do you take to be the imposters?"

"I'll never tell," his recorded reply followed. "That way, you can admire them equally and be less apt to reveal—"

"Turn that damn thing off!" Gladstone shouted, returning to life. Looming over Madame D, he seethed, "How the hell did you get this fucking lawyer to play into your entrapment farce?" He bent lower, glowering, their faces almost touching; she, refusing to flinch. Without waiting for an answer, he snapped to attention. "Give it here!" he ordered the man in possession of the recorder.

"I think not, Mr. Gladstone. Let me introduce myself. My name is Oliver Schmidt, agent with the Swiss Federal Office of Customs and Border Security."

"Bullshit!"

"Hardly batting an eye, Schmidt responded. "My credentials are on the premises, in safekeeping with the Freeport's insurance consultant. His extension is eight-seven-three. Feel free to call him. To continue. With reasonable suspicion of your having misrepresented the authorship of art works, and furthermore, for your having expressed a clear intention of perpetrating fraud on one or more consumers of said art works, I have the authority to bring you in for questioning, with or without your consent."

There were three men present who had not yet contributed to the exchange. They were speechless, as Gladstone had been, but unlike their host, they had been physically animated—faces shifting into exaggerated phases of shock and alarm, like actors in a silent movie.

Suddenly one of them leaped out of his chair—the individual that had been introduced as Police Officer Marcel Meyer, representing the authority of the canton of Geneva. "You heard the man! Hand over the effing recorder to Mr. Gladstone. Now!" No smile arose from the somber resting face this time around, only grim turning grimmer.

Erika's heart was racing, but still, she was thinking ahead, trying to decide on a move, physical or verbal. But first, who was this man? *Surely not a police officer! Gladstone's strongman? One of his hitmen? God, no—the biker who hurt* Harrison?

"What the hell is going on, Schmidt, or whatever the hell your name is," Victor Simms cried. "Are you implying my client's paintings are forgeries? While Mr. Keller is lying in a hospital in critical condition and unable to defend himself?"

"I'm on it, Simms!" the man thus far claiming to be a police officer snapped. "Keep your mouth shut!"

"Present your proof of identity at once!" Agent Schmidt ordered.

Gladstone's champion whipped a wallet out of his pants pocket, flipped it open, and held it up in front of Schmidt's face. "Take a look. There's a magnifying glass on the table. Take a *closer* look!"

Erika laid her hands on Madame D's shoulders in protective assurance. In reciprocation, Madame D reached back with her right hand and, after a decisive pat, placed it on Erika's left. Steady as can be.

After a quick appraisal of the ID presented to him, Schmidt's facial expression was proof enough. Marcel Meyer was who he said he was. "Your behavior is unbefitting an officer of the law, sir. You'll be obliged to explain yourself to the Federal Office for Customs and Border Security."

"The FOCBS has no authority over me. You could use a refresher course, old man." Officer Meyer shoved his wallet back into his pocket, reached further back under his jacket hem, and—Erika saw it coming from where she stood—pulled a gun from his belt. Aiming it at Schmidt, he said calmly, "Easy now. Let's not lose control of the situation. There are ladies in the room. Who knows what could happen? Hand over the recorder."

"No way."

Meyer swung his arm forty-five degrees left to point the gun at Madame D's head. "Care to rethink that? Hand it over."

"You wouldn't dare," Madame D, cool as a cucumber or putting on a good act, directed at Meyer. "You're hurting my shoulders, Ellie," she said, breaking her train of thought as Erika's grip tightened in a useless attempt at urging her companion to be silent. Finishing the thought, Madame D asked Meyer, "How would you explain bumping off a helpless old lady to your superiors?"

"Touché. Giving them a scare is all." Meyer swept the revolver back in Schmidt's direction. "Gutsy lady, right? Time to stop playing games, Schmidt. Hand over the device."

"Give it to him!" Madame D demanded with show-stopping sternness. It was a voice used by a parent who meant business. *Trust* me."

It sounded to Erika like Madame D had something up her sleeve, or better still, an ace in the hole. She hoped Agent Schmidt had gotten the idea as well.

Whether he had gotten the idea, or out of fear of escalating the situation, Schmidt extended the hand clutching the drop earring and opened his palm. "Here. Now put the gun down."

Without budging the hand holding the weapon, Meyer reached out with his free hand to retrieve the recording device.

Diving forward, Gladstone grabbed it out of Schmidt's palm. As the group looked on in anxious curiosity, he strode to the table desk, pushed aside a few scattered items to form a clearing, and in it, placed the earring. "Fuck this," he snarled. He picked up the bronze discus player, and with three carefully aimed strikes with the edge of the statue's base, crushed the offending object.

It was difficult to assess the reaction in the room beyond sheer surprise. Erika waited for a definitive response. She expected one was coming and wondered how she would play into it.

"Before any of you get any ideas," Officer Meyer warned, I have the right of way here. Anybody thinks he or *she*"—with a piercing glance at Madame D— "can shoot their mouth off about what they heard here, think again." He twirled the gun around on his trigger finger like a Hollywood cowboy, ending the spin with the gun once again pointed at Schmidt. "Fact is, I could take any of you out, including Agent Schmidt here. All I have to do is testify that after making false accusations of forgery in an attempt to blackmail the parties engaged in a peaceful transaction, you resorted to violence when your efforts appeared to be failing."

"How unoriginal," Erika heard herself saying, "since blackmail is already *your* game. That is, if it isn't a mutual agreement you have with Mr.

Gladstone. You cover for him; he gives you a kickback." So much for the wise advice to keep silent, she had tried to convey to Madame D!

For one long instant, it was impossible to predict what would happen next.

And then Officer Meyer erupted in a hearty laugh. "Damn, this one's as gutsy as the old lady!"

"And then some!" Madame D added.

"I bet!" Turning serious, Meyer pointed the gun haphazardly at one, then another of the group. "Are we ready to continue the proceedings in an orderly fashion?"

"No, we are not," Madame D said. "I must inform you all that Mr. Gladstone and I had a most revealing conversation six days ago, at which time he made a number of comments as incriminating as those he uttered today. I was wearing the recording device on that occasion and—"

"And it has been destroyed," Meyer said.

"Don't complete my sentences, young man. No, it has been saved." She frowned. "What's the word I'm looking for?" She glanced at Agent Schmidt for help.

"Download?"

"That's it, download. We downloaded the conversation."

"You downloaded the conversation to your phone?" Gladstone asked. "Then let's find that phone." He grabbed her satchel from the table desk.

"Of *course* not to my phone. The phrase 'we downloaded' was a figure of speech. I wouldn't have a clue how to download my own name, let alone a conversation. It was downloaded by the Prefecture of Police of Paris onto a computer at its headquarters, where it remains in safekeeping." Again, she glanced at Agent Schmidt. "Your Federal Office for Customs and Border Security has an excellent rapport with our Directorate-General of Customs and Indirect Taxes, I believe."

"We do, yes."

Gladstone sought Meyer's attention with a panicked look.

"I'll take care of it," Meyer assured him, adjusting his aim more accurately at Schmidt's head, possibly as a warning, possibly with deadly intention.

With a movement so unexpected and quick, Darien Roth's passage from his chair to Meyer's erect form seemed not to have taken place. The gun fired as Meyer hit the floor, the bullet striking high up on the wall opposite. Darien, lying across Meyer's body, reached desperately for the gun.

Like a bear startled from his winter's sleep, Meyer let out a growl and flipped Darien, helpless as a turtle, onto his back, holding him down with his free hand, gloating as Darien kicked and punched blindly, failing to make contact.

No more than five seconds had gone by since Darien had initiated his attack. During this time, Victor Simms had fled the room, Gladstone and Schmidt had stepped closer to the combatants—from the look of it, each preparing to make his move—and Madame D had placed her hands on the wheels of her chair and pushed forward an inch or two, whispering "Gladstone," just loud enough for all to hear, but not loud enough for anyone to attend to, what with the commotion. Except for Erika, who knew Madame D well enough to know what was on her mind—not exactly, but close enough. One way or another, they were going to attempt to impede Gladstone and improve Schmidt's chance of overtaking Meyer unopposed.

Erika pushed Madame D in the direction she had indicated they should go—toward Gladstone. He wasn't far, at most three or four feet away. His back was toward them, and his attention was glued to the men going at it on the floor. As the wheelchair drew up behind their target, Madame D reached for a lever on the outer right side of the chair and gave it a yank. The metal footrests snapped up into their extended position, whacking Gladstone on the back of his legs, and as his knees buckled, Agent Schmidt, who had been distracted by the floor fight as Gladstone had been, sprang toward him and caught him under his arms, hoisting him to his feet only to get proper leverage to deal him a massive punch to the jaw.

Agent Schmidt unceremoniously dropped Gladstone's limp body to the floor. No need to check if he was out cold.

Meyer saw Schmidt coming. Darien, pinned on his back and still struggling to land a blow, could not have seen Schmidt, Erika realized, as she instinctively flung herself protectively over Madame D. What Darien *must* have seen was Meyer's *response* to whomever he saw coming: the eyes widen, the hand holding the gun jut forward, the trigger finger poised. Without knowing who was about to be upon them, only that this person was about to be shot, Darien reached up and grabbed Meyer's gun arm, shoving it to the side, at the same time attempting to turn to his side just enough to allow him to reach out and secure Meyer's lethal arm with his other hand as well. He had nearly managed it, Erika saw, but as Schmidt descended on them, Meyer's hand swung free. In a mighty effort to prevent Schmidt from being shot—if he indeed knew, in that millisecond, that it was Schmidt he was attempting to save—Darien rose up like a breaching whale and brought Meyer down, and as he did so, a shot rang out.

An anguished howl arose from the heap—not from the victim, Darien Roth, but from Oliver Schmidt. "Fucking damn!" he cried, wrenching the gun from Meyer's hand, training it on him as he rose to his feet.

Meyer shifted to a more balanced sitting position. "Son-of-bitch attacked me. Had it coming to him."

Schmidt tautened the arm holding the revolver. "Not a sound out of you. Don't move a goddamn muscle!"

Erika glanced anxiously from Gladstone, still out cold, to Darien. "You okay?" she asked Madame D, needing confirmation before rushing to the wounded man's side.

"Go!"

Darien was lying by Meyer's feet. His suit jacket was flapped open and he was pressing a hand to his chest to staunch the flow of blood. "We're getting help," Erika said, crouching by him. "Hold on. You know you just saved a man's life?" Sounded idiotic—but *anything* would have. She sprang to her feet.

"Phone!" Schmidt barked.

"Didn't bring one—yours?"

"Right pants pocket!"

She jumped to his side. Retrieved the phone. "Password!"

He gave it to her. She punched it in.

"Dial one-one-two. Ask for police and medical assistance. Freeport's main office will direct them to where we are."

Erika followed his directions and rushed back to Darien, detouring to grab a throw pillow from one of the chairs. "Stay awake, Darien," she said, gently lifting his head and placing the pillow under it. His eyes were closed, and his hand had fallen away from the chest wound and lay on his abdomen. Erika pressed down on the area with her own hand.

"Harder!" Schmidt directed. "Harder than you think is sufficient! Use both hands!"

She placed her left hand on top of her right and compressed the area as hard as she could. "They're coming, Darien. Stay awake!"

Darien opened his eyes and lay his bloody hand on hers. "It's okay," he said, patting her hand—comforting *her*! "He good? Schmidt?"

"He's fine. You saved him."

"Good, good. No more. It's over. Gladstone?"

"Out cold."

He smiled weakly. "You'll see to it, won't you?" His voice fading.

"See to it?" she repeated, feeling like a fool for not instinctively knowing. But how *could* she know?

"Ezra. You tell him I'm sorry. I didn't mean him to…"

"Darien?"

"Be a good boy, Richie."

No, no. She exerted more pressure on the wound. Had she relaxed the pressure? She panicked. "Darien!"

"He's fucking dead," Meyer said.

Gladstone stirred, his groan mocking the sound of grief.

* * *

The detective and police officers arrived on the scene ten minutes after they'd been summoned; same time as the emergency medical crew. Gladstone had fully gained consciousness by that time and appeared to be fine—physically—but the authorities decided to have him hauled off to the local hospital for evaluation before grilling him, after which, Erika supposed, he would be expedited to England, where his fate would ultimately be determined. Or not. Maybe not. Her mind was in turmoil; her concerns bouncing in and out of focus. How was Denise holding up—*I mean, truthfully?* Would Meyer's colleagues believe his story? Where had Victor Simms run off to? Was Harrison worried? To shield her identity, she hadn't brought her cell phone with her and had called him on Denise's phone only once before they'd left Paris. Had Lucas cried for her? The paintings—who was in charge of them, Agent Schmidt? And Darien, the steady rumble beneath it all. Why hadn't she compressed the wound more forcefully? What if she *had*?

One blessing, a small one. For whatever reason—maybe their uncontested innocence—she and Denise would be interviewed on the premises and dismissed.

There was blood on her hands—Darien's blood. She asked the detective if she could wash it off. An officer escorted her to the restroom and waited outside the door for her.

She looked in the mirror. "I want to go home," she confided to her Bohemian likeness. *I want to go home!*

Chapter Twenty-Three

"Mommy, you're back!" Lucas exploded, running out the door to greet her.

"Yes, I am!" Erika sang out, an octave higher than her normal voice. He ran into her arms, and she picked him up—her son, still in one piece!—and clutched him to her chest.

And there was Harrison, supported by two crutches, standing—*standing!*—albeit on one foot, the left leg stuck out like a footballer frozen in mid-kick— at the front door, dressed in a T-shirt and those useful oversized sweatpants.

Twenty-six hours earlier, her interrogation at the Geneva Freeport had been drawing to a close. After that, she'd accompanied Madame D to Paris, stayed with her overnight, and taken a morning flight back to New York. It was noon in her world, dinnertime in Madame D's. Who could believe it?

She put Lucas back down, and he proudly helped her pull her carry-on to the door and pop it over the threshold. "Thank you, honey!"

"Back safe," Harrison murmured, embracing her with his eyes, aware of the tragedy that had taken place, but grinning helplessly. She'd called him from Paris before her flight had left for New York and had told him what had taken place, omitting details. That would come later. "I wish I could hug you, but I'd fall over," he said.

Erika cupped his face in her hands and kissed him lightly on his lips. "I can't believe you've advanced to crutches."

"I've been working on it."

"How was your physical therapy session?"

"Good. I asked him when I could expect to get on one of those anti-gravity treadmills Jeremy Renner used after his snowplow accident."

"And?"

"He told me not to get ahead of myself; that the doc said it'll be about three, four weeks before I'll be ready for even *partial* weight-bearing with the left leg. Never mind that. What's important is that Lucas has been a big help to me—right, Lucas? Tell Mommy about this morning."

"I made Daddy breakfast, and I brought it to him in bed."

"Fantastic!" Erika praised. "What did you make?"

"Orange juice and toast and ice cream."

Harrison cocked his head. "Aren't you forgetting something?"

Lucas scrunched his brow. "What?"

Harrison briefly let go of the crutches' hand grips and fluttered his fingers in the manner of falling rain. "On the ice cream?"

"Sprinkles! I put sprinkles on the ice cream! Kate said it was too much, and so did Kate's boyfriend, but Daddy said it was just right. Kate's boyfriend went home last night. Daddy said I'm a much better helper, right Daddy?"

"Right, you are. And now I think I'd like to sit down for a bit. Let's take the elevator up to the living room. You can have play time and then lunch, and Mommy and I can talk about some grownup stuff. How's that?"

"Okay—wait. I forgot to tell you, Mommy. Jake stole some of Daddy's ice cream. It was vanilla. Chocolate is bad for dogs."

* * *

After checking in with Grace and Kate and delivering Lucas to their care, Erika and Harrison rode up to their bedroom, her carry-on in tow. Jake was lying at the foot of the bed. He jumped off to greet Erika as vigorously as his old bones would allow.

Harrison dropped gratefully into his wheelchair, and Erika propped his crutches against the wall alongside the headboard.

"Let me give you a proper hug," he said.

She bent toward him, and they languished in a mutually rejuvenating embrace.

"Now, tell me the whole story," he said. "Not the elevator pitch. You made it back, and you're standing in front of me so I can take anything." He maneuvered the wheelchair close to the bed. "Sit."

She sat down on the edge of the bed. "First, tell me how Morris Keller is doing," she said.

"Last thing I heard—yesterday—is that he hasn't regained consciousness, but that his vital signs are stable. Interpret that any way you like. His wife, Naomi, is by his side day and night."

"I'd like to be there when he wakes up," Erika said, as if it were a done deal. To his look of surprise, she replied, "My excuse, I'll tell him what went on in Geneva. After all, he was supposed to have been there. I'd like to see his reaction when I tell him six out of eight of his paintings are not Monets."

"You're assuming a lot. Keller's ability to communicate. His willingness to communicate with *you*. His *wife's* willingness. Permission from the guard sitting outside his room—"

"I know all that. I'll check how he's doing tomorrow. No harm in trying."

"Are you trying to deflect, darling?"

"From what?"

"From telling me all about what happened in Geneva."

"Maybe. It was a horrible experience. Darien's death is haunting me. I was pressing down on the wound—the Customs agent told me to press harder, harder, and I did, but what if it wasn't hard enough? What if I let up, even for five seconds?" She pressed her fingers to her temples, if only to press *something*.

"Oh, sweetheart, please don't! You couldn't have done anything more!"

"I know that. The medical team—they said nobody could have saved him—but still!"

"It was a traumatic experience, Erika. That's what you're reacting to—the sheer trauma of it." He rolled closer, reached out, and grasped her legs just above the knees. She was wearing jeans, and he wished he was touching her more directly, as if that might make his words more convincing.

"I know, I know," she said, laying her hands on top of his. "I'll be okay.

Maybe it'll help to talk it through—what happened in that room, I mean. Even afterwards—determining the fate of the paintings—in whose custodial care they'll be while all the legal issues are sorted out, who's in charge of verifying their authorship—*everything*." She took his hands in hers and raised them to her lips one by one, kissing them ceremoniously before placing them back in his lap. "First of all," she began. "I know I told you on the phone last night that Denise is doing fine. Still, you may be worried that she isn't. She is."

He smiled. "Good."

"She's a real trooper, Harrison. I really love her."

"Yeah. So do I."

* * *

She told him everything. From her initial impressions of the warehouse to Agent Schmidt's projections of what would happen in the days and months to come. Her narration was both a report and a catharsis. She saved the issue needing immediate attention until the end because it required an interchange.

"I have to find Ezra and Richie," she said.

"You feel obliged to pass on Darien's messages to each of them."

"I *am* obliged."

"I know—of course. The names aren't familiar to me. You?"

She shook her head. "No idea. I think his friend Meagan Dunne might know. Let's call her. We can't tiptoe around any longer. The people most likely to cause harm to us or anyone we associate with are either in custody or under surveillance. Their jig's up. We're no longer a threat. Their *hitmen* are probably the ones who should watch their backs!"

"I agree, but warily," Harrison said.

"Good enough. Listen, I don't want to upset Meagan any more than she surely is. If we call her published telephone number, will she be scared it'll be intercepted? She was so nervous on that last call."

Harrison shook his head. "If she's still worried about calls, she'll have kept her burner phone. If we call her burner phone number, it's routed through her regular cell phone number without revealing it to us. That should be of some comfort to her."

"Let's not overthink this. Would you call her now, while it's still a reasonable hour in England? And put me on?"

Harrison retrieved his cell phone from the pocket of his sweatpants, scrolled through the incoming calls until he found the number he associated with the memorable call from Meagan, and tapped it.

"Ezra Fisher was Norman Blethmore's partner," Meagan informed Erika after Harrison had put her on. Meagan had no worries about phone interceptions, but had not yet gotten rid of the burner phone. "Negligence, my excuse," she said. "I heard about Darien's death last night. If I sound a little careless—carefree? —it's because I took a sedative of some sort—I think an Ambien. A friend's offering. I was reeling with the news, you see, and…oh dear, I really am feeling woozy. Who else did you ask me about?"

"Richie," Erika said. "Are you sitting down, Meagan? You don't want to fall…Meagan?"

"I'm fine. Yes. Richie. Richard is Darien's younger brother. He's very attached to him. Poor boy's in prison for a crime—a murder—he swears he never committed. Darien has been working on getting him the best representation for his appeal. What did you say Darien said about him in the end?"

"He said, 'Be a good boy, Richie.' They were his last words. They were said with love. Richie should be told his brother was killed, saving another man's life."

"Do you want me to relay the message? It might be easier for me to reach him—and easier for him to hear it from someone he knows."

"Thank you, Meagan."

"I'm going to write this down now, so I won't forget."

Erika waited.

"Done," Meagan said. "Anything else?"

"If you could possibly give me Ezra Fisher's phone number, that would be great."

"I have their landline number in my contacts, not Ezra's cell." Meagan audibly yawned. "Oh dear."

Good enough. "Is the name spelled with an 'i-s-h' or 'i-s-*c*-h'?" Erika asked—regretting it instantly—after being told the number.

"Could you repeat that?"

"Never mind, Meagan. Thank you so much. I hope we can talk again under happier circumstances."

"Always!" Meagan replied, in what may have been her last hurrah before the sedative had its way with her.

Lest she over-think her approach to her call to Blethmore's partner, Erika did not hesitate a moment before punching in his landline number.

A somber "Ezra Fisher here" opened the exchange.

Erika introduced herself and expressed her belated regrets. She asked Ezra if he had heard that Darien Roth had been shot to death the day before. He had not. She explained the circumstances. "I was with him in the end," she said. "He wanted me to tell you something."

"Can you tell me his exact words?"

"He said, 'Ezra. You tell him I'm sorry. I didn't mean him to….' He lost the thought—or consciousness—for a second. So that's all of it."

"What do you think he was trying to say?"

'I didn't mean Norman to die!' she silently answered. "I don't want to guess the exact thought in his mind because I don't think it would be fair," she stated aloud.

"He said to tell me he's sorry," Ezra said. "He was being repentant."

"Yes."

"What the hell for? Did he kill Norman?"

"No." She wondered if she should have been so blunt, worried he'd probe for information she should not be revealing at this point in the investigation. Her fears were unfounded. He did not probe; he did not have a chance to. Instead, Harrison asked if he could have a word with Ezra about Norman, whose lecture on Pissarro he'd attended at an N.Y.U. conference—maybe seven years ago.

"*Exactly* seven years ago," Ezra corrected at the start of his conversation with Harrison. "I know because that's where he and I met. I was teaching an art survey course at Brooklyn College at the time. I followed Norm to London. I'm now at Slade School of Fine Art."

Harrison told Ezra how much he'd admired Norman and had never forgotten him.

"Nice guy," Harrison commented to Erika after his conversation with Ezra had ended. "He seemed really grateful to be talking at length about Norman, maybe because I'm a virtual stranger. He returned his cell phone to his pocket. "Listen, when you were relating your experience in Geneva, you mentioned your technique of retaining—or trying to retain—the images of the eight paintings."

She gestured toward her carry-on, standing by the recliner chair. "On the flight to New York I drew a few sketches—bad sketches—to help in the process. They're in the bag."

"We have to discuss this."

"Can we have lunch first? I'm starving." She rose from the bed and, without thinking, took her place behind the wheelchair.

"Hand me my crutches, please," Harrison said, like a child who'd just learned to walk and did not require a helping hand.

She fetched his crutches and handed them to him. "I'm so proud of you," she praised, instinctively in just the tone his request had prompted.

Chapter Twenty-Four

After lunch, Erika and Harrison decided on a change of venue—Harrison's den. It was where they kept their notes, lists, and assorted documents on the investigation and where there was a desktop on which Erika could line up the sketches of her cerebral snapshots. It was also where their collection of art books resided and where Jake's shelter—his familial womb, the knee-hole of Harrison's desk—provided him warmth and safety and where his slumbering presence cast an indefinable stability on whatever was happening around him.

Harrison waited by his desk while Erika transported the wheelchair, which provided the most comfortable resting position for his legs, down to the first floor. She removed her drawings from its seat, and Harrison lowered himself into the chair. The crutches were stowed behind the couch.

Harrison maneuvered the chair so that he'd be parallel parked alongside the rear of the desk. "Let's see what you've got," he said.

Erika stepped around to the head of the desk and sat down, careful not to disturb Jake. She moved Harrison's computer aside and lined up her eight sketches facing him. "Not a word of criticism out of you."

"Beauty is in the eye of the beholder," he countered. "Let's leave it at that."

She made a move like she was about to throw his computer at him. Turning serious, she declared, "To begin with, I did not take along a thing to Geneva that would give me away. That includes the list of eight paintings that were railroaded into Monet's catalogue raisonné by Chauncey Gladstone and friends. The list Greg gave us. Did we put it in a side drawer?"

"Middle left."

She fetched it. "Here goes." She pointed to a rough drawing of men and women, a few standing about, most sitting on a blanket. "This is obviously either *Picnic on the Lawn*, the painting Morris Keller's ex-wife, Lois, alleges is promised to her, or *Luncheon Party*. In the background, dense treetops, abundantly green with touches of yellow and white. On the blanket, an array of food and wine. All the participants are dressed formally." She pointed from one to the other, describing the styles and colors of the dresses—this one green, this one lavender." She paused. "I performed this exercise hoping it would be of some use to us. Now I'm not so sure."

"It'll come to us," he said. "Meanwhile, I'm enjoying the presentation as an end in itself. Continue."

She shrugged and pointed to another of her rough sketches. "This one can only be *Wedgewood Vase with Flowers*. It was its youthful exuberance that drew me to it. The vase is alive with purple and mauve gladioli and pink and red lilies—and wildflowers spilling over its lip—yet they're delicately outlined, as if the artist was attempting to contain his ebullience, not quite independent enough to let it fly. This scribble here represents a goddess strumming on a lyre. An innocence here, too—the pristine whiteness, the tilt of her head." Another pause. "Tell me when you've heard enough."

"Won't happen. Go on."

"Here's another sure thing. *Girl at the Piano*—although granted, my piano looks more like a footstool. The gentleman standing over the young girl at the piano is dressed in a brown suit. He has brown hair, neatly parted on the right—wait—*left* side. His forehead is slightly sloped; nose long— aristocratic, I suppose it might be called. The girl looks as if she's fifteen or so. She's wearing a dress that reminds me of our Mary Cassatt painting, *Girl in the Blue Dress*—I guess because of the age of the girl and the paleness of the blue. The dress actually appears to be white with blue polka dots, but the fabric is touched with the barest tint of blue where the sunlight is not striking it directly. The long sleeves are of the same pattern, but are transparent. I've never seen a dress quite like this in a painting. It seems summery, airy, yet formal in a way, especially by today's standards, given its billowy, floor-length skirt. The finishing touch is a blue sash tied around her waist, bow in the back, its ends trailing to the floor. The girl's slender hands are poised above the keys and"—Erika glanced from the drawing to Harrison—"What's wrong? What did I say?" If there was a look that epitomized the state of surprise, his was it.

"Nothing's wrong," Harrison said. "I want to show you something. You'll understand why in a minute." He maneuvered the wheelchair to one of the book-case lined walls, Erika walking around the desk to follow him. "If I can't find what I'm looking for here, we might be able to find the images on the internet, but they won't be as sharp." He scanned the shelves. "Let's see, the books are relatively organized—well, in groups, sort of. Art movements. Ah, here we are, fifth shelf. *A Comprehensive Study of Impressionism.* See it? Lying on its side? Can you reach it?"

"You mean can I *lift* it," Erika said, sliding it from the top of a trio of volumes of similar heft.

Harrison realigned his wheelchair alongside the rear of the desk and slid Erika's drawings out of the way. Erika lay the volume faced in his direction on the desktop and waited by the foot of the wheelchair.

Harrison headed directly to the back of the book, to the catalogue of works, finding what he wanted pretty close to the beginning of the impressive list. He heaved the bulk of bound pages to the right, then skipped forward a few pages. "Here we go."

The painting comprised a two-page spread. It portrayed a group of people seated and standing—posed—on a patio in a country setting.

It was Erika's turn to be taken by surprise. "That's the exact polka-dot dress—worn by *two* of the figures in this painting!" There was no identifying text on the display pages. She squinted at the hard-to-read signature at the very bottom edge of the reproduction; 'F,' the initial of the first name.

Harrison turned to the previous page and pointed to the reference: "Frédéric Bazille, *The Family Gathering*, 1867-68, oil on canvas, Musée d'Orsay, Paris."

Erika was dumbstruck. She'd seen references to Bazille when she'd done her cramming in preparation for her trip to the Geneva Freeport, but it had never entered her mind that the artist would serve as a clue in their criminal investigation. She turned back to the spread.

"The girl in the center of the arrangement even looks like the girl at the piano," she said.

"This is Thérèse, Bazille's cousin." He smiled. "But wait, there's more. Let me find something else for you to take a look at." He flipped back a few pages, then a few more—where he found what he was looking for. A portrait of a man reading. "Does this look like the man standing by the girl at the piano?"

"Yes, it does!"

"This is Bazille's portrait of his friend, Edmond Maître, a musician with whom he played four-hand piano compositions."

"Really?"

"Really. I'd like you to take a look at another portrait of Maître, one by Renoir. I don't think we'll find it in this book." He took his cell phone out of his pocket and punched in a few key search words. "Here it is." He handed her his phone. On its screen appeared another portrait of Edmond Maître reading. "What do you think? Which style of painting is closer to the one you saw in Geneva—Bazille's or Renoir's?"

Erika spread her fingers on the screen to enlarge the image. "Without question, Bazille's. Renoir's is much freer, the outlines less pronounced— more advanced on the Impressionist spectrum." She handed him back his cell phone. "I'm puzzled. I knew Bazille had met Monet in Paris around the early 1860s, but so had Pissarro. So had a number of *other* painters—Renoir, Cézanne, Sisley, to name a few. Who would have thought Durand-Ruel's ledger entry of 'plus x's six' was a reference to works by Bazille!"

"The Monet-Bazille tie was more than casual," Harrison said. "They shared studio space. On many occasions, Bazille provided the down-and-out Monet with cash. Bazille was Monet's son, Jean's godfather, in fact. Nevertheless, it would never have entered my mind that Bazille could have been the painter 'x' Durand-Ruel had referred to in his ledger. He didn't know Bazille from Adam, nor did he ever have any dealings with his art work!"

"So odd," Erika said. You know, I thought maybe the Manet-Monet connection was involved somehow. I'd read that their paintings had often been mistaken, one for the other, which enraged them both. But I asked myself, why would Durand-Ruel have omitted Manet's name when referencing the six paintings, and I couldn't come up with an answer, so I rejected the idea."

"The anonymity factor is an enigma no matter *who* the artist is," Harrison said.

"Focusing on Bazille, you think maybe we're barking up the wrong tree?"

"What I'm thinking is, maybe we wandered into the wrong forest!"

Chapter Twenty-Five

"Here's my first sedentary assignment of the day," Harrison announced at breakfast the next morning. "I'm going to track down the person at the Metropolitan Museum of Art in charge of determining which six of the eight paintings were fraudulently attributed to Monet."

"And report our thoughts on Frédéric Bazille?" Erika asked as she buttered her bagel. "I thought we'd tabled the subject for the time being."

Harrison took a sip of his coffee. "We did, but I don't want to sit idly by while you gum-shoe about town. You're planning to drop in on Morris Keller at Langone, Brooklyn, come hell or high water. Am I right?"

"You are."

"And ,of course, you'll be allowed to see him since you checked with the nurses."

"Well, no. I decided if they tell me over the phone that I won't be allowed, they will be even less accommodating when I arrive in person."

He flashed her a wry smile. "They don't stand a chance with you. Tell Morris I said hi."

* * *

Morris Keller had been moved out of the intensive care unit to a private room. He was making progress by leaps and bounds, the head nurse informed Erika—conscious and breathing on his own. However, he appeared to be somewhat agitated. This was worrisome. She was reluctant to allow Erika to visit the patient for fear of agitating him further. She would have a word with his wife. Mrs. Keller's feelings on the matter would help determine her verdict.

While the nurse was seeing to the patient's needs and incidentally conferring with Naomi, Erika was to wait in the visitor's lounge at the end of the hall, just outside the ward proper.

The lounge was comfortable yet uninviting. Erika sat down on one of the padded leather chairs. She was the only person in the room. She gazed at the abstract canvas whose prominent color matched the wall paint—or vice versa. In her tailored navy suit, white silk blouse, and conservative low-heeled navy pumps, she felt like she was waiting for a job interview—and not likely to get the job.

"Erika, come," the nurse beckoned from outside the lounge's archway.

Erika stepped up beside her. "Is there a problem?" she asked, seeing the nurse's troubled expression.

"I'd say so, yes. When I informed Mr. Keller you were here to see him, hoping he'd understand, he became very excited."

Erika was incredulous. "*Excited* excited, or excitable?"

"*Excited* excited. At the very mention of your name. His wife tells me they met you once, and only briefly. Is this true?"

"It is, but our meeting dealt with an important matter."

"May I ask the nature of your meeting?"

"It's a pending case"—double-checking the nurse's name badge—"Cayleigh—so I'm not at liberty to say."

"I see. Well, Mrs. Keller believes her husband is in shock and behaving irrationally and is worried your presence will stress him further."

"And what do *you* think, Cayleigh?"

"I'm inclined to agree, but I think my not allowing the visit might cause the patient even *greater* stress. I'm going to override Mrs. Keller's wish to bar you from the room and hope that I'm making the right decision." She touched Erika's back. "Come along."

Cayleigh informally attested to Erika's legitimacy, but the security guard posted outside Morris's room insisted Erika show him her driver's license and let him poke around in her shoulder bag before she was allowed entry.

The moment Cayleigh opened the door to the room, Morris spotted Erika and raised his head from his pillow, only to have it drop back with the effort. He was attached to an intravenous tube, electrocardiogram leads, and a chest drainage tube. The gauze dressing covering the wound site was partially visible at the opening of his hospital gown. Nothing obstructing his mouth, however, so there was a chance he might try to convey something crucial to Erika. *Ruling out a break with reality, why* else *would he have been excited to see me?* flashed through her mind.

Naomi was sitting in a molded plastic chair jammed up alongside the bed. Since Erika had last seen her, she had gone from slender to wraith-like. She was wearing a crew-neck polo and slacks that looked like they'd been bought for her to grow into. "Cayleigh, I told you my husband is not up to seeing visitors!" she reprimanded.

Morris shook his head and flailed his arms wildly before programming them into a motion for Erika to come near.

"You'll rip out your IV tube!" Cayleigh warned. "Calm down, Mr. Keller!"

Naomi grabbed his wrist and pressed it against the top of the bed railing, holding it still. Morris winced—from pain or simple frustration. He lasered his wife with a look and, with his free hand, pointed toward the door. His lips formed the word "out" while an unintelligible rasp escaped them.

"He's delirious!" Naomi cried. "Get that woman out of here!" She released her husband's wrist. "Calm down, like Cayleigh says—please!"

Cayleigh grasped Naomi's elbow. "Look at the monitor, Mrs. Keller. Your husband's systolic is two-twenty-five. Does it matter if he's delirious? Your presence at this moment is causing his pressure to go sky-high. I understand perfectly how you must feel—all your caring, all this time. Did you hear the sound he made? I guarantee he'll be talking in no time, and we'll be able to pinpoint the nature of his disturbance. Come out in the hall, hon. Let's just let him be for a few minutes. You'll be coming back in a jiffy. I promise." She lifted up on Naomi's elbow, encouraging her to rise.

Naomi grabbed onto the bed railing with both hands. "I'm not leaving. I know what's best for my husband!"

"Maybe *I* should leave?" Erika put forth, hoping her suggestion would be ignored.

"Stay where you are. Mrs. Keller—*Naomi*—understands the situation. Don't you, hon? She just needs a moment."

Naomi clung to the railing for dear life, as if she were on a boat tossed in a raging sea.

The situation was at an impasse. An unexpected act was called for. Erika, who had been hanging back, hastened to the unoccupied space beside the bed and briefly rested her hand on the patient's shoulder. "Do you have something to say to me, Mr. Keller?"

Naomi's grip went slack; her mouth opened, but no sound was produced.

Morris tried to speak, but he touched his throat, indicating, Erika deduced from his look of exasperation, that it was too much of a strain. She supposed his throat was sore from his having been intubated. He took hold of her jacket lapel and pulled her toward him. When their faces were almost touching, he put his mouth to her ear.

"She fools them all," he whispered.

"Who?" Erika asked aloud.

"Wife. Don't leave me alone with her. Call the police."

"What the hell is she doing?" Naomi raged, finding her voice. She jumped out of the chair, prepared to spring to the other side of the bed.

Cayleigh thwarted her with a restraining embrace. "Doesn't matter what he's going on about. It seems to be calming him down."

"Stay until they come," Morris whispered.

"What is he saying?" Naomi demanded.

"Your husband wants to talk to the police," Erika said, rising to her full height.

"Really? Bring them on," Naomi challenged. "Let's set the records straight." Without a word of explanation, she strode to the narrow closet used to stow the patient's belongings and pulled open its door. Sitting on her haunches, she removed a canvas bag from the floor of the closet, unzipped it, and felt around until she found what she was looking for. She re-zipped the bag, returned it to the closet, and slammed shut the door. Rising to her feet, she held up the extracted object and waved it at her husband. "Why, if it isn't your cell phone!" she vamped.

A look of fearful disbelief flashed across Morris's features. "Ivan too!" he hoarsely expelled under his breath—or at least that's how Erika interpreted the utterance.

"I've summoned the police," Cayleigh announced. "They'll be here shortly. I want you two to leave the room now. Mrs. Keller, you'll, of course, be allowed back in momentarily."

Neither moved.

"At once! I'm paging the physician on call. I need orders—stat! —to bring down Mr. Keller's blood pressure, which has become very unstable."

"Mr. Keller wants me to stay with him until the police arrive," Erika protested.

"Mr. Keller will have to put up with me."

The three women—two reluctantly—headed for the door.

Does he know there's a security guard posted outside his room? Erika wondered. "There's a security guard just outside your door, Mr. Keller!" she called back as she exited the room. *That should provide some comfort.* Of course, she had no intention of leaving the premises until the police arrived, but verbalizing this would only have caused trouble.

* * *

The full import of the hospital incident did not hit Erika until after she'd related it to Harrison, two hours after it had taken place. "I guess because I was more involved with the interplay," she reasoned. "Plus, Cayleigh and Naomi acted like Morris's mumblings were post-trauma delusions, or some such."

"And what was that 'Ivan too' quote of his all about?" Harrison posed.

Erika shrugged. "Who knows? He may have said, 'IV tube.' What I heard could have been influenced by what was on my mind. It's going to be interesting, seeing what comes of this—Morris's interview with the police, the significance of Naomi's ta-da! moment when she waved his cell phone at him and his look of genuine horror when she did so. What a mystery."

"Rest assured, John will be on it. Give him a minute." Harrison smiled, an element of roguery in it.

His smile, clearly more than a tag to his snappy reference to John, put Erika in mind of the prelude to this talk. She had called him from Brooklyn Heights to give him her Uber car's estimated time of arrival. He'd been waiting for her on the couch in the lobby, crutches propped against the arm of the couch. Each of them had been eager to relate what had transpired in the other's absence. He had insisted she go first. "You were going to tell me something," she said. "What is it?" She cocked her head; studied his face. "I think it's big."

"Oh, it's big, alright."

"A breakthrough in our investigation?"

He shook his head. "What's bigger than a breakthrough?"

"Harrison!"

"I got a call from Norman Blethmore's partner, Ezra Fisher. We must have made a good impression. He says he trusts us. Also, he says he distrusts most of Norman's associates since his death and will feel safer sharing his discovery on US soil.

"What is the general nature of this discovery?"

"For security reasons, he won't say—only that he'd like to divulge it as soon as possible. I told him in two days we've got an appointment to speak to the Metropolitan Museum of Art conservator in charge of analyzing the eight paintings you had a chance to examine in Geneva. As a Hail Mary pass I threw out the suggestion he join us, and he grabbed it. Being in direct contact with individuals at the heart of the investigation would make him feel useful, he said."

"This is all news to me, but I'm in."

"I knew you would be. You were in Brooklyn when I finally got through to the conservator—name's David Boyd—and I didn't want to miss my chance to gel plans on the spot. David is being very accommodating. The paintings were flown to him posthaste out of Geneva, but still, that hasn't given him much time to analyze them. He asked that we meet him at two in the afternoon, give him a couple more hours to work on them."

"I'm looking forward to this meeting," Erika said, her glance randomly lighting on Harrison's crutches at the peak of her anticipation. She remembered how the news of his assault had hit her like a thunderbolt, right in the middle of a promising phone call. Without rational cause, her anticipation was struck by a clap of foreboding.

Chapter Twenty-Six

Harrison's stamina on crutches was improving, but for long hauls, the wheelchair was the most practical means of conveyance. "Does this elicit a feeling of déjà vu for you?" Harrison asked Erika as she guided his wheelchair through the maze of basement corridors of the Metropolitan Museum of Art.

It was a world hitherto unknown to her, but she got the point. "You're a more challenging character than Denise," she jested, "but yes, it does." Once again, she and a seated companion were trailing after someone—a conservator, this time—who knew his way around a maze of hallways leading to a den of secrets.

By prior arrangement, the Wheatleys had met the conservator, David Boyd—bespectacled, well-groomed, with an air of confidence—and Norman's partner, Ezra Fisher—good-looking, with the bearing of one who gracefully acknowledges it—just inside the ground floor entrance of the museum, recognizing each other through texted mug shots. Ezra, who was attached to a computer case with a white-knuckled grip, had checked into the Park Lane Hotel earlier that morning and had sat in his room brooding over the time he and Norman had last visited New York. It was good, he said, to "get out of myself and meet you people." The Wheatleys planned to ask him and David out for a late lunch or early dinner, depending what time their meeting ended.

As David led them through the subterranean grid of tunnels and corridors, Erika marveled at the diversity of activities taking place in them and their adjunct nooks and offshoots—the storing and moving of books, packages, mail, food products, art works—in and via carts, crates, shoulders, dollies. In an open room off one corridor, a worker stood atop a stepladder repairing the upper arm of a marble statue; in another, a bunch of food carts were being loaded for transport to the museum's dining rooms— "via passageways and through doors unknown to the public," David informed them. "How is this possible?" Erika wanted to ask, but didn't, figuring his answer would be as confounding as her ignorance. Several times along the way, she noticed an alert posted on the corridor walls, which said it all: YIELD TO ART IN TRANSIT.

David stopped before a closed door midway down a corridor, where by now, Erika guessed, all but David had lost their bearings. "I would have brought you to the lab," he announced, "but we're working on a da Vinci portrait, and there wasn't time to get you security clearance to enter. Besides, this private"—air quotes—"'showroom'—provides us with the freedom to speak our minds." He dug for a key in the pocket of his jeans and unlocked the door.

Erika understood the reason for the air quotes once the room was revealed. This was essentially a large storeroom for chairs, folding and non, lined up six to eight rows deep against the walls. Eight metal H-Frame easels dominated the center of the room. On them were seated the eight paintings. The room was windowless. Five floor lamps were stationed among the easels, their extension wires plugged into a power strip, which in turn was plugged into a wall socket. David first clicked on a wall switch to turn on the overhead lights, then turned on the five floor lamps. "Careful you don't trip on the wires," he cautioned.

"Splendid!" Ezra exclaimed, speaking for them all at the sight of the paintings. "They appear to be illuminated as much from within as without, don't you think? I'm so glad I came to see them in person."

Erika and Ezra followed David to the wall area where a regiment of high-back wood chairs stood at attention. Each retrieved one—Ezra, awkwardly, still holding fast to the computer case—and set it down within the display's viewing area. Erika placed hers next to Harrison. "You good?" she asked softly, touching his arm. "More than," he replied, squeezing her hand.

A folding table, likely imported for the meeting, stood at the end of the easel line-up. On it lay several pairs of plastic-encased white gloves, an assortment of magnifying glasses and flashlights, a leather art portfolio, and pencils and mini-notebooks.

"You mind if I record this session?" Ezra asked.

"You're all welcome to."

"Thanks." Ezra lay his computer case on his lap and drew his cell phone from the breast pocket of his suit jacket.

Harrison fetched his cell phone from the side pocket of his baggy— "relaxed-fit"—chinos he'd recently purchased from Amazon. "I've got this," he said, eliminating the need for Erika to dig for her own device.

When the phones had been set up to record the meeting, David placed them out of the way on the folding table and returned to his seat. "Our first premise," he began without further ado, "is that we have two Claude Monet paintings in front of us— *'plus x's six,'* as Harrison quoted the dealer Durand-Ruel's stock ledger when we spoke on the phone. Harrison's educated guess was that the mysterious six were Frédéric Bazille paintings, and I'm eighty-five percent with him on that. Feel free to interrupt at any time."

"They are Frédéric Bazille paintings with one hundred percent certainty," Ezra stated flatly. In answer to his audience's audible expressions of surprise, he patted his computer case and added, "Later."

"You have proof," David said.

"I do, but it'll keep. Please go on."

David obliged. "Another premise from the Wheatleys' research, close to airtight, it appears, is that the individual who tampered with the six *Bazille* paintings by replacing his signature with a likeness of Monet's, was an art expert—Ryan Jacobs—who perished under questionable circumstances in August 1872. Jacobs, it may be assumed from the story's context, was hired to perform the signatory alterations by the couple who purchased all eight paintings in 1871, James and Abigail Scott of Greenwich, Connecticut. That said, to date, I have not seen or gotten wind of any document categorically attesting to which among the eight paintings passed off as Monets actually originated from his palette. Anything, Ezra?"

Ezra shook his head. "Sorry, I have no such document."

David gave a hapless smile. "Of course. What did I expect? If there were such documentation, there'd be no reason for our having to subject the paintings to meticulous x-radiography and other techniques, scientific and intuitive, to come up with relatively certain verdicts of authenticity."

"I have faith in the process," Ezra said.

"So do I. But before I report on my findings thus far, why don't you tell us what *you've* got for us."

"Certainly." Ezra unzipped his computer case and removed a laptop from its central space and a flash drive from one of its two side pockets. He re-zipped the case and set it on the floor beside his chair, then turned on his laptop and inserted the flash drive into its USB port. The dialogue box appeared on the screen. "Before I open the folder, let me explain how I came into possession of this flash drive." With the barest cough as introduction, he let drop: "Common law marriage does not exist in the UK. It would have been wise of Norman and me to have set up a cohabitation agreement, but who said we were wise? There was a safe deposit box at a local bank. It was in Norm's name—rented before we met. After he died, I submitted a request for its contents. My request remained in limbo for nearly a month while the contents of the safe were held in custody at the bank. A few days ago, my request was denied, and Norm's belongings were delivered to his sister, Ann. On her own initiative—with an apology, in fact—Ann ceded ownership to me of all items in the safe deposit box except a diamond necklace that had belonged to their mother. The flash drive was one of the items handed over to me. It will speak for itself."

The listeners took a collective breath as they waited for Ezra to punch the "open folder" in the dialogue box. They were kept in suspense as he angled his laptop first toward the Wheatleys, seated to his left, then to David, on his right. "This seating arrangement is awkward," he concluded. "If I pull my chair forward"—he did so— "and you move closer to me, the view of my screen will be in all your lines of vision without my having to shift about."

Ezra's directive was followed, and the much-awaited folder was promptly cued to *Pissarro Exhibits/Archives*. "There are several files in this folder that don't pertain," he said. "They relate to Pissarro exhibits Norman curated or assisted in curating. He was working on one for the Connaught Brown gallery in London…he was looking forward to it, opening in just two months and…damn!" He shook his head. "Sorry."

"Nothing to be sorry for," Harrison said somewhat forcefully. "You can't be expected to shut yourself off for us."

"Appreciate that." Ezra closed his eyes in a pause to reset. Opening them, he composedly suggested, "If any of you are interested in reviewing the folder in its entirety or at your leisure, I'll make copies of the flash drive for you. Now, let's take a look at the file we're here for." He clicked on the title *Archival addition/ son Lucien Pissarro source*, and it lit up the screen—or appeared to, to Harrison, as another image ignited memory—Norman Blethmore, an envelope of documents held to his chest, walking into the print room, the barest spring to his step.

"I could have printed a copy of this letter," Ezra said as he scrolled down to reveal the file's contents, "but I wanted you to see it direct from Norman."

An address, a date, the day of the week, and a salutation appeared at first glimpse:

> *Montfoucault, Brittany*
> *26 août 1870 vendredi*
> *Mon cher Camille,*

Scrolling further, the letter appeared in its entirety. It was signed: "F. Bazille."

"This is Norm's handwriting," Ezra said. "He copied Bazille's letter word for word. Norm's English translation is below, also written in longhand." He scrolled further, and it appeared.

"This is one of the letters that was stolen," Harrison noted in a hushed voice. "It was written one month before Bazille's death. It will be history-making."

"Can you all see it properly?" Ezra asked.

"This is too significant," Harrison said. "It merits a recitation. Read it aloud, Ezra. As a memorial—to Frédéric Bazille and Norman Blethmore."

Ezra drew in his breath. "I'll do that, yes." He rose to his feet and faced his audience. "To set the stage, let me begin by saying that Bazille is writing to Camille Pissarro in Montfoucault, where he is temporarily staying at his friend Ludovic Piette's family home. The Franco-Prussian War had begun in July, and Montfoucault had been providing a safe haven from war-torn Paris. I might also add here that although Camille Pissarro spent most of his life in France, he was born in St. Thomas in the West Indies, and remained a Danish citizen. He, therefore, could not be drafted into the French armed forces." Ezra smiled. "Thank you for not stopping me to tell me you knew all that."

"I didn't know all that," Erika confessed. "So thank *you*."

Ezra nodded acknowledgment, then looked down at his laptop screen, poised at chest level, and began. "'My dear Camille. I hope you and your family are well. Forgoing any attempt at a graceful turn of phrase, I will come right to the point. Ten days ago, I enlisted in the Third Zouaves Light Infantry Regiment. My friend, Edmond Maître tells me I am mad, and others, perhaps you included, keep silent, but think it. I am sure others ascribe various peculiarities of character to my decision, and even a few may believe the Zouaves' colorful uniform played a part in it. But the truth is deeper and more somber. I feel stalled, artistically and in life. I fear there is an effeteness to my disposition, which if not dispelled, will come to define me. I want my art to have a real impact on the world, and for that, I have come to believe it must be informed by the redeeming power of experience on the cusp of life and death.

"'Which brings me to the reason why I am writing to you. It is a request I wish you to fulfill in the event that I am killed in battle. (Yes, I have said I have no intention of being killed because I still have much to do with my life, but surely you must know this statement was made in a fit of hubris or infantilism.)

"'Contrary to what you might surmise from my gloomy thoughts, I do think much of my work is quite competent. My fear is that it will either stagnate or deteriorate if I do not take proper measures. I would like to ship to you my *Still Life with Flowers*—the one you admired, with the lyre-strumming goddess motif on the Wedgewood vase—and five other of my best paintings for your safekeeping while Paris is in turmoil. In the event of my death, I wish you to see that they are sold and that the proceeds be given anonymously to Claude Monet—as a gift from an admirer or through a ruse you find more suitable. Monet is a great artist, my mentor, my dear friend, the father of my godchild, and, unfortunately—unjustly, in light of his genius—often in need of funds. He is very unhappy with my decision to enlist, and I know he will feel guilt, albeit unwarranted, if I am killed in battle. Guilt for not having been more forceful in persuading me not to enlist. Guilt for not having enlisted himself. I would not want to compound that guilt with the spoils garnered from my death. Anonymity at all costs! If possible, I would like my name omitted from all records of sale.

"'I cannot ask this favor of my parents because I cannot trust them to fulfill it. Though well-intentioned, their motives would be governed by grief and sentimentality. They would not part with my paintings while they mourn my death, and if ever they would, certainly not in this manner. Please let me know if you agree to take this task upon yourself. If you do not, I will understand. If you do, I will be forever in your debt.' It is signed 'F. Bazille,'" Ezra concluded.

He was greeted by the silence that follows the performance of a symphony, a dead silence that predicts the eruption of applause.

Ezra's small audience burst into simultaneous exclamations. "What did I say—history-making!"—Harrison. "Sure goes easy on Monet!"—David. "Wow!"—Erika.

"What did you mean by 'easy on Monet'?" Erika's follow-up.

"Bazille's gentle reference to Monet's often being 'in need of funds,'" David replied. "He doesn't mention the fact that Monet often asked him for funds, sometimes aggressively. Did you know that to help him out, Bazille bought one of Monet's paintings for a whopping 2,500 francs when Monet was getting about fifty for one of his works?"

"I don't suppose it would have been discreet of Bazille to have reminded Pissarro of Monet's aggressiveness or, for that matter, of his own generosity," Erika said.

"That's true. Consider me chastened. And Harrison, I agree with you when you say this is history-making—at least within the confines of *art* history. Bazille was prescient when he suggested the variety of ways people might interpret—and, by implication, argue over—his decision to enlist. He puts the controversy to rest here."

"Amen," Harrison said. Addressing Ezra, he asked, "In Norman's notes, does he reference Pissarro's letter in answer to Bazille's?"

"He does, yes. He copied a portion of Pissarro's gracious response, but for the sake of efficiency, let's not review it. As I said, I can make you all copies of the flash drive. The only other item in the file that sheds light on your investigation is an excerpt from Pissarro's letter to the art dealer, Paul Durand-Ruel, asking him to sell the Bazille paintings. The letter is dated December the fifth, 1870—seven days after Bazille was killed in the battle of Beaune-la-Rolande."

Harrison sat bolt-upright in his wheelchair. "Finally! A clue to what Durand-Ruel referred to as 'that brilliant idea of yours'!"

"We hope," Erika said. "Don't keep us in suspense, Ezra."

Ezra scrolled down to the notes on order. "Norm says here that the letter is written from Pissarro's temporary home in Lower Norwood, South London, where he moved after staying a few months with the Piette family. He says Pissarro asked Durand-Ruel if he'd handle the sale of Bazille's six paintings in the manner Bazille requested and that he'd see to it the paintings were safely transported to the dealer's rented gallery on New Bond Street." Ezra paused.

Harrison's face fell. "That's it?"

Ezra raised a hand. "Patience. Here's the excerpt. To quote— 'If the opportunity arises, you might consider selling any number, optimally all, of Bazille's paintings along with a Monet or two. When you reimburse Monet, credit the total income solely to the sale of his art work. He will be pleased with the generous figure! You might suggest to a prospective buyer that if he admires Monet, whose works you've predicted will one day be among the most sought after in the world, he should take a look at the work of another artist with a similar technique.' There's an ellipsis," Ezra said, "and then Norm quotes the following lines. 'In my eagerness to follow Frédéric's wishes to their fullest, I fear I have been guilty of advising a master dealer in a matter about which he knows best. Forgive me.'"

"Another question answered!" Harrison rejoiced. "Thank you, Camille Pissarro—and you, Ezra—and Norman!"

"Erika nodded in agreement. "To Norman's sister, Ann, as well."

"I'm wondering if Durand-Ruel did indeed use the painters' similar techniques as a selling point," David mused.

"And if from it, the Scotts spun off their misattribution scheme," Erika said, taking David's thought to its natural conclusion.

"Something we'll never know," David said. He rose to his feet. "Now that we've come full circle to the question of forged signatures, I say we move on to the paintings themselves." He squeezed Ezra's shoulder. "What you've given us has been invaluable. Thank you."

"No problem," Ezra said. Taking the cue, he returned to his seat.

David stood before the display of paintings. "The obvious place to start is with the painting we know without a doubt is Bazille's. The one Bazille refers to in his letter as his 'still life with flowers'—Ezra, in the letter, does this appear to be a title or a descriptive?"

"A title; written as such."

"I see. So. Greg Smith forwarded me a list of the eight paintings entered into Monet's catalogue raisonné under suspicious circumstances—the list he'd originally given the Wheatleys, I believe." (Confirmative gestures from the Wheatleys.) "The floral still life is entered as *Wedgewood Vase with Flowers*. Therefore, I believe we can safely assume the culprits thought to change the titles of at least six of the paintings."

"Think of it," Harrison proposed, "if it had not been for Bazille's description of the painting—the only painting he *does* describe in his letter—Norman would not have been so taken aback when he saw it credited to Monet on the cover of Lazlo's auction catalogue, and would not have, in effect, set off the alarm."

"Exactly," Ezra replied somberly. "And Norman would be alive today, and the misappropriation might never have been discovered. Given the power, I would have chosen Norman's life over historical accuracy."

"I understand," David said. "But here we are, in this moment, morally, and yes, historically, obliged to continue on the course Norman has set for us."

"A thought I keep having to remind myself of. It doesn't come naturally."

"I realize that," David said, briefly locking gazes with Ezra. "And now, let's continue our journey. I've got good news and bad news. The good news is I think I know how Bazille's signature was eradicated. The bad news is I reached the answer through inference; I can't be absolutely certain. Through x-radiology, I saw no signs of an underlying signature—on *any* of the paintings. I believe Bazille's's signature was removed with turpentine, fresh paint dabbed onto the area, and Monet's signature added."

"Turpentine evaporates," Harrison said. "Monet himself, in fact, often began a painting with rather thin paint spiked with turpentine. Leaves no trace."

David nodded vigorously.

"Any difference in the paint ingredients detected?" Erika asked. "I mean between the original paint and the paint freshly daubed on, and in the freshly applied signature?"

"Good question, and I wish I could give you a definitive answer at this time. So far, I've done infrared imaging on several paintings without positive findings. I'd like to complete the study, but also supplement the data from other spectroscopic methods—and they abound. Still, we've got enough to work with today to come up with a couple of reasonable conclusions. On the topic of paint variants, I'm hoping to hit on evidence of Léon-inspired pigments in my extended testing."

"'*Léon*-inspired'?" Erika queried.

"Sorry. Léon was Monet's older brother. He was a chemist focusing on synthetic dyes and pigments used to color fabric. He came up with new, vivid synthetic colors, which Claude would often use."

"Any of the canvases recycled?" Harrison asked. "I know Bazille, for one, regularly painted over his rejects."

"Yes, he did. Monet did, too, at times. Although"—little laugh injected—"I think he may have been partial to destroying a canvas rather than reusing it. In answer to your question, yes, there are a few underpaintings among the group—but not under the floral still life. In fact, before we move on to the next painting under discussion—*Girl at the Piano*—let me fetch an X-ray photograph of its underpainting." From the leather art portfolio lying on the table, he produced a photograph and held it in front of them. It was a black-and-white image of a somewhat indistinct landscape.

"Ghostlike," Erika commented. "As if raised from the dead."

"Which indeed it has been," David said.

"The *over*painting is one Harrison and I talked about," Erika said. "Thanks to him, I'm aware it's a portrait of Bazille's cousin Thérèse and his good friend Edmond Maître. So I guess the conclusion is, it was painted by Bazille."

"Not so fast. Monet knew both of these individuals. Unless we decide authorship based solely on the painters' distinguishing techniques, we can't be sure which—"

"Wait," Harrison interrupted. "The underpainting—the landscape—is greater in width than in height. The portrait is the opposite."

David's pale cheeks bloomed pink. "Oh, dear—of course!"

"No worries," Harrison comforted. "We've all had our purloined-letter moments."

"Please explain," Ezra said.

Harrison deferred to David.

"When Bazille was about to paint over an image he wasn't happy with, he often rotated the canvas ninety or one hundred eighty degrees," David said. "In this case, ninety, obviously. It was an unusual practice." He raised his hands in concession. "That breaks the deadlock. The painting's a Bazille." Adding, with a restorative grin, "Well, at least beyond a reasonable doubt." He returned the landscape photo to his portfolio and brought out another photo. "Let's proceed to the two beach paintings, *Seaside* and *At the Shore*." The paintings' easels stood side by side in the center of the line-up, and he pointed out which was which. "They are almost identical in subject matter and perspective, and the two friends did paint side by side at the shore—at Saint-Adresse, for instance, which may, in fact, be the location depicted here." He gestured for the threesome to come nearer.

Harrison was the first to move, aligning the side of his wheelchair with the row of easels in order to be as close to the paintings as possible. "Let me know if I'm in anybody's way," he said as Ezra and Erika stepped up to the display.

"What do you think?" David posed. "Compare the two. Often, we instinctively know at a glance—without knowing why. Afterwards we run tests and analyze, only to come to the answer we first *beheld*."

"I have a sense *At the Shore* is a Monet," Erika said almost at once. "I've seen these eight paintings before, in Geneva, so I guess this qualifies as cheating."

David smiled. "Putting aside the question of whether your pick was instinctive or studied, how did you arrive at it?"

"In *At the Shore*, the brush strokes look like they've been applied more confidently—more quickly, maybe, as if the painter wanted to capture the light in that very instant, the demarcation of sand and water, sea and sky, less important than the, well, the *transition* from one to the other. In *Seaside,* the brush strokes are fewer and more deliberate, the scene itself more studied, but at the same time more tentative—about the artist's commitment to go all out, I mean. In *At the Shore*, I see stirrings of Impressionism. In *Seaside*, I see a cautious exploration of style." Erika shrugged. "I may be off by a mile."

"Or not," David replied, a note of slyness in his voice. He held up the last photo he'd removed from his folder. It was another ghost-like black-and-white image, this one a portrait of a gentleman in formal attire. "This is *At the Shore*'s underpainting," he said. "Do you know who it is?"

"I don't. Harrison, you want to help me out?"

"I don't know who it is," Harrison said, "but from the wily expression on David's face, I'm guessing it might be Monet's brother."

"The infamous Léon; right you are. And at first blink," David added, addressing Erika, my reaction was not unlike yours." Scanning the group, he asked, "Is it unanimous, then? *At the Shore* is a Monet; *Seaside*, a Bazille?"

"I'm agreeing, though with reservations," Harrison said. "I'd like to see more concrete evidence—the smallest bit would come close to sealing it for me."

A mischievous grin appeared on David's face, seemingly from out of nowhere. "One second." He removed another sheet from his folder. "Take a look." It was a document entitled "Samples of Claude Monet's Signature." He passed it around.

They were all familiar with Monet's signature, but looking at multiple examples served to highlight its unique features. Within seconds, the giveaway was discovered. In all of the samples of Monet's signature, the crossbar of his "t" consistently sloped in the same direction—downward, from left to right, like an accent grave. The crossbar in *Seaside*'s signature sloped in the opposite direction, like an accent aigu.

"How did this pass notice all these years?" Ezra asked.

"The painting, along with its siblings, were kept out of the public's eye," David said. "The experts who took stock of them in recent times, either missed or intentionally overlooked the crossbar slip-up. Are we ready to accept *Seaside* as a presumptive Bazille and move on? As I see it, after that, we need look at only one more painting—*Luncheon Party*—which I'm quite certain we can assign to Monet. In which case, we will have found our two Monets, and thus by default, we can credit the remaining three works— *Woman Reading, Picnic on the Lawn,* and *Woman in the Garden*—to Bazille. All in favor?" he asked—to which he received a chorus of ayes. "Excellent. Now take a look at *Luncheon Party*. It must look familiar to you, am I right?"

"With minor variations, straight out of Monet's *Luncheon on the Grass*," Harrison said without a moment's hesitation.

"Sorry my stick figures didn't clue you in, Harrison," Erika said.

"For the most part, they were extremely helpful—truly!"

Giving the two a quizzical look, David said, "I won't venture to ask. Now, as for *Luncheon Party*, I'd say it's just about a twin—well, fraternal twin—to the painting we're familiar with. The configuration of the foliage is the same as it is in the full-scale version. The two standing women whose backs are facing the viewer are wearing the same dresses here, only in colors more vibrant. He took a slow, deep breath, as if the air were manna from heaven. "Do you realize what a find this is? After the indignities suffered by the full-scale version—for one, mildew in the basement of a landlord who held it for years as collateral for unpaid rent?"

Erika did not want to disrupt David's seemingly transformative experience, but the question needed to be asked: "It's a given, then, that this painting could not have been Bazille's respectful spinoff of Monet's painting—one that Monet never completed?"

"You're on the ball, Erika," David remarked, gratefully unperturbed. "That may very well have been a possibility, but this was the first painting I analyzed, and I took my time with it. The brush strokes down to the first contact on blank canvas are, I'm quite certain, those of Monet. Nevertheless, as I've said, there's more work to be done on all eight of the works, and if I change my mind about any of the attributions, I'll, of course, let you know. How's that?"

"That's great. Thanks."

"Before we close shop, anyone know who the tall gentleman on the far left of the painting is? The word 'tall' should give you a hint."

"That's Frédéric Bazille," Harrison replied, again without hesitation.

"Six feet two inches," David confirmed. "Damn tall for his time. In that colorful uniform and at that height, poor fellow was an easy target at Beaune-la-Rolande." He sighed. "Not the best way to wrap up our meeting, but there we are. As it stands, our Monet paintings are *Luncheon Party* and *At the Shore*. Once again, I'll let you know if further research prompts second thoughts."

"Harrison and I were hoping you and Ezra would join us for a bite to eat," Erika suggested, as she went to pick up Harrison's cell phone from the table, where it had been recording their discussion. "Your choice of venues."

"Very kind of you, but I should stick around and see that the paintings make their way back to the lab safe and sound. This might take a while, and I don't want to hold you people up—but say! If you care to relax and surf the menu right here at our Balcony Lounge, I can swing by if I'm not held up. How does that sound? It's open until eight-fifteen tonight, so you can loll about indefinitely. By the way, the lobster roll is to die for."

"We know," Harrison said, pocketing his cell phone, with a nod of thanks to Erika for fetching it for him. "Sounds like a good idea. We haven't been there in a while. Erika? Ezra? You on board?"

They were.

David gave them instructions on how to get back to the elevator, and after only one wrong turn, the trio was on its way up to the second floor.

* * *

The Met's Balcony Lounge is a sanctuary steps away from the balustrade of the museum's grand staircase. Looking in from outside its massive glass doors and seeing pairs of face-to-face creamy beige sofas sharing long glass tables upon which rest drinks in long-stemmed glasses, and here and there art books perched on strategically placed console tables, you might predict an ambience a step above clubby—more like genteelly snobbish. The Wheatleys knew from experience you could not be further from the truth. The staff, as genuinely friendly and caring as your favorite relatives, banished any preconceived notions of exclusivity based on genealogy or class. Despite—and here was the kicker, along with its attendant guilt—you needed to be a member at the "evening hours" level or above to gain access.

"I'm not a member," Ezra advised the host, an approachable-looking man with salt and pepper hair, who was in the process of scanning the Wheatleys' membership card.

"No problem," the host replied genially. "You're a guest of the Wheatleys." He handed the card back to Erika. "We're wide open. Where would you folks like to sit?"

They chose the nearest sofa pairing and were escorted there by the host.

Erika and Ezra sat down opposite each other. Harrison maneuvered his wheelchair close to the arm of Erika's sofa.

Ezra placed his computer case beside him, right up against his thigh. He reached into the breast pocket of his suit jacket. "Oh no!"

Erika lurched forward in her seat. "What is it?"

"My cell phone," he expelled, struggling to keep his voice down. He jumped to his feet and dug into the jacket's side pockets. "Thought I'd need it to see the menu."

"No QR code here," Harrison said. "You think you left your cell in the basement? I thought I saw you pick it up."

"I need that phone—can't lose it!" Ezra went through the pockets of his pants, two at a time, the side, the back, as if he were after a live grenade. Nothing.

"Let me call David," Harrison said. "He's in my contacts."

"Fine, but first, let me try my computer case." Ezra sat back down. With trembling fingers, he pulled open the zipper.

A young woman in a colorful print dress approached the table. "Hi. I'm Lori." She placed three menu cards on the table.

"Here it is!" Ezra uttered breathlessly, extracting his cell phone from one of the side pockets of his computer case. "How did I not remember?"

"Everything okay?" Lori politely inquired. "May I help you with anything?"

"Give us a minute, Lori—thanks," Harrison said

"Of course." With an endearing smile, Lori retreated.

"Sorry for that display," Ezra said, slipping his cell phone into his breast pocket. "It's just that I've saved Norman's voice message—he was at the supermarket, asking what brand of yogurt I wanted; they were out of my usual. I didn't realize he'd called until he got back, and by chance, I never deleted the message."

"You should make a more permanent copy of it," Harrison suggested.

"I've been meaning to." Ezra picked up the menu, turned it over. "I think I need a drink."

Harrison leaned forward to grab one of the remaining two menus. They were just out of reach, right under Erika's nose. "Erika?"

Erika did not answer.

Ezra reached over and retrieved a menu for him.

"Thanks," Harrison said, taking it from him, while still focusing on Erika, who was sitting stock still and staring intently into space. "Erika?"

"That's it!" she exclaimed. "I've got to call John! They'll never take my word for it at the hospital—Naomi's got them eating out of her hand!"

"Erika, sweetheart, what's going on?"

She spoke in hushed tones. "Morris is in danger, and I believe he was, in effect, telling me his wife had tried to kill him and that she's responsible for

Ivan's death as well! When he said 'Ivan too' he was not talking about IV tubes or any such nonsense, he was saying 'Ivan,' comma, 'too!' That is, my wife shot me as *well* as Ivan!"

"How did this suddenly occur to you?"

"It was when Ezra couldn't find his cell phone—first, his look of surprise and fear, and then, when he unzipped his computer case and found it there—it took me back to the hospital. Naomi unzipping her husband's canvas bag, bringing forth the phone, Morris's look of disbelief and fear. I believe this was not her plan A. This was a plan she kept in reserve, should he wake up and start blabbing. Which he did!" Erika pulled her cell phone out of her bag. "I'm wasting time." She scanned the room. In a corner niche were two sets of loveseats, abbreviated versions of the sofa pairings that occupied the greater portion of the venue. She rose from the couch. "I'm going to go sit in that secluded area," she said, with a head tilt in its direction. "I'll be back in a few minutes. Order me something—anything." She took a few steps, then stopped to turn around. "Thank you," she said, addressing Ezra before walking off.

Two of the loveseats faced the open area of the lounge; their mates faced the wall. Erika settled in one of the latter. She punched in John's number. *Please answer!*

"Hey, Erika, what's up?"

"Okay, listen carefully." She began reeling off what had occurred at the hospital. John asked her to slow down. With difficulty, she did. She tried to stick to the salient points: Morris, in effect, accuses Naomi of trying to kill him. At his insistence, but mainly to humor him, the police are summoned. Naomi responds to these events by producing Morris's cell phone from his canvas bag. Morris is visibly surprised and fearful. Naomi issues an unspecified, but unmistakable threat.

"So, what's the scenario you pieced together from these observations?" John asked.

"These are not the only observations making up my scenario."

"I'm listening."

This was not going to be easy because her epiphany had come to her in a flash, like an instant rewind of an explosion. Now, she was obliged to enumerate the scattershot. "I thought back on our visit to the Kellers in Brooklyn Heights," she began. "Remember? Morris's ex, Lois, was demanding to know what was going on—why was the insurance canceled, where the hell are the paintings. Naomi wasn't asking a thing. Why? Because she knew. *How* she knew is another story. I can guess, but it would be pure conjecture."

"You're saying Naomi knew—what's that, if not conjecture?"

"*Informed* conjecture, okay? Hear me out, John!"

"Sorry."

"So. Regarding Ivan's murder. Morris's alibi is that he was home with his wife that night. His business call made from their landline is proof he was home. I ask you, how many people use a landline these days as anything more than a backup? I think Morris couldn't find his cell phone, and that's why he used the landline. I'm thinking Naomi took his cell phone to Manhattan that night and that she sent a text or email from that phone—maybe the very message Ivan Brooks received at the Laszlo auction. A message which she could use to incriminate her husband, should the need arise."

"And you're saying the need arose—at the hospital—when he ratted on her."

"Exactly. At which opportune time, she produced the cell phone, which knocked him for a loop. He was probably somewhat disoriented, coming out of a coma, and may have even forgotten about their deal—for surely they had a deal."

"He would corroborate her statement that she was home that night," John expanded. "And she would see to it his cell phone remained *lost*, so to speak."

"That's it, yes. I'm not going to guess what went wrong between them for Naomi to decide she had to bump him off, but I think there's still a window for the police to search for evidence based on that assumption. From what I've heard, she hasn't left his side for a minute since the shooting took place, so there's a chance she didn't sufficiently clean up the scene. If they haven't already taken the house apart searching for evidence, they better get on it before it's too late. You've got to use your pull, John!"

"Any other directives for these guys?" John asked, the words delivered as a friendly barb.

She pretended she didn't catch the inflection. "Yes. Most important, they should keep a close watch on Naomi. She might decide to pull a fast one in the hospital while Morris is too weak to defend himself. They should check out the usage on the Kellers' landline. The more infrequent, the more significant a clue. They should also check out the phone Naomi seemed ready to hand over to the police. If they spot an incriminating message made from the phone the night of Ivan's murder, they should see if they can discover from what location it was made. If Manhattan, it's a hit. Murray Hill, a bull's eye."

"Whoa, I should have been taking notes," John commented—again, with that touch of sarcasm. "Have you given any thought to the little matter of motivation?"

"I think we can both come up with believable motivation, John. Let's hear what Morris has to say. And for that, you have to see that he stays alive."

"A tall order, but I'll see what I can do."

"Think you can manage it without the detectives in charge losing face? The Murray Hill guy seems to have tunnel vision when it comes to the Ivan Brooks case. Can't seem to see past that senior account executive at Laszlo's—Sheldon Adams."

"I can be tactful, Erika."

"I didn't mean to imply—"

"I know. Look, I'm impressed with your hypothesis. I'll do my best to sell it. Does Harrison know the full story?"

"No, but he will."

When she got back to the table, the food and drinks had already been served. Three lobster rolls and three glasses of white wine. "Thank you!" she said, sitting down.

"How'd it go?" Harrison asked. His plate was resting on his lap, but neither he nor Ezra had begun eating.

"It went fine. You shouldn't have waited for me."

"Don't mistake us for gentlemen. The food just arrived. You want to talk about your phone call?"

"Not right now. I'm all wound up. Let's just hang out."

When they were done with their food and wine and were reviewing the dessert options, David arrived. "I was afraid you'd left," he said. He sat down beside Ezra. "It went well today. Collaboration. It can be a real boon, wouldn't you say?"

"Oh, yes," Erika agreed, seeking eye contact with Ezra. "Especially when it's serendipitous."

Chapter Twenty-Seven

It was the conservator, David Boyd's idea to arrange a private showing for all those who'd had a stake in what he'd dubbed The Monet Operation or who'd played a part in its execution. What prompted the idea, he said, was a call from Agent Oliver Schmidt's superior at the Swiss Federal Office for Customs and Border Security, who'd asked if he might have a look at the eight paintings himself. David had asked the Wheatleys to make up a list of names they thought should be included in his email notice. "I'm just now learning what a multi-faceted investigation this has been—and continues to be," he said when he'd called with his proposal three days after their conference at the museum. "You've been in the thick of things from the start, I hear. The paintings will not be under one roof very much longer, and I believe it would be, at least for some, a rewarding experience. What do you think? You supply the list. I'll take it from there." The Wheatleys were all in favor. In fact, Harrison, with Erika's blessing, thought it would be a nice gesture to provide complimentary dining at any of the museum's restaurants to the invitees and their companions, provided he be permitted to pick up the tab.

And here the Wheatleys were, twelve days later, at 10:25 a.m., pulling up in front of the Metropolitan Museum of Art, about to attend an exhibition of paintings that had been at the nexus of a series of art-based crimes.

Erika exited the rear seat of their driver, Bill's car, then slid Harrison's crutches out. By this time in their relationship, Bill knew the pair were uncomfortable with what they deemed over-solicitousness, so, contrary to instinct, he remained glued to the driver's seat.

Once Harrison had exited the vehicle—right foot planted firmly on solid ground, left, tentatively—Erika handed him the crutches. "You okay?" she asked. It had been less than twenty-four hours since his legwear had been revamped. The right knee's long rigid brace had been replaced with a shorter, flexible one, and the sidebars on the left knee brace Greg had likened to a Rube Goldberg gizmo had been removed, allowing limited knee flexibility. Although he was still allowed only partial weight-bearing on the left leg, his stamina had improved since his last visit to the museum, and nothing was going to stop him from testing it to the max. "I'm okay," he assured her.

Through the closed car window, they mouthed goodbye to Bill, then set off for the museum's ground-floor entrance. The paintings would be on display all day, from 10:00 to 5:00, on the ground floor, in one of the study halls of the Uris Center for Education. David would be on hand for the duration. If he needed to take a short break now and then, his assistant would spell him.

Greg had flown in from London for the occasion, and he, John, and the Wheatleys had planned to meet at the exhibit around 10:30. Madame Denise Fontaine was given to understand that her invitation included, under no uncertain terms, a two-week stay at the Wheatleys. She and Gretchen would be arriving at JFK at 11:00 a.m. and stopping by the Wheatley residence to freshen up before continuing on to the museum. Bill would be on call for them.

More than to revisit the paintings, Erika and Harrison were hoping for updates on the criminal investigations. Although over the past two weeks, they'd been privy to a scoop or two from their cohorts, it was a fluid situation. They hadn't heard from either John or Greg for at least thirty-six hours. During this period of radio silence, there must have been breakthroughs.

Entering the room hijacked for the exhibit, they were greeted with affectionate hugs from David—Harrison's, more cautiously bestowed. "Glad to see you up and about," he said.

"Progress," Harrison replied. "Thanks for arranging the event. Great idea." He hailed John Mitchell, who'd turned from his study of Bazille's *Woman Reading* on hearing Harrison's voice.

The paintings were arranged as they'd been in the museum's catacombs—only this time, with ID labels glued to the lips of their easels. They were lined up two to three feet from a wall gridded with chalk-and cork-board. "Amazing how they elevate the environment," David commented, nodding toward the art work.

"That they do," John said, approaching the group.

Ezra joined them with a diminutive young woman at his elbow—David's assistant, they were shortly to learn. "I've just been told you and Laura have discovered traces of Léon Monet's dyes in one of Monet's paintings," Ezra said, addressing David. He grasped each of the Wheatleys' hands in turn. Erika sensed the tension below the cordial manner, jaw clenching, the outward sign. Not a chance in hell Ezra came all this way to discuss chemical dyes. He was here to get concrete answers regarding Norman's death. And she would do her damnedest to see that he did.

David nodded in response to Ezra's comment. "In *Luncheon Party*, yes, there are traces of those innovative dyes. But not in *At the Shore*, a less exuberantly bright piece, to be sure." He hastily introduced his assistant, Laura Keane. "By the way, I should tell you, our list of attributions remains intact. I will see to it that the putative Bazilles are removed from Monet's catalogue raisonné as soon as possible."

"I was wondering," Erika said. "What about the fake Monet signatures on the Bazille paintings? Are you going to remove them?"

"Excellent question. I am going to remove the fraudulent signatures, but will not be compounding one forgery with another by applying a likeness of Bazille's signature—or, for that matter, as has been suggested, printing his name with some self-serving proxy notice with reference to yours truly. Attribution will be noted on the back of each of the canvasses, and certification, along with copies of letters from Bazille, Pissarro, and Durand-Ruel will be attached."

"Sounds like the best solution," Erika replied. She scanned the room. Aside from the present company, there were only three other people in the room. The one she recognized was holding a cell phone out in front of him.

"It's still early," David said, noticing her distraction. "I'm sure it'll get livelier around here as the day progresses. The couple standing by *Woman in the Garden* are museum personnel and friends of mine. The imposing gentleman trying to conceal his stature in a slouchy suit is Oliver Schmidt, an agent with Switzerland's Federal Office for Customs and Security."

"I know him," Erika said. "I met him at the Geneva Freeport—under extraordinary circumstances."

"Ah, yes, of course. You were there. Oddly enough, it was Schmidt's superior officer who suggested we stage this event, but at the last minute, he had to attend to a family matter. Schmidt is on a FaceTime call with him now. Giving him a virtual tour, I suspect."

"Speaking of family matters," John said, "I hope you don't mind if I steal the Wheatleys for a minute or two." He took hold of Erika's elbow and turned her toward the seating arrangements at the other end of the room.

"'Family matters'?" Harrison questioned when they were out of hearing.

John shrugged. "A tactful segue." He pointed to one of the several four-chair semi-circles at their disposal. "What are you trying to prove, standing about? Sit the hell down."

Harrison smiled. "I thought you'd never ask." He arranged himself on one of the armless tufted chairs and lay his crutches beside it.

Erika indicated John sit between them. When they were settled in, she rattled off the questions she'd been stifling. "Are the detectives from Murray Hill and Brooklyn Heights coming? You said they were receptive to my ideas about Naomi's role in Ivan Brooks's murder and her husband's attempted murder, but you didn't tell me if they followed through. *Did* they? Are they stalling?"

"Hold on, Erika. It's all good. Where is Greg? I thought he was coming at ten-thirty."

"He'll be here. You're not going to wait for him to give us an update, are you?"

"No. I'm just curious to hear what news, if any, he's got from the art front. Or if he's been hit by a bus." He sat back. "And no, the detectives from the Manhattan and Brooklyn precincts will not be coming today. They say they don't want to be pressed for answers they're not ready to divulge in public. Frankly, I believe they'd rather not take the chance of bumping into each other. There's history between them—a dispute over a transfer or a promotion. I don't probe. But this is a good thing. Each is vying for the competitive edge. Neither cares where the brainstorm sprang from. Only thing that matters is which one ends up a hero in the headlines."

"Seems you're implying they acted quickly," Erika said, grabbing Harrison's hand.

"Bats out of hell. Naomi's nailed on all counts."

Erika felt like throwing herself into Harrison's arms. Another factor played into her elation, but she'd get to that later. "Was the usage frequency of Keller's landline determined?" she asked.

John nodded. "Once in a blue moon. Morris had to use it the night of the murder. His cell phone was nowhere in sight. This came out in the story he gave the police when he was feeling physically able to withstand a grilling."

"What about his cell phone? Was there a message to Ivan Brooks found on it? I was sure that's what Naomi was planning to pin on her husband if she had to."

"Right again. A message saying, and I'm paraphrasing: 'Meet me in the courtyard, we've been set up. There's a plot to steal the Monet in transit after the sale. I have an idea, need your help.'" John shook his head. "Sounds phony as hell in retrospect, but tell that to the geniuses out there who've lost their shirts to online scammers. And yes, Erika, the origin of this message was traced to the Murray Hill area." Erika opened her mouth to speak. He raised his hand to stop her. "Let me guess—you want to know if they found any incriminating evidence in the top-to-bottom search of the Keller home, which you so avidly proposed. The answer is yes. Speed was of the essence the morning Naomi shot Morris, plus she hardly, if at any time, stepped foot in the house after Morris was hospitalized. For one thing, the contents of the laundry hamper were examined with a fine tooth comb. Gunshot residue—gunpowder particles, nitrite, nitrates—were found on one of Naomi's shirts."

"'For *one* thing'?" Harrison repeated, taking the words out of Erika's mouth.

John grinned. "For another, the striations on the bullets removed from Ivan Brooks and Morris Keller are likely matches. This will probably be contested, but even so, it's persuasive evidence, if not one hundred percent reliable. Unfortunately, the weapon itself has not been found."

"My head's spinning," Harrison confessed. "Morris originally covered for his wife the night of the murder by reporting she was home with him."

"Covering his ass," John affirmed. "She'd threatened to implicate him in the murder by handing over his cell phone to the police if he didn't."

"I get that," Harrison said. "What I don't get is exactly how and when they adapted their individual stories to jibe with emerging evidence that contradicted them!"

"Understandable. There are a lot of moving parts to this case, and I should have presented their contortions in chronological order. I'll try to do that."

"I heard the word 'contortions,'" a familiar voice sounded from behind. "I'm intrigued."

"Where've you been?" John asked Greg as he came round to claim the unoccupied chair next to Harrison.

"For the last five minutes, studying the paintings. Fantastic lot. Monet's *Luncheon Party*—what a find. I predict it'll go for more than the one hundred million ten *Haystacks* fetched in 2019 at Sotheby's. Don't wince, Harrison. I don't mean to be boorish; simply making an observation. Say, my friend—sans wheelchair, looking good!" He leaned forward to address Erika. "You, too, luv. Radiant as ever." To John: "Carry on, old boy. Sorry for interrupting."

"No problem, *old boy*. Now, where was I?"

"Contorting."

"Right. Let's begin with Morris's account—the one he gave after his wife tried to pin Ivan's murder on him, and he was forced to retract the statement that she'd been at home with him that night. Mind you, he had to admit to some shady dealings—minor compared to murder—in order for his story to ring true. Now then. As Morris tells it, according to my source, the evening before the Laszlo auction—and Ivan's murder—Ben Laszlo met him at his home in Brooklyn Heights. Each had an urgent matter to discuss. Earlier that day, Laszlo had gotten a call from a professor, one Norman Blethmore, who informed him that he knew for a fact that the Monet still life up for auction was not a Monet. He had proof. That same afternoon, Morris had gotten a similar call from a Chauncey Gladstone, in attributions with a firm in London, though this call had come with a threat. Gladstone would expose the fraud unless Keller hired him to broker the fake Monet and any other suspect Monet paintings in his possession. He would sign, seal, and deliver their Monet accreditation. Keller had yielded. He reported this to Laszlo at their meeting in Brooklyn—which Naomi attended, it should be made clear. Laszlo agreed to remove the still life from the block, but he wanted to wait until the auction was in progress so he would not run the risk of attendee drop-outs beforehand.

"Morris admitted both he and Laszlo were worried about Ivan's getting wind of this plan for the same reason Morris had insisted on Ivan's being his agent at Laszlo's—his unwavering moral fortitude! Ivan, sentiment aside, would have no choice but to report them if he suspected foul play. Laszlo cracked a joke about *taking care* of Ivan, which shocked Morris. No comment from Naomi. In the end, Laszlo said he'd see things went smoothly with Ivan and would keep his own mouth shut, provided that when a sale went through with Gladstone, he'd get a piece of the action. A case of blackmail squared, I'd say."

"Laszlo's a mega-bully," Greg commented. "This story makes sense, but there is no way he's going to admit to any of it. He'll deny every word."

"He already did," John said. "To get back to Morris's story. Naomi went into the city the next day on the pretext of visiting an old high school chum, and as luck would have it, her date had been arranged the week prior. No suspicions aroused—that is, not until Naomi returned the next morning issuing her order to Morris: when the cops come around to question you, tell them I was home with you—or else!"

"Got it," Harrison said. "So what went wrong? It was working for her. Why did she try to kill him?"

John raised his finger in a silent "Aha!" He looked from one to the other of his companions, drawing them into his force field. "The fact is…" he began slowly, "there was no high school chum waiting for Naomi in Manhattan. There was only her lover—the one she'd promised never *ever* to see again after she'd had a row with Morris. My Brooklyn Heights connection suggests Morris found out about her ongoing affair via an overheard phone conversation, but I'm not sure he got that from the horse's mouth. No matter. Morris and Naomi had a major argument about her clandestine meeting, during which Morris informed Naomi that he was divorcing her; she'd had her chance to reform and had failed. Since they had signed a pre-nuptial agreement stating that in the event of a divorce, the wife has no claim on art work purchased by the husband prior to the marriage, Naomi would be out the fun of spending down the more or less half a billion selling the eight"—air quotes— "'Monets' would add to the Keller nest egg." John smiled. "There was nothing in writing excluding Naomi's claim to the art work in the event of her husband's *death*."

"I see now," Harrison said. "After the irrefutable evidence emerged pointing to Naomi's guilt—in *both* cases, thanks to Erika—Naomi had to scramble for a new narrative. Or did she just…fold?"

"She scrambled—desperately. Pointed the finger at her boyfriend, who, she claimed, admitted he had acted on her behalf. Boyfriend blew that one out of the water with an airtight alibi. He did see Naomi earlier in the day, but at the time of Ivan's murder, he was at his neighbor's apartment on Columbus Avenue and One Hundred Ninth Street, five miles from the scene of the crime on First and thirty-eighth. As for her husband's near-fatal, quote, 'accident,' Naomi went for the oldest plea in the books—self-defense. I'll spare you the details. Bail set at a big number."

By the end of John's de-briefing, the study hall had become more populated. Among the newcomers, Harrison recognized only Aubrey Devan, the assistant chief of archives at the Ashmolean who'd introduced him to the documents recently added to the Pissarro collection—or rather to those documents that had survived the sleight of hand of pseudonymous Professor Nadine Lowery. Erika, on the other hand, recognized any number of individuals—among them, Lois Keller, Morris's ex-wife, itching to get her hands on *Picnic on the Lawn*, and Max Rayburn, Laszlo auction attendee and first in line to purchase *Wedgewood Vase with Flowers*. (*How did they react on learning neither of their heart-throbs was a Monet?* she wondered.)

Aubrey was the first of the new crop of guests to saunter up to the seated group. Harrison introduced him to Erika, John, and Greg, and a conversation easily flowed from there, beginning with Harrison's coverage of his "misadventure" in London and his progress since. Max Rayburn was next to drop by, and soon, others gravitated toward the group, Oliver Schmidt among them.

"Glad to see you're doing okay after our Freeport ordeal," Oliver said, giving Erika a gentle version of a bear hug when she rose to greet him. "I have to say you did brilliantly, given the circumstances."

"Good to see you," she said, eliding the subject. She introduced Oliver to the immediate group.

"Mind if I sit with you?" Oliver asked. "I'm sure you've got questions."

"Please—grab a chair." She noticed Ezra sitting alone at the remotest seating arrangement, clenched fists resting on his knees. She supposed he had finally succumbed to his mood. Determined he be given some answers about his partner's death, she decided he must be brought into the fold. Surely Oliver—or John, with his connections—could provide him with a progress report, even if the investigation was still under wraps. "Be right back."

Moments later, two chairs had been added to the original four, with Oliver and Ezra completing the Wheatley clique. They formed what must have looked like a closed circle now. Though they could hear David Boyd holding court on the other end of the room, conditions were aligned to ensure the conferees' privacy.

* * *

The position of Chair at the group's ad hoc meeting had logically fallen to Oliver Schmidt. Oliver was in a pivotal position, both as a reliable witness-cum-reporter of the Freeport event and as an officer with the Swiss Federal Office for Customs and Border Security. He was a needed resource and an invaluable investigator. Which meant he had top-security access to all agencies, including his own, with an interest in the present tangle of art crimes. For starters: The United Kingdom's National Crime Agency; the French Republic's Directorate-General of Customs and Indirect Taxes; the United States Federal Bureau of Investigation Crime Theft Division.

"I'll share what I know, provided you hold the information in confidence," Oliver said in answer to Ezra's plea for news regarding the hunt for Norman's killer. "This goes for all of you," he added, focusing on each of the group in turn. "All cases under investigation are connected, one way or another, and all are at once sensitive and ongoing." He waited until he'd heard a convincing avowal from each of them before continuing. "I won't keep you in suspense, Ezra. Norman died by means of a lethal injection of abrin. Darien Roth leaked Norman's research findings to Chauncey Gladstone, which he knew Gladstone, and as informer, he himself, would profit greatly from. Gladstone hired his enforcer to eliminate Norman and retrieve the computer containing his critical Pissarro file."

"Which Darien felt guilty about to his last breath," Erika felt compelled to add.

"He did," Oliver said. "I heard him, too." Addressing Harrison, he said, "The enforcer is the same individual who attacked you and Darien in the parking garage."

"The *biker*?"

"Yes—one Rock Nelson. Gladstone meant the assault to be a warning to you. Darien was supposed to have suffered a bruise to deflect guilt from his having played a part in the plot. His skull was collateral damage." Oliver let that sink in. "And do you know who played the role of Professor Nadine Lowery?"

"You know I don't."

"Rock's wife, Natalie. Natalie was working in the red light district in Paris when Rock discovered her. She was a newcomer—a runaway with no ties, no one looking for her. Smart, beautiful, unattached. Rock saw the potential. Ten years of grooming later, she's a full-time character actor in Gladstone's stable."

John let out a guffaw that got heads turning from the display area. "How in God's name did you pick up all this information?" he asked, turning down the volume. "In a damn confessional?"

Oliver smiled. "Hardly. To get it, you have to understand we're dealing with a food chain in reverse—individuals spitting up those below them in the chain and being spat out by those above. All to acquire clemency in one form or another. Take Chauncey Gladstone. We've got the incriminating tape Madame Fontaine—Denise—recorded during her visit to Gladstone's London office, subsequently downloaded by the Prefecture of Police of Paris. Regarding the Freeport meeting some of us will testify to having heard Gladstone's recorded self-incriminations before the fellow smashed the recording device. Then we have Police Officer Marcel Meyer of the canton of Geneva, who we—Erika, I and Denise—heard incriminate himself as Gladstone's partner in crime prior to shooting Darien Roth dead. To catch a break—short of immunity, of course—he spat out all he knew about Gladstone's criminal activities, including his employment of Rock and Natalie Nelson.

"Fortunately for Gladstone, he did not take Meyer into his confidence about *all* of his criminal behaviors—and *connections*. There was much left in Gladstone's craw to regurgitate on his own behalf. Especially when the need for bargaining chips rose exponentially when Rock came up with a recorded phone call in which Gladstone is advising him on the manner and means of terminating Norman Blethmore."

"All in all, screwed by the sound of his own voice," John bluntly summed up. "I'm curious, what did the man give up—or should I say *spit* up—for a scrap of kindness?"

"A feast. Gladstone's workplace, Richardson Gallery and Conservation Studio is, as Gladstone confessed, not the only entity with an embedded criminal in its midst hiding behind the skirts of the mother company, Global Arts Research Corp. Gladstone gave up the names of individuals with whom he networks on staff at two other companies, one in France, one in Germany. These people share trackers, who search social media, museums, universities for novices and seasoned pros in the art field who might be—well, *bought,* for lack of a better word."

"This is the way Darien was…acquired," Harrison said.

"Exactly. Vulnerable and useful. The perfect target. They have it down to a science. The tracker does the research. The recruiter approaches the target. Once an individual is signed on, the enforcer ensures his or her loyalty."

"I've been speaking to the president of Global Arts," Greg said. "She assures me that the company has begun an investigation of its own into the personnel associated with each of its affiliates worldwide."

"Where is Chauncey Gladstone right *now*?" Ezra asked through gritted teeth. "Walking free?"

"Initially, he was detained in Geneva," Oliver replied evenly. "He has since been remanded to the London courts. More for his own safety than punishment, he is presently on remand in Pentonville Prison, London."

Ezra looked disappointed, as if he'd expected such an answer to satisfy. "Alright."

"As for Officer Marcel Meyer," Oliver continued, "he'll be prosecuted in Switzerland. Rock and Natalie Nelson will, like Gladstone, be tried in England. United States citizens"—with a glance at the Wheatleys—"as well as other witnesses of foreign parts—like Madame Denise Fontaine—will, for their convenience, be deposed remotely for whatever trials or hearings their testimony is required."

Harrison frowned. "I don't mean to throw you off course, Oliver, but…"

"I've completed the course. Shoot."

"I'm wondering about the fate of the eight paintings in all this turmoil. Does Morris Keller's collusion with Gladstone strip him of ownership? I would think he'd be arguing two points in his favor for maintaining it. One, that he and his father had always assumed all eight paintings were authentic Monets; that they had no idea six of the signatures had been tampered with back in the 1870s. Two, that if he did not go along with Gladstone's scheme, harm would come to him and his wife. I know this may be out of your bailiwick, but are you aware of any judgments having been made in this area?"

CHAPTER TWENTY-SEVEN

"Out of my bailiwick, but I am in the loop."

"I have had experience dealing with contested ownership," Greg said, grinning. "But in this instance, being in the loop carries more weight. What news from the lawyers, Oliver?"

"Not much need for them," Oliver said with a corresponding grin. "The process of adjudication is just about running on automatic; the lawyers, essentially scribes. There's still some friendly arbitration regarding valuations going on, but I'll tell you where it's heading. To inspire goodwill, Morris Keller is gifting Frédéric Bazille's *Girl at the Piano* and *Woman in the Garden* to the heirs of Frédéric's younger brother, Marc. The Bazille family has elected to distance itself from any controversy and will be donating these paintings to the Musée Fabre in Montpellier, France."

"A thoughtful move," Harrison said. "The Bazille family estate, Meric, is right outside Montpellier."

"Homeward bound, yes," Oliver said. "As for *Picnic on the Lawn*, Morris will be honoring his promise to his ex-wife, Lois, and gifting the painting to her. No audible complaints from her about the painting not being a Monet. Max Rayburn, who has had his eye on *Wedgewood Vase with Flowers*, will be purchasing it, and Morris will be using a portion of the payment received to defray his anticipated fines handed down by your government. Rayburn is actually quite excited about the painting turning out to be a Bazille because of its unique historical value."

"It'll make for some great cocktail talk," John said, with somewhat of a class-scorning smirk.

"I bet," Oliver returned, a touch of backlash in his smile. "Moving on to the remaining two Bazille paintings—help me out here—anyone?"

"*Woman Reading* and *Seaside*," Erika said.

"Thank you. Morris will be gifting one of these paintings—the choice under discussion—to Robin, Ivan Brooks's widow. I suspect to assuage his conscience. And so we come to the two legitimate Monet paintings, *At the Shore* and *Luncheon Party*. The former will be—ah, your ladyship!" he declared, the first to catch Madame D's entrance.

"'Your ladyship,' indeed, you rascal," Madame D replied as Gretchen steered her toward the group, and those who were able jumped up to move around chairs to provide an opening in the circle. Introductions and reunions followed—Harrison and Madame D's, the least limber and most affectionate. Gretchen was tactfully advised by Madame D to go have a look at the paintings—"I'll join you in a moment, dear." To the group, she announced, "As you were, people. No need for a recap."

"We were discussing the fate of the paintings," Oliver said. "You came in on the tail end."

"How suitable for one at *her* tail end."

Oliver wagged his finger at her in protest. "To resume. Morris Keller has agreed to sell Monet's *At the Shore* to the Metropolitan Museum of Art for what I've been told is a very modest price."

"Which is?" Greg asked.

"I wasn't informed. Sorry. As for *Luncheon Party*, apparently the more valuable of the two due to its reference to Monet's *Luncheon on the Grass* is scheduled to be an outright gift to the Met, in memory of Morris's father, Lewis." Oliver clasped his hands. "That about does it. If you have any questions, Denise, don't hesitate to ask."

"That won't be necessary, your lordship," she teased. "I'll be staying with the Wheatleys for two weeks and will be grilling them mercilessly." She started to back her wheelchair out of the circle. "I'm going to have a look at the paintings. Who's the fellow that appears to be holding forth?"

"David Boyd, a Met conservator," Erika said, rising to come to Madame D's aid. "The final arbiter on attribution. I'll introduce you." She grabbed the handles of the wheelchair.

"Excellent. But then you must leave me in Gretchen's care. She is still smarting from my having, as she said, 'rejected' her as my caretaker on the Geneva Freeport excursion."

On the way back to rejoin her group, Erika was thinking she must do everything she can to dispel Gretchen's sense of rejection, for which she herself felt a share of guilt. Her thought was cut short by a stentorian *"Veni, vidi, vici!"* as Ben Laszlo threw open the door and entered the room, diminishing everything in sight with his blustering presence. Following in his wake: a jean-clad young man with a hand-held camera; a studious-looking woman harnessed by a large cross-body bag and holding a pen and spiral notebook; Ivan Brooks's widow, Robin, burdened only by a sheepish look.

All heads turned toward Laszlo and his entourage.

"Accompanying me is Molly Jones," he announced. "Molly is the journalist who's writing a piece on me for *New York* magazine. She's brought along her cameraman, Gary. Last and definitely not least"—he smiled at his snappy turn of phrase—"is Robin Brooks. You have Robin to thank for my presence. Who's in charge here?"

David stepped forward. "I am, sir. David Boyd, conservator with the Met Museum. I sent out the invitations, if that's why you're asking. And you are…?"

"You familiar with the Laszlo Auction House?"

"I am." David reddened. "Are you…?"

"Yes. Was it an oversight, or did my invite get lost in *junk* mail? I'm not a petty man"—he stroked his chin—"but on the other hand, I do not appreciate being passed over. If I hadn't called Robin to let her know I was looking for a venue—for variety, one other than my own—I would not have known of your plans." He moved closer to the line-up of paintings. "Will you move away, please," he ordered the visitors occupying the immediate area. "I will be making a presentation—why, hello, there," he said, noticing one of his clients among the group retreating on command. "I see the still life you admired is on display. By Frédéric Bazille, as it turns out."

"I intend to purchase it," Max Rayburn replied.

"Wise choice," Laszlo said. "You'll be the talk of the town. You know, Molly will be describing the part I played in exposing the Monet signature fraud," he lied with aplomb. "A terrific writer, Molly. Terrific writer." With a wave, he beckoned Robin to come stand by him at the midpoint of the display. "I see a twist of hair has escaped from Robin's bun, Molly; want to tuck it in?" Molly obliged. He withdrew an envelope from his breast pocket. "Gary, can you get at least four of the paintings in my handing-over-the-envelope shot?" he asked the cameraman. "Without minimizing the main subjects, that is?"

Oliver Schmidt, along with Greg, John, and Harrison, had moved closer to the action, reuniting with Erika, Madame D, and Gretchen at the crowd's periphery. Oliver stepped forward. "We will not be taking photographs of the paintings today…Mr. Laszlo, is it? Negotiations regarding the art are incomplete."

"Will they be complete in one month?" Laszlo demanded.

"I'm quite certain they will."

"Then we're in compliance. Molly's piece is not due for release until then." Laszlo returned his attention to the cameraman. "Are we set?" Gary gave him a thumbs-up and started snapping photos, directing Laszlo and Robin to move this way and that. "Smile, Robin," Molly suggested.

Erika wondered if Robin knew what was in the envelope—and if so, was that the reason for her uneasy demeanor?

Laszlo withheld the envelope while he delivered a short speech extolling his empathy and generosity vis-à-vis the tragic death of Ivan Brooks. "Robin's loss is also a loss for the Laszlo Auction House family," he said. The way he saw it, his grief could be assuaged "only in part by a gift of sustenance in the amount of two million dollars." He handed her the envelope, and Gary snapped a dozen photos in a span of ten seconds of her weeping.

Erika still did not know if Robin had been aware of the contents of the envelope beforehand, but something about the way she avoided eye contact and held the unopened envelope between her thumb and forefinger led her to believe she felt something akin to shame, or at least embarrassment, in accepting it. "Thank you," Robin finally said, almost inaudibly.

Erika was about to dash over to Robin and give her a hug, but Laszlo preempted her by embracing Robin himself—long and diligently, as Gary snapped a dozen more photos.

"'The part I played in exposing the Monet signature fraud,'" Harrison grumbled under his breath, as Laszlo's empty boast echoed in his head.

"People who hold themselves in high esteem can be very seductive," Madame D replied. "Don't be surprised if he's believed."

"That's comforting," Harrison said, smiling in spite of himself.

As abruptly as Laszlo and his entourage had arrived, so did they depart; Robin Brooks bent over in their midst, as if she were seeking shelter from the rain.

After Laszlo's performance, the ebb and flow of the gathering changed. Several of the guests prevailed upon David to resume his lesson in art conservation and trotted him off to the sitting area. Others decided to take advantage of Harrison's anonymous pledge and wandered off with their maps and coupons to one of the many dining venues on offer. A group of newcomers arrived, and David's assistant, Laura Keane, was on the spot to provide them with in-depth analyses of the paintings, along with a crash course on art forensics.

As for the Wheatleys' coterie…they bid individual goodbyes to all those whom they knew or had just met and promised to remain in communication. Once outside the room, they discussed immediate plans. Greg was headed for Art Loss Register's New York office, where he was scheduled to interview a candidate for a position that had been vacated by a retiree. John was due to meet a prospective client—"a woman who suspects her husband is cheating on her. So what else is new?"

"Where to?" Harrison asked after he, Erika, Madame D, and Gretchen were left to themselves. "Think fast. My legs are about to give out."

"Oh dear," Madame D said. "We need to get some nourishment into you."

"We need to get me a place to sit down."

"Want to go back inside, darling?" Erika asked, frustrated she couldn't single-handedly lift him off his feet. "You can sit there for a while?"

"I didn't mean to sound the alarm—but lunch on the premises may be the way to go. Okay, everyone?"

Five minutes later, they were looking out at the treetops of Central Park from the vantage point of their window table at the Met Dining Room. Another ten, and they were sipping iced tea and waiting for their cauliflower soup and crab cakes—all except Madame D, who, ever marching to the beat of her own drum, had ordered beet salad and charcuterie.

* * *

Somewhere between the clearing of the plates and the group decision to skip dessert, Erika, Harrison, and Madame D found themselves alone—all alone. The couple that had been sitting nearby had left a while ago. Their waiter—the only waiter who appeared to be in attendance—was out of sight, giving them unhampered time to debate over the dessert offerings. Gretchen was off on a restroom break.

In that delicate interval of intimacy—bound to be short-lived—Madame D said, "I do hope neither of you will want to order dessert—and Gretchen—I must convince her, too."

"Why?" Harrison asked, worry in his voice. "Are you feeling ill?"

"Heaven's no. I only want to get back to that darling child of yours. I feel such a bond with him. It's hard to explain."

Erika, sitting between them, leaned toward Madame D and planted a kiss on her cheek. "From both of us. We do love you, Denise."

"I know, dear. As I love you. I want to thank you for this blessing."

"Lunch was that good?" Harrison asked.

"Naughty boy," Madame D pretended to scold. "I'm ancient. I can be as sentimental as I like. Thank you—both of you—for blessing me with a great-godchild."

The moment was impossible to pass up. "How would you like being blessed with a second great-godchild?" Erika asked—casually, just for the teasing joy of it.

"Oh, my word, yes!" Madame D exclaimed as Harrison's jaw dropped.

"If it's a girl, I'd like to name her after you, Denise. Okay, Harrison? I didn't put you on the spot, did I? You look like a deer in the headlights."

"No, no, that's great!" Harrison squawked, coming to. "Denise, a great name!" He rocked toward Erika to give her a hug without jamming his left leg into the table's pedestal. She scooted her chair closer to make it easier. A kiss was managed.

"And if it's a boy?" Madame D asked, sticking to the subject. "What will you name the baby if it's a boy?"

Erika separated from Harrison, held him at arm's length, gave him a look serious as all get out. Capped it with a dramatic pause. Finally, with the coyest tilt of her head, she asked, "What do you say we go with SpongeBob SquarePants?"

Harrison burst out laughing.

For the first time in living memory, Madame D was at a loss for words.

A Note from the Author

Across the street from my apartment building in Manhattan, there's a huge swath of undeveloped land known as The Mud Pit. I've been wanting to "develop" this plot for years, and, without lifting a finger, I finally have.Of course, it remains the same old desolate expanse, but in my imagination it's become a flashy art auction house called Laszlo's.

For this fusion of art history and fiction, I read a variety of books on Claude Monet and the Impressionist movement, including *Monet and His Private Muse* by Mary Matthews Gedo, *Monet by Himself*, edited by Richard Kendall, *Camille Pissarro* by Joachim Pissarro, and *Memoirs of the First Impressionist Art Dealer* (1831-1922) by Paul Durand-Ruel.

Thanks, as ever, to Verena Rose and Shawn Reilly Simmons of Level Best Books for their insightful input. Thanks, too, to Jeanne Thornton for her helpful read-through.

To my son, Eric, much appreciation for allowing me to bounce plot twists off you whenever the mood strikes, and for cheering me on whenever the need arises.

About the Author

Claudia Riess is an award-winning author who has worked in the editorial departments of *The New Yorker* and Holt, Rinehart and Winston, and has edited several art history monographs. *Stolen Light*, the first book in her art history mystery series, was chosen by Vassar's Latin American history professor for distribution to the college's people-to-people trips to Cuba. *To Kingdom Come*, the fourth, will be added to the syllabus of a survey course on West and Central African Art at a prominent Midwestern university. Claudia has written a number of articles for *Mystery Readers Journal*, Women's National Book Association, the Sisters in Crime *Bloodletter*, and *Mystery Scene* magazine. She has been featured on a variety of podcasts, blogs and Zoom events.

SOCIAL MEDIA HANDLES:
  Twitter: @ClaudiaRiess
  Instagram: @claudiariessbooks
  Pinterest: claudiariessbooks
  Email: claudiariess.w@gmail.com

Also by Claudia Riess

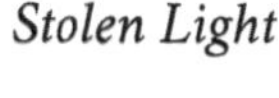

Stolen Light

False Light

Knight Light

To Kingdom Come

Love and Other Hazards

Reclining Nude

Semblance of Guilt